UNRAVELLED

ISABELLE MACDOWALL

Ebook ISBN-13: 978-1-7641054-0-8
Paperback ISBN-13: 978-1-7641054-1-5
Hardcover ISBN-13: 978-1-7641054-2-2

Cover design by Miblart Illustrations by Bibi Illustration First Printed June 2025

*For everyone who falls asleep each night with a movie playing
in their head.
This one's for you.*

Ebook ISBN-13: 978-1-7641054-0-8
Paperback ISBN-13: 978-1-7641054-1-5
Hardcover ISBN-13: 978-1-7641054-2-2

Cover design by Miblart Illustrations by Bibi Illustration First Printed June 2025

*For everyone who falls asleep each night with a movie playing
in their head.
This one's for you.*

THE FIVE KINGDOMS OF THE NAVIGATORS

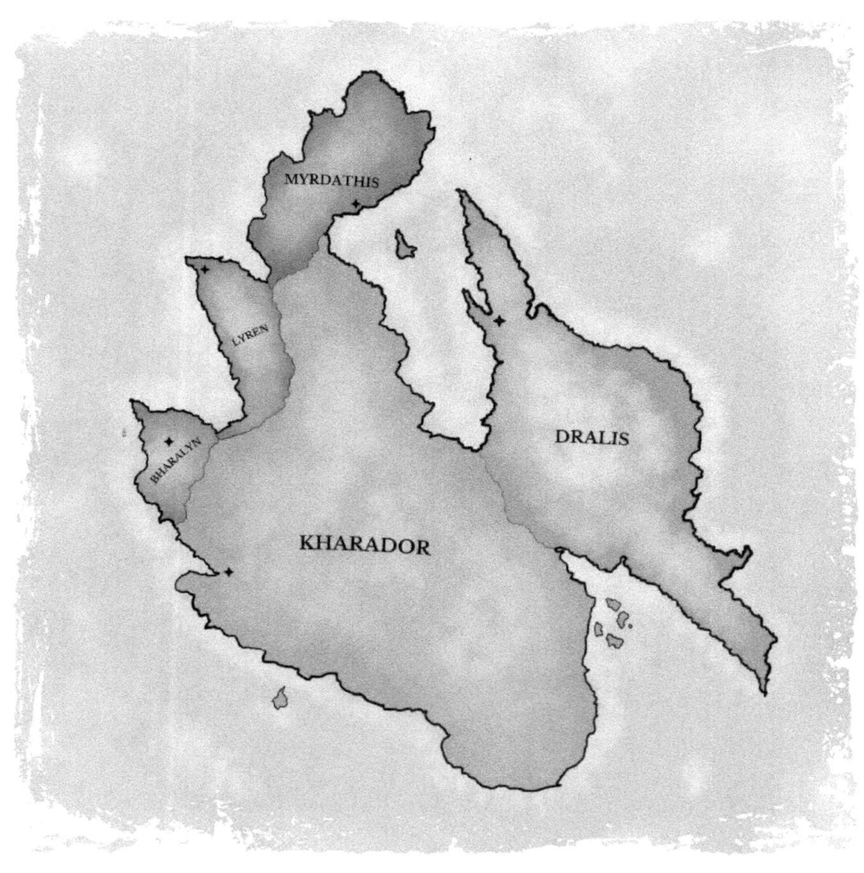

PROLOGUE

EONS AGO, WE FLED the chains, across a sea vast and silent, where stars stretched endlessly, watching as we sailed into the unknown.

Storms rose to meet us, waves crashed with fury, but our Navigators held the course, their hands steady, their eyes unyielding.

Bharas led us to the water with unshaken resolve, his gaze steady, though the stars wept for him. His heart aflame in the darkness, burning with the weight of all he left behind.

Kharad whispered, and they forgot their fear, His voice laced with echoes older than oceans He turned wrath with a silver tongue, Guiding the many with silver words and steel.

Drala's hands moved through the unseen, plucking fate with no knowing touch. She chose the paths of all who sailed, unaware of the weight she wove into each thread.

Lyren was the price the sea demanded, dragged down by fate's cold, closing hand. He drowned so others might be spared, His name now sung beneath the waves.

And Myrran, gentle with a thousand stars, heard futures the world would never hold. She walked the wind with unseen grief, a dreamer burdened by what might have been.

When they passed beyond the veil, they left us gifts shaped in sorrow. Bound in blood, carried by whispers, their power waits in those who listen.

We give them our faith in silence and fire, our children born beneath their names. We carve their memory into stone, and live within the echoes of their sacrifice.

* * *

Eleven years before.

The wind was warm, and sunlight streamed through the leaves of the tahla tree. Though the summer was drawing to a close, the bees still hummed, lured by the sweet scent of flowers twining around the tree's hanging vines.

The tahla tree, one of the few trees to bloom in the peak of summer, offered more than just beauty. Its bark was perfect for climbing, small knots of wood jutted out at odd angles before giving way to a cascade of branches and green-blue leaves. The tendrils of leaves hung low, creating an ideal hiding spot from parents and caregivers.

A young girl stood at the base of the tree, her gaze calculating as she studied the tree trunk. A stray wisp of her auburn hair fell across her face, but she paid it no mind.

Instead, she searched for the perfect knot to start her climb.

Her father had warned her not to wander too far that morning, but the looming lessons in etiquette, history, and, worst of all, ballroom dancing had driven her out here. The dance lessons had started when she turned twelve and she detested every moment, especially since her older brother was her dance partner.

The second her morning chores were done, she had darted through the palace hallways, escaping into the gardens. She was quick, easily outrunning her brother and disappearing past the hedges.

Her eyes landed on a large knot, just out of reach. She leapt and caught it with ease, her fingers gripping tightly. A perfect ledge sat just a few knots higher. Climbing with practiced skill, she ignored the sound of her dress snagging on the rough bark.

The rip did not matter to her either. Even as she reached the perch high enough to risk a broken arm or leg if she fell, she felt only exhilaration. A broken leg would mean no dancing for a while, but it would also mean no gardens.

She closed her eyes, taking in the summer. The sweet smell of tahla flowers mixed with the heat of the day. She knew this would be one of her last opportunities to be part of the garden. Beginning next year, they would expect her to admire the garden, not climb in it.

A shout broke her thoughts, distant but growing closer. She poked her head above the canopy of leaves. The gardens surrounded the palace on three sides. She could see the hedge maze that filled most of the back gardens, the fountains of the Navigators, the lawn where the Queen and her Crowned Betrothed held balls. A shrill voice carried clearly through the air, laced with annoyance.

"Boys! Missing another appointment with your tutor will disappoint me! Return at once! Do not make me search all day again!"

By the edge of the royal gardens, a woman moved hurriedly among the hedge maze and bushes, her apron smudged with dirt and leaves.

The girl's ears caught hushed whispers below her. Two boys, only thirteen years old or so, huddled together at the base of the tree, half-hidden by its trunk. They looked like brothers. Their dark hair and noble attire marked them as children of the court. She glanced at her own dress, made of the same silk and gold trim.

"What do we do now, idiot?" one boy hissed. "We can't keep hiding in the same spot every time!".

"I'm thinking, okay?" the other snapped back. "She's

better at finding us than the last babysitter."

A smile tugged at the corners of her lips. They were like her, fleeing their lessons and courtly duties. The woman steadily advanced, her eyes scanning every shrub and tree as she glanced back. Mira sank below the canopy. Watching the boys fight, she thought it wouldn't be too bad having friends to hide away with.

"Hey," the girl whispered. "Up here."

Both boys froze before looking up at her, their eyes wide with surprise. "How did you get up there?" the shorter one asked.

"Wait!" the other said, grabbing his shoulder. "Don't talk to her. She might be a tree sprite"

The girl glared at him. Tree sprites, according to the stories, were small, ugly creatures that delighted in tricking humans. Her sharp tongue got the better of her, as it often did.

"I am not a tree spirit," she snapped, her voice cutting. "And for all you know, I am a Navigator, and since you have insulted me, I will curse your life to sail forever through chaos."

The curious boy grinned up at her. Without hesitation, he reached for the knots in the tree, ignoring his friend's frantic protests. She raised her eyebrows in anticipation, watching as he struggled to find the right handholds.

Finally, she pointed to the correct one, and soon, he was face-to-face with her. Below, the guardian's voice rose sharply.

"There you are!" The boy ducked down close to the tree trunk. She glanced down to see the guardian grab the smaller boy by the shoulder.

"Now where is he?" the woman demanded. "You know

we cannot attend without him." The boy below shrugged.

"Don't know. We split up to make it harder for you to find us." The guardian grumbled in frustration but began dragging the boy away, lecturing him on the consequences of his antics.

Above, the girl turned back to the boy in front of her. His green eyes bore into hers, and for a moment, neither of them spoke.

He smirked, "I wouldn't mind being cursed, as long as it's you doing the cursing."

1

Mira

THE GREAT HALL STRETCHED before Mira. A space so vast and elegant it seemed to hold echoes of the past within its stone floor. It was her favorite room in the palace, a place where history and grandeur intertwined. The ancestors had crafted the hall with intention. Long and open, its sheer size lending itself equally to grand balls and solemn ceremonies. At the far end, above the dais, five towering stone arches framed magnificent stained-glass windows.

As the summer sun spilled through the glass, the room bloomed into life. Ruby, gold, and sapphire dancing across the stone. Each window was a masterpiece in its own right, depicting the legendary navigators who had guided their ancestors to safety in ages long past.

There was Kharad and his silver sword, Drala with her hand outstretched, Lyren under the waves, Myrran with her frosted eyes. But in the center window stood Bharas, the kingdom of Bharalyn's namesake, portrayed with a heart of flame in the dark.

Mira's gaze lingered on Bharas. The dark and grey glass depicted him kneeling, hands outstretched, with a radiant red glow at the center of his chest. She had often visited this room to admire how the streams of sunlight made his heart seem alive, flickering and shifting, as if truly ablaze. It was a moment frozen in time, showing him at his most distraught, burning with everything he had sacrificed and left behind for her ancestors.

A testament to his ultimate duty.

A sharp cough interrupted her thoughts.

Mira blinked and looked over towards the sound. Cleric Perrin stood nearby, waiting. A woman in her mid-thirties, composed and steady, with the presence that quiets a room without asking.

Her white robes were simple but finely made, flowing in clean lines that spoke of ritual and reverence. She measured each movement, as if bearing the weight of tradition and memory. She hid her hair beneath a ceremonial headdress. An ivory silk veil, sheer yet dignified, embroidered with silver threads in the shape of ancient sigils and soft celestial curves. Tiny crystal beads lined the hem, catching the light with each breath she took.

Mira drew in a steadying breath and stepped forward, the black folds of her gown swirling softly at her feet. She came to stand beside Torvyn, their mirrored auburn hair a clear echo of their mother's. His was slicked back with ceremonial precision, while hers fell in waves.

Torvyn wore deep crimson and silver robes, cut to reveal his broad chest and shoulders. He was regal, imposing, a figure carved for command. Yet Mira knew better. Beneath the sharp lines of his face lived a gentleness, a steady warmth he shared with everyone. She met her brother's gaze for a brief, grounding moment, before turning to face the crowd, the weight of tradition settling over her like a second cloak.

With a steady voice, she declared for all those gathered in the hall, "I have seen this pair and know they are as one." Perrin nodded, her voice solemn as she addressed the couple.

"Torvyn and Branh, you are both past your twenty-seventh year, and so I ask this of you in earnest. You enter this bond knowing you cannot break it, you cannot escape it, it will be with you always. This bond will irrevocably link you as one. Not even in death will this bond break. In the eyes of the Navigators, you will be one soul, in two parts."

Torvyn took Branh's hands, his movements slow and measured, a calmness radiating from him that Mira had never seen before. In this moment, standing with Branh, he seemed unshaken, at peace in a way that felt brand new. Branh, shorter and stockier than Torvyn, stood solidly at his side. His blonde hair caught the light, and his presence was a steady contrast to Torvyn's imposing stature.

They had grown up together, first as companions, now as betrothed. Their bond, built on years of laughter and shared silence, showed in the way their voices rang out together.

Clear and resolute. "We do."

Torvyn smiled softly, his gaze fixed on Branh as if nothing else existed. Slowly, he leaned forward and Branh met him halfway. Their kiss was tender, yet filled with the unspoken promise of their bond. Unshakable, eternal.

For a moment, the crowd seemed to hold its breath. Mira glanced at the empty seat the Queen would have occupied. She shifted her gaze to Caelric, the Crowned Betrothed. His head lulled down, just slightly. She wasn't sure if it was a nod of acknowledgment, or a quiet slump of grief?

Perrin stepped forward with purpose, her voice a calm current guiding the moment back to the ceremony. "We are witness," she said. "And the bond is sealed."

A roar of celebration filled the hall. Voices echoed against the marble walls as the crowd cheered. Torvyn pulled back and took Branh into the center of the great hall. The hall's edge held a feast, its tables laden with food and drink. Somewhere above, music played, filling the air with a lilting melody. As the crowd dispersed into merriment, Mira watched them dance and smiled. They looked so in love, moving as though the rest of the world had melted away. Mira lingered for a moment, watching them, then turned toward the feast.

"Mira!" a voice called from across the room. "Come sit with us!" She turned to see Lady Elendra waving her over to her small group.

A confection of glittering sheer fabric, more suggestion than substance, draped the plump, middle-aged woman. The gown hugged her curves with bold confidence, its delicate silk strategically placed to maintain a semblance of modesty. Jewels adorned her neck, wrists, and ears, catching the glow of the chandeliers with every subtle movement.

Beneath layers of silk and jewels, Elendra, known for her sharp wit and manipulative charm, was the court's most cunning collector of secrets. She could disarm even the most guarded, and by the time they realized how effortlessly she had drawn their confessions, it was already far too late.

Mira smiled and drifted towards her as she wove between twirling couples and the flutters of velvet and satin. Laughter mingled with the soft swell of string music, sunlight catching in the crystal chandeliers above.

She approached a velvet-cushioned alcove near the towering windows, where Lady Elendra lounged like a cat at ease. With a graceful dip, Mira settled beside her on a plush seat, the scent of rosewater and spiced wine lingering in the air between them.

"Poor thing," Elendra cooed, lightly patting Mira's hand. "Is it strange, watching love bloom again when yours was so tragically pruned from your memory?"

Mira resisted the urge to sigh. She knew this game too

well. Elendra's velvet-tongued questions, dipped in honey and sharpened with intent.

Since her own bonding a year ago, she'd learned to deflect, to wear the mask the court expected. A scandal, they had called it. Whispers still clung to their names like perfume.

She had been just twenty-two, too young by tradition, and far too young to convince a cleric to perform the bonding. And yet, somehow, they had done it. Bound without a navigator's witness. She turned to Elendra with a polite smile, her voice calm but carefully measured.

"If you're looking for another scandal from me, Lady Elendra, I'm afraid I'm retired." Mira smiled as her gaze drifted across the room to where Torvyn and Branh stood, laughing together in the center of the hall.

They really looked like they belonged together, their bond natural and unshakable. A pang of grief tightened her chest, sharp and undeniable. "Besides, today is about them, not about what I can and can not remember."

"Strange, isn't it?" Lady Elendra said with a feigned tone of reverence, her fingers idly tracing the rim of her goblet. "How could anyone do something so sacred without a sacred witness? No one's quite figured it out."

Her sharp eyes, however, glinted with curiosity. "And the late Queen, Navigators guide her home, hiding both of your memories of the ceremony ... harsh, even by her standards."

She leaned forward then, her voice dropping to a whisper. "But you must remember something. Indulge us." Her voice was velvet, but Mira felt every syllable like a needle.

Mira's lips slipped into a sly smile. "Tharion and I have always been... resourceful. But if we shared our secrets, Cleric Perrin would be confined to her study, with nothing to do all day."

Elendra laughed, and she continued, "But I will admit, Tharion has his way of keeping things... interesting." Mira let the words hang, vague enough to tantalize, knowing full well how much Elendra enjoyed filling in the gaps.

But what they hadn't shared, what they didn't dare speak aloud, was that Queen Sarelle's punishment had dulled more than just the memory of their bonding. She had hidden pieces of them, too. Stolen the fragments of their love, their laughter, their quiet moments. No warmth in the touch, no color in the scene. Mira's thoughts drifted back to the story of how they met. In the palace's tree gardens. How they had crossed paths again over the following years, drawing together until they finally gave in. After that they couldn't keep away from each other. Courting in secret until they bonded to each other, heart and soul. Just the hollow facts, stripped of feeling.

"Oh, Mira, you are wicked." Lady Elendra turned to her group, "But I wouldn't expect anything less from a former Royal Guard" Mira's answer had satisfied the woman's appetite, for now. It would be more than enough.

By morning, the court would be aflame with whispers of how she and Tharion had spent their first year as bonded betrothed. Wildfire had nothing on Elendra's brand of rumor.

Since their punishment, Tharion had felt so distant, like a stranger wearing a face she used to know. They still shared living quarters in the palace, but it was like living with the ghost of a man she could almost remember.

She hadn't seen him in days. He was assisting the townships surrounding the palace, his duties pulling him further away.

Elendra's hushed tone drew from her thoughts Mira "And it's good the Crowned Betrothed held this celebration.

Nobody has since him since the queen passed. This kind of weak leadership hurts the people."

He hadn't moved since he had entered at the start of the ceremony. His chair, though carved with care, was noticeably smaller, less ornate than the one beside it. The empty throne next to him, crowned in dark iron and etched with the sigil of the bloodright line, remained untouched.

It was Queen Sarelle's by legacy, and no one had dared occupy it since her death. They had no children. No heir. And so, by law and absence, ruling had fallen to him. A title passed not by blood, but by grief.

He looked pale beneath the sunlight, his posture rigid, his eyes glassy and distant. It was the look of a man who wasn't truly seated in the hall, but somewhere far away, searching the caverns of memory for a voice, a touch, an echo of her that refused to answer.

"Exactly. He needs to put plans in place for succession. The kingdom is in peril if nothing is done. I refuse to let the Khardradorian's swallow us whole just because Caelric is grieving." Mira whipped her head towards her brother's voice. Torvyn met her gaze, his eyebrows raised in challenge. The smirk tugging at his lips made it clear. Mira's jaw tightened as she resisted the urge to rise to Torvyn's bait.

His smirk was all too familiar, just like when they were children and when he'd dared her to steal an extra honey roll from the kitchen without getting caught. She drew a slow breath, then turned her words to the others.

"Has anyone actually thought about what he's going through? He lost his bonded. Six months might seem like enough, but grief doesn't work on a timeline."

"Ah, there she goes again, passionate as ever," Torvyn chuckled, nudging Mira like she'd just made some harmless joke.

Mira rolled her eyes and nudged him right back. "Don't mind him. He's always been the dramatic one."

Torvyn clutched his chest in mock offense. "Wounded! And after I've been nothing but charming."

He turned to the group with a grin, then extended his hand to Mira with a flourish. "My sister and I will now put all those dance lessons to good use."

"Oh, but Torvyn," Elandra said with a smile, her fingers lingering on his sleeve, "just a moment longer? I was hoping you'd share the latest from the council, unless you can't, of course?" Her voice dripped with charm, each word honeyed.

Torvyn only laughed, gently freeing his sleeve from her fingers. "Sorry, Lady Elandra," he said easily. "I gave Mira my word." He caught his sister's eye, still teasing, and took her hand. "Come on."

The waltz was effortless, a rhythm they had perfected in countless lessons. Their steps glided seamlessly across the room, as if no time had passed at all. Mira felt the corners of her mouth lift, warmth rising in her chest. For all his teasing and bravado, this was her brother. Steady, familiar.

She glanced up at him, her voice sincere. "Congratulations, Torvyn. Anyone could have witnessed your ceremony. I'm honored you chose me."

He smiled down at her. "I still can't believe this. The bond is different than I expected." His eyes grew distant. "It's like he's always with me, like I'm whole in a way I never was before. Never alone."

Mira's gaze fell to the floor, her smile dropping for the briefest moment. Her bond with Tharion was dim. She felt it in moments, like a warmth, then a strange emptiness. Like a moment withdrawn before it ever landed. Another consequence of Queen Sarelle's punishment.

Torvyn paused, his gaze dropping to her face, and then softly said, "Mira, I'm sorry. I didn't mean to bring up… you and Tharion…"

She cut him off with a quick, practiced smile. "Today isn't about me. It's about you." Her tone shifted, nudging him toward lighter thoughts. "Where is Brahn?" He looked above her and searched the crowd behind.

Mira forced a laugh. "Don't look for him. Listen for him. Find the pull of him with the bond."

Torvyn looked at Mira with worry, but closed his eyes and turned. Directly in front of him, the crowd parted, clean and deliberate, until Brahn appeared, deep in conversation with Lord Edric. And just like that, Mira no longer existed. Torvyn dropped her hands without a word. She let him drift back to his bond, drawn not just by love, but by something deeper, ancient and unshakeable. The pull Mira used to feel.

She stood alone, the music still swirling around her. The dance floor shifted around her like a tide, couples sweeping past in pairs. A flicker. Regret and longing.

A voice rang out across the room. "Mira Solwynd! You can't be on the dance floor alone! It will cause a scandal!" She rolled her eyes, a smile tugging at her lips as she turned toward the source. That voice could only belong to one person.

Her eyes landed on Ren, the bastard son of the Crowned Betrothed. The court's infamous heartbreaker, all charm and flirt, with a laugh that promised nothing real.

Ren was the mirror image of Caelric. Tall, lean, with dark hair that curled just enough to soften the sharpness of his features. The stubble of an unshaved beard shadowed his jaw, a constant reminder of his indifference to courtly expectations. It sent whispers fluttering through the court, faux disapproving glances filled with heat trailing in his wake.

He had the playful arrogance to match his reputation, sharp-tongued, self-assured, and always carrying himself with the quiet confidence of a man who knew exactly what he was capable of. A presence that demanded attention, whether or not people welcomed it. He was a man who wielded charm like a weapon, cutting down judgment with a grin and a well-placed jest. Courtly gossip had never bothered him. He had remained Tharion's closest friend throughout their scandal. He thrived on the court's discomfort. Everyone knew the truth about his origins.

Caelric had fathered him outside his bond to Queen Sarelle, a product of what many assumed to be a moment of desperation for an heir. The bond between the Queen and the Crowned Betrothed was said to be unshakable. A bond not born of treaty or bloodline, but of the navigators' will and heartfire. Yet even their bond could not prevent Caelric from straying.

When Queen Sarelle learned of Caelric's indiscretion, she had reportedly shattered several priceless artifacts in her private chambers. The announcement of Ren's impending birth escalated the scandal and shocked the court. Sarelle, once the unshakable figure of grace and composure, refused to hold court for months. Leaving the realm to be governed by her advisors and Caelric himself.

The court murmured that she had contemplated banishing Caelric's illegitimate son altogether. But in the end, she allowed Ren to remain, though not without making it abundantly clear that he would never inherit the throne. His very presence became a reminder that no matter how eternal a bond claimed to be, fallible hands still carried it.

Her eyes moved beyond Ren to where Tharion stood, a sentinel in worn leather and shadow. Mira stepped off the edge of the dance floor and began weaving between the dancers, her dress catching on the occasional breeze as music continued around her as she kept her eyes on him.

Tharion's armor, dark as aged bark and at his side, the hilt of his sword shone dully, an extension of the man who had become a shield for them both. He had neatly cropped brown hair, framing a hardened face. His steady, watchful eyes, which seemed to take in everything without betraying emotion, offset his sharp jawline and strong features.

Tharion was a man who radiated quiet strength, a guardian whose very presence promised both protection and loyalty.

She stopped in front of him, lifting her chin to meet his eyes. He towered over her, a wall of quiet strength and unreadable calm.

"Welcome home," she whispered, the words gentle. Tharion nodded, taking her hand. He lifted it to his lips in a gesture so formal it almost made her laugh. But this was Tharion since they bonded. Steadfast and reserved, even in moments like this.

She missed the Tharion who once wore his heart so openly. The one climbed the viewing seats to kiss her. The one who would pull her into the dark recesses of the library, where his restraint melted, and every moment felt like a secret just for them. Now, it was as if the bond had refined him into stone. Polished, cold, and just out of reach.

"Great Navigators above Tharion. Are you going to just stand there? She clearly wants you to ask her to dance." Ren rolled his eyes. Tharion shot him a glare, a sharp warning.

Ren only grinned, utterly unbothered. For a moment, Mira thought Tharion might ignore him. His jaw tightened, and his eyes flicked to her like he was bracing for something.

He relented, stepped forward, every movement deliberate, measured. His hand reached for hers, steady and sure, and she placed hers into it without hesitation despite the stiffness that lingered between their fingers. He said nothing, but the air around them shifted as he led her onto the dance floor.

The music wrapped around them. To anyone watching, it looked effortless. Seamless. Like nothing had ever fractured between them. But Mira could feel the distance in every perfectly placed step. Tharion moved with the grace of an accomplished dancer, his steps confident as he guided her effortlessly across the room. Mira followed with ease, yet something about him felt different. His movements were deliberate. Unlike balls they'd attended before, he maintained a careful distance between their bodies.

"How were the villages?" Mira asked gently, her gaze lifting to meet his. "Which ones did you visit?"

Tharion's jaw tightened, not in anger, but weariness. "Three along the border," he replied after a moment. "Anyerit, Emreth, and Hallen's Reach." Their steps glided in time with the music, elegant and practiced, even as his voice dropped. "They're struggling, Mira." Mira nodded, her brows drawing together as she let him lead her through a graceful twirl, skirts sweeping around her legs.

"Struggling with what, exactly?" she asked carefully. "If the Crowned Betrothed understood the scale, he might step in."

Tharion exhaled through his nose, the sound soft but

weighted. "He won't," he said, quieter now. They turned again, his grip gentle but sure. "We've been fighting Kharador for almost a year. He hasn't spoken to a single township in months. He's... not responding to the requests."

"Torvyn could help if you tell him what's needed." she mentioned. Tharion's steps faltered slightly, and for the first time, his composure slipped.

"He can't do anything Mira, they need everything." he said, the word brittle with restrained exhaustion. "Blankets. Food. Tools. Anything that reminds them that even without the Queen, Bharalyn is still standing." He looked away. "They're scared, Mira. And I don't know how much longer I can keep promising things I don't have the power to give."

The Queen's punishment had given them one mercy. Sparing them both from complete disgrace. Mira had been relegated to the service of Cleric Perrin. Her position as the daughter of a royal advisor had once poised her to become a lady-in-waiting, her future rooted in courtly grace and political promise. Perrin, who oversaw the palace staff and the affairs of the Altar of Bharas, had accepted Mira under her authority. The cleric directed Mira's days, serving both the palace and the altar, as she moved between dust- laden books in the library and the meticulous preparation of ceremonial rites and the endless rhythm of invisible work that kept the palace breathing.

The Advisory Council had presented Tharion the position of Underguard Steward, a shadow of his former role in the Royal Guard. Now he led hastily trained volunteers from scattered border villages. Coordinating defenses and the delivery of scarce resources. He had borne the demotion with quiet fury, channeling his energy into the villages he now served.

But the spark that once defined him had begun to fade, dimming with each passing day.

The joy that used to light his eyes, the cheeky jabs and charm she once expected, had vanished. He no longer reached for her hand, no longer pulled a smile from her with a well-timed grin. What had once been effortless between them now felt fragile, distant, as if their bond was being slowly burned beneath the ceaseless flame of obligation and loss.

Mira's chest tightened as they returned to the practiced steps of their waltz. She followed his lead, but each step felt like a fading memory of something that used to be brighter.

He was still Tharion, but the weight of his burdens was slowly eclipsing him, and she didn't know how to stop it.

* * *

They left not long after the dance ended, and Mira could already see the exhaustion hanging off Tharion like a second skin. It trailed behind him as he walked, heavy and silent, all the way to the washroom. His steps were slow, too slow. She knew he hadn't touched the heated bath in days, choosing instead the chill of a bucket and sponge. The punishment he thought he deserved.

Mira sat on the edge of the bed, watching him. He undid his armor piece by piece, fingers moving with a kind of bone-deep fatigue. Each strap took longer than the last. His hand paused over his chest, like even undressing cost him more energy than he could afford. When he struggled with the chest piece, Mira stood and crossed the room to him.

Her voice came softly, carefully. "Let me help," as she reached for the clasps, wanting to take even one burden from him. But he leaned away before she could touch him.

"I've got it," he said, quiet but firm. The wall between them rose in an instant. Mira froze, her hands suspended between them before she let them fall.

Her voice wavered. "Tharion…" He wouldn't look up, and the words withered on Mira's tongue.

He pulled the chest piece free and let it fall to the floor with a dull, final thud. Then his tunic followed, peeled away with a grunt, exposing the scars across his back and chest. So many. So new. All of them had come after they were bonded. And just for a moment, their eyes met. Mira saw him. Guilt. Pity. Regret. He turned away and disappeared into the washroom.

The door clicked shut. Mira stood there, staring at the door, feeling the weight press deeper into her chest with every second that passed. She shut her eyes and reached for a prayer with desperation. A plea to the Navigators. To fate. To anything. Something to hold her still. Something to keep her from letting go.

The silk of her gown sliding off her shoulders like a sigh. His steady, reverent hand anchored her to the moment, to him, its warmth a grounding presence. Tangled with the wild heat between them, the sweet and heady scent of tahla blossoms still clung to the air. His laugh sounded raw and breathless. The way it cracked her heart wide open. The taste of him on her lips. His breath against her throat, every word a vow he branded into her skin. The way the bond sang, alive and surging, threading through her like wildfire. Her own fingers in his hair, clinging, grounding. The moonlight on his skin.

✳ ✳ ✳

She opened her eyes, her breath hitching. Fragments of the memories Queen Sarelle had locked away had flickered at the edges of her mind since her death. Even through the haze, glimpses surfaced occasionally. Like cracks in a window.

Moving with careful purpose, she undressed, her hands deftly loosening the ties. The dress slipped off, pooling silently at her feet. Barefoot, she stepped lightly across the room. She reached out, pushing the door open just enough to peek inside. The soft sound of water floated towards her and through the crack, she saw him.

Tharion was standing chest-deep in the water, his back to her, muscles taut and unmoving, his head in his hands. The faint mist from the bath curled upward, cloaking the air in a humid warmth. With a quiet inhale, she stepped inside, the cool tiles beneath her feet a stark contrast to the heavy warmth that filled the room. She didn't speak, letting the steady rhythm of her heartbeat and the soft drip of water from the faucet fill the silence.

Carefully, she slid into the water. The heat enveloping her up to her neck. She moved toward him, her presence barely disturbing the surface of the water until she was close enough to reach out. Her fingers grazed the scarred planes of his back. He tensed beneath her touch, the motion sharp and instinctive.

Undeterred, she began tracing the roughened muscle with all the gentleness she could. Leaning in, she pressed a featherlight kiss to his shoulder, her lips against the warmth of his skin.

"Mira, don't." Tharion's voice was low. His hand caught hers, not rough, but firm, and slipped her hand away from his skin.

"Why won't you let me touch you?" she asked, barely above a whisper.

Tharion turned slowly, deliberately. The surrounding water stirred with the shift, rippling outward as if it, too, felt the quiet change in the air. Mira was still heart pounding. She met his eyes and searched for something behind them. A reason. A truth. Anything that would explain the distance he kept putting between them.

"Mira," he sighed, exasperated, but more weary than anything. Her chest clenched at the look on his face. The pain etched into every line. The way his brow furrowed. She shut her eyes. A single tear slipped free, tracing a silent path down her cheek. "You don't see it, what I see," he said, voice low, frayed at the edges. "All I see is…" He trailed off, jaw tightening. The silence between them stretched, heavy, trembling.

"…suffering, Mira. That's all there is. It's everywhere. In the streets. In the shadows. People being torn apart for bloodlines, for crowns, for pride." His voice cracked, just barely, but she heard it. Felt it. The gentle slosh of water stirred between them as he shifted. He shook his head, trying to drive the images away. "I can't let it go. Every loss.

Every failure." His jaw tensed, the frustration in his eyes dimmed by exhaustion. "Every day, I try to do something, anything, to help" His breath faltered. He looked at her then, truly looked. "So when you look at me like that" His voice faltered, softer now. "I don't know what to do."

For a heartbeat, he didn't move. The water lapped gently between them, quiet and echoing. His gaze lingered, just long enough for her to feel the weight of everything he wasn't saying. Everything he couldn't. Tharion turned. The motion was slow, careful. The water broke around him in soft splashes, trailing behind his retreat.

She didn't follow. She didn't breathe. Each step sent ripples radiating toward her, cool and soundless, as if the space between them had widened into something vast and permanent. He stepped out of the water, out of her reach. The echo of dripping water followed him, the wet sound of his footsteps fading against stone. Until there was nothing. Only the soft ripple of water around her.

2

MIRA CALLED OUT, her voice sharp with frustration.

"Torvyn, must I wear this? It's completely indecent. Father would lose his mind." She gestured dramatically at the gown hanging before her.

At first glance, it seemed modest enough. A floor-length black dress with sleeves that ended just below the elbow. But that illusion quickly fell apart. A daring seam ran up one side, exposing her leg nearly to mid-thigh. The neckline plunged dangerously low, and the back dipped all the way to the small of her spine, utterly bare.

Outside, the spring breeze drifted in through the open balcony doors, carrying the scent of blooming roses and wet stone from the recent rain. Birds sang somewhere in the garden below, oblivious to her wardrobe crisis.

Crossing her arms, Mira glared at the dress like it had insulted her. "Do you want me to scandalize the entire court?"

Torvyn appeared in the doorway, arms folded, one brow arched in that older-brother way that never failed to grate on her nerves.

"Frankly, I'm more scandalized by your whining. It's a dress, Mira, not a death sentence."

Her scowl deepened. "Easy for you to say. You're not the one being shoved into half a dress and told to look regal."

30

"No," he said dryly, stepping into the room, "I'm just the one who has to track every courtly smile and veiled threat so I can advise Father which allies won't stab us in the back at dinner."

She opened her mouth to argue, then let out a breath instead. He moved to stand beside the dress, considering it.

"Look," he said, his tone softening. "I get it. It's bold. But today matters. And like it or not, you'll make a statement just by walking in."

Mira hesitated, glancing back at the dress as the breeze stirred its hem, making it flutter like a challenge.

"And what statement is that?" she muttered. "Here I am, future political pawn, now with a revealed leg?"

Torvyn chuckled, moving to lean against the edge of her dresser. "No. The statement is, Here I am, look closely. Because Solwynd's won't be ignored."

She fell silent, lips pressing into a thin line.

"And," he added, that familiar smirk tugging at the corner of his mouth, "if you scandalize the court a little, it will remind them you're not just another pawn."

Mira rolled her eyes. "If I have to wear this, every champion had better ask for my favor."

Torvyn pushed off the dresser with an easy shrug as he headed for the door. "They will," he replied.

* * *

Mira sat next to Torvyn in the Queen's viewing box, the prime seat for the championship duel. The spring air was warm against her exposed skin. She had twisted her hair back with silver pins, leaving her neck bare to the sunlight.

The championship duel, held every five years, was the

most anticipated event of the spring. Aspiring guards battled for honor and the chance to become a royal guard, while young court members offered their favors. Being unable to attend and with no heirs of her own, Queen Sarelle had requested Mira and Torvyn sit in her place and bestow two royal favors on her behalf.

Mira's eyes tracked the champions sparring in the practice ring, their blades clashing and flashing in the bright midday sun. The championship barred the use of armor. No protection meant the fighters had to rely entirely on their skill, speed, and precision. Most of the contenders wore simple tunics and shirts, their movements unencumbered as they danced between strikes and parries.

Leaning closer to Torvyn, "Which one is the Queen's Champion?" she asked.

Torvyn pointed toward a man moving fluidly across the field. Mira was only a little younger than him. He had neatly tied back his hair, a familiarity about him that tugged at the edge of her memory, yet she couldn't place him. Shirtless, pants and boots, his every move was swift and precise, each strike and parry carefully planned. He was a strong, agile fighter who never gave up against his opponent.

"Over there," Torvyn said. "He was the Queen's ward until he came of age a few years ago, I think."

Mira tilted her head. A ward of the queen. No wonder he looked familiar. There were only so many children in the palace that they must have run into each other at some point. She studied his effortless precision. His muscles contracted smoothly as he deflected an especially aggressive blow.

"Impressive," she murmured, more to herself than to Torvyn. "What's his name?"

But something diverted Torvyn's attention. Another

contender was approaching the Queens box, a young man, smaller and stockier than the Queen's Champion. His blond hair caught the sunlight as he adjusted his grip on his sword.

"Brahn," Torvyn said, standing to get a better view.

Brahn tilted his head up. "Torvyn," his voice carrying easily over the noise of the crowd, "would you care to bestow upon me a royal favor?" Torvyn beamed, leaning over the railing.

"I've seen you fight, Brahn. You're going to need it." With a flick of his wrist, Torvyn tossed a blue flower tied with a golden ribbon down to the young man.

Brahn caught it effortlessly, his grin widening as he tucked it securely into the waist of his pants. Mira observed the exchange. She saw the way Brahn's confidence softened slightly under Torvyn's smile.

She'd been watching the two of them for a while now, and their connection ran deeper than just friendship, and yet, they still danced at the edges, like naming it might break the spell.

"Lady Solwynd," a deep, smooth voice interrupted, "would you care to give me a royal favor?"

She turned to see the Queen's Champion himself, standing just below the royal box. His eyes locked with hers. His stance was confident and calm. Mira rose to her feet, meeting his gaze with a smile.

Do you really need my favor, Champion? From what I've seen, you're doing just fine without it." He smiled back, "True," he said smoothly, "but even the most practised champions need luck."

"Wait!" The shout rang out from the sparring field, sharp and commanding enough to turn heads. Mira looked toward the source of the voice. A young man standing tall

amidst the other contenders. His clothes were simple yet well-tailored. A simple tunic and pants paired with polished boots. But it wasn't his attire that held her attention. It was his eyes, bright green and burning with an intensity that seemed to pierce straight through her.

She hadn't seen him since that day in the tree. He was no longer the boy Mira remembered. His frame carried strength and confidence. Sweat beaded on his brow, matting his dark hair to his forehead as he advanced toward the Queen's box. The glint of steel from his sword caught the light with every deliberate stride, his presence commanding silence. He called up to her again, his voice clear and laced with daring confidence.

"Lady Solwynd, grant me your favor?" The boldness of his words sent a ripple of murmurs through the crowd, but Mira remained composed, tilting her head slightly as she studied him. His challenge piqued her curiosity.

"Be careful what you ask for, champion. Are you sure it wouldn't curse you instead?" His green eyes sparked in challenge.

"Grant me the disadvantage, then." Mira's heart skipped. She leaned back, her fingers brushing against the blue flower tied with a golden ribbon in her hand. Her mind raced. Should she do as she was expected and offer the favor to the Queen's Champion, or defy expectations and choose the newcomer?

She glanced at Torvyn, his wide eyes silently urging her to make the smart choice. Her gaze shifted to the Queen's Champion. He stood poised and calm, his expression unreadable as he awaited her choice.

"If this is truly a curse," she said, her voice carrying over the crowd, "then I'll be helping you by bestowing it on *another champion." The Queen's champion gave a slight bow, graceful and polite, before stepping back without protest. Mira's attention turned to the newcomer as her decision settled in her chest. "I will bestow my curse on you, champion." She declared, holding the flower aloft.*

As she prepared to throw it, the young man suddenly scaled the side of the royal box with surprising ease, his boots landing softly on the edge. Gasps and whispers rippled through the onlookers as he leaned over the railing to be face-to-face with her. Mira held the blue tahla tree flower between them, her fingers brushing his as he took it. The crowd moved on, their energy shifting to the next spectacle, oblivious to the moment.

For a moment, he lingered his hand against hers, and then, in a swift movement, he dipped his head close to hers. His lips brushed lightly against the edge of her jaw. Mira's breath caught, her heart racing as he pulled back slightly. To anyone watching, it would have seemed like nothing more than a whispered exchange.

"I am sure this won't be the last time you curse me", he murmured, his voice below, tucking the flower securely into his belt.

✳ ✳ ✳

Mira stirred as the soft glow of dawn filtered through the window, coaxing her from sleep. Blinking slowly, she tried to cling to the remnants of her dream, a memory of the first time she met Tharion. A smile tugged at her lips as she closed her eyes, hoping to recapture the fleeting moment. But the persistent knocking at her door shattered the peace.

Sighing, she slipped out of bed and hurriedly pulled on

her robes. Tharion hadn't stayed here in months. His side of the bed remained untouched, made up with careful precision. When she opened the door, she found Nerra standing there, her youthful energy barely restrained.

The girl, just eighteen, had dark hair and bright brown eyes that always seemed to hold a spark of mischief. "Cleric Perrin sent me to fetch you. Ready to start the day, Mira?"

Mira sighed, still caught between sleep and the demands of reality. "As ready as one can be at such an hour," she said, her voice smooth, wryly composed. "Let me change". With practiced efficiency, Nerra helped Mira into a plain brown dress and tied the apron snugly around her waist.

Mira spent her days with the dwindling number of attendants. Many had returned to their villages over the past months. Working alongside them gave her a chance to hear their concerns and quietly pass them along to Cleric Perrin, circumventing the usual fears of reduced earnings or retribution. "What's on the agenda for today?" Mira asked as Nerra tied the last knot of her apron. Cleric Perrin had granted her a reprieve from her usual responsibilities over the last few days, assigning her instead to assist with Torvyn and Brahn's ceremony preparations.

"Well, we've all the meals to prepare, naturally," Nerra began, her tone bright and animated as she opened the door and stepped aside for Mira to follow.

They exited her quarters and began their walk down the long stone corridor, the sound of their footsteps echoing softly beneath the vaulted ceilings.

"Then there are the noble beds to make, linens to wash, not to mention the new shipment of candles that needs sorting. Oh! And someone mentioned that the storeroom direly needs a proper inventory…"

She continued, barely pausing for breath, her voice a cheerful rhythm that filled the quiet space around them. Sunlight filtered through the high stained-glass windows, casting shifting patterns of color along the worn stone floor as they passed. Mira couldn't help but smile. Nerra's chatter was an odd comfort in the early hours. The girl could talk endlessly, weaving mundane tasks into a stream of words that made the day seem less daunting. Mira nodded occasionally, half-listening, content to let Nerra's voice fill the quiet spaces.

The heavy wooden door creaked softly as Mira and Nerra stepped into the Altar of Bharas. It wasn't large, but it felt vast in the way sacred places often did. Even silence seemed to echo. The domed ceiling arched overhead in smooth, pale stone, its surface painted with fading constellations and depiction of the navigators, their edges blurred by time and candle soot. Small alcoves carved into the circular walls held offerings, bundles of dried herbs, polished river stones, folded prayers etched on linen parchment. Light filtered in through narrow stained-glass slits, casting pools of soft color across the floor, muted rose, indigo, and gold. The scent of old incense hung in the air, sharp and spiced with a faint trace of amber and lavender, grounding and ethereal all at once.

At the heart of the room stood the altar. A low, circular platform of moonstone, ringed with etched sigils that glowed faintly beneath the morning light. It looked less like something built and more like something uncovered. Cleric Perrin stood beside it, her white robes trailing in clean lines across the stone, every movement quiet and exact. She stood before a gathered cluster of attendants and novices, calmly distributing the day's duties with the gentle authority of someone accustomed to being obeyed.

She spotted Mira approaching, her tone remained even, but her gaze softened slightly. "Ah, Mira. Good timing." She consulted the parchment in her hand, and her smile deepened. "I know you were hoping for a quiet start today," she said, looking up, "but the storeroom is still a mess from the last shipment. I wouldn't trust the others to sort through the chaos without mistaking dried elderroot for ceremonial incense." Her eyes twinkled. "Besides, I know you've a talent for finding order in disorder."

Mira let out a soft laugh. "That's just because I don't trust anyone else to label things properly."

"Exactly," Perrin said, satisfied. She placed a hand lightly on Mira's arm, a brief, grounding gesture. "Take Nerra and Harwen with you. You'll have more than enough company." Her tone held something more than command. A kind of camaraderie. Trust.

Mira nodded once, more touched than she let on. "We'll handle it." Perrin gave a final nod, already turning to intercept another flustered attendant.

As they continued on, Nerra glanced sideways at Mira. "She really likes you, you know."

Not long after, Mira was in the storeroom, the cool air heavy with the scent of dried herbs and aged wood. She stood beside Nerra and Harwen, another young handmaiden, carefully counting the fruits, vegetables, and dry goods stacked in neat rows on the shelves.

Harwen, ever precise, moved with the steady grace of someone used to swaying decks and uneven tides. Her skin was sun-kissed, and her pale blonde hair, salt-lightened and stubbornly wavy, was bound in a loose braid that fell over one shoulder, often catching on the collar of her apron.

"Three crates of apples, but these here look like they've

seen better days," Nerra said, lifting a bruised apple with a grimace. "Maybe we can set these aside for the pies?"

"Better than letting them rot," Mira agreed, making a note on her list. As they worked in the storeroom, the only sounds were the soft scratch of chalk against slate and Nerra's steady stream of chatter, weaving through the otherwise quiet rhythm of their task.

"So, Harwen, Saltcliff, huh?" Nerra said, glancing over her shoulder as she scribbled down the count of potatoes. "What's it like? I've always imagined it's all cliffs and waves and salty air. Oh, and those little seaside markets with fresh fish. Do you have those?"

Harwen paused, her fingers brushing over a sack of grain as she counted. "It's... quieter than here. The markets are nice, but it's mostly just fishing boats and long days." Her voice was soft but steady, with a faint provincial accent.

"Long days, huh? What, like hauling nets and mending sails?" Mira asked, curious. "Sounds a lot harder than sorting crates of candles."

Harwen's lips curved. "Harder, yes. But simpler, in a way. There's a rhythm to it. You learn to listen to the sea, it tells you everything if you pay attention."

Mira looked up from her notes, "The sea speaks to you?"

Harwen shrugged, her eyes flicking back to the crates of apples. "Not in words. But the tides, the waves, even the gulls... they tell you when the fish will be plentiful or when a storm's coming. You just have to know how to listen."

"That's so poetic," Nerra said dreamily, leaning on a barrel. "I'd be hopeless at it. The only thing I'm good at listening to is gossip. Speaking of gossip," she continued, her voice dropping to a whisper, "you will never guess what I heard last night at the ceremony. The people in the towns are growing restless and that they might stage an uprising. Could you imagine? Why would anyone want to overthrow the Bonded Betrothed?"

Mira's hands stilled, her eyes shifting to Harwen, who was now inspecting an apple a little too intently. "I suppose people might feel differently if they don't think he's listening to them," Mira said carefully. Her tone was light, but her words carried an edge.

Nerra hesitated, fiddling with her chalk. "I mean… maybe," she muttered, her usual brightness dimmed. "But that doesn't mean it makes sense to rebel. Things aren't that bad,".

With her gaze at her half-rotted apple, Harwen's voice was low, "It depends on where you're standing, doesn't it?" The sickly sweet, tart scent of the apple filled the air. Her voice was calm but firm, cutting through the tension. "In Seacliffe, we don't see many of the comforts you have here. It's easy to think everything is fine when you're not the one struggling."

Nerra flushed slightly, her shoulders stiffening. "I didn't mean it like that. I just… I don't understand why they'd go that far, is all."

Mira watched the exchange, her brow furrowing as she watched Nerra's embarrassment. "Maybe it's worth understanding," she whispered. "Before it's too late to do anything about it."

Nerra glanced at Mira, her expression self-conscious and ashamed, before changing the subject. "Anyway, we've still got to finish counting these apples. No time for worrying about things like that, right?"

Mira didn't press further, but the unease hung in the air. Harwen caught Mira's eyes briefly as they returned to their work.

3

THEY WORKED STEADILY until mid-afternoon, finally finishing the tedious task of documenting and cataloging every item in the storeroom. By then, the other attendants had scattered, retreating to spend the quiet hours with their families.

Cleric Perrin, satisfied with the day's progress, had dismissed Mira and she wandered the halls, her thoughts preoccupied. Her feet carried her toward the library, the worn stone halls cool beneath her steps.

Torvyn had taken up their father's mantle after his passing, now serving as one of the Queen's advisors. Rows of ancient scrolls and heavy tomes surrounded his office, a place of quiet strategy and sharp decisions. He was all she had left now. The last of her blood.

Mira quickened her pace, hoping to catch him before the afternoon swept him into court affairs. She needed to speak with him about the growing strain in the outer villages. The shortages, the unrest. Rebellion, once unthinkable, now lingered at the edges of conversation like smoke before flame.

Turning a corner, she collided hard with someone, the impact sending her stumbling back. Before she could fully lose her footing, a firm hand snaked around her waist, steadying her.

"Mira," She looked up and found herself face-to-face with Ren. "It seems I can't walk and read," he said, the corners of his mouth lifting into a grin. He ran his hand through his hair, slightly dishevelling it. He wore a dark tunic tucked into well-worn riding trousers, the edges of his sleeves dusted faintly with ink and parchment dust, as if he'd come straight from the archives without bothering to change. A thin leather satchel hung at his side.

"Ren," she said, straightening and stepping out of his grasp, brushing imaginary dust from her sleeve. Her cheeks were warm, but she lifted her chin, voice light. "You should really watch where you're going. That book nearly took me out."

He laughed, unbothered, and pointed the leather-bound volume at her like a sword. "Or maybe you should stop sneaking around like a ghost."

Mira smiled, "Maybe you're just easily startled," she shot back, arching a brow. "

Untrue," he said, solemnly. "I'm startled exclusively by rogue noblewomen launching sneak attacks in narrow hallways."

"It wasn't an attack," she said, brushing off her skirts again. "I just don't expect people to come barreling around corners with their noses buried in books. What's so important it couldn't wait?" she asked, eyeing the cover.

"Light reading," he said, far too casually. He tilted the book toward her, the gold- embossed title catching the light. Legends of the Navigators. "Nothing that warrants knocking someone over, though."

Ren's grin softened, his expression shifting to something more sincere. "Are you all right? I didn't mean to startle you," he said, reaching out to touch her arm.

"I'm alright" Mira gently stepped just out of reach with a light shrug. The movement was subtle but intentional, and his hand dropped back to his side.

For a fleeting moment, his expression changed. She saw the flash of regret in his eyes. An attendant passed behind them, casting a brief glance their way. Ren's posture didn't change, but Mira felt the shift in the air. How visible they suddenly were.

"Where are you headed?" he asked, recovering quickly, his casual tone returning. "The library," Mira said, glancing back at him. "Torvyn's office, specifically."

Ren's expression shifted slightly at the mention of Torvyn, his brows lifting with mild curiosity. "Important business?" he asked, voice casual but clearly interested.

"Potentially," she said, careful with her words. "Just something I need to discuss with him. Things for the villages, to help Tharion."

Ren studied her for a moment, his scanning her face as if searching for more than she was willing to share. Then he nodded, the teasing grin returning, though it didn't quite reach his eyes. "I'll accompany you," he said lightly, holding up the book in his hand. "I need to return this." Ren spun on his heel and started down the hallway, the faintest bounce in his step as if he'd already decided she wouldn't argue.

Two acolytes passed them in the opposite direction, slowing slightly to whisper behind their hands. Mira sighed inwardly. "Didn't you just collect that book?"

Over his shoulder, he called back to her, "Potentially..."

Mira huffed. As much as she wanted to avoid the gossip that seemed to follow Ren wherever he went, she also knew arguing with him would only draw more attention.

With a glance at the onlookers behind her, she followed him down the hall.

The occasional rustle of parchment and the distant hum of a passing steward beyond the arched doorway broke the stillness in the library. Towering shelves lined the walls from floor to ceiling, their wooden frames worn smooth with age, each filled with books and scrolls that smelled of dust and ink. High above, arched windows let in golden afternoon light, their glass panes casting shifting patterns across the floor. A narrow outdoor balcony wrapped along the upper level, its wrought-iron railing twisted into curling vines.

Tucked among the rows were small reading nooks, some barely large enough for a single chair and a lamp, others hidden behind heavy curtains or shelves that curved inward like a secret waiting to be found. Mira had spent many hours here under Cleric Perrin's direction, copying records, translating half-crumbling scrolls, and losing herself in texts far older than herself.

Torvyn had stepped out but was due to return shortly. Mira had waited. The conversation ahead weighed too heavily on her mind to be postponed. Ren, to her mild surprise, had waited with her. He lounged comfortably in a cushioned chair by the window, one leg slung casually over the other, the golden sunset light pooling around him. It caught in the tousled strands of his hair, and painted warm shadows across the spines of the ancient tomes behind him, giving the entire corner a quietly enchanted glow.

In his hands, the book he'd claimed earlier hung open but forgotten, resting on his knee as his gaze drifted idly to the gardens beyond the glass. Across from him, Mira sat upright in one of the high-backed reading chairs, a worn leather-bound book open in her lap. Her fingers turned the pages with practiced ease, but her eyes barely skimmed the words. Her mind buzzed with the things she needed to say to Torvyn, the warnings, the unrest.

The silence between them wasn't uncomfortable. It had a kind of ease to it, the kind that only came with long-standing familiarity. Every so often, Ren would glance her way, never long enough to break the moment, but just enough to let her know he was still there, choosing to wait with her.

"Do you ever think about the Navigators?" Ren asked, his tone light, almost dismissive, as he thumbed lazily through the pages of his book.

She barely glanced up from her own reading. "Of course. Everyone does."

He shrugged, the movement casual, almost careless. "They're just stories, aren't they? Tales to keep children in line," He lifted his chin. "Honor the Navigators, or the storms shall rise and sweep you away." An unmistakable imitation of Cleric Perrin.

Mira laughed, the sound soft but genuine. She glanced up from her book, a faint smile tugging at her lips. "That's actually pretty good," she said, amusement flickering in her eyes. "You've clearly spent too much time eavesdropping on altar sermons."

Ren gave a mock bow from his chair. She could have buried him in the theological history of The Navigators, quoted passages, recited the sacred texts, lectured him until his eyes glazed over. But that would've been too easy. Too expected.

Mira closed her book with quiet purpose and set it aside. "They're far more than stories to scare children," she said evenly, her voice steady but edged with something warmer, even reverent. "The Navigators aren't just names carved into shrines. They were visionaries. Thinkers. Leaders. They were classically, unapologetically human." She met his gaze, calm and unwavering. "And that's what makes them worth remembering."

Ren leaned forward, resting his chin on his palm. His eyes lit up with amusement. "Alright, then. Who's your favorite?"

"Bharas," she said without hesitation.

"Of course it's Bharas." Ren leaned back in his chair. "Everyone loves Bharas here. He's the kingdom's namesake."

She shook her head, brushing off his dismissal. "It's not because of that. Pass me your book, I'll show you."

He raised an eyebrow but handed over the well-worn copy of the kingdom's shared mythos. Mira flipped through the pages with practiced ease until she found what she was looking for.

"Bharas wasn't like the others," she began, her voice softening as her fingers brushed the illustration on the page.

"He was the only Navigator who was royalty. Everyone else was a slave or servant."

She turned the book toward Ren, revealing the image of a young man, Bharas, standing high on a hill, his royal robes billowing in the wind as workers toiled in the fields below.

"But he didn't rule from a throne," she continued. "He helped our ancestors build their boats, gave them food, shelter, and protection."

She flipped to another page, showing Bharas hauling heavy timbers into the hull of a ship, his royal finery replaced with simple work clothes.

"And when it came time to leave," she said, her voice lowering as if the words themselves carried weight, "Bharas had to make a choice. He could stay and keep everything he'd ever known, including the woman he loved. Or he could sacrifice it all, his crown, his home, his heart, to do what was right.

Mira's hand lingered on the last page, her gaze fixed on the image of Bharas kneeling on the shore, one hand resting on the edge of a boat. The illustration showed his heart as a blazing flame, illuminating the surrounding night. In the background, a shadowy figure stood on the hill. Her face turned toward him as he departed.

Ren touched the book, thumb trailing over the woman, "Why didn't he stay for her? Shouldn't love be the right choice?"

"That's why he's my favorite." Her voice held a weight as she confessed. "Because he didn't just give up a crown or a place. He gave up his entire life, the person he loved. All for something greater than himself."

A deeply thoughtful silence settled between them. As if some ancient presence had subtly altered the atmosphere. Ren looked up at her, it wasn't his usual smirk or the teasing grin he so often wore. It was a real, warm, unguarded smile. As though she had pulled something genuine from him without even trying.

He leaned back and tilted his head. "For someone with so many hidden memories, you're surprisingly sentimental." She rolled her eyes and he continued, "But he's not my favorite."

She tilted her head in interest, "Who is yours then?". "Myrran," he breathed.

She raised an eyebrow, surprised. "The Seer?"

Ren brushed a hand through his hair, that effortlessly casual gesture he always seemed to make when he knew he had an audience. It made him seem confident, almost careless, but Mira was starting to see through him. The way his fingers lingered just a moment too long, the slight shift in his posture. He was nervous. He hid it well, but not well enough to fool her.

"Myrran wasn't a fighter, a leader, or a builder." His voice was low and thoughtful, "She was a dreamer. Looking beyond what was, to what could be. And while the others focused on the storms, the stars, the ships… Myrran saw something else entirely. She saw the world they were sailing toward before we knew it existed."

He reached for the book lying between them, his fingers brushing lightly against hers. The touch was brief, barely more than a whisper of contact, but it sent a jolt through her, sudden and sharp. Her heart skipped. She froze.

Across from her, Ren said nothing. If he'd noticed, he gave no sign. He opened the book to a page worn thin at the edges, the paper soft from countless turnings. With care, he turned it, revealing an illustration, still vibrant despite the age of the book, of Myrran standing at the bow of a ship, arms outstretched into the darkness, her white hair streaming behind her like silk caught in the wind. He slid the book closer to her.

"Some called her foolish," he continued, his eyes lingering on the image. "Said her head was too full of fantasies. But Myrran didn't care. She didn't just believe in the dream of a new land. She made everyone else believe in it too. Myrran had this way of reaching people. She'd look at you, and you'd swear she could see everything you were hiding.

Every fear, every doubt and somehow, she'd make you feel like all of it didn't matter. Like you could still be something more."

Mira glanced up at him. He was caught somewhere

between the story and this moment. There was a softness in his expression, an attentiveness in his eyes that felt dangerously close to affection.

Her fingers drifted along the edge of the book's cover, the motion slow, thoughtful. She wasn't entirely focused on the story. It was the weight of his focus. The quiet hush of his eyes on hers.

Ren whispered, "You know how it ends, right?"

Mira nodded, whispering back "Tell me anyway," something inside her needed to hear Ren tell her.

"She was the first to step onto the new land," Ren said, his voice barely a whisper. Mira looked down at the illustration of ships listing in the shallows. Waves crashing against jagged rocks, and Myrran standing barefoot in the sand, her staff anchored in the earth like a promise.

Ren's breath fanned her face as he narrated the image, "The storm had taken Lyren, but she stepped onto that shore like it was exactly as she'd always seen it. She planted her staff in the ground, turned back to the people who had followed her through the darkness, and smiled. She told them this was home. That they were going to be alright." Mira met his eyes.

"And then she was gone." Ren flipped the pages without looking away, slowly, revealing the image. Myrran lay encased in a glass coffin, surrounded by the ancestors who had made it to the new land. Their faces were solemn, grief stricken. One little girl stood in the back, eyes clouded with white.

"It had all taken its toll," he whispered. "The Storms, the journey, the weight of keeping them together when everything was falling apart. She gave too much of herself, and she knew it." Ren paused. "But she didn't stop. Not until she gave them what they needed." He glanced at the image. "Not until she passed on her gift. Only then… did she let go."

For a moment, the library felt impossibly quiet, the weight of his words settling between them.

"She broke hearts without meaning to," he said, his voice barely a whisper. "The way she made them believe in something bigger than themselves. Something beautiful. Something impossible."

His gaze never left her, the space between them seeming to shrink with every breath. For a heartbeat, the world stilled. Her pulse fluttered, sharp and unexpected, as something cracked in her chest. A memory not fully formed, just the edge of one.

✳ ✳ ✳

The scent of parchment. Afternoon light painting the shelves in gold. And then, heat.

The warmth of hands at her waist, steady and sure. The solid press of her back against aged wood, the faint scent of cedar rising from the shelves. Her fingers had curled into the fabric, anchoring herself.

✳ ✳ ✳

Her breath caught. The edges lingered hot in her chest, but it wasn't whole. It felt stretched, distorted. But the emotion wrapped around her all the same: want, tension, anticipation. Ren brushed his nose against hers. Mira didn't move. His breath brushed her face, warm, fleeting, and her heart lurched. Her lips parted, unsure whether to breathe or speak or fall. His hand lifted, slow and steady, hovering just above the curve of her neck. Not touching. Not yet. But she could feel the warmth of it.

The door creaked open suddenly. Mira jerked back, the moment shattering in an instant.

Heat rushed to her face as she turned toward the sound, breath caught somewhere between her ribs and her throat. She hadn't even realized how far she'd leaned in.

Torvyn's voice filled the quiet space, casual and utterly oblivious. "Mira! Sorry to keep you."

Ren's hand hovered in the air, suspended in the space where she had been. Slowly, his fingers curled into a fist, as if catching something that had already slipped through. He looked down at the table, his expression unreadable. He leaned back into his chair slowly, his movements measured, though his shoulders sank slightly.

Mira looked away, busying herself with the book on her lap. Her ears barely registered the words Torvyn was saying. Still, she could feel it, Ren's gaze lingering on her, silent and steady. Just for a moment longer. Then he pushed himself up from the chair, the easygoing facade sliding back into place.

"Well, don't let us keep you waiting, Torvyn," he said lightly. "Mira and I were just keeping ourselves entertained." A reflex. A shield. He reached for the book they'd been sharing, tucking it under his arm as he straightened. "Enjoy your conversation," he added, flashing a quick grin that didn't quite reach his eyes.

Mira's lips parted, as if to say something, but the words caught in her throat. She watched him leave, his footsteps soft against the library's stone floor, until the door closed behind him.

4

As Mira stood and stepped into Torvyn's office, the last light of day spilled through the narrow windows, painting long slashes of amber across the stone floor. Shadows crept along the walls, stretching with the setting sun.

Torvyn stood by the desk, striking the flint with quiet precision. A small flame bloomed to life in the brass oil lamp beside the open ledger, casting a soft glow that flickered across the room. The polished wood caught the light unevenly, broken by stacks of parchment and half-rolled scrolls. The lamp's light danced across his face as he straightened, the weight of the day settling on the slope of his shoulders.

The encounter with Ren still clung to her like perfume, light and dangerous. It had unearthed a memory of Tharion that had been intoxicating. A ghost of a feeling she'd once known. Guilt and longing pulsed through her in equal measure.

Nothing had actually happened between her and Ren. And nothing would. Mira straightened, exhaling slowly as she pushed the lingering warmth of the moment aside. Her heart settled. Her mind cleared.

Mira leaned against the edge of the desk, arms crossed, her expression cool but her voice teasing. "Why aren't you off with your bonded, basking in blissful domestic peace?"

Torvyn looked up from the scattered papers, a corner of his mouth lifting. "And leave you to talk circles around every advisor here? Not likely." Mira's smile faded.

She straightened slightly. "Torvyn." A beat. "How bad are things in the villages?"

His reply was a slow exhale. Shoulders sagged. A weight he'd been carrying too long. "Worse than I've seen in years." he admitted.

She tilted her head, eyes narrowing. "How bad?" He hesitated.

A flicker passed over his face, there and gone before he met her gaze. "The Kharador soldiers have stripped them bare. Grain. Livestock. Tools. Everything. Families won't survive the winter, let alone see the next harvest." He paused, his jaw tightening. "And the ones who tried to fight back?" Her stomach clenched. "They're being made examples of," he said flatly. "Publicly. Heads on pikes. One in every village square along the border. The message is clear.

He didn't need to finish. She already knew. Mira's hands curled into fists at her sides. "How many?"

His voice lowered. "Most of the border villages. They're starving, Mira. Dying. And no one is coming to help."

The silence between them chilled the air. Finally, she straightened, voice sharpening. "We can't let this continue."

Torvyn tilted his head. There was something in his eyes, part wariness, part admiration. "No, we can't," he said. "But tell me, little storm, what do you think we can do?"

The words hit her with more force than she expected. Little storm. It had been her father's name for her. Spoken with exasperated fondness when she'd thrown tantrums unexpectedly fierce for her small frame. Or when she challenged rules with the force of someone twice her age. The pet name had always come with a look, half pride, half warning. She hadn't heard it in years. Her chin lifted, resolving stitching itself back into her spine.

"Tharion said they need supplies," Mira said quickly. "Food. Shelter. If the advisors knew they could help,"

Torvyn gave a snort. "They'll offer sympathy and nothing else. They're very generous with their pity. Not so much with grain or resources."

"There has to be something. Can you convince the Crowned Betrothed to meet with them?" Mira's tone sharpened, a plea.

"Convince him?" he echoed, brow arching. "Do you think anything can convince Caelric in his current state? Mira, he doesn't even speak anymore. He hasn't left his chambers in days. They're moving him around like furniture." Mira looked down. She didn't have an answer.

Torvyn's voice lowered, gentle but firm, the way only an older brother could manage. "The people don't need more kind words, Mira. They need someone who gives a damn. Someone who'll actually do something." A pause. "You know that. I know you do."

Her gaze flicked to his. "What exactly are you saying Torvyn?"

He spoke slowly, choosing his words, "Sometimes, the only way to fight corruption and abuse of power at this scale… is to dismantle it."

Mira stiffened. "You already know about the rebellion." she whispered "You're involved..."

He didn't confirm it. He didn't have to. "I know as well as you, that a letter to Caelric won't save anyone," he said.

She pressed her lips into a line, her voice softer now. "He's hurting, Torvyn. Losing the Queen, it broke something in him."

"Mira," he said, and this time it was a little sharper.

"There's no more time. People are dying, right now. And your compassion for them?" he said, almost sadly. "It's surprising considering what they did to you." A beat. "To our father."

Mira remembered standing in the center of the great hall, trembling, not from fear, but from fury. Her fists had clenched at her sides, her chin lifted in quiet defiance, even as the sentence was passed. Their father, once the Queen's most trusted advisor, had been named the scapegoat. Punished for his lack of supervision of his kin.

He had accepted it without protest. Exile. He had gone gladly to protect what remained of their family's standing. To shield Torvyn's future. To preserve Mira's. She remembered the moment he passed her on his way out, silent, composed. The whole court watching, the Queen silent on her throne. He had paused only for a breath, placing his hand gently against her cheek. No words. Just that. And that memory… Queen Sarelle had left untouched.

"Just because they hurt us, Torvyn… doesn't mean we have to become like them. We can still choose compassion."

Torvyn let out a low, almost disbelieving laugh. "You think this is about us?" he spoke slowly, softer but the edge was still there. Buried beneath the warmth of his voice. "Mira." Her name was a sigh, gentle, fond, familiar. "You've always had a good heart.

You want to believe the world can be better. That people will choose mercy if you show it first. But those people out there? The ones starving? Dying?" He looked up now, his gaze steady, serious, almost sad. "They don't need hope or compassion. They need help. Real help. Food. Shelter. Protection."

He let the words settle. Her chest tightened. "You're not

wrong to want compassion, Mira," he added, voice low. "But sometimes? The most compassionate choice… is to stop giving it to the people who've already taken everything." He paused, come with me to Anyerit in a few days," he asked. "See it for yourself. And then decide if you still believe the Crowned Betrothed and council deserves your compassion more than them." His words pressed on something deeper in Mira than guilt. It felt like duty.

Mira's gaze drifted toward the window, where the palace banners stirred in the soft hush of evening. Gold and ivory, embroidered with the symbols of the court. So familiar they felt like part of her skin. These walls contained everything she had ever known, every rule, every duty, and every truth she'd been raised to believe. Torvyn wasn't pushing her out the door. He was standing beside it, waiting. Asking.

Her voice was quiet when it came. Measured. But not uncertain. "If Cleric Perrin approves … I'll come."

Torvyn's brow lifted, just slightly, surprise flickering there, quickly masked by something warmer. Pride.

* * *

As Mira stepped back into the library, the door closing softly behind her, a thought lingered in the back of her mind.

She hadn't seen pride on Torvyn's face since before she was bonded.

Mira turned the corner into the attendant's wing at a brisk pace and nearly collided with a solid figure rounding the same bend. She skidded to a halt just in time, her shoulder grazing his as they both jerked back in surprise. Brahn let out a soft grunt, catching himself against the wall to steady his balance.

"Brahn!" Mira gasped, reaching for him instinctively. "I'm so sorry, are you alright?"

"I've had worse," he said lightly, brushing off the front of his chef's apron with one hand. "Though I think you've gotten stronger since the last time you ran me down."

She gave a small smile, embarrassed. "That wasn't exactly a graceful entrance, was it?"

"No, it was not," he replied, a touch of warmth in his voice, though his expression remained mostly neutral.

Her gaze flicked past him toward the kitchen door. "Is Tharion inside?" He nodded, stepping aside, giving her room to pass.

The scent of stew met her as she stepped into the kitchen, warm, familiar, spiced with rosemary and salt. Tharion sat at the far end of the kitchens at a small rounded table. He sat hunched over a steaming bowl, his dark hair damp at the ends, likely from the barracks wash.

Mira approached slowly. "Didn't know the kitchens were open for private service."

He glanced up, spoon halfway to his mouth. "They're not." He gestured toward the bowl. "One apprentice slipped me a helping."

Mira sank into the seat across from him. "So now I'm out of stew," she said, half- teasing.

"You didn't cook it," he said without looking at her.

"Neither did you." That earned the barest twitch of a smile from him, but it didn't last. He went back to eating, silent and methodical.

Mira rested her elbow on the table, tracing a worn knot in the wood with her fingertip. The silence between them was familiar, heavy but familiar. She swallowed. "Torvyn asked me to go with him to Anyerit in a couple of days."

Tharion froze, the spoon in mid-air. His eyes snapped to hers. "The village?" He lowered the spoon and set it down with deliberate care.

"Yes." Mira didn't acknowledge the tone in his voice.

His voice darkened. "Mira, that place was under siege less than a day ago. Half of it's rubble. Why would you,"

"Because I want to help," she interrupted, her voice certain. "They need healers. Supplies. I may not be a cleric, but I have been with Perrin for almost a year. I can dress wounds, stop bleeding. Comfort people."

He stood abruptly, the chair scraping back. "That village is not a place for you to go right now."

She stood too, eyes meeting him. "You don't get to decide that." His jaw flexed. "I'm not deciding. I'm protecting you."

"I'm going to that village. I have to do something ..." she declared. His eyes searched hers. "If there's a way to make even a piece of this a little better for them then I have to try."

He exhaled. The fight drained slightly from his frame. "Fine, but you stay with me. No wandering off. No foolish risks. You do not leave my sight. Understood?"

"Fine." The word came clipped firm with purpose, not defiance.

"Good." Tharion was quieter. More worn. He sat again, the bowl in front of him remembered as he began to eat.

Mira didn't push further. She just watched him, watched the way his shoulders stayed tense, the way his jaw clenched even in silence.

"Does Perrin know?" he asked, not quite meeting her eyes. She shook her head.

"I'll ask her tomorrow." Tharion let out a dry huff, half doubt, half resignation. He leaned back with a sharp breath, jaw still tight.

Mira saw it now clearly. He wasn't angry she was going. He was terrified she wouldn't come back. Tharion was still trying to protect her, always had, but this wasn't about her safety anymore.

* * *

Beneath the soft hush of morning the altar hall was quiet save for the hum of cicadas outside the tall, arched windows. Warm sunlight spilled across the polished stone floor in golden ribbons, flickering through leaves swaying in the breeze. The scent of sun- warmed dried herbs clung to the air, grounded by the ever-present burn of the incense curling from the altar door.

Mira pushed open the carved door, boots tapping impatiently on stone. Cleric Perrin didn't look up immediately. She was finishing the last loop of a careful sigil in pale chalk along the edge of the dais. Her veil fluttered slightly in the cross-breeze, catching the light like woven moonlight.

"You walk like the day's already behind you," Perrin said mildly, still crouched. "And the sun's barely cleared the sky."

"I've been arguing with myself for the past two hours about how to ask you so you will say yes..." Mira said, striding forward, barely bothering to lower her voice.

Perrin rose slowly, dusting her fingers off with a linen cloth. "I assume this is your way of saying you've come with a request for time away."

Mira nodded once. Firm. "I want to go with Torvyn to Anyerit. He's leaving tomorrow." Perrin studied her, saying nothing at first.

Mira continued, "The village was hit hard. There's nothing left standing. They need aid. I'm not trained like you, but I can help. Even basic healing makes a difference."

The cleric moved to light a summer candle, tallow and lavender, low and slow-burning. She cupped her hand around the match and waited for Mira to keep speaking.

When she didn't, Perrin turned. "Tell me what you're really hoping to find there"

Mira's voice was quiet. "The people there have nothing. And I... I have the luxury of choice. I want to use it to help them."

Perrin regarded her with a gaze that saw more than it revealed. Her expression softened. She walked to the basin beside the altar and dipped her fingers into the water. "You know what you'll witness there won't be easy," she said, turning back to face Mira.

Mira nodded, "I do."

"And that there may be more to Torvyn's purpose than simply relief work?" Perrin spoke with no judgement.

Mira's jaw tensed, but she didn't flinch. "Yes."

There was no rebuke in Perrin's silence, only thoughtfulness. She stepped forward and gently placed a hand over Mira's. "Then go. See it with your own eyes. But don't just look at what's broken." Her voice was softer now, almost reverent. "Look for what still stands."

Mira took a breath, nodding. "Thank you."

Perrin offered the smallest of smiles, though her eyes held firm. "Don't thank me until you come back." She looked at Mira through her veil for a moment, eyes narrowing before moving on. "You'll be in the sanctum today. The central stacks need reordering, and the tomb ledgers are waiting to be archived properly." she paused, "Take it as a quiet place to think, before the noise of the road."

Mira hesitated. Perrin had never allowed her in the sanctum before. It was usually reserved for her acolytes. Mira nodded and turned away toward the rear alcove. Here the dust smelled of old vellum and the tomb ledgers sat in solemn, uneven stacks. The space was quiet, removed, lined with arched shelving and narrow nooks carved into the stone. A single narrow window spilled sunlight across the floor like a golden blade, catching on the edges of faded ink and brittle parchment.

And Mira let herself exhale. It wasn't punishment she assured herself. It was a pause. A breath. A place to be still before she faced fire. She rolled up her sleeves, laid her palms on the first stack of ledgers.

5

ALL THREE HAD AGREED. Cleric Perrin, Torvyen and Tharion had insisted that Mira ride in the convoy of carriages, a decision she accepted with visible reluctance. She'd argued, of course, but none of them had budged. Riding in a carriage felt stifling compared to the freedom of a horse, where the wind and open air would have been her companions. But with Tharion stationed on one side of the carriage and Torvyn on the other, they'd made their point clear. There would be no sneaking off to commandeer a spare steed.

Through the small carriage window, she caught sight of Tharion riding beside her. He sat tall in the saddle, his dark cloak shifting slightly in the breeze, revealing black leather armor marred with faint scratches, silent testaments to the battles he'd fought out here. His sword rested against his hip, the hilt worn from years of use.

Once, she might have felt a spark of heat seeing him like this, a steadfast warrior, commanding and unshakable. But now, she felt only the faint ache of something unspoken, something muted and distant. Whatever connection they shared was buried deep in their memories. Her gaze lingered on him as he turned his head, scanning the horizon with sharp eyes that always seemed to search elsewhere. Once, his unwavering devotion to duty had impressed her. Now, it felt like a wall shutting her out.

The journey to Anyerit was short, just a few hours, but to Mira, it felt endless. She sat stiffly, her chin resting on her hand as she gazed out at the changing landscape. The lush gardens and towering trees near the palace gave way to the township surrounding the palace, then to orderly farmland. The neat rows of crops stretching across rolling hills. Sunlight bathed the fields, and for a fleeting moment, Mira allowed herself to believe that the rumors about Anyerit might have been exaggerated. But as the convoy pressed on, the scenery changed. The crops grew sparse, their leaves curling and browning.

Vibrant green turned to dull yellow, and yellow gave way to brittle brown.

Mira leaned closer to the window, her brow furrowing as she watched the life drain from the land. There were no signs of fire or war, no scorched earth or smoldering ruins. These fields should have been thriving, feeding the people who worked them, but they had simply withered, as if the land itself had been drained of vitality.

The convoy slowed near a small rest point, the drivers pausing to water the horses. Mira welcomed the stop, stepping down from the carriage as the heavy fabric of her simple gray dress swayed around her legs. The design was practical for travel, with a fitted bodice and loose sleeves that gathered at her elbows. Tharion dismounted his horse with practiced ease, his boots crunching on the gravel as he approached her. His eyes scanned the horizon, his hand resting on the hilt of his sword.

"What happened here?" Mira asked, her voice low as her gaze drifted to the barren fields.

"They poisoned the fields," Tharion said grimly. "It's a classic Kharadorian tactic from a few hundred years ago. Kill the land, starve the people, weaken the kingdom."

Mira frowned, stepping away from him as her curiosity

pulled her toward the field's edge. She knelt down, brushing her fingers over the dry, cracked soil. Her brow furrowed as she surveyed it.

"No," she murmured, more to herself than anyone else. "This isn't poison. It's salt." Tharion stepped closer, his tone skeptical. "Salt?"

"It's like the salt we use in the rituals," she murmured, rising to her feet and brushing the dry soil from her palms. She held a small pinch of the coarse white substance out toward Tharion, her hand steady. He took some without hesitation, his glove brushed lightly against her fingers as he did. "Why would they salt the fields instead of poisoning them?" she asked, turning the granules over carefully in her palm.

"Poison would be faster. Far more effective." Tharion glanced down at the earth. From behind her, "Salt can eventually be removed."

Mira turned as she caught sight of Ren. He wore a dark travelling cape. The high collar framed his sharp jawline, and beneath it, his black tunic clung to the lean muscle of his chest. He always carried his strength so effortlessly.

Her eyes caught Ren's, and he tilted his head. A glint in his eyes. He'd caught her admiring him. Mira snapped her eyes to the salted filled ground. Mercifully, he said nothing, but she could feel his satisfaction rolling off him.

He continued, his voice calm yet sharp as he adjusted the leather gloves on his hands. "If they wanted to use the land for themselves one day, salting it would make more sense. It ruins it for now, but not forever."

Mira looked at the soil, the weight of Ren's words settling heavily on her chest. The Kharadorians weren't just mindlessly destroying, they were planning, thinking for the future. This wasn't just an attack. It was a calculated move to strip the land of its people and their hope while keeping it primed for their own future use. Tharion's jaw tightened, his voice low and hard. "They've condemned these fields to years of suffering."

A whistle rang out, cutting through the birds. The drivers signaled it was time to move on. Mira hesitated, her gaze lingering on the desolate fields for a moment longer, before turning away. She left Tharion and Ren where they stood and climbed back into the carriage.

A few moments later, the door creaked open. Ren stepped inside, Mira looked up, her eyes widened slightly in surprise.

Ren's lips curled into a smile as he shut the door behind him. "Looks like you'll be stuck with me for the next leg," he said lightly, his tone teasing as he removed his cloak and gloves, settling into the seat across from her. Mira shifted in her seat, trying not to stare as Ren sprawled out comfortably across from her.

The carriage jolted slightly as it began moving again, the rhythmic sound of hooves and wheels filling the silence between them. She forced her gaze out the window, determined to keep the silence, but she should have known better than to expect quiet from him.

"You know," Ren began, his voice laced with playful mischief, "this feels familiar, doesn't it? You and I, in close quarters." He leaned forward slightly, resting his elbows on his knees. Mira spun her head, her lips pressed into a thin line, but she didn't speak.

Ren's grin widened, and his voice dropped lower, making the already-small space between them feel impossibly intimate. "The way you looked at me. The way we..."

"We did nothing," Mira's cheeks warmed as heat crept up her neck. Crossing her arms tightly over her chest. "It was nothing."

Ren let out a soft, knowing laugh, shaking his head as if he found her reaction endlessly amusing. "Nothing?" he repeated, the word dripping with disbelief. "Funny, that's not what I remember. In fact, it seemed like we were…"

"I wasn't doing anything," Mira snapped. Her body stiffened as she shifted in her seat, suddenly aware of how close he was. How his presence seemed to fill the entire carriage.

Ren chuckled, leaning back with that infuriating ease of his, the glint in his eyes unmistakable. "You can keep pretending all you want, Mira... but I know we both felt it." His gaze lingered on her lips.

"What are you doing here, Ren?" Mira's voice, sharp and trembling with fury.

"Do you think I'd miss the chance to ride alongside enemy territory with you?" he drawled. Mira shot him a look sharp enough to cut. Heat prickled at the back of her neck anyway. Ren's grin only widened, "Tharion needed someone who knows the streets of Anyerit and let's be honest, I'm prettier than the rest of the underguard."

Mira snapped back at him, "Do you have no respect, for me, for Tharion, for the bond we share?" Ren didn't answer. He sat across from her, his elbows on his knees. She shook her head, the heat behind her words softening just enough to let the hurt bleed through.

"We're friends... but" She leaned forward slightly, eyes locked on his. Her voice rose again, more bitter now. "he is more than your friend, he's practically your brother."

✳ ✳ ✳

The slam of the doors startled Mira so violently she nearly dropped the brush from her hands. She'd just stepped out from the bathing chamber, steam still clinging to her skin, the warmth of the water a fading comfort. The silk robe at her waist hung loosely, damp tendrils of hair curling against her collarbone. She saw the figure standing in the doorway, even though candlelight flickered across the walls. Ren. His chest was heaving, eyes wild, searching the space as though expecting something, someone. Raw and unguarded, his presence was a stark contrast to his usual effortless charm. His gaze landed on her, and for the briefest second, something passed over his face, something so open and full it made her breath catch.

"Mira," he said, the word ragged, broken. She froze, confusion knitting across her brow. Why was he looking at her like that? Like he was seeing a ghost. As if she were lost. Before he could speak, she tilted her head and called lightly over her shoulder.

"Tharion?" Ren flinched. It was barely a twitch, but Mira saw it. His expression cracked. Something inside him crumpled. Her brows drew together. She took a tentative step forward. "Ren...?"

Tharion stepped into the room. His eyes flicked between them, and Mira caught the tightness in his shoulders, the stillness in his face. Ren swayed, and suddenly he was on the floor. He dropped to his knees like something had buckled inside him, hands curled against the stone as a sound tore from his throat, a sound that didn't belong in any palace chamber. A sob. Raw. Gutting.

She moved forward instinctively, but Tharion was faster.

He stepped in front of her, blocking her view, kneeling at Ren's without hesitation. His hand clamped around Ren's shoulder. Not harsh, not forceful, steady. Like a pillar. Mira stopped, stunned. Ren collapsed into Tharion's arms, his body shuddering as though it couldn't hold the grief inside him.

Mira stood there, unmoving, watching the way Tharion gripped him, not just holding, but anchoring. Containing the storm. She felt like she was watching something intimate. Something she wasn't supposed to see.

"I know," Tharion murmured, his voice level. Too calm, too carefully held. "I'm sorry, Ren." The bells tolled. One slow, sonorous note after another, each strike of bronze reverberating through the stone walls like a dirge. Mira's eyes snapped toward the tall windows. Not a celebration. Not a warning. Death. One ruler had passed. One of Ren's parents, adoptive or not, was gone. And in that tolling, Mira realized it didn't matter that blood hadn't bound them. The grief she saw in him was when the person who loved you despite everything, was suddenly gone. She knew that grief.

Mira's chest tightened, and her heart dropped. She could feel it now, the grief hanging thick in the room like smoke after a fire. She glanced down at Ren, curled into Tharion's arms, and the pang in her chest deepened. Tharion's hand cradled the back of Ren's neck, his other arm firm around him.

Mira had seen Tharion calm soldiers, seen him carry wounded boys home on his back without a word. She'd never seen him like this with Ren. Not protective. Not commanding. Brotherly.

Tharion's voice lowered. Meant only for Ren. Mira didn't catch the words, but they sank into the space like a balm. Ren's sobs didn't stop, but they slowed. Less jagged. Less loud. Still, Mira stood frozen.

"I should go," she began, but her voice didn't carry. Neither man looked up. She stepped back into the steam-warmed shadows of the chamber, her robe still damp, her heart thudding in her chest.

✳ ✳ ✳

"After everything he does for you Ren, this is selfish. And you know it." Ren shifted like he was about to speak, but Mira cut him off before the words could form, "We are struggling, Ren." Her voice dropped colder. "He's barely holding himself together. And instead of helping him, you're here playing games with me."

A pulse of guilt beat beneath her ribs, because part of her knew she wasn't just talking to him. This anger, this outrage, it wasn't only for Ren. It was for herself, too. Because she'd let herself feel it, even if only for a moment.

Ren tilted his head, and something filled in his gaze. It curled in his eyes like smoke, wrapped tight around the edges of everything he wasn't saying. Regret. Desire. Longing. The ache of knowing this was wrong, but wanting anyway. His face shifted, more serious now than she'd ever seen him.

"Let me be clear," he said, his voice steady but low, each word deliberate. "Whatever you think of me, of Tharion, of our brotherhood. This is not a game. You are not a game." His gaze burned through her and she tore her eyes away.

Searching outside the carriage window to where Tharion rode beside them. His figure was rigid, as always. His dark cloak trailing behind him, his hand resting on the hilt of his sword.

Her fingers curled against her lap, her nails pressing into her palms. "What happened changes nothing," she said finally, her voice barely above a whisper, "I love him" though she wasn't entirely sure if she was saying it to him, or herself.

Ren didn't reply immediately. He leaned back in his seat. His expression shifted. It was raw, quiet, and genuinely him. For a moment, he just looked at her, like he could see past every layer she tried to shield herself with. He sighed, "I know Mira," he said, his eyes dropping to the floor. "I know."

Neither of them spoke again after that. The road stretched on in uneasy quiet, the rattle of the carriage wheels their only company. By the time they crested the ridge, the sun had slipped behind a veil of cloud, and the air had cooled.

* * *

They arrived at a town that was barely standing. Houses were reduced to crumbling walls, their foundations exposed to the grey sky. People gathered quietly in the few places where roofs still held, their faces gaunt and hollowed with exhaustion. Fires had been lit not in hearths, but wherever there was dry wood, corners of broken rooms, patches of clear ground, even in the streets. The air was thick with smoke and the sharp tang of ash.

As the carriage rolled to a stop, Ren was the first to rise. His movements were composed, but Mira could see the tension in his jaw.Outside, Tharion stood beside the carriage, his broad frame soot-smudged from travel, arms crossed as he took in Ren's appearance with a scrutinizing gaze.

"You made it," Tharion said with a grunt, his voice roughened by travel and wear. "Thought maybe court life had made you too soft for the road." His words were edged with dry amusement. The kind of jab that came from years of brotherhood, all bark and no bite.

Ren grinned, stepping down and clapping a hand to Tharion's shoulder, a gesture so familiar it came without thought. "Please. I've been cramped in that carriage so long I might never ride again."

Tharion snorted, the corner of his mouth twitching upward. "That's what happens when you get comfortable."

Their exchange was effortless, the rhythm of old friends who'd traded bruises and stories under too many skies to count. Mira watched them, a tight twist curling in her chest.

"You wound me," Ren said, mock-offended, bumping his shoulder lightly against Tharion's. "I'll have you know I was perfectly capable of riding."

"You didn't want to. Typical of a spoiled court boy." Tharion muttered as he turned toward the carriage, already reaching for Mira's hand.

Mira was already there, waiting at the threshold, the scent of smoke and ash drifting in around her like a warning. Tharion's hand appeared in her view steady and gloved.

"Careful," he said simply, his voice softer. She placed her hand in his, and he guided her down. No ceremony, no flourish, just the same quiet strength he'd always offered her. As her boots touched the cracked dirt road, her gaze flicked up to meet his, and for a heartbeat, they simply looked at one another. Mira's fingers lingered a moment too long in his before she let go.

When she turned to look back, Ren was gone. He'd already slipped into the convoy, swallowed by movement and noise. Like he'd never been there at all.

Mira's boots crunched over the rubble as they made their

way through the remains of the town square. Tharion followed behind her. Mira didn't need to look back to know he was there. She could feel his presence, like a weight that followed her steps. She scanned the scene, the huddled groups of survivors, the makeshift tents fashioned from ripped cloth and splintered wood, the faint cries of children mingling with the moans of the injured. A large canvas tent stood near the edge of the square, marked with a crude red cross painted on its side.

Inside, the cries of pain were louder. Mira rolled up her sleeves as she approached. The moment she stepped into the tent, the smell of blood and sweat hit her. A harried woman, her hands coated in grime, glanced up from tending to a man with a splinted leg. She looked at Mira with suspicion, her eyes darting to Tharion.

Recognition flickered across her features, followed by a palpable wave of relief at his presence.

"Tharion?" Her voice cracked, half disbelief, half relief.

He stepped forward, giving her a nod. "Ena, we came as fast as we could." She stood slowly, wiping her hands on a blood-streaked apron, her breath catching as she truly took him in. Tharion's jaw tightened. "I brought what I could. Grain, water, blankets, salve."

Ena looked toward the filled stretchers, "It won't be enough," she muttered. Not unkindly, just tired. "But it's something."

Mira looked around the tent, the crowded stretchers, the bloody linens, the desperate eyes of those waiting for help, and her shoulders sank.

"I know it's not enough," Tharion said quietly, his voice heavy. "I'm sorry."

Ena shook her head, stepping past him to check on

another patient. "It's more than we've had in days." Then, almost gently, without turning back, "And you being here… that counts, too."

"What can I do?" Mira asked.

Ena looked at Mira and hesitated, then nodded. "There's more than enough work. If you can sew, clean, or carry. Take your pick."

Mira chose to clean wounds. Her hands moved quickly and efficiently as she worked her way through the injured. She didn't ask questions. The people were too weary to speak. It wasn't until she knelt beside a young boy that the silence broke.

"Hi," Mira said gently, her voice soft like the touch of a breeze. She crouched to his level, careful not to loom over him. He couldn't have been more than seven, his slight frame nearly swallowed by a tattered cloak. He clutched a threadbare doll to his chest, his knuckles white. Dried tears and soot marred his face. "What's your name?"

"Samir," he mumbled, barely audible. He didn't look up.

"That's a strong name," she said, her tone light but warm. "My name is Mira, and this is Tharion." At the mention of his name, Tharion stepped forward, lowering himself into a crouch beside her. He said nothing right away. He just offered a small canteen of water, uncapped and held out with both hands, so the boy wouldn't feel pressured to take it.

"You don't have to talk if you don't want to," Tharion said softly, his voice roughened by the smoke in the air. "But you should drink something. It helps." Samir blinked up at him, wary. But after a moment, his fingers uncurled just enough to take the canteen.

Tharion didn't push. He waited as the boy took a slow sip, then another. When Samir looked up again, Tharion managed the faintest smile, not bright or forced, just steady. Reassuring. "That's it," he said. "You're okay."

She reached for his arm, noticing a fresh scrape running down the length of it, crusted with dirt. "May I?" Samir hesitated but gave a small nod, his grip on the doll tightening. Mira cleaned the wound, working slowly and carefully to avoid causing him pain.

"You're very brave," she told him as she wrapped a clean bandage around his arm. "Most people I know would have been louder than thunder over me cleaning a scrape like this."

She glanced at Tharion, his gaze was warm as he looked at Samir. "She's not wrong.

I've seen knights twice your size whimper like pups over less." Samir looked between them, the hint of a smile ghosting across his soot-streaked face. "You're tougher than half the guard already."

His smile vanished quickly at the mention of guards. "They came at night," Samir said suddenly, his voice barely above a whisper. Mira paused but didn't interrupt, letting him speak at his own pace. "People with torches and capes. And swords." His wide, brown eyes darted to the tent flap, as if expecting them to burst through it at any moment. "They broke everything. They burned..." He swallowed hard, his small frame shuddering.

Mira's chest tightened, but she kept her face calm and kind. "That must have been very scary."

He nodded, a tear slipping down his cheek. "Mama told me to hide. She told me not to come out, no matter what. But I saw... I saw it from under the stairs. I saw what they did." Mira's hands stilled for a moment before resuming their work.

"Samir," she said softly, "you did everything your mama asked you to do." "But I didn't help her," he choked out. "I didn't do anything."

Mira placed a gentle hand on his uninjured arm, her voice firm but kind. "You're here, and I am sure that's what your Mama wanted most.'

He looked at her, eyes shimmering with unshed tears. "Will they come back?" Mira couldn't lie to the boy. They might come back. And when they did, this town, these people, they wouldn't be ready. They didn't have the resources or people to defend themselves.

"You're safe right now," she whispered, brushing a stray lock of hair from his soot- streaked face.

Samir stared at her, his small frame trembling beneath the weight of fear too old for his years. "Will you leave?"

Mira hesitated. The truth was there, quiet, inevitable. "In the morning." she said gently. Samir's lower lip quivered. His voice cracked. "I want to stay with you."

Mira opened her mouth, but no words came. Her eyes shimmered, and she blinked hard, trying to hold back the tears threatening to fall in front of the boy.

Tharion spoke, his voice calm, grounded. "You won't be alone, Samir," he murmured. "Ena will be with you. She's strong, and she knows how to keep people safe."

Samir sniffled, nodding slowly, the fear still there but dulled just slightly by Tharion's presence.

Mira leaned in closer, lowering herself to sit on the stretcher beside him. "We'll stay," she said. "Until you fall asleep."

Samir looked at her, searching her face for any sign she might disappear the moment his eyes closed. She offered a small, soft smile. "Promise."

Samir's small shoulders relaxed just a fraction, the weight of exhaustion finally overtaking him. Mira held his trembling form and murmured a few soothing words until his breathing evened out. His grip on the threadbare doll loosened, though he still held it close.

When she rose, her legs felt heavy, as if the weight of his words had settled into her own bones. She turned away, fighting back the sting of tears, but it was no use. They slipped free, streaking silently down her face.

Tharion's voice, low and steady, spoke from just behind her shoulder. "You did well."

Mira shook her head once, a bitter breath catching in her throat. "It wasn't enough." He didn't argue. He didn't offer empty comfort. Instead, his hand came to rest gently on her back, between her shoulders, solid and grounding.

"It was enough for Samir." he said quietly. When she closed her eyes, all she could see was Samir's face and fear.

For a few breaths, they stood there in silence. The world around them continued. Murmurs of the injured, the soft rustle of fabric in the wind, the distant crackle of fire.

Tharion shifted slightly, his voice low but certain beside her. "Our tent should be ready. There'll be a meal waiting."

Mira didn't answer right away. Her body ached, her heart even more so. But his words, quiet, practical, grounding, eased something in her. She nodded and let him guide her towards the exit. As Mira stepped out of the tent, she stopped short. Torvyn was waiting.

He stood just beyond the firelight, arms relaxed at his sides, posture calm but purposeful. His expression was soft, but there was something resolute in it. He didn't speak. Just looked at her. And in that look, she felt the concern and the pride from days ago.

She stepped toward him. As soon as she was close, Torvyn pulled her into a firm embrace. She didn't resist. She let herself lean into him, surrendering the tired weight of her grief and all the strength she'd spent holding it together. Tharion stood nearby, his arms folded. But after a moment, he shifted his stance and quietly turned away, giving them the space they needed.

"This is what we're fighting for, Mira," his voice in her ear. "This is why the rebellion matters." Torvyn released her. "There are so many more towns like this," he continued, his tone heavy. "Places that are barely holding on." He sighed. "The raids hit them harder every day. Food is running out, trade is a distant memory, and they don't have enough hands to rebuild. We're not just fighting for survival. We're fighting for the chance to rebuild, to give towns like this a future."

Mira took a deep breath, her fingers brushing away the remnants of her tears. She nodded, a flicker of fire reigniting in her eyes.

"You're right," she said quietly but firmly. Torvyn offered her a faint smile. She stepped back, her gaze sweeping over the tent where Samir rested, then to the ruins of the town square, where survivors clung to what little they had left. She turned back to Torvyn, her voice low. "Where do we start?"

He looked at her, a glint of pride in his eyes, "Meet me tonight," he whispered. "Behind the granary, once the others have turned in."

✳ ✳ ✳

Mira followed Torvyn through the skeletal remains of the town, her breath coming fast as they weaved through the wreckage. His grip on her hand was firm, guiding her over fallen beams and shattered stone as they put as much distance between themselves and the granary as possible.

Shadows stretched long in the fading light, casting jagged shapes against broken walls where windows once framed laughter and life. Now, those homes stood silent, their stories buried beneath soot and ash. They ducked beneath a collapsed archway, moving low as charred beams jutted from the ground like blackened ribs. The scent of smoke clung to the air, thick and acrid, but the fires had mostly burned out, leaving only ruin in their wake.

Once Torvyn was sure they weren't followed, he led her to a small cottage on the outskirts of town. It had fared better than most. Its walls still stood, though the roof had been burned away, exposing the empty sky above. Smoke curled lazily from a smoldering hearth fire within.

They entered quietly. Inside, the dim light cast flickering shadows along the stone walls. A handful of townsfolk huddled close around the hearth, their faces hollow with exhaustion and fear. Mira's chest tightened. These people, these survivors, were all that remained of a place that should have been thriving. Someone stepped forward. Mira froze.

"Brahn?" The name barely escaped her lips, a whisper of disbelief. He wasn't supposed to be here.

Brahn was the principal chef at the palace. He had spent years crafting elaborate dishes, serving meals fit for royalty and nobles alike. His hands shaped feasts that were praised and envied. Overseeing preparations and barking orders to apprentices. He was always in the kitchens, ensuring every meal met the court's impossible standards. He never left the palace.

And yet… he stood near the fire, his dark eyes sweeping over the group before speaking.

"This isn't the end of our story. Not if we refuse to let it be." His voice grew stronger, each word deliberate. "We're not just fighting to endure this. We're fighting to rebuild what was taken. To forge something stronger than what they've tried to destroy. We fight for the future."

Mira watched from the doorway. This wasn't the Brahn she thought she knew, the one with boyish charm and the easy going demeanor that she saw with her brother. This Brahn was calculating, persuasive and every bit a leader.

"Look around you. This is one town, one among so many, but the story isn't unique. You've heard. The raids grow fiercer every week and it feels like we're losing more than we can bear, yet the Crowned Betrothed does nothing," a low murmur stirred among the gathered.

It began as breath, but grew. Anger. Agreement. Determination. He let it swell before he spoke again. "Even what we brought today…" His voice dropped just slightly, but the words struck harder for it. "It was siphoned from other allocations. Redirected. Quietly. By people I trust." That drew stares and murmurs of disbelief. Tension thickened in the air like a coming storm.

"There's no royal approval for this," he said. A flicker of silence followed and for a heartbeat, Mira felt panic spike in her chest. A sharp, breathless jolt. "No decree. No signatures." Brahn's voice deepened, quiet yet firm, each word laced with conviction. "We are not victims who will simply lie down and be forgotten. We are more than survivors clinging to what's left. We are the hands of freedom. The ones who will rise from the ruin and forge something new, something stronger, something ours."

He glanced toward the children huddled near the fire, his tone softening "We fight for them. For the chance to give them a life free from fear. For a tomorrow where they can dream of something greater than just survival." The fear that had gripped the room began to fade, replaced by something quieter, but far stronger. Hope. Brahn straightened, his presence filling the small space as he finished. "This is not our end. This is where we begin again."

A ripple moved through the crowd, not of noise, but of energy. Heads lifted. Shoulders straightened. The quiet murmur of agreement rolled forward Faces that had been slack with despair hardened. A man near the back straightened, his weathered hands clenched into fists. "For Freedom!" he called out, his voice cracking with emotion. The quiet murmur of agreement rolled forward like a tide reclaiming the shore. Hope. Not loud, but rooted, grounded. Real.

One by one, the villagers unfroze, not in haste, but with purpose. Someone returned to tend the fire. Another picked up a hammer, slinging it over their shoulder. A woman wrapped her child in a blanket and pressed a kiss to his forehead, her eyes no longer distant. They dispersed in pairs and trios, back into the square, back into the broken homes and makeshift shelters.

Brahn's gaze swept over the dispersing crowd, steady and piercing, until it locked with them. Torvyn had barely smiled before Brahn stalked over, pulling him into a fierce kiss. For a fleeting moment, the weight of the destruction surrounding them lifted, replaced by the overwhelming shock of familiarity and relief. They pulled apart breathlessly, foreheads brushing, neither quite ready to let go. Torvyn's hand lingered at Brahn's collar, and Brahn's eyes searched his face.

Mira took a tentative step forward, her voice carrying quiet admiration. "That was a powerful speech," she said, her gaze steady. "You've reignited their hope."

Brahn's gaze shifted sharply to Mira. His expression darkened as he took her in. He turned back to Torvyn, his voice laced with disbelief. "You brought her here?"

"She's ready," Torvyn said quickly, stepping between them. "She can help us."

"Help us?" Brahn's laugh was bitter, almost hollow. "Do you have any idea what's at stake here, Torvyn? What could she cost us if you're wrong?"

Mira stiffened. "If you have something to say about me, say it to me," he shot back, her voice sharp.

Brahn's eyes narrowed as he turned fully toward her. "I don't need to. You don't have a rebellion in you," Brahn said, with a hard stare. "You're a walking scandal, not a fighter." He glanced back at Torvyn. "You shouldn't have dragged her into this."

"She's not just a her Brahn," Torvyn said, his voice low. His gaze held Brahn's steadily. "She's my sister and the only family I have left. Mira can help us."

Brahn turned his full attention to Mira. His gaze was sharp, assessing. His jaw worked silently for a moment before he nodded, slowly, as if coming to some unspoken decision. "Then prove it," he said finally. Mira blinked, "Prove what?"

"Prove you have a rebellion in you," Brahn repeated, his words deliberate, his gaze fixed on hers with unrelenting intensity.

Mira lifted her chin, refusing to flinch under his stare. Her heart hammered in her chest. "What do you need?" she asked, her voice clear and unwavering, her resolve unshaken.

For the first time, Brahn's lips curled into a grin. Not the charming, calm smile she was used to, but something sharper, predatory. "The key to the convoy's weapons chests," he said. "Your bonded never lets it out of his sight." Mira's hands stayed still at her sides, but a jolt went through her.

"You're asking me to betray Tharion," she said, her voice low.

Brahn shrugged, the motion as casual as if he were discussing the weather. "I'm asking you to make a choice," he said. "If you want to prove you're ready to stand with us, this is how you do it. Betrayal comes with a rebellion, Mira. If you're not willing, then you don't belong here."

Torvyn stepped forward, his expression torn between anger and concern. "Brahn, this isn't..."

"She asked what I needed," Brahn snapped, cutting him off. "This is it."

Mira's breath came slower now, measured, though her heart thundered behind her ribs like a war drum. The key. Tharion's trust. She could still see him kneeling beside Samir. He wasn't the one responsible for this destruction, but he was trying. It wasn't changing anything though. She looked at Brahn again. At the hard glint in his eyes. At Torvyn, who wouldn't meet her gaze. And then past them, to the survivors outside.

She inhaled. Slowly. Sharply. "You're right."

Torvyn's head lifted. Brahn's grin returned, full and razor-edged. Her voice was steady, "This is a choice." A pause. Her fists uncurled. "You'll have the key before morning."

Torvyn's expression shifted, relief tangled with concern, but he said nothing. Brahn gave a small nod, like a commander acknowledging a soldier's oath.

The fire crackled louder and Mira turned away before the guilt could root too deeply, before doubt could unmake her choice.

Her boots carried her toward the door. By the time Torvyn fell into step beside her, she didn't look back. They moved through the shattered streets, the silence pressing between them.

"You don't have to do this, you know," his voice breaking the stillness.

She let out a quiet sigh. "Yes," she replied, her gaze drifting up to the stars. "I do. Not to prove myself. It's for them", Mira gestured to the houses around them.

They continued in silence, the crunch of their boots on shattered stone the only sound between them.

After a while, she asked, her voice barely above a whisper, "When did you know? About Brahn."

Torvyn glanced down at their feet, his brow furrowed. "He's always been passionate," he began, his voice thoughtful. "You know he came from the border villages himself.

But after the queen died... something in him changed. The villages had always been… worse off, but now they were suffering in ways he couldn't ignore." He paused, his expression softening, a flicker of something between awe and sorrow crossing his face.

"Something in him shifted. He became decisive, focused, strategic. He became a leader."

Torvyn's voice grew quieter, laced with a bittersweet admiration. "When he asked to bond with me, after all those years, I thought it was a dream finally realized. I thought it meant we could build something together, something lasting. But it turns out it was more than that."

Torvyn paused and took a slow breath. "He was becoming the man I always knew he could be. Strong.

Brilliant. Someone the people could follow, someone they would look to and believe in Mira."

He looked at Mira, his eyes glinting with the faintest sheen of unshed tears. "That's who you saw tonight. Not just a leader... but the man I've loved all along." Torvyn's voice was a quiet murmur beside her. "I've been smuggling him into villages since the Queen died. He has this ability to rally people. To make them believe in a better tomorrow."

His words held a deep weight as he carried the burden of every promise made and every sacrifice taken in this war. Mira smiled softly and nodded.

She turned her gaze back to the broken streets ahead, her thoughts clouded. Brahn's presence, his conviction. It was magnetic, even beautiful in its intensity. But it was that same intensity that deep down, that unsettled her. A fire could burn as easily as it could light the way.

They turned the corner and froze. Ren stood alone in the narrow street, half-lit from a torch spilling light from somewhere above. His back was to them, one hand resting against the hilt of his blade, his body unnaturally still. The air was silent, heavy with the tension that made every breath feel too loud. For a beat, he stood there still as stone, like he was waiting. He didn't move.

Mira spoke. "Ren?" He whipped around.

And in the space of a heartbeat, whatever composure he'd held snapped cleanly apart. The sharp set of his jaw faltered. His eyes found hers and raw emotion rippled across his face. Relief. Anger. Fear. All of it tangled too tightly to separate. He crossed the space in three long strides, urgency rippling off him like heat. No words. No hesitation.

"Mira," he breathed her name, cutting through the silence like a blade. Then his hands were on her face, rough but heartbreakingly gentle with her. Like he needed the feel of her skin beneath his fingers just to believe she was real.

"Where have you been?" His voice was low, strained, each word dragged from somewhere deep. "And Tharion?"

"I…" she started, but her voice wavered, barely rising above the sudden ringing in her ears. The moment pressed in too fast, too close. His touch. His words. A memory flickered to life within her.

✳ ✳ ✳

Starlight, the sweet scent of flowers, summer breeze, Tharion taking her arm, standing under the tahla tree, bright green eyes. A declaration, hands holding her face, a heated kiss…

✳ ✳ ✳

Mira blinked, startled as vivid memories surged through her, unbidden and sharp. But before she could say a word, Torvyn stepped forward, placing a firm hand on Ren's shoulder and shifting slightly to stand between them. Not aggressive, purposeful.

"That's enough, Ren." His voice was even, but carried a sharp edge. A warning wrapped in civility.

Her breath caught. Ren's eyes locked onto hers, searching, unrelenting, like he could see straight through her. His hands dropped from Mira's face, but his jaw clenched, as if holding something back. His gaze remained locked on her. Torvyn didn't flinch. He didn't move from between them. Mira took a slow breath, grounding herself. The heat of Ren's touch still lingered against her skin, but she pushed it down, pushed it back.

"I went for a walk with Torvyn," she said, voice calm, the weight of the moment still pressing against her chest. "I don't know where Tharion is."

As if her words had summoned him, Tharion stepped out from the alley behind her, his approach smooth, measured. Mira turned toward him and froze. His leather armor was streaked with dirt and ash, but he moved with an easy, almost careless stride. He wasn't looking at her. His gaze swept past her like a patrol checking the perimeter, not the people.

Ren's eyes flicked sharply to Tharion, his voice tight and low. "Where the hell have you been?"

Tharion's expression didn't flicker. "Patrolling the outskirts," he said. His eyes shifted to Mira just a glance, then back to Ren. That brief glance had landed like a blow.

Distant and detached. Not suspicion. Not concerned. Just… nothing. Only hours ago, his voice had been softer. His touch had calmed her. There had been warmth. Real, steady warmth. But that version was gone now.

"It's late," Tharion said evenly, turning to her. "I'll take Mira back to our tent." She nodded numbly, falling into step beside him. She didn't look back but she felt both Torvyn and Ren watch her walk away.

The walk to the tent was steeped in silence, every footstep marked with quiet tension. Tharion's movements were precise, controlled. When they reached the tent, he held the flap open for her. He didn't speak as she passed, simply stepped in after her, letting the canvas fall closed behind them.

Inside, the lanterns cast a soft, flickering glow across the tight space. Shadows danced along the seams of the walls, folding them in. Mira stood still. The warmth of the tent did nothing to chase off the cold knot forming in her stomach. She watched Tharion, but he was shut off, like a gate slammed closed behind his eyes. Distant. Controlled. Like that afternoon hadn't happened at all. Why had he even come after her if he was going to look right through her? And then it hit her, he hadn't come after her. He'd been following her.

Her thoughts twisted in on themselves, spiraling between confusion and anger. He hadn't just followed her. He'd watched from the shadows, silent, like she was someone to be kept in check. Like she wasn't worth trusting to breathe on her own. He hadn't taken her choices outright, no, he was smarter than that. He let her believe she had freedom, gave her the illusion of choice… while keeping a hand on the reins the entire time.

Mira turned to him. "What was that back there?" she asked, voice sharp. She took a step forward, arms crossing tightly over her chest. "You were watching me."

"Not you..." Tharion replied, voice calm, but low. Mira froze. Torvyn, he was watching Torvyn.

He continued, "I didn't know for sure. Not until I heard it myself." Mira's chest tightened. The truth settled over her like ice. He'd heard the speech, their whole conversation. He knew she'd been ready to steal from him, and he didn't seem to care. She didn't know why, but this landed like a bruise on her heart.

She looked at the floor, "I don't want to betray you, Tharion, but these people…".

He cut her off, "You're doing what I should've done." He reached for her hand. She flinched, but didn't pull away. His touch was gentle. When he let go, something small and metallic remained pressed against her palm. She looked down.

The key.

Surprised, she looked up at him. He nodded once.

"These people need a chance, Mira. A fighting chance. I've been trying to protect them, but it's not enough"

She shook her head, heart pounding. "This is treason."

"No," he murmured. "This is their survival."

Without another word, Tharion turned away and began removing his armor. Unfastening the buckles with steady hands. The leather creaked softly as he laid it aside, piece by piece, breastplate, vambrace. Mira watched him in the dim light, the lantern glow catching on the sharp angles of his face, the worn creases of his expression. The silence between them pulsed like a second heartbeat.

For a moment, just a flicker, she saw him, the Tharion she remembered. Not the soldier who kept her at arm's length, but the man beneath it all. The strong, clever, and quietly steadfast man. The one who cared deeply, not just for her, but for the kingdom, its people, and the duty he bore with pride. She swallowed hard. "Come with me,"

Her voice was soft, but it carried. Tharion's hands stilled for a moment, then resumed setting the last piece of armor down beside the bedroll. He straightened and met her gaze.

"Please" she whispered. He gave a single nod.

They left the tent with quiet precision, Mira tucking the key into her sleeve. The town was muted now, the fires dying low, the murmurs of voices thinned to hushed rustles and the occasional voice of a distant watchman. The air was cooler than before but the scent of smoke clung to everything.

They moved in silence, Tharion weaving between the scattered tents and broken beams.

Mira realized just how easily Tharion followed her. No searching. No stumbling. The path she'd taken with Torvyn earlier had felt instinctive, like slipping into shadow. But now she wondered if it had ever truly concealed them.

When they reached Torvyn's tent, Mira hesitated just for a moment. Tharion stepped forward and tapped the canvas wall twice. There was a rustle inside. Shadows moved. The flap lifted a few inches, and Torvyn's face appeared, brows furrowed. Surprise flickered across his features when he saw who stood beside her.

"Tharion," he said, guarded. "I didn't expect…"

Mira extended her hand. The key gleamed faintly in the lantern light as she held it out. Torvyn's gaze dropped to the key, then to Tharion, then back to the key again. His expression hardened slightly, in disbelief. Still, he reached out and took it from her, closing his fingers around the metal.

No more words were exchanged. Mira felt something inside her shift as the key left her hand, something irreversible. A thread pulled taut. Torvyn gave a tight nod. The tent flap dropped shut once more.

They stood there a moment longer, feeling the chill in her arms. Tharion didn't speak, only turned beside her, waiting for her to lead the way back.

As they walked, two shadows in the dark, bound together by a shared act of rebellion neither of them could ever take back.

6

MIRA SPENT MOST OF the following morning in the medical tent, her hands busy as she moved from one wounded to the next. She worked quietly but efficiently, offering small words of encouragement where she could.

The scent of herbs and salves mingled with the sharper tang of blood and sweat. She forced herself to focus on the people. By late morning, the town was a hive of activity. The convoy was being re-packed. Supplies and belongings strapped tightly to the carriages, voices rising as orders were barked and tasks delegated. The tension in the air was palpable. It clung to everything like the weight of an approaching storm.

Once Mira had washed and changed into a simple travelling pants and shirt, she made her way toward the carriage. Weaving through the chaos, until she spotted Tharion checking the straps on one of the supply carts. He hadn't noticed her yet, his head bent, his fingers tugging at a stubborn buckle. She hesitated, her feet rooted in place for a moment before she forced herself forward.

"Tharion," she called, her voice steady but loud enough to cut through the surrounding noise. He turned, his expression guarded but calm as he straightened to face her. For a moment, neither of them spoke, the air between them heavy. Her gaze flicked to the cart he was packing. Their theft wouldn't be reported until they were already back at the palace. Tharion's eyes briefly met hers, and after a heartbeat of hesitation he stepped toward her, holding her upper arm and guiding her toward the other side of the cart.

Mira stumbled slightly, glaring up at him. "What are you doing?" she hissed.

"Just keep walking," he muttered under his breath, steering her around the back of the cart, away from the watchful eyes of the camp. Once they were shielded by the bulk of the wagon, he released her arm, his touch softening as his hand lingered just a moment longer than necessary.

Lowering his voice. "Mira, we can't afford to slip up" he said, his tone softer now, though it still carried the weight of his concern. "If they notice anything off about this cart, it's over." Mira glared up at him, her frustration bubbling to the surface.

"I know what's at stake, Tharion. I wasn't going to…" The sound of approaching boots cut her off. Mira tensed, her eyes darting toward the noise. Quickly, Tharion moved closer. His forearm rested on the wood, not quite touching her, as he leaned in further, his face inches from hers.

Her heart leaped, catching her off guard. For a fleeting moment, she thought he might kiss her, for the first time since they were bonded, right there in the middle of this chaos. The thought sent a surge of heat through her, unbidden and impossible to suppress. She stretched up on her toes to meet him, trying to close the small gap between them. He shifted, his lips brushing her cheek instead. The gesture was quick, almost casual.

The sound of the boots stopped. Both Mira and Tharion looked toward the source of the noise. Ren stood a few steps away. The air between them crackled, charged. Anger.

Disbelief. Hurt. It all twisted through Ren's expression like lightning caught behind storm clouds. His jaw tightened.

His hands clenched into fists at his sides as he took a slow, deliberate step forward.

Tharion didn't move. Didn't flinch. His expression remained calm, but Mira recognised that calm. It was armor. Worn and polished. Ren stopped just short of them, his breath shallow. Mira didn't dare speak. Ren's eyes narrowed.

"What have you done, Tharion?" His voice was low, almost a whisper.

"Is a bonded couple kissing really your concern right now, Ren?" Tharion asked, his tone calm but pointed. He shifted, just enough to place himself between them. Subtle, deliberate. A silent barrier. A protector.

Ren's eyes slid past Tharion to her and then the cart. He blinked. A flicker of realization passed over his face.

"Give me the key," Ren said, voice flat, deceptively calm. Tharion didn't answer right away. His gaze locked on Ren's, jaw tensing as the silence stretched. One hand dropped just slightly, toward his belt. Not obvious. Not overt. But Mira saw it.

"You already know I can't" Tharion replied evenly, his voice steady as stone. "The people deserve a way to fight back." Tharion said quietly.

Ren's gaze flicked past him to Mira. Her cheeks burned. Tharion hadn't said we. He hadn't exposed her. He'd shouldered the blame alone, like he always did for her. For all of them.

Mira was finished hiding behind the sacrifices of others. She stepped forward, past the shield Tharion had built around her, until she stood at his side, as an equal. Her fingers slid into his steady, deliberate.

She lifted her chin as she met Ren's stare. "What we've done," she said, voice clear, sure. "We chose this. Both of us." The words struck like flint. Sharp. Unapologetic.

Ren didn't move. His face was stone, but the fire in his eyes blazed for a moment, before it was replaced with quiet grief.

Ren shook his head, "You think this is noble," his voice low but sharp. "But stealing those weapons, lighting the match before the people are ready, it's not a rebellion, it's a slaughter."

Mira didn't blink. "You think they have the luxury of waiting? They're already dying, Ren."

Ren took a step forward, his tone rising. "And you think putting swords in the hands of terrified people will stop trained soldiers? You're leading them into a bloodbath."

"We're giving them a chance," Tharion replied calmly. "To defend themselves. To stop waiting for help that clearly isn't coming."

Ren's eyes narrowed. "You're giving them hope without strategy. You're going to burn everything they have left."

For a long moment, nobody moved .

Ren exhaled, fists unclenching. His voice was quieter now, but no less weighted. "I don't agree with this," he said, eyes stayed locked with Tharion's. "Not your methods, or the timing. Not this whole Navigators-damned gamble."

"But?" Mira prompted, barely above a whisper.

Ren looked at her. His eyes gently held hers, unflinchingly. "But I believe in the people," he said. For a beat, the words hung between them. Honest, vulnerable, and final. Then his expression hardened and without another word Ren turned sharply and stormed off, the echo of his boots fading into the distance.

Mira exhaled, the air feeling lighter but no less charged. Next to her, Tharion's steady presence remained unmoving.

He didn't speak. He just watched the corner where Ren had disappeared, the tension in his shoulders slowly ebbing. He exhaled through his nose, a faint huff that was almost a laugh if there'd been any joy left in it.

Mira turned to him, her voice quieter now, edged with something uncertain. "Do you believe him?"

Tharion turned to face her. "Yes," he stated simply. "I do." She studied him, waiting for more.

His gaze returned to the space Ren had just vacated, his jaw working slightly before he added, "He's always had the people at his center. Even when it didn't look like it. Even when no one else believed it."

His voice softened, something almost fond tugging at the edge of his words. "The court sees a troublemaker. A flirt. A loose thread." Tharion sighed "But I grew up with him. He's always known which walls needed shaking."

Mira's brows knit together, questioning "Even if that means breaking the rules?"

Tharion shrugged, "Someone has to. We all have our roles, Mira. Mine's the soldier but Ren?" He glanced at her again, more certain now. "Ren can see the bigger picture. What needs to be done."

By the time they regrouped with the others, the sun had risen higher, shadows extending across the camp as wagons were loaded and final instructions given. They didn't speak about their betrayal the night before. Their words were easier now, casual. Small things, shared observations as they prepared her carriage. How the horses were restless and a quiet comment from Tharion about the uneven axle on the left wheel. Mira replying that it had leaned a little on the way. Nothing urgent, nothing heavy. Just small threads of conversation. There was comfort in it. An echo of familiarity she had missed.

The convoy set off soon after.

✷ ✷ ✷

Mira inhaled deeply, letting the crisp evening air fill her lungs. After the stifling confines of the carriage during the first half of the journey, it felt like freedom. She had managed to pester Torvyn into letting her ride for a while, and she savored the sensation. The steady rhythm of her horse's movements beneath her, the open road stretching ahead, the world bathed in the golden hues of the setting sun. The farmland rolled in soft waves around them, trees casting long shadows in the fading light. For a while, she simply listened. The rustle of the wind through tall grass, the distant call of a bird settling for the night. Peaceful. But beneath it all, something stirred. A restlessness. A whisper in the back of her mind that wouldn't quiet.

She turned toward Tharion, riding next to her. "Are our memories returning?" His head snapped toward her, his expression surprised. She hesitated. "I've been seeing pieces. Flashes of us from before." He went rigid. His grip tightened on the reins, his knuckles whitening. He didn't answer right away, didn't so much as blink. Mira swallowed, pressing forward. "We lost them together.I thought you'd remember too...".

Tharion exhaled through his nose, a slow, controlled breath, but the tension in his frame was obvious. "What exactly are you remembering?"

"Nothing clear," she admitted. "Just… impressions. A feeling, the weight of a hand that isn't there. Sometimes I hear voices, but I can't make out the words... and then it's gone."

Tharion yanked his horse to a stop. Mira had to pull hard to stop with him, her mare nickering in protest. The road fell silent as the convoy progressed slowly around them. Even the wind seemed to hold its breath.

He turned to face her fully. His gaze locked on hers, searching. She continued, "But I dream sometimes," the words barely more than a breath. "And in the dream, it feels real. But when I wake up… it slips away. I try to hold on, but it's like… trying to catch smoke."

His stare sharpened. Razor-edged. Careful. "And how do you feel afterwards?"

She hesitated. "Disoriented. Sometimes confused about where I am." A shiver crawled down her spine. "Tharion," she murmured, unsettled now. "Do you dream of me too?"

His reaction was slight. So slight, she might have missed it if she wasn't watching him. A flinch. A flicker of something in his eyes, gone too fast. Mira's breath came fast, uneven. A knot of unease tightened in her chest. "Tharion…?"

A sharp whistle cut through the air, fast. Deadly. Tharion grunted. An arrow jutted from his shoulder, buried deep in the muscle. He jerked sideways in the saddle. Sliding down, he reached out and dragged Mira down between the horses. They hit the dirt hard. Her breath knocked from her chest. He threw himself over her, his body a shield as chaos erupted, shouts, boots pounding, the crack of panic splitting the air. The whinny of horses, the heavy sound of hooves striking the dirt as figures emerged. Kharadorians.

They emerged from the trees, from the road behind them. Mira looked around as the horses bolted. Tharion lay over her breathing in quick gasps, gritted his teeth against the pain. She scrambled out from underneath him and helped him behind the nearest cover, the cart. The same one he'd almost kissed her against.

Blood seeped from the wound, darkening the fabric of his sleeve. Without hesitation, Mira gripped the arrow and snapped the shaft cleanly near the wound. Tharion let out a raw cry of pain, his body tensing beneath her hands. Mira's pulse pounded in her ears. Her hands, covered with Tharion's blood. She twisted to see their men rush toward the cart, fumbling at the latches. They were breaking it open. For weapons. For protection.

She and Tharion exchanged a glance. They both knew. The guard yanked open the chest. Empty. The moment stretched, then shattered as fresh panic swept through the group like wildfire.

Hooves pounded against the earth. Ren's horse tore past in a blur of motion, mud spraying as he held the reins, circling the group. "Fight with your swords! We outnumber them!" His voice was a blade, sharp and commanding.

He barely glanced at her. "Tharion! Her carriage!" Then he was gone, vanishing into the chaos of ambush.

Mira's pulse hammered against her ribs. Her breath came too fast, her hands shaking. She had nothing, no weapon, no armor. A firm grip closed around her arm.

Tharion. Standing, his sword drawn, his face tight with pain. His hold was steady despite his wound. He didn't speak, just pulled her with him, pushing forward, shielding her as they wove through the chaos.

Swords clashed. Soldiers fell. Somewhere, someone screamed. Mira stumbled, nearly slipping in the churned mud made from dust and blood beneath her feet. But Tharion kept her upright, his grip on her arm unyielding.

They moved in bursts, darting past the chaos, ducking beneath swinging blades, pressing through gaps before they could close. A Kharadorian reeled toward them, clutching his stomach where his leather armor had been split open, eyes wide with shock. Tharion shoved him aside and kept moving.

A sharp whistle. Tharion spun and pulled her to his chest. An arrow buried itself in the wood where she had been standing a heartbeat before, vibrating from the force of the shot. Her breath caught in her throat. Tharion's head snapped towards the shot, scanning the battlefield like a predator. He let go and moved, slipping through the chaos like a shadow. Mira barely registered what was happening before she spotted him closing in on the archer too late, hidden in the press of bodies, already reaching for another arrow. Steel flashed. The archer's body went stiff, then crumpled.

Tharion staggered as he stepped back, breath ragged. The wound in his shoulder was still bleeding, the dark patch spreading down over his leather breastplate, but he didn't stop. He knelt, yanked the archer's bow from their fingers, and turned. Without hesitation, he tossed the weapon to Mira. The quiver followed, slung from the dead man's shoulder.

Did she know how to use this?

Her fingers tightened around the wood of the grip. The weight was familiar. Her sharp eyes locked onto a Kharador dragging an underguard behind a burning cart. He couldn't have been more than seventeen years old. Without hesitation, she raised her bow and let an arrow fly. A sharp cry confirmed the hit.

She did.

∗ ∗ ∗

The night hummed with stillness. A silver mist curled

across the ground, rising in tendrils around Mira's boots. Shadows pooled at the edges of the practice ring, swallowing the world beyond. The torchlight flickered once, dim and distant, painting everything in shades of bone and ash.

She exhaled. The air kissed her skin with an icy whisper, slipping beneath her clothes, raising goosebumps in delicate swirls along her arms. Her fingers curled tighter around the crossbow, the worn grip familiar against her palms. Ahead, the targets loomed like ghosts, faceless, unmoving, half-lost in the dark.

"You call this difficult?" she murmured, voice soft, almost amused. She could make this shot blindfolded.

A low hum stirred the silence behind her. A sound like velvet over stone, familiar, indulgent. "Is this too easy for you, Mira?" The rasp of his voice slid along her spine like smoke, curling warmly in her chest. She turned her head slightly, enough to catch the ghost of him in her periphery, his shape outlined in gray scale, all shadows and angles.

"Oh, absolutely," she purred, every syllable dipped in heat.

He stepped closer, the world seeming to hush around them. A breath. A pause. "Try one-handed," he murmured.

The words spilled against her ear like silk. His hand slid over hers gentle, coaxing, guiding. Down. To him. The moment stretched, suspended. Her fingers brushed heat beneath the fabric of his waistband.

His breath caught, sharp and quiet. A moan from his chest, low and rough, vibrated against her fingertips. He bowed forward, pressing his face to her shoulder, his arms encircling her waist like gravity itself.

"Am I distracting you?" he asked, voice a broken whisper of silk and smoke. It wasn't the darkness that was the

challenge tonight.

She smiled, lips parting in slow amusement. "Not at all." She squeezed. "I'm just enjoying you." She stroked him, slow and languid, her movements precise, like aiming. His body shuddered.

He clutched her tighter. "Mira..." he groaned, her name escaping like a secret. He moved his hips, rocking subtly into her hand, breath catching again. Her eyes stayed locked on the shadowed target ahead. A breath. A beat.

"I don't think you have it in you," he whispered.

She laughed. "The shot?" she said. A pause. He groaned, the sound rumbling from deep in his throat as her fingers tightened.

Her name slipped from his lips again, reverent. "Let's make a wager," he breathed. His voice was darker now, threaded with desire.

"If you miss..." His fingers traced slow, hypnotic circles against her hips. "I get to draw out every moan and curse from your lips. However," he punctuated the word with a sharp thrust. "I." Another. "Want." Another.

"And if I make it?" He stilled, breath trembling. "Then I'm all yours," he said, voice rough "and I'll beg you" he said, voice rough, low. "On my knees if that's what you want"

She inhaled. He knew exactly what that would do to her. The image hit her before she could stop it. On his knees, looking up at her, his hands trailing slowly along her back, chin resting against her stomach. Waiting, wanting.

Her aim faltered. Just for a second. She blinked hard, breath catching, the crossbow's weight suddenly more difficult to center. But she didn't let it show. Focus snapped back into place like a drawn wire.

She lifted the crossbow. Her other hand still moving. And then, release. The arrow split the silence, a streak of silver in a world drained of color. It struck the target dead center, right through the heart. Silence fell again. Only their breathing remained, layered and uneven.

✳ ✳ ✳

It wasn't a crossbow but Mira barely noticed. She scanned the battlefield, chaos churning around her. Instinctively, her gaze swept the wreckage for Tharion. A glimpse of his armor, his stance, anything. But he was nowhere. Just bodies. Just fire. Just noise.

Soldiers clashed, metal rang against metal, and the acrid scent of smoke burned her nostrils.

She pivoted on instinct, losing two more arrows in rapid succession, one finding its target. Then she moved, darting through the fray, weaving between bodies and blades. Sparks flashed as Kharad weapons clashed around her, the heat of the burning wreckages licking at her skin.

A towering figure loomed before her, clad in a battered steel breastplate, his presence commanding even in the chaos. The leader of the ambush. His red cape danced in the wind behind them. For a heartbeat, neither of them moved. Their gazes locked. Mira grinned. Adrenaline surged through her veins, sharpening her focus. Without breaking eye contact, she raised her bow and loosed an arrow, deliberately off-mark, the arrow slicing past his shoulder. A taunt. A challenge. His expression darkened.

He lunged. A flash of steel. Mira twisted, barely evading the sword's thrust, but pain seared across her side as the blade skimmed her flesh. He barely had time to register the move before she spun, deliberate and precise. She aimed the bow mid-turn, directly at the back of his head.

The moment stretched thin. She let the arrow fly. She didn't linger to watch him fall. There was no time. Blood soaked the earth. They were winning, but they had not yet won. Mira tore through the fray, her mind already on her next move. She needed more arrows.

Thunder, a rhythmic pounding against the earth. Mira spun towards the sound just as Ren charged through the chaos. His horse cut a path like a blade through flesh. His eyes met hers. No words needed. He reached a hand out and she grasped his wrist. In one swift, practiced motion, he hauled her up behind him. Ren wheeled the horse around, driving it hard toward her carriage.

The battle still raged, the air thick with screams and steel, but he didn't slow. His grip on the reins was iron, his posture rigid. As they reached the carriage storage box, Ren yanked the horse to a sharp stop, using the stallion's hooves to break it open.

Wood splintered, the latch giving way with a sharp crack. Inside lay a crossbow. Smaller, more ornate. Dark, knotted wood gleamed beneath the dimming light, its form elegant yet deadly. A quiver of bolts rested beside it, ready. Ren didn't hesitate. He leaned down and snatched the weapon, turned, and shoved it into Mira's hands.

"Now," he barked. Ren was already kicking the horse forward, back into the chaos.

The moment her fingers closed around it, something surged through her. Recognition. She had just seen this crossbow in her memory. It was hers. She raised the crossbow, loading the first bolt.

They moved as one. Ren rode with effortless control,

weaving through the battlefield, while Mira took aim, losing bolt after bolt. Each shot found its mark, picking off the worst of the Kharadorians with deadly precision. Before the sun could fully set around them, the remaining fighters scattered, their resolve breaking. Shadows swallowed them as they fled into the trees, leaving behind their dead and dying.

∗ ∗ ∗

Throughout the night they counted their dead and burned the bodies, the acrid scent of smoke curled into the blackness. Shadows flickered across the battlefield, cast by the flames consuming the fallen. The distant cries of the wounded echoed through the clearing, a stark reminder of the cost they had paid.

Mira stood by her overturned carriage, her fingers idly tracing the grain of the crossbow's wood. She should have felt something more, grief, horror, even exhaustion, but none of it settled in her chest the way she expected. The battle had raged, blood had been spilled, and yet, she wasn't shaken.

For the first time in a year, she had moved without hesitation. It wasn't just the thrill of battle. It was the way she and Ren had moved together. Seamlessly and instinctive. She had felt like herself again, just for a moment.

She watched as Tharion, Torvyn, and Ren discussed the way forward, their voices low but urgent. Mira couldn't hear their words over the crackling of the fires and the murmur of the wounded. She could see the tension in their postures.

Tharion stood with a stiffness that betrayed the pain beneath his bandages. His jaw was set, pride keeping him upright.

Ren, in stark contrast, looked every bit the warrior fresh

104

from battle. Sweaty, disheveled, his dark hair damp and tangled, the scruff on his jaw seemed rougher than usual. Blood smeared his arms and clothes, some his, most not. His usual cocky smirk was absent, replaced by a quieter, more intense look.

And then there was Torvyn. Untouched. His leathers gleamed in the firelight, not a scratch or stain to be seen. Even his hair remained perfect, as though the battle had been nothing more than a mild inconvenience. She shuffled closer to hear.

"We need to figure out how to move everyone without the carriages." Torvyn stated.

"That's going to be difficult. We have too many wounded to walk on their own." Tharion nodded. "We'll have to redistribute. The strongest of us can walk or double up on horseback, while the injured ride in the carriages that still have wheels. But it's added a few more hours with the horse pulling so much weight."

Torvyn crossed his arms. "We take turns. Rotate the riders to keep a steady pace. We can make it work if we're careful."

Ren sagged against the broken wheel, "That only works if we don't run into more trouble." Ren's gaze slid to Mira.

She turned away from him. Shame, deep and painful, settled in her chest. People were dead, Bharalyn people. A consequence of her choice. Their blood was on her hands. Mira stared at the fire, jaw clenched so tight it ached.

Ren continued, "If we're ambushed on the way back, we're slow and exposed. We need a better plan." Mira exhaled through her nose.

"Also the supplies? We lost most of them when the carriages went down and we can't carry what's left." Torvyn warned.

Tharion's lips pressed into a hard line. "We take only what we need to get home. Anything else, we leave behind. It's not worth slowing us down."

Ren pushed off the wheel. "We can stash what we can't carry. Mark the location and send a retrieval party later."

Tharion nodded, "We can send word ahead, have them meet us halfway."

Torvyn's shoulders relaxed slightly as he agreed, and Ren exhaled. They would make it work. As the conversation continued, the exhaustion that Mira should have felt crept in.

Slow, suffocating but it wasn't just weariness pulling at her. Her choice had gotten people killed. That fact pressed against her ribs, hollowing her out from the inside.

She lowered herself to the ground against the carriage. The motion stiff and reluctant, knees drawing up slightly toward her chest. The fire's warmth reached for her, but it couldn't thaw the ice settling under her skin. The voices around her dulled, like a storm rumbling far away. She sat with it the weight of what she'd done, the silence of those who would never speak again. Her limbs felt heavy. She let her eyes fall shut. Just for a moment.

She heard Torvyn brushing dust from his palms. "I'll get the scouts moving. We'll need eyes on the next pass before dawn." His voice was low, firm, and efficient. No one argued. Mira listened as his footsteps disappeared into the darkness.

A moment later, Ren's voice cut through the low hum of the fire. "You gave away our weapons."

Tharion's voice remained calm. "I gave them to people who needed them more than we do."

"We're right alongside of hostile territory," Ren hissed, "People died, We could've held our own if we'd had those arrows." Mira's eyes cracked open.

Tharion didn't flinch. "Anyerit would've been protected in the first place if someone in Bharalyn had actually assigned resources to protect them." Silence.

Tharion sighed. "We can argue about it all night Ren, but I did what I thought was right. If that's a problem..."

Ren's snap could have cut through iron. "It is a problem when your version of right gets people killed."

The hushed argument rolled on, sharp and low around her, but Mira barely heard it. The exhaustion she'd been holding at bay finally settled in, heavy and certain. She sank deeper into it, the words blurring at the edges of her mind, until they faded into something distant and harmless.

✳ ✳ ✳

The market pulsed with life, a vibrant tapestry of color, scent, and sound. Silk banners of crimson and sapphire billowed overhead, casting shifting shadows over stalls brimming with sun-warmed fruit, fragrant spices and delicate trinkets that glimmered like captured starlight. The air carried the sweetness of honeyed pastries and roasted almonds, mingling with the rich, familiar scent of tanned leather and parchment.

Mira moved effortlessly through the crowd, the weight of her coin purse against her hip. Torvyn had left her to search for some specific items, muttering something about rare herbs, but she had little patience for potions and elixirs. Instead, she lingered by a stall of leather-bound books, their gold-embossed spines catching the light.

A flash caught her eye. Its edges worn, its cover softened by time. She reached for it, fingertips grazing the spine. A sudden force barrelled into her. Her breath was knocked from her chest. She gasped, tilting off balance, but before she could fall, a firm hand caught her wrist, steady and unyielding.

"Easy," a voice murmured, laced with amusement. "Wouldn't want you falling." She spun, the beginnings of a sharp retort on her tongue, only to find him. Recognition struck her like a whispered storm. Taller than she remembered. Strength carved into every inch of him, the kind earned through battle training. His dark tunic clung to lean muscle, his belt riding low on his hips, the hilt of his sword worn smooth from use. Strands of unruly hair curled down to his jawline, but it was his eyes, green, sharp, knowing. The tournament, the way he fought as though victory had already chosen him. The fiery intensity in his gaze, each perfect strike a dance of destruction.

"You," she breathed. The corner of his mouth lifted in a slow, knowing smile. "I recognized you at the tournament."

He nodded. She caught the faint, intoxicating scent of steel and cedar. "I wasn't sure about you at first either," he admitted, voice smooth, deliberate. "You looked every bit the noble. Poised. Untouchable. Stunning" A pause, his smirk deepening. "But then I saw the way you leaned forward during the practice duels. The way you watched every strike, every dodge." Mira's lips parted slightly. He had noticed that?

"You assume I wasn't watching the champions. They were all so attractive," she teased, masking the way her pulse raced.

His smirk didn't falter. "I remember you climbing trees at twelve years old. I can't imagine you're happy sitting on the sidelines."

Her breath hitched. He remembered. For a moment, the world around them faded. The laughter, the music, the shouting of merchants, it all blurred into the background, like a painting smudged at the edges.

His expression shifted, something heavier, something unspoken settling between them she couldn't quite see.

"You were meant to give your favor to the Queen's Champion," he murmured, the words careful, measured. "Everyone expected you to."

Mira lifted her chin, feigning indifference. "I don't enjoy doing what people expect." Something flickered across his face, something between amusement and relief. He exhaled, a quiet laugh escaping him. There was something else there too, something he hesitated to say. He shifted on his feet, the confidence from before giving way. His throat worked as he swallowed, his green eyes searching hers, as if looking for an answer before he even spoke.

"Come with me tonight," he said, the words almost shy, almost daring. Mira's brow furrowed. "What?"

His fingers brushed the back of his neck, a small, nervous gesture. "You didn't have to choose me. But you did."

Her chest tightened. She could have brushed him off, could have made some witty remark, but the way he was looking at her. Like she was something he had no right to hope for but couldn't stop himself from wanting.

His breath was uneven now, his voice rougher, lower, barely a whisper, "You don't owe me anything, Mira." Then he took a small step closer, closing the already small gap between them. He leaned in, his breath warm against her ear, his scent wrapping around her. Steel, cedar, and something deeper, something that could only belong to him.

"Please." His voice brushed her ear, sinking into her like

a hook. "Meet me at the Tahla tree. Midnight."

A slow, treacherous shiver coiled through her. She should have made him wait, made him chase, made him ache for it. And Navigators, how she wanted to. She let the silence stretch, tilting her head just slightly, her lips curving into something wicked and teasing.

"Tonight, you say?" she mused, tapping a finger against her thigh as if considering. "I don't know... I might have other plans."

He pulled back to look at her, his gaze sharpening, amusement flickering in the green depths of his eyes. "Other plans?" he echoed, one dark brow arching in challenge.

Mira lifted one shoulder in a careless shrug, her smile nothing short of wicked. "I might have better offers," she teased.

His green eyes narrowed in playful doubt, his smile deepening. Slow and dangerous. He circled around her, until he stood behind her.

"How can I convince you," he said, his voice dropping low, almost a purr. Mira didn't so much as flinch. She turned her head just enough to catch him over her shoulder, her smile sharpening.

"Just a flower," she said lightly. "But not just any flower. Bring the Tahla I gave you."

A low, rumbling chuckle left him, not frustrated, not annoyed. If anything, he looked like he was enjoying this far too much. He reached into his pocket, movements unhurried, and drew out a small, folded scrap of cloth. Nestled inside, perfectly preserved, was the tahla flower.

"You think I'd ever let it out of my hand?" he murmured, his smile slow and sure.

7

S OFT VOICES PULLED HER from the haze of sleep. She kept her body still, the fire's warmth brushing against her knees.

"You saw her tonight," Ren murmured quietly. "She remembered. Not pieces. That crossbow shot was all her." Mira's chest tightened. She could hear the smile.

Tharion's low voice followed, "She's always been in there. Even afterwards." Another silence. Heavier. "She's not ready." Tharion's voice stammered.

"There might not be a choice much longer, The Navigators will decide eventually..." A low sound of agreement.

Mira strained to catch the words. They were both whispering so quietly she could barely tell who was speaking.

"If you push this if it all comes back at once, she won't survive it..." The fire popped, and she shifted.

Tharion cleared his throat. "We should get ready to move." Ren made a vague sound, neither agreement nor denial.

Mira heard the soft clatter of gear and the rustle of worn packs as the two men began gathering their things. They knew. Both of them. And they were keeping her in the dark. Why did Ren know but she didn't? Tharion called out to Ren again, this time loud enough for Mira to hear.

"Mira rides with me."

A moment later, footsteps retreated, leaving her alone with the quiet. She kept her head down for a beat longer, inhaling trying to center herself. The anger simmered, low and steady beneath her skin, but she forced it down. They had people to move. They needed to get home. Now was not the time for confrontation.

She sat up, rolling her shoulders, shaking off the lingering ache from the fight. The air was already warming, the kind that tasted like the hot summer buzz. Around her, the others moved quietly, voices low as they secured their gear and strapped down what little they had left.

Mira rose, gathering herself. She took the half-empty canteen from beside her bedroll and poured the remaining water over the fire, listening to the soft hiss as steam curled up into the morning light. The embers darkened, the last warmth fading. She tucked away the anger behind her ribs as neatly as the supplies on their carts.

She spotted Tharion by the horses, tightening a strap. His jaw set in that focused, too- still way that meant he wasn't really thinking about what he was doing. She crossed to him, silent until her boots crunched softly over the dried grass. He didn't look up.

"Good Morning," she said, voice calm. Tharion's hand paused on the saddle. He turned just slightly, eyes meeting hers.

"Morning." He paused, "I know you heard us." The words were simple. Not accusing. Not apologetic.

Mira nodded once, slow. His eyes searched hers, checking, maybe, for how much she'd taken in. How much she understood. All she gave him was anger, clear and steady, burning just beneath the surface. He looked away first, adjusting the saddle strap with a last tug. "We'll talk more privately"

"Fine," she said. A beat passed.

His voice was soft, almost careful. Without looking at her, he asked, "Are you alright after yesterday?"

Her throat tightened. The memory of yesterday twisted through her chest. Grief, guilt, a helpless fury. She shoved it down, burying it "Yes." A lie.

She moved toward Tharion's horse, expecting to mount behind him as usual. But before she could reach for the stirrup, Tharion was already moving, swinging up into the saddle with practiced ease, his silhouette steady against the rising morning light. She paused, confused for a half breath, until he turned, reached down, and extended a hand to her.

No words. Just an open palm. Not commanding. Not coaxing. Just offering. Her gaze flicked to his face, but he gave nothing away. She placed her hand in his. His grip shifted in an instant, sliding to her waist and with one fluid pull, he hauled her up into the saddle in front of him.

She landed lightly, instinctively bracing herself, but his arm was already there. Strong and steady around her. Her breath caught as his body settled close, his chest firm against her back, the warmth of him soaking through the anger. His arms moved to collect the reins, one on either side of her.

✳ ✳ ✳

The convoy moved slowly. Wounded riders. Weak horses. Wagons rigged with salvaged wheels and fraying ropes. They kept to the treeline, following a winding path that cut through low hills and over ridges. The hush of early morning, of grief settling thick over the road. Mira sat still, tucked into Tharion's body as they rode at the rear of the line.

Mira's gaze drifted over the line of weary riders ahead. Over the hollow-eyed people, the stretchers, the damaged but

113

functional carts. A heavy cloak of silence settled on them, each stifled sob an echo of their pain. She exhaled slowly, pressing her spine a little deeper into Tharion's chest. His breath shifted against the crown of her head. A soft inhale.

The horse shifted beneath them, jolting slightly over uneven terrain. Tharion snaked an arm around her. Mira sucked in a sharp breath, a startled sound escaping before she could bite it back. Pain flared sharp and hot where the blade had sliced through her yesterday, a brutal reminder that her body was still catching up to her mind.

Tharion froze. The reins went taut for half a second before he pulled them to a halt. His grip softened, his touch becoming featherlight, afraid to cause her more pain. He shifted in the saddle to look at her side.

"You're hurt." The words slipped out, sharp with sudden realization. "You don't say." Mira forced a smirk, though it was tight.

Tharion exhaled through his nose, his jaw tightening. "Mira, you should've told me." He traced his fingers just above the wound, through the tear in her shirt, careful but assessing. His expression darkened. "You're bleeding." Mira gritted her teeth.

"It's fine. Just a scratch. There were more serious wounds to tend to" Tharion's eyes bore into her wound, "You're bleeding, Mira. That's not fine "

Before she could argue, he was already reaching for bandages from his horse's pack. He slowly raised her shirt up to the wound. He moved with practiced efficiency, looping it around her waist, tying it off just tight enough to stop the bleeding. His fingers never lingered for a second longer than necessary, his touch warm even as he lowered her clothes back. Tharion met her gaze, his voice quieter this time.

"You can tell me when you're in pain..." The words landed harder than she expected, striking a place she'd fought to keep sealed. To avoid wanting. Without another word, he nudged the horse forward.

The silence stretched between them, thick with all the things neither of them dared say. The steady rhythm of the horse's hooves filled the space instead, a hollow sound against the brittle quiet of the morning. Mira let it go on, her thoughts looping back to the questions she couldn't ignore.

She turned her head slightly, catching the sharp lines of his face in her peripheral vision. "Why do you and Ren seem to know more than I do?"

Tharion's voice came again, low. "We didn't mean for you to hear that."

She didn't respond right away. Her fingers curled lightly over his arm. "But I did," she said, turning back to the road. He shifted behind her, just slightly. Enough for her to feel the tension in his chest.

Tharion sighed, "We didn't know what had happened," he started. "What the punishment took, what it left behind?" Mira's throat tightened. The road curved, and their horse adjusted without command. She stared ahead, jaw set.

"It's our memories Tharion, I deserve to know," she said, quiet but firm. Tharion sighed. A warm wind tugged at his cloak. Trees passed like ghosts in the early light.

"It wasn't only the memories of the bond that were contained, Mira," he confessed. "What happened... it wasn't... clean." Mira's stomach turned. "Bonds can't be broken," he said, his voice rough. "But the memory of them can be." His hands flexed once on the reins. "Sarelle's punishment didn't just contain the memories. It carved through them.

Through you."

Mira stared ahead, her jaw locking tight. Rage coiled hot beneath her ribs, sharp enough to burn. "But you knew," she said, voice low and shaking. "You and Ren. You both knew, and said nothing." Her fingers curled into fists against her thighs. "Why?"

Tharion paused, trying to find the right words. She felt the tension in him, in the way his hand twitched on the reins.

"We don't know everything," he admitted. "But there's a power in a bond. And we think they were afraid of what it would become if it grew unchecked. Especially given the extra time it had to develop."

Mira's anger still burned, but underneath it, something else broke through. She heard the way his voice roughened, in the careful distance he kept. He hadn't been hiding the truth to betray her. He'd been trying to protect her from it. Like he had said all along. She exhaled slowly, the fight draining out of her ribs, leaving only the ache. She turned her head slightly, catching him over her shoulder.

"You were afraid I wouldn't survive remembering it," she said softly. Mira gave a faint smile, more tired than angry.

"I still am." he whispered.

"But I can," she replied, her voice steady. "You don't have to protect me." Her chest and ribs ached.

She turned slowly, shifting just enough to meet his eyes fully. They were shadowed beneath his brow, tired. But not cold. Not unkind. Just… exhausted. And before she could stop herself, before she could think it through, she leaned in and pressed her mouth to his. A soft, seeking kiss. Gentle.

For a heartbeat, she let herself believe he might meet her there, might remember something, feel something. The world held its breath around them.

But there was nothing in return. The touch was only skin-to-skin. She felt no weight, tug, or sensation. He didn't pull away. His mouth was warm but unmoving, his body still as carved stone.

Mira pulled back slightly, blinking. Confusion swept through her like ice. She'd expected something. Anything. He didn't speak. Neither did she. The silence between them stretched.

Frustration swelled inside her, pressing against her ribs, curling hot in her chest. Her throat ached with the sting of embarrassment. It felt like a rejection. Worse, like erasure. Like she'd reached for something she thought was there and found only emptiness. Mira whipped around to face the front, her hands clenched in her lap.

Silence dragged between them. Heavy. Suffocating.

She turned, sharp and sudden, hoping to distract them both. "Are your memories returning?" she asked. Tharion blinked once.

His expression didn't change. "It's not that simple." "That's not an answer." His jaw tightened. Just slightly.

"It's the only one I have, Mira." Something in his tone, flat, steady, weary, made her anger roar back to life. She swung her leg over the saddle and slid down, her boots landing softly on the packed earth.

He called out, "Mira…"

"I can walk, carry someone who can't," she snapped, the words quick and hard. She didn't look at him. Instead, she stepped forward and raised a hand toward a rider near them. Within moments, someone else had taken her place on Tharion's horse without question or fuss. She didn't look back. Not when she heard the subtle shift of his weight in the saddle. Not when she felt the heat of his gaze press between her shoulder blades like a question left unspoken. She kept walking, despite the pain in her side.

∗ ∗ ∗

The road stretched before her throughout the day of travel. Winding through fields that should have been bursting with life. Past villages that should have been filled with voices, with laughter, with people. But Mira walked in silence, her boots kicking up dust from a path that had seen too many leave and too few return.

The land had not been burned. No scars of war marked the soil, no remnants of battle lingered in the air. And yet, the damage was there, etched into the wilted crops, the cracked earth, the abandoned homes with shattered windows and doors left hanging open like silent screams. The once-rich soil had turned brittle, the fields now nothing more than skeletons of what they were.

In the distance, the palace and surrounding city remained untouched. The towering spires gleamed in the light of the setting sun, banners of gold and ivory catching the wind like delicate things that had never known hardship. Even from afar, she could see the intricate embroidery shimmering along their edges. Each thread woven with wealth, with indulgence. The palace walls, carved from pale stone and inlaid with veins of lapis and quartz, glowed as if they had captured the last remnants of daylight. Pristine, whole, unscathed by the suffering that occurred just beyond their reach.

Mira did not see any of it the way she once had. Not after what she had seen. The villages of hollow-eyed children, the fields that yielded nothing. A resistance that fought not for victory, but for change. And yet, here, the palace stood, unmoving, unwavering, wasteful.

Perfumed air curled from the city gates as they approached. Thick with jasmine, honeyed wine, and incense. She could hear the fountains before she saw them, their crystalline waters spilling endlessly into sculpted basins adorned with images and statues of Navigators. Symbols of wisdom. Of peace. A laugh almost slipped from her lips.

Footsteps sounded beside her, slow and careful. Tharion moved to her side.

"Not everyone believes a ruler should live in luxury while their people suffer." Mira didn't respond. The anger in her chest hadn't left, it just found a new target, coiling beneath her ribs like a blade half-drawn. Her gaze swept the palace walls, the glittering halls, the lavish banners fluttering in the warm breeze. All of it built on the backs of people who had nothing. All of it flaunted without thought, without shame.

Her rage burned hotter now, cleaner. It wasn't just the secrets, the betrayals. It was the sheer waste. The carelessness. The way the nobility treated survival like a game they had already won.

"Then let's give the ruler a reason to pay attention." Her voice didn't rise. It didn't need to.

She turned her head, watching him through the haze of incense and evening light. Tharion held her gaze for a breath longer, then nodded, just once. Quiet. Certain. He turned and moved ahead, weaving through the slow-moving column of riders and wagons, his stride purposeful as he made his way toward the stables beyond the gates. Mira watched him go, the distance growing between them again, not out of anger this time, but necessity.

Mira's steps were slow as she moved through the grand

halls of the palace, exhaustion creeping into her bones. The polished floors gleamed under the soft glow of candlelight, the distant hum of stringed instruments practised. Her fingers brushed against the stone as she walked, grounding herself against the reality of it all, the stark contrast between her and what lay beyond the gates. A memory surged forward, unbidden, sharp and searing, cutting through the exhaustion that clung to her limbs. It struck her like the lingering warmth of a dying fire, familiar, intoxicating, dangerous.

One year ago

The scent of spiced mead and salt filled the air, mingling with bursts of laughter and the steady hum of conversation. Lanterns flickered against the walls, casting everything in a golden haze, though maybe that was just the drink settling in. Their corner booth, half-hidden from the chaos of the main room, had seen countless nights like this. Debate and drink.

"The way Dralis treats its fishing towns, the way the wealth from their catch never seems to make it back to the people hauling the nets, is a disaster waiting tohappen." Mira leaned forward, tapping her fingers against the table for emphasis, conviction slurring slightly with drink.

"If we keep pretending, this isn't a problem, refusing to negotiate fair trade, the harbors will fall apart. And when that happens, guess what? Everyone loses. Trade benefits everyone."

Across the table, a cup tilted, mead sloshing dangerously close to the rim, nearly spilling onto an already drunk companion.

"Maybe," came the lazy response, voice smooth, amused. *"Still doesn't mean it has to be our problem."*

A pause, then a slow tease, *"Bharalyn thrives because it doesn't get tangled in other kingdoms' affairs."*

Mira scoffed, rolling her eyes. *"You cannot seriously believe that."* Her hand swept in a grand gesture, too grand, sending a half-finished drink dangerously close to toppling.

"These people, our ancestors' people, deserve better! They should be able to sell their fish for a fair price! FAIR. PRICE."

Another wide sweep of her arm, nearly knocking over a candle this time. *"Not get scraps while some fancy bastards swim, swim, in their profits like smug little fish kings!"* She paused, frowning. *"Wait. Do fish have kings?"*

A loud thunk as a cup slammed onto the table. A slow, wicked grin followed. *"You know what I care about?"* A hand clapped to a chest, fingers splayed dramatically. *"Getting more mead before you convince me to overthrow the fish monarchy."*

"I would never. For I Am a Fish King Loyalist!"

With great drunken conviction, a fist was raised. *"Fish King! Fish King! Fish King!"*

A sudden tilt, a hushed, conspiratorial whisper breathed against Mira's ear. *"But... are there fish kings?"*

Another gaze flicked to her, full of mischief, urging her on, daring her to take it further. Mira smirked, locking eyes.

"If so..." she mused, leaning in, voice heavy with conspiracy. *"They must be stopped."* A spark of inspiration flared, eyes widening, the fire of a grand mission taking hold. A finger jabbed toward nothing in particular.

"That's it. I'll find him. I will find the Fish King... and I will steal his mead." A pause, a slow, knowing nod. *"Because*

you know he's hoarding the good stuff."

And then, with all the conviction of a drunken hero, one of them pushed to his feet, swaying slightly before straightening and marching toward the bar, half-shouting, "Fish King! Show yourself, you fishy coward!" Laughter, low and warm, curled around her.

A shift. A change in the air. The firelight flickered, shadows stretching, twisting as something unspoken crept between them. A voice, low, edged with need.

"You get this fire in your eyes when you argue." A pause, a breath, hot and deliberate. "It's addictive." A beat. A glance, closer now. "Navigators, I need to touch you."

A slow drag of lips against her neck. A sharp inhale. Fingertips tracing over the fabric, up her thigh, teasing, unhurried. The scandalous slit of her black dress, the one they loved, had already ridden up around her legs, granting easy access. A soft, breathy sound escaped her as she shifted, hips pressing instinctively into the touch.

Another hand, warm, curved around her back, pulling her closer, fingers skimming over the bare skin. Hot breath at her ear, voice thick with hunger. "I adore you, Mira... particularly with you in my lap." She felt his fingers slide inside her as she gasped. She couldn't help clamping down, nails digging into his arms. Her gaze flicked toward the crowd, toward the oblivious revelers just feet away.

"We're not alone," she whispered, breathless, a warning laced in her voice. A quiet chuckle, sinful, unrepentant.

"They can't see us," came the response, low, teasing, hungry. Hands tightened at her hips, holding her in place. "But if they could?" A slow thrust, a deliberate drag of sensation. "Let them watch."

Heat shot through her, spiraling, unrelenting. She let her head fall back against a shoulder, breath catching in a soft, helpless sound. A mouth ghosted against her throat. A deep, knowing chuckle. The words purred against her skin.

"Do you need more?" Her answer was a shuddering gasp, fingers grasping at the fabric of someone's tunic. Desperate, needy. The hand on her back shifted and she was pulled fully into a lap, as his fingers leisurely pumped into her.

Lips brushed the shell of her ear. "Beg Mira. " came the demand, dark and dangerous. Pleasure was building rapidly. "I'll give you want you want, if you beg me "

Her pleasure peaked through her like a storm, leaving her shaking, her body arching into him as the world blurred around her. She collapsed back against a broad chest, breath unsteady, still reeling.

A slow exhale. She felt his fingers withdrawing with deliberate care. A low, indulgent hum. Then, lips parting around slick fingers, sucking them clean with slow, sinful reverence.

✳ ✳ ✳

Mira jolted, the memory clinging to her skin like a phantom touch. The warmth of her memory with Tharion vanished too quickly, leaving only the echo of their last kiss. The stillness, the unmoving weight of his lips against hers.

Tharion had wanted her once. She knew that. Felt it in every memory, but now? Beneath the sting of rejection bloomed a deeper fear. What if he doesn't remember? What if the version of him she'd loved was gone? What if the man she was seeing in fragments had been buried beneath fractured memories and the wreckage Sarelle left behind? What if all that remained now was this silent stranger, this echo, who barely looked at her, who didn't kiss her.

She exhaled slowly, rubbing a hand over her face as she finally reached their quarters. The moment she stepped inside, exhaustion crashed over her, her body aching, her mind still tangled in the web of past and present. She collapsed onto the bed, boots still on, the sheets too soft beneath her.

As she closed her eyes, Mira tried, tried, to summon a memory of Tharion. When he had looked at her like she was the only person that mattered. When his touch had made her feel wanted, known, loved. But nothing came. No warmth. No clarity. Only shadows.

Ren flashed through her mind. Unbidden. Unshakable. The ghost of him lingered in the library, where golden light spilled across ancient stone and dust danced in silence.

Where his voice had wrapped around her name.

No matter how hard she tried to force the memory she wanted, all she could see was Ren.

8

IRA AWOKE WITH THE lingering heaviness of exhaustion clinging to her limbs. Sleep had not been kind. Her dreams had been vivid, pulling her back into memories she couldn't quite recall. Balls, celebrations, the scent of perfume and sweat, the low thrum of violins beneath laughter and silk. She could still hear the music. Still feel the weight of stares, the press of expectation. Still feel the echo of Tharion's hand on her back.

She groaned as it slipped away. Her dreams always remained just out of reach. A melody half-remembered. She shifted, glancing to the other side of the bed. Tharion had not returned, not that she'd expected him to.

A sharp knock at the door pulled her fully from the haze. She sat up slowly, stretching against the stiff ache in her spine. The door creaked as it gave slightly under pressure, and on the floor lay an envelope. Small. Plain. Sealed in crimson wax.

She held her breath as she rose and crossed the room, fingertips brushing over the seal as she collected the message. The wax bore Torvyn's insignia, but the handwriting within it, was Brahn's. Her stomach tightened as her eyes flicked over the hurried script.

Meet me in the kitchens at the ninth bell toll this evening. Bring your bonded. Burn this letter.

Her pulse quickened. Brahn wouldn't risk this message unless it mattered. She crossed to the brazier near the window. With a flick of her fingers, she dropped the letter into the embers. It caught immediately, curling inward like a drying leaf, the message vanishing in a soft rush of smoke and flame.

Mira washed and dressed slowly, wrapping herself in layers of soft, flowing fabric. Appropriate for the day's duties. When she exited, the stone halls were already alive with movement. Courtiers and stewards swept past with arms full of fabrics and scrolls, the scent of cut flowers and incense growing thicker the closer she drew to the great hall.

Mira slipped in, just as the second bell tolled. The space was already crowded with attendants, clerics, stewards, and apprentices, all gathered in a loose half-circle around the thrones. The scent Mira had followed was drifting from brass burners nestled between the marble columns. Golden light streamed in through the stained-glass windows, casting fractured sunbursts across the floor.

Cleric Perrin stood at the altar, her voice rising above the hum of the crowd, measured and certain. Every syllable polished with practiced authority.

"...The Festival of the Final Sun is not merely a celebration," she intoned, "but a sacred reflection of balance. Light and dark, warmth and cold, life and rest. The Navigators guide us not only through seasons of the year, but through the seasons of the self."

Mira lingered at the back of the crowd, folding her hands before her. No one had noticed her arrival.

Perrin continued. "The preparations are already underway," she said. "we will open great hall to the townships at sunset this evening. In a few days, the Lantern Rite will begin after the sun sets on the western hills. Thereafter the garden canopy will be opened to noble guests only." Perrin surveyed the room.

"The great hall will be adorned with petals by midday. The floral weavings must match the five Navigators, no substitutions." Perrin continued, her gaze sweeping the crowd with steel-backed grace. "The Altar must be redressed each day before the third bell. I expect precision from everyone, not improvisation."

A few scribes scribbled faster. One apprentice paled visibly. Perrin's voice cut through Mira's drifting thoughts.

"We do not falter in the shadow of endings," the cleric said. "We rise to meet them. That is the legacy of the Navigators."

Applause rippled politely as Cleric Perrin gave a slight nod, and with smooth, rehearsed ease, an apprentice acolyte stepped up. Her voice was soft but clear as she began calling out roles from a folded list in her hands.

"Household stewards to the Pavilion. Lanternists report to Master Arlis near the southern courtyard. Florists are to begin in the great hall under Vesra's direction…". The applause was quickly replaced by the shifting murmur of movement as instructions rippled outward.

The rhythm of work resumed as people peeled off, footsteps echoing beneath the high vaulted ceiling. Perrin's robes whispered as she moved, her presence like a shadow slipping through the crowd. She moved with quiet purpose until she was standing beside Mira at the edge of the hall.

"Mira," her voice low but kind. "Walk with me." Mira hesitated only a breath before falling into step beside her.

They walked in a companionable quiet for a few strides. The bustle behind them faded slightly as they turned toward the quieter alcove beneath the side windows, where dappled light streamed across the floor in softened gold. The noise of the hall fell away behind them.

"I expected you earlier," Perrin mused. "But I understand there was a complication when you were returning."

Mira gave a slight nod, unsure how to respond. Her silence had never seemed to offend Perrin. They stopped just before the open altar doors. Perrin looked at her. Not as a superior, not even as a cleric, simply as a friend. Mira stood beside her, unmoving.

"You're not sleeping well, are you?" Perrin said gently. Mira's throat worked, but no sound came. She stared down at the fractured light at her feet.

"Not well, no." she whispered finally. "Not really."

Perrin didn't press. Mira swallowed, the burn rising behind her eyes sudden and hot. The silence made it worse. The weight of everything unsaid pressed against her chest until it ached.

"I kissed him. And he didn't even move. Just… nothing. Like it meant nothing. Like I don't..." Mira tilted her head to her chest. Perrin didn't fill the silence with platitudes. She let the words settle. Let the hurt live where it needed to.

"I don't know who I am to him anymore," Mira's voice cracking. "I don't even know who I'm supposed to be." Still no tears, but her fingers trembled where they were clenched in the folds of her sleeves. Perrin reached out, gently taking Mira's hand in hers. Not pulling, not pressing, just holding. Warm. Present.

Mira stared out the window, blinking against the weight behind her eyes. That pulled a shaky breath from Mira. Perrin gave her hand the lightest squeeze.

"Let him have his silence a little while longer. Perhaps it is the best option, for you both" Mira nodded once. The ache didn't ease.

"Tell me of Anyerit?" she asked. Mira blinked, startled by the timing of the question.

"It was…" Mira's voice faltered. "Worse than I imagined. But there's still people there. People worth helping." Perrin nodded, her hands folding before her.

"It's strange, isn't it? To see destruction and still feel hope. Like trying to carry water in your hands."

Mira swallowed, her throat suddenly tight. "I wonder if I did enough. If I was enough."

"I am sure you did everything you could," Perrin said. "and you saw the truth of what is happening out there." She let the words linger, then turned back toward the altar, her voice shifting back into a lighter lilt. "Now go, they'll need you to collect the petals from the gardens." Mira nodded, she didn't reply, only turned to go. The echo of the temple's quiet halls stretching ahead of her.

Mira spent the rest of the morning in the lower gardens, where the sun had finally crested above the palace walls. The scent of earth and blooms was heavy in the warm air, and her fingers were already stained with pollen and crushed petals.

She moved slowly, basket in hand, brushing her fingers over each bloom before plucking its petals carefully. She looked down at her full basket. Colorful. Balanced. Beautiful. Repetitive. A task that asked for nothing more than her hands, her breath, her patience. The soft whisper of bees, the rustle of a breeze, they helped her forget the weight of eyes and expectations, even for a moment.

She bent to gather a cluster of bright amber marigolds when the sound of hurried footsteps and fabric brushing against stone reached her.

"Mira!" a familiar voice sang out, far too cheerfully. Mira looked up just in time to see Nerra round the edge of the archway, arms loaded with neatly folded fabrics and a grin as wide as the sun. Nerra laughed, unbothered.

"We've been given flower duty, and I am delighted." Mira tilted her head, eyes narrowing with mock teasing.

"Of course you are." She couldn't help the slight lift at the corner of her mouth.

Nerra dropped the stack of linens onto a nearby bench, then clapped her hands together. "I already have a vision, by the way. I'm thinking of floating garlands. Maybe arrange the petals by color gradient? You know, to mirror the sun's descent."

Mira grinned. "You've put too much thought into this." Nerra's energy could level an army, and she loved her for it.

"I've put exactly enough thought into this," Nerra replied with a wink. "Now come on. I saw a basket of twilight orchids near the fountain that would look divine along the entrance to the great hall." Mira hesitated, glancing down at her half-filled basket of quiet simple flowers. Her plan was different from Nerra's celebratory vision. Quieter. Still... the energy in Nerra's smile was impossible to resist.

"All right, come on then" as Nerra brushed her palms on her skirts. Mira followed, the warmth of the sun curling over her shoulders like a shawl. And for the first time in days, her mind felt just a little lighter.

∗ ∗ ∗

By the late afternoon, Mira and Nerra were knelt on the floor of the great hall, surrounded by baskets overflowing with petals and trailing vines. Sunlight filtered down through the high stained-glass windows, washing the flowers in waves of color that changed with every passing cloud.

130

The vast chamber had changed under their hands. Its stone bones softened by color and scent, transformed by ritual and intention. The hall bloomed. Petals swept in deliberate arcs and swirls across the floor, winding toward five offering pedestals positioned beneath each stained-glass panel. Five paths. Five legacies. Five Navigators.

They had chosen each flower offering with care. Violets for Myrran, arranged in drifting constellations across the eastward steps, reflecting soft light with a faint shimmer. Fire lilies for Bharas clustered in bold spirals at the center, their orange-red petals radiant beneath the dome. Stormbells for Kharad lined along the base of the columns, their delicate deep blue flowers catching the breeze from the open archways. Sea glass poppies for Lyren, set in low bowls of water that mirrored the ceiling's painted skies. Star-vine for Drala, woven through the throne dais railings, its silver strands trailing like spun fate.

Nerra sat back on her heels, hands streaked with pollen, and let out a long breath. "A little behind schedule but, if this doesn't please the Navigators, I'm sending a complaint."

Mira let herself smile. It was true, but she couldn't help poking Nerra. "You said that in the garden."

"And I'll say it again at my funeral if the arrangements are ugly," Nerra replied. "No one wants to ascend surrounded by wilting greens and some sticks." Mira laughed, brushing a smear of pollen from her wrist. But the levity barely had time to settle before she caught the sound of boots echoing on stone. She looked up to see Tharion.

He paused just inside the hall, caught mid-step by the transformation. His eyes swept the petals, the light, the impossible quiet. For a moment, he simply stood there, looking at the space she and Nerra had shaped.

His eyes landed on Mira's. "I didn't mean to interrupt."he said quietly.

Nerra nudged Mira gently and stood, brushing off her skirt. "I'll go check the stormbells. Again."

Tharion drifted further into the hall, gaze shifting toward the star-vine woven across the dais. "It's beautiful."

"It was Nerra's vision," Mira said. "I just followed her orders." His eyes flicked toward her. She stood. "What are you doing here?" she asked, keeping her voice low.

He paused for a moment, then nodded toward Bharas. "I came to pay my respects." She nodded him forward, and Tharion moved to the image of Bharas and knelt.

For a moment, he was still, his head bowed in silent reflection beneath the shifting light. Mira watched him quietly, saying nothing as he rose.

"I need you to come with me tonight." she blurted out. That caught his full attention. She lowered her voice, "Ninth bell. Kitchens. Back entrance." Tharion's jaw tightened slightly. "It was Brahn's request," Mira added quietly. "He asked for both of us."

He studied her for a beat. "Do you know why?"

Mira shook her head and looked down, then met his eyes again. "Please." He hesitated, just for a breath. Then, softly, "I'll be there."

She released a breath she hadn't meant to hold. "Thank you." He glanced at the petals one last time before turning. He gave Nerra a brief nod on his way out, and was gone.

✳ ✳ ✳

The ninth bell was just beginning to stir in the distance. Deep and low, a sound that rolled through the stones of the palace

132

like a slow heartbeat. Mira stood at the rear entrance to the kitchens, half-shrouded in shadow, her hood drawn low over her face.

The door before her was old and thick, worn smooth by decades of heat. It smelled of flour, oil, and soot, even from the outside. Behind her, Tharion was silent. Still in his guard's cloak, though, his hand hovered casually, deliberately, near the hilt of his weapon.

"You sure he's here?" Tharion asked, voice low, pitched just above the breeze.

Mira hesitated, then nodded. "He wouldn't risk sending a note if he wasn't ready for us." Tharion's jaw flexed.

The final peal of the ninth bell echoed and faded. Mira raised her hand. Knocked once. The door remained closed for several heartbeats. Just as Mira reached to knock again, there was a soft scrape, metal sliding free, and the door cracked open.

Only a sliver. The warm scent of bread and herbs rushed out, strange and comforting against the night air. A single eye peered through the gap. Sharp. Familiar. Then the door opened fully.

Brahn stood at the threshold. His hair was tied back hastily, and his face was more worn than Mira remembered. No armor. No weapons. But the weight of responsibility clung to him all the same.

"He came?" Brahn asked, almost disbelieving. "You asked for my bonded," Mira replied.

Brahn's mouth twitched, a half smirk. "Come in."

He stepped aside, and Mira pulled her hood down and crossed the threshold first. Tharion followed without a word, closing the heavy door behind them. Heat poured from the hearths, and the scent of baking bread curled in the air. A few cooks worked at the far end of the preparation bench, too absorbed to notice them.

Mira glanced around. "The kitchens?"

Brahn gave a smile. "No one listens in the kitchens. Just clatter, flame and mouths to feed. Makes it the safest place in the palace to speak."

Tharion stepped up, next to Mira. "Then say it. Why are we here?" Brahn leaned back against the preparation bench, folding his arms.

"Because our people are being squeezed dry, by rations, by fear, by a council more interested in posturing than protection. I've tried diplomacy with Torvyn. I've tried patience. Neither buys food, or keeps the Khadrador blades off our borders."

Mira had known things were bad, heard the murmurs in corridors, seen the guarded looks on attendants faces. But Anyerit was the truth laid bare. People were going hungry. Families were being torn apart. The council's silence wasn't strategy, it was neglect.

Brahn turned to her, expectant, waiting for a suggestion. For the first time, Mira saw a path forward. She wasn't just sitting at the table as Tharion's silent shadow, absorbing strategy and watching others lead. She had a voice, and she could use it. She could act. An old instinct to defer, to stay quiet, flickered and died. She met Brahn's gaze. His eyes sharpened, and the faintest nod told her he was with her. Encouraging. Ready.

She drew a breath and spoke, "We need something that shakes the council into seeing the consequence of what they refuse to."

Brahn moved past the hearths to a door tucked behind a rack of drying herbs. He opened it without a word, revealing a narrow alcove. A single small box sat in the corner. He crouched and opened it, pulling free a thick roll of parchment, its edges worn. He brought it to the table and spread it open. A map of the region, hand-marked with inked trails, ridgelines, and trade paths.

Mira and Tharion stepped in close. Brahn tapped a thin route carved along the eastern side of the mountains.

"There's a Khadrador supply convoy running this path. We think it's small. Fast-moving. Carts. If they're cutting through the Ridgelands, they're doing it to stay out of sight." Brahn looked between them. "I want to hit it. Clean. No bodies. Just enough damage to throw off their schedule and send a message. To them and to our council."

Tharion studied the route. Mira leaned in, scanning the map. Her fingers hovered over the lines, the terrain shifting in her mind from ink to stone in her mind.

"They wouldn't use the lower pass," she murmured. "Too exposed. If they're smart, they'll take the spine trail and keep low."

Brahn nodded. "That was my guess."

She traced a bend higher up. "What about here? It bottlenecks between the hills. Steep on both sides. Sheltered from the wind. Perfect for an ambush."

Tharion stepped closer. "You're right. It would muffle the sound, too. That trail's brutal. Easy to trap, hard to escape. No other path for miles." Brahn gave a curt nod. "We wait there. Let them come to us." Mira's hand lingered on the map. "We can go in fast.

Scatter the horses, cut the reins, take what we can. No deaths. Just confusion."

"No witnesses," Brahn agreed. Mira looked up at the two men beside her. She felt the weight of the moment, not as a burden, but as something solid she could carry. This was a choice. Her chance to make something right.

"Then it's settled." Brahn rolled up the map and set it aside. "Midnight. Horses will be at the south gate. No one else joins us. No one knows we've gone."

Tharion raised a brow. "Just the three of us?"

"Just us," Brahn said. "Fewer voices, fewer mistakes."

Mira looked between Brahn and Tharion, heart steady. She felt like awakened to what this fight truly was.

Tharion stood beside her, his voice low. "You sure about this?"

"I am," she said, without hesitation. Tharion held her gaze a moment longer, then gave a single, firm nod.

* * *

Hours passed, and the night air clawed at Mira's skin as they rode away. Behind them, the palace loomed high, its windows aglow with festival lanterns. Silks fluttered from balconies. The scent of crushed petals lingered in the gutters, sweet beneath the press of night.

The Festival of the Final Sun was everywhere. Even now, the celebration pulsed beneath the city's skin, soft music drifting from closed tavern doors, low laughter winding between alleys, the occasional flicker of a lantern released too early, drifting upward like a lost prayer. Garlands hung across narrow streets. Ribbons of gold and rust-blood red. Chalk sigils drawn for protection and offering in doorways were already smudged by footsteps. The entire city was caught between the revelry and ritual. Mira tugged her hood lower over her brow.

The rhythmic thud of hooves against the dirt road along

the town's border, a steady drumbeat that matched the quickening of her pulse. She was seated behind Tharion, her arms wrapped tightly around his waist. His back was solid, a wall of warmth and strength between her and the uncertainty that lay ahead. With every jostle of the horse, she pressed closer, grounding herself in the steadiness of him. He said nothing, but his hand would occasionally brush against hers as he held the reins. A small that they were still together in this.

Ahead of them, Brahn rode alone, his silhouette a dark cutout against the pale wash of moonlight. His horse moved with controlled grace, each stride deliberate, as if even the beast knew not to disturb the stillness too much. Brahn didn't look back. His focus was honed to a blade's edge, his silence a tether that held them all taut with unspoken command.

They rode for what felt like hours, the city's lights swallowed by rolling hills and thickening trees. The air cooled slightly, wrapping around them like damp wool. When Brahn finally pulled his horse to a stop, they found themselves on a small rise overlooking a well-traveled road. The trees parted just enough to offer a view of the dirt track below, where wheel ruts ran deep and the stones reflected the moonlight.

Mira slid off the horse, her legs protesting as she found solid ground. Tharion followed, his movements fluid, but his eyes remained fixed on Brahn. She mirrored him, watching as Brahn easily dismounted his steed. The air seemed to still around them, the trees a wall of shadows, eavesdropping on secrets.

Brahn crouched at the edge of the hill, his eyes fixed on the road below. His gloved fingers tapped against his thigh, a slow, thoughtful rhythm that seemed to echo inside Mira's chest. "They can't be much longer." he whispered.

The minutes stretched, each one a coil tightening in Mira's chest. She exchanged a glance with Tharion, his expression a mirror of her own confusion. The wind tugged at her hair, strands slipping from beneath her hood, and she fought the urge to shift, to fill the silence with something, anything.

A convoy slowly came into view, the creak of wheels and the soft clinking of metal are hooves breaking the quiet. Three wagons, sturdy and loaded with crates, rolled along the road. Each was flanked by a guard, their armor catching the light in dull silver flashes. The sigil of Myrdathis, a star encircled by a ring of laurels, adorned their breastplates. Their faces were obscured by helms, but their postures spoke of weariness, of duty-bound men simply following orders.

Mira narrowed her eyes at the passing convoy, her gaze locking on the sigils etched into the guards' breastplates. "They're not Khadradorian," she said sharply. "That's the crest of Myrdathis. They're Myrdath."

Brahn stepped slightly in front of her, his hand hovering near his sword. "No, they want you to think that."

"What?" she turned to him, incredulous. "Brahn, that's not the Khadradorian symbol."

"It's a disguise," he growled, eyes fixed on the convoy. "Khadradorian scouts have done it before. Borrow the colors, wear the sigils. It's a trick to get close, to pass unseen."

Mira exhaled through her nose, sharp and controlled. Doubt flickered through her head, but she didn't step back. "You're sure?" she asked, voice low.

Brahn didn't look at her. "As sure as I've ever been."

That was enough to clear her doubts. She nodded once, jaw tight. "Then we do it clean. No blood"

Tharion crouched, drawing a quick diagram in the dirt

with his knife. "We set a trap. A tree downed across the road, nothing too obvious. When they stop, we create a distraction." He glanced at Mira, a question in his gaze. "You're an excellent shot. Can you light a fire with a bow?"

Mira nodded, her mind already rifling through her pack. A small flask of oil and a set of arrows fletched with dark feathers. "I can."

Brahn interjected "And if you add a bit of powder to the oil, it'll burn hotter. The smoke will be thick. Give us cover."

"Perfect." Tharion's knife moved again, sketching out positions. "We'll take out the rear guard first, quietly. When the smoke hits, they'll panic. We knock them out, bind them, and take the wagons." Brahn considered for a moment, his face unmoving. Then, slowly, he nodded.

Mira let out a breath. She reached for Tharion's hand, her fingers brushing against his, before he took her hand and squeezed. Quick, reassuring. They had a plan. And they could do this without bloodshed.

Brahn rose, brushing the dirt from his gloves. "Then let's get to work."

Surrounded by deep shadows, they settled in as Mira prepared the powder-laced arrows, the gravity of their mission dawning on her. Not thieves. Not killers. They were striking back, a warning to Kharador and a message to the council. We will fight for our kingdom, for our people.

They moved quickly, each of them slipping into position along the tree line like shadows cast by the moon. The fallen stick tree lay across the road, its branches tangled and gnarled, appearing as though it had been brought down by the wind rather than the careful work of Tharion's blade.

Mira crouched behind a cluster of rocks, her crossbow resting against her thigh. Her fingers moved deftly, wrapping the oil-soaked cloth around the arrowhead, smearing the head with powder. The scent burned her nose, acrid and sharp, but it would do the job.

The smoke would billow thick and dark, a veil between them and the guards. Her heartbeat steadied, the rhythm aligning with the quiet sounds of the forest. She struck a flint, the spark catching, and the cloth ignited with a soft whoosh. The flame was a tiny, hungry creature, gnawing at the arrow. She took aim at the brush on the opposite side of the road.

The arrow flew true, arcing through the night. When it struck, fire bloomed, a bright, sudden flare that devoured the dry leaves and sent a plume of smoke curling into the air. The forest shifted around it, shadows dancing in the orange glow.

Voices rose from the approaching convoy, foot guards scrambling as the smoke thickened. They moved as expected, some towards the fire, others back toward the rear of the convoy where Tharion and Brahn waited. Mira moved, slipping from her cover and down the slope. The soft leather of her boots made no sound against the earth. She kept low, her body a line of shadow against the forest, eyes fixed on the convoy.

Tharion and Brahn moved through the chaos with practiced efficiency. They slipped between wagons, their dark forms blurring against the smoke and shadow. Tharion struck first, his arm curling around a guard's neck, his other hand pressing against the man's temple. The guard crumpled to the ground without a sound, his breathing deep and even. Unconscious. Brahn was a step behind, his blade hilt knocking against another guard's helm, a quick and precise blow that sent the man slumping against the wheel of the wagon. The metal clattered softly, but the smoke and sounds of fire swallowed the noise.

Mira's breath hitched, but not from fear. There was a fluidity to Tharion's movements, a predatory grace that she couldn't look away from. Each step he took was calculated, his movements an artful blend of power and silence. His hair, clung to his forehead, and his expression was one of calm focus. There was nothing brutal about his actions. Each strike was measured, every guard left breathing, their bodies only temporarily surrendered to the dark. She slipped closer, her eyes darting between the few guards who remained. Two were still near the lead wagon, their swords drawn, the silver blades reflecting yellow in the wavering light of the fire. They spoke in hushed tones, their attention divided between the blaze and the rear of the convoy where their comrades lay.

Mira reached the edge of the wagons, pressing her back against the wood. The heat from the crates radiated against her, and she forced her breathing to slow. She needed to focus, needed to keep her thoughts clear. But even now, as Tharion moved ahead, her eyes lingered on him. The strength in his shoulders, the careful way his fingers gripped the hilt of his blade, not to stab, but to strike with the flat edge. A weapon used for subduing, not killing.

She moved silently, flanking Tharion ahead of her. He moved with a predator's grace, his form slipping through the smoke like a shadow. Mira crept forward, her crossbow in hand. She loaded an arrow, aimed, exhaled and released. The arrow found its mark, sinking into the wood above a guard's head. He looked up, confusion clouding his expression, suddenly Tharion was there, a spectre that appeared through the smoke. The guard turned, but Tharion's hand struck the side of his neck, and his body folded gently to the ground.

Mira loaded another arrow, her breath a controlled pace. She mirrored Tharion's movements, shifting to the left, her eyes fixed on the wagon. If she could draw the guards' attention, just a moment's distraction, that was all they needed. She aimed, her focus narrowing to the sliver of wood between the guards. The arrow was in flight just as she sensed something wrong. Her fingers still curled against the trigger as time stretched, the arrow slicing through the air. It struck the wagon with a hollow thud.

The cart erupted. The explosion tore through the night, a violent storm of fire and shrapnel. The world tilted, sky and earth tangled into a blur, until she hit the ground. Pain radiated through her, a shockwave of agony. For a heartbeat, everything was still. The flames licked at the sky, shadows dancing across the wreckage. Then Mira's world rushed back, in a wash of heat and nothing but a high-pitched buzzing where the sound should have been.

Mira's limbs felt distant but she forced them to move. She rolled onto her stomach, coughing against the grit and ash. Tharion lay just ahead, crumpled.

"Tharion…" She clawed at the earth, dragging herself forward. Each pull of her arms sent fresh stabs of pain through her chest. Her fingers found the edge of his sleeve, and she used it to haul herself closer. "Tharion…"

His face was slack, a thin line of blood trailing from his closed eye. She pressed her fingers to his neck, his pulse beat strong beneath her touch. Relief flooded her heart.

Brahn appeared through the smoke, his figure a blur of movement. His lips moved, his hands grasping her shoulders, but the ringing in her ears swallowed his words. She blinked up at him, his face etched with fury, his mouth forming shapes she couldn't understand.

"Mira!" The sound broke through, sudden and raw. "Move! Now!"

She shook her head, the world tilting, and Brahn's grip tightened. He pulled her up, her knees buckling. The ground beneath them trembled, and the heat of the flames clawed at their backs.

"Tharion," she started, but Brahn was already reaching for him. He knelt beside him, hefted Tharion onto his back, and rose with a grunt, the weight heavy but manageable as he staggered forward.

The forest lay beyond the flames, a promise of shadows and safety. Her legs moved, though each step jarred her bones. The trees swallowed them whole, the firelight fading behind like a dying star. Branches clawed at Mira's arms, leaves slick with dew catching her skin as they moved through the forest. The horses waited where they'd tethered them, restless and snorting, ears twitching toward the smoke and chaos behind.

Brahn reached them first. He shifted Tharion's weight with practiced strength, long enough to ease him down into the bed of moss and leaf litter. Brahn cradled Tharion's back against his chest.

Mira collapsed to her knees beside him, lungs burning. "He's breathing," she gasped, brushing his hair back, fingers trembling.

"He needs water. Pack's behind the brown mare, get it." Brahn;s growl held none of his usual sharpness.

Mira hesitated, watching him. Brahn's hands moved steadily over Tharion's body, checking for broken ribs, wounds, burns. He was thorough, careful in a way she hadn't expected. When he found the gash under Tharion's eye, his jaw tightened. He ripped a strip of cloth off his shirt and pressed it against the bleeding, muttering something under his breath.

Mira stumbled toward the horses, still reeling from the blast. The forest felt too quiet now, every sound muffled beneath the dull ring still echoing in her head. She found the pack, her fingers fumbling over the buckles, and returned with the waterskin. Brahn took it without a word, lifting Tharion's head slightly to trickle a few careful drops between his lips. Mira knelt beside them, her hand brushing Tharion's cheek.

"Why… why did it explode?" she whispered.

Brahn didn't answer immediately. His gaze remained on Tharion, his hand still cradling the back of his skull. When he finally looked up, something like guilt flickered behind his eyes.

"A trap. Or fuel. We didn't scout it close enough." Mira's breath caught.

"He could've died." she whispered, her voice trembling as tears welled in her eyes.

"He won't." Brahn said quietly. Tharion stirred, a soft grunt escaping him as his eyes fluttered open. Mira leaned in, clutching his hand.

"You're alright," she reassured. "You're okay." His gaze was hazy, unfocused, but he found her for a moment before drifting on to Brahn.

"You dragged me out?" he rasped over his shoulder.

Brahn gave a short, humorless huff. "You're welcome." Tharion turned his head, blinking slowly toward the blur of Brahn's silhouette. Silence settled between them, tense, layered, but oddly grounding.

"He needs to rest, we all do." she said softly, replacing Brahn's hand with her own "recover for a moment. Then we can ride."

Brahn gave a small nod. "We'll move in an hour".

9

THE JOURNEY BACK was slow, Brahn rode ahead scouting the path in case any patrols had seen the fire, while Mira kept close to Tharion. He sat slumped in the saddle, barely conscious, his weight swaying with each step of the horse. Mira rode behind him, one hand wrapped around his waist, the other gripping the reins with white-knuckled focus.

By the time they reached the outer edge of the palace gardens, dawn had lightened the sky. A soft pink bled across the horizon, a gentle indifference to the night just past. As they entered the kitchens, the scent of baked bread and cooking meats clung to the air. The warmth of the ovens wrapped the room in a deceptive comfort, but fear still curled low in her stomach like smoke trapped beneath stone.

Brahn lay Tharion on a cot beside the hearth, wrapping him in Mira's cloak. His chest rose and fell in shallow, even breaths, but his skin was still too pale, his brow slick with a fever that refused to cool.

"He needs a healer," Mira said, nearly trembling. Brahn leaned against the cot, arms crossed, shadowed by the flickering firelight.

"And bring someone else into this? One wrong word, Mira, and we lose more than just him."

"He's burning up," she hissed.

"He'll survive, he always does" Brahn muttered, though the words felt like a prayer more than certainty. He crouched beside Tharion, one hand hovering for a moment before tugging the cloak higher, tucking it just beneath Tharion's chin.

Mira had turned away. She didn't wait for permission or another argument. Her boots echoed down the stone hallway, each step ringing with urgency. The corridors were hushed in the early morning hush, but the palace never truly slept. She slipped through the attendants' stairwell, avoiding the main passageways, until she reached the door of the altar.

She knocked once, sharply. Then again. It was Cleric Perrin who opened the door, still dressed in her night robes, though her veil had already been pulled over her hair. Her face was calm but curious, but Mira could see the tension in the way her fingers gripped the doorframe.

"Mira," she said, voice low but alert. "What's happened?"

"He was training," Mira said quickly, the words tumbling from her tongue before she could second-guess them. "Out past the lower range. He fell. I think he hit his head. He hasn't woken properly."

Perrin studied her in silence, eyes sharp behind the thin curtain of her veil. Mira didn't flinch beneath the weight of it. A long moment passed.

The cleric stepped forward, and gestured for her to lead. "Show me."

They moved fast, cloaked in quiet and wrapped in the chill that clung to the early dawn. Mira led her through the passages, keeping their route away from the usual patrols and watchful attendants. Perrin said nothing, her steps soft but swift, robes trailing like whispers behind her.

Inside, the warmth of the hearth reached for them, comforting but heavy with worry. Brahn looked up from where he still sat by Tharion's side, his face etched with concern. He didn't speak as Perrin crossed the room and knelt beside the cot. She pressed a hand gently to Tharion's temple, her fingers moving with practiced grace. Her movements were soft, almost reverent.

"He's lucky. He will recover in a few hours," she murmured. "But the swelling is dangerous. He needs rest. I'll mix a poultice to draw the heat and an elixir for the pain if he stirs." Mira exhaled shakily and sank to her knees on the other side of Brahn.

Perrin glanced between them. "He will recover, but you'll need to keep him cool and still. And next time," her voice dipped with quiet steel, "Don't train so recklessly." Perrin didn't soften. But there was a thread of understanding beneath her words, thin but present.

Mira offered a tight nod, relief surged beneath her worry. Tharion was going to be all right. She brushed a hand gently against his arm, needing the contact to anchor her. Her jaw clenched to keep the emotion from slipping out. Perrin's curiosity hung heavy in the air, she asked nothing. For that, Mira was quietly grateful. Perrin stood, brushing a hand down her robe.

Mira stood with her and dipped her head. "Thank you."

Before she could lower herself back to Tharion's side, Perrin touched her arm lightly, halting her. "You can not tend to him"

Mira blinked. "But I…".

Perrin continued "Go to the east corridor and send for Acolyte Vesra. She's to oversee the morning delegations." Perrin paused, assessing Mira. "No one will question you," Perrin said briskly. "And you'll raise suspicions if you're seen outside the kitchens too often." There was no room to argue, not with Perrin's tone, and not with the logic she so effortlessly wielded. "Get some sleep, and then find Harwen."

Still, Mira hesitated, her eyes drifting to the cot where Tharion lay unmoving. Mira nodded slowly, pressing her palm to Tharion's chest one last time before turning. She crossed to the door. Brahn hadn't moved, but he looked up, his eyes rimmed with something that might have been exhaustion... or guilt.

∗ ∗ ∗

By mid-afternoon when Mira woke, the palace hummed with its usual business. Soft footsteps echoing along the corridors, silks brushing against stone, voices low and measured behind arched doors. Mira stepped into the great hall, chin lifted, her dress gathered neatly at the waist by her apron. No one would guess she had been out all night. No one would see the worry still coiled at the base of her throat.

Across the room, Harwen waited near the eastern archway, her hair freshly braided, her apron a more formal wrap of pale blue linen. She looked every inch the perfect attendant. Calm, organised and collected.

"Hello Mira," she said softly, stepping closer. "I hoped they'd pair us for the lantern placement."

Mira gave her a smile. "You don't think I'd let you place the lanterns crooked on your own, do you?" she joked, though she felt her eyes lingered a little too long, trying to hide the fear still clinging to her.

Harwen huffed a quiet laugh. "I heard they are only crooked because you tie the strings too short. Which is why I'm doing the tying today," Harwen declared cheerfully. "You'll do the placing. Teamwork."

They retrieved the four wicker baskets, brimming with carefully packed lanterns, small glass bowls of oil, reed floats, and silk cords already trimmed to length. The halls had become quieter, most courtiers and attendants wrapped in pre-festival duties or final preparations, leaving the gardens and balconies theirs for the afternoon.

The sun had dipped low in the sky by the time they made it out into the open air. Golden light dappling through the gardens and catching the fine threads woven into the lantern silks. The fountains trickled quietly, and bees hovered near the star-vine hedges. To Mira, it felt like one of those lazy summer afternoons that might stretch on forever, just as the summer began slipping away, soft and slow.

"I've decided I'm going to catch one this year," Harwen announced as she knelt beside the reflecting pool. She was arranging a trio of lanterns along its edge. "After they're released. I've been practicing my timing."

Mira arched a brow and paused, tying a cord around a hook. "You know they're designed to float away, right?"

"Which is exactly why it's impressive," Harwen said smugly. "I almost had one last year."

Mira paused, she watched Harwen tuck a wisp of hair behind her ear, her face lit with excitement and determination. It was rare to see that kind of joy in anyone lately.

"You would get a request of the Navigators if you did. What would you wish for?" Mira asked gently.

Harwen didn't answer right away. Her hands were steady as she placed another lantern at the edge of the path, fingers brushing the delicate sides with care. She sat back on her heels, eyes drifting toward the open expanse of the garden.

"For someone to listen to my village," she said at last.

Mira stilled. Harwen didn't meet her gaze, not at first. Her voice remained soft, even. "They send requests. Petitions. One after the other. Shortages. Sea rot. And the council sends back scrolls full of reasons.

Policies. Delays." She looked up then, and her eyes met Mira's with a quiet smile, bittersweet. "So if I catch one, that's my wish. We just need someone to listen." Mira nodded back.

They didn't speak for a while after that. The wind shifted gently, tugging at their hair, ruffling the corners of their sleeves. Together, they worked steadily through the rest of the garden, placing each lantern with quiet precision. Some were strung from the arching iron hooks above the flower beds. Others were placed on reed floats, ready for the evening release. The air grew slightly colder, golden with the slanting light of afternoon.

When the last lantern was set, Harwen stepped back and wiped her hands on her skirt. "That's all of them," she exclaimed, satisfied.

Mira looked around, heart swelling with the beauty of the garden covered in lanterns. The palace felt transformed. Not just prepared, but hopeful.

"Thank you," Harwen replied, voice quieter than before. "For listening." Mira met her eyes. Harwen's expression brightened again, cheeks a little pink from the wind and sun.

"I hope your wish finds its way to someone. Navigator or human." she offered gently. There was a beat of silence between them. Mira gave a small nod, the kind that said she understood more than she would ever put into words.

"I need to change. If I show up to the release looking like a stable hand, Perrin will have a fit." Harwen smiled before waving as she disappeared into the palace.

Mira turned and took in the gardens. Beyond the

carefully tended flower beds and labyrinth of hedges, the land sloped gently upward toward the tahla tree on the hill. Its branches stretched wide and ancient. The tendrils of leaves swaying in the breeze like an old sentinel watching over the palace grounds.

It stood alone at the crest, its green-blue leaves caught the last of the sunlight, turning them into shimmering coins of light. Delicate blue blossoms clung to its boughs, their fragrance carried on the warm breeze. The scent tangled with something half- remembered, half-forgotten.

The trunk thick with age, knots twisting through its bark. Its branches stretched wide, as if trying to embrace the sky. Strong yet flexible. Built to endure, to bend but never break. A realization struck. Her crossbow. It was made of Tahla wood. She hadn't been to the Tahla tree since…since...

The memory slipped away before she could grasp it. Mira lingered at the edge of the path, her fingers idly brushing her sleeves, eyes drifting over the tahla tree, the forgotten memory pressing against her mind like a whisper she couldn't quite hear.

"Lost in thought again, Mira?" That voice broke her concentration. Smooth, warm, laced with lazy amusement. She didn't turn immediately. She didn't have to. Ren. A soft chuckle, the rustle of fabric as he stepped closer. "You get that unfocused look on your face." Slowly, carefully, he leaned in, his breath ghosting over her ear as he inhaled the subtle fragrance of her hair.

"Ren," she started, but her voice wasn't as sharp as she wanted it to be. Ren let out a hum of questioning, barely pulling back.

Mira exhaled slowly before stepping away and turning to face him. Ren stood in the center of the path, dressed in effortless finery. Midnight-blue waistcoat and pants, embroidered with faint gold constellations, an open collar dress shirt underneath, revealing the sharpness of his collarbones. His ever-present smirk played on his lips.

Steadying herself, "We've been over this, what happened in the library changed nothing." She meant for her voice to sound firm, final. But the words wavered. The memory lingered between them, pressing against the space she had tried to create. She could still feel the ghost of his almost touch, the way he had looked at her.

Ren's expression darkened, his voice dropping lower, rougher. "You really think it didn't change anything?" Ren ducked his head to meet her eyes. His gaze locked onto hers, searching, relentless. "If you do, then why are you looking at me like that?" he asked softly, the words nearly a plea.

Mira swallowed hard. She wasn't sure how she was looking at him, only that thread by thread, beneath the weight of his stare, her strength was fading. His fingers traced up her arm, slow, deliberate, until they curled at the side of the neck. She nearly shivered at the tenderness in the gesture.

"I can't," she whispered, the words fragile, uncertain. Ren let out a quiet sigh, shaking his head. She flinched but continued, "I can't betray Tharion like that." His hand lingered on her throat, his fingers twitched, like he wasn't sure if he had the right to hold on.

"Mira," he said, voice low. "He's not waiting for you." She stilled. Ren continued gently. "I can see it." Ren's thumb stroked along her jaw. "And I know you'll tell me it's not like that, that it's just the bond or the past or whatever you need to believe. But… he is." He swallowed.

She didn't answer. Couldn't.

His tone was barely above a whisper. "He's not yours." Her breath caught. "But I can be..." The flickering lantern light danced across his face, soft shadows, warm gold. His eyes searched hers, not demanding, but asking.

The wind stirred the trees overhead, rustling through the garden like it, too, was holding its breath, waiting for her reply. Her pulse pounded beneath his fingers, an echo to the weightless feeling creeping over her. There was a familiar sensation of something flickering at the edge of her mind, just out of reach.

She wasn't sure if she was recalling a memory or something Ren was weaving into her now.

"Why?" she asked quietly. Ren's fingers slid from her neck to her hand, threading his fingers through hers.

"It's always been you..." Ren murmured, his voice a low, steady vow. Each word was woven with a quiet commitment and a depth of adoration she hadn't expected. He continued, "Even when it couldn't be, it was always you". His fingers tightened around hers, warm and sure.

Mira longed to hold onto this moment. The quiet urgency in him, echoing the ache she'd carried for so long. The yearning to be wanted, and the depth of her wanting him in return. She swallowed hard, her pulse thrumming. Her world had been uncertain for so long, memories slipping through her fingers like sand. Frustration burned beneath her skin, curling tight in her chest. She was tired. Exhausted with the effort of chasing memories that dissolved like mist, of reaching for someone who should have felt like home. Whose hands were once meant to reach for her and yet now felt like a stranger.

And worse than the frustration was the loneliness. She needed to be wanted. Deeply, unquestionably, to be seen and adored. Needed someone who looked at her like she was theirs, and who, in the same breath, was hers. Like she mattered. Like neither of them was slipping away.

"I...," she faltered. He was closer now, leaning in. His breath warmed her skin, and his hands, steady, certain, slid to the sides of her neck, one after the other, as if holding something precious in place. His body radiated a heat that called to her, that threatened to pull her under.

"Please," Ren murmured, the tip of his nose brushing against hers like he had in the library. "Mira..." The sound of her name on his lips, raw and unguarded, undid her.

She closed the space between them. His lips met hers slowly, deliberately, as if savoring every second of contact. As if he had waited years for this moment. But the moment her fingers tangled in his shirt, pulling him closer, he snapped.

Ren moved her with sudden, unrelenting urgency. Backing her until her shoulders hit the ivy-covered wall. A soft gasp escaped her against her mouth, and he laughed into the kiss, low and rough, as if the sound pulled something deeper from him. Heat curled low in Mira as his lips parted against hers, his tongue sweeping over her lower lip before coaxing her into a slow, intoxicating rhythm.

Ren didn't hold back. His body pressed into hers, his hands framing her waist, holding her there, anchoring her to him. His fingers curled against her hips, firm, possessive.

Grounding himself in this moment. Slowly his hands moved, trailing up her sides, his touch slow, teasing. His fingertips tracing the dip of her spine, up the sides of her ribs and across her shoulders before settling at the base of her neck. His thumb brushed against her jaw, tilting her face and deepening the kiss. Her knees weakened, her breath unsteady. Ren must have felt her because his arm returned to slide around her waist, pulling her flush against him again. The fire between them built, burning away reason, blurring the lines between past and present.

A flicker of a candle against stone walls. Laughter, warm and familiar. Fingers laced together in the dark. Tharion's hand.

No, Ren's hand. Her body tensed, the world tilting as memories collided with reality.

Stolen fruit between shared breaths. Her whispered name.

Everything overlapped, blurred at the edges. She couldn't tell what was real, what had belonged to who.

Ren pulled back slightly, his breath ragged, "Mira…"

She tried to breathe, tried to steady herself, but the past wasn't just creeping in, it was crashing into her, pulling her under.

✳ ✳ ✳

She moved soundlessly, her steps sure, her pulse thrumming with anticipation. The night stretched quiet and heavy around her as she slipped through the side of the palace. Past the towering hedges and marble archways, into the dimly lit garden tucked away from the grand hall. It was secluded. Hidden from prying eyes, perfect.

And there he was, facing the stone wall. His back was to her, one hand braced against the cool stone, shoulders rising and falling with slow, measured breaths. The tension in his frame was unmistakable.

Mira stepped closer, deliberately silent, savoring the quiet thrill of catching him off guard. She was right behind him when she finally let her voice slip into the night, smooth and teasing.

"Running away so soon?" He jolted, twisting around, and for the first time since she'd known him, she saw something rare in his eyes, genuine surprise.

For a flicker of a second, his usual composure faltered. His sharp, green eyes widened, something almost embarrassed flashing behind them. It vanished as quickly as it came, replaced by the usual smirk, by the narrowed gaze that always met her with a challenge. She tilted her head, brow furrowing slightly, until her gaze dropped, until she noticed. His hand. Just above his waistband.

Heat flushed through her, realization striking like a spark to dry kindling. She should have looked away, should have let him have the dignity of pretending she hadn't seen.

But she didn't. Instead, she stepped closer, gaze lifting to him as she reached out, trailing a single finger down the front of his jacket.

"Poor thing," she murmured, her voice laced with amusement, with challenge. His breath hitched. Just slightly. But she caught it. She was going to enjoy this.

He let out a quiet curse under his breath, his jaw tightening as Mira's fingertip ghosted over his chest, trailing lower, teasing. His body was taut, every muscle wound tight as if caught between retreating and pressing forward.

He didn't retreat.

He exhaled slowly, schooling his expression into something resembling control, though his green eyes betrayed him. They darkened, locked onto her like she was prey.

"You really enjoy this, don't you?" he murmured, laced with frustration and desire.

Mira feigned a thoughtful expression. "Enjoy what?"

Her finger traced an idle path down his stomach.

His lips curled into something caught between a smirk and a grimace. "Torturing me."

She laughed softly, the sound slipping between them like silk. "Oh, this?" she murmured, leaning in just enough for her breath to warm his skin. "It's not torture if you like it." And navigators above, she could feel just how much he did.

His hand shot out, catching her wrist firmly before she could go any further. Just enough to make her pulse quicken. She met his gaze, steady and unflinching. He was always composed. Always smug and in control. But now? Now she had him unravelling.

She could see it in the way his throat bobbed, in the way his grip flexed around her wrist. And then, with a deliberate slowness that sent heat pooling low in her, he lowered her hand to his waistband. A dare. A challenge. Her fingers curled just slightly, teasing at the edge of the fabric, and she felt the tension ripple through him, his muscles coiling tight beneath her touch. His hands found her hips, fingers pressing in, gripping her like she was the only thing tethering him to the earth.

It came out barely a whisper. "Mira, please... touch me." His voice was low, wrecked.

The sound of him begging sent a rush of heat through her, igniting something deep and dangerous in her chest. What she would do to hear him beg again. A wicked smile ghosted across her lips as she reached inside his waistband, her fingers wrapping around him.

She began stroking slowly, deliberately. His head dropped forward, a sharp inhale breaking into a low groan. He tightened his hold on her. An involuntary jerk of his hips met her touch. His self-control crumbling with each passing moment.

"Mira," His voice was a rasp, desperate, pleading. His forehead rested against hers, his breath ragged, uneven. "Don't stop."

She wouldn't. She kept her movements measured, torturously slow. Drinking in every reaction, every shudder, every sharp inhale, every curse that slipped past his lips. He moaned, his body tensing, his hands flexing against her hips like he was trying so damn hard to hold on. He growled low in his throat before moving. Smooth, sudden. She gasped as he spun her, pressing her back into the ivy's cool embrace.

Before she could tease him for losing control, his hands were already on her thighs, rough and impatient. He lifted her skirts, fingers dragging up the bare skin of her legs, setting her nerves alight. Then he lifted her, and she wrapped her legs around his waist, their bodies pressing flush against each other.

"Mira," he breathed, his lips barely brushing her jaw, his voice thick, wrecked. "If you don't want this you need to tell me.."

She exhaled shakily and nodded, "I want this," she whispered, every word laced with longing. Her fingers tightened in his hair, pulling him closer. "I want you." Their mouths met in a kiss that was anything but tentative. Urgent, consuming, a collision of desperation and desire. Her focus narrowed to him. Hard and insistent against her, pressing exactly where she needed him. A gasp slipped from her lips, pleasure sparking through her, and he chuckled, low and dark.

"You feel that?" he murmured, rocking into her just enough to make her whimper. His mouth ghosted along her skin, his breath warm, teasing. "That's what you've done."

Another roll of his hips, slow, deliberate, making her eyes roll back. His grip on her thighs tightened, his fingers digging into the soft skin as he held her against the wall, as if anchoring himself. His lips skimmed the column of her throat, his voice rough with frustration and want.

"Do you have any idea," he rasped, rocking into her again, and she matched him, grinding back, pulling another gasp from both of them, "what it was like to watch you tonight?"

She tried to form words, but he rolled his hips again, and all that came out was a sharp inhale, her fingers tightening in his hair.

"That damned dress..." His voice was almost a growl. "Every damn man in that room wanted to devour you." He bit down gently at the curve of her neck, then soothed the mark with his tongue. Mira swallowed hard, her body thrumming.

"And you didn't like that?" she teased breathlessly. His grip on her thighs flexed. Another thrust, rougher, harder. She moaned. He let out a sharp growl, his hand sliding up her thigh, fingers pressing in possessively. His fingers flexed against her.

"You had to dance with him." His other hand fumbled at his waistband, urgency roughening his movements. A sharp breath, a low curse. He freed himself, the heat of him pressing against her. Mira bit her lip, with a satisfied hum. "You sound jealous."

A low growl rumbled through his chest, and in an instant, he snapped his hips forward, forcing a gasp from her lips as she arched against him, her nails digging into his shoulders.

"You wanted me to be," he accused, his voice a husky

rasp. His breath came fast, uneven, his grip bruising as he rocked into her again, making her feel exactly how much she had undone him. The heat between them was overwhelming, intoxicating. She could barely think beyond the pleasure building between them, but what she did saw was him dancing with a daughter from the Vaeloria family.

His lips curved, dark and sharp. He could tell what she was thinking about. "I danced with her," he murmured, his voice low, "because I wanted to see you break first." His lips ghosted over hers, teasing, never quite closing the distance. "I wanted to see if you'd come to me, if you'd show even a flicker of jealousy." He thrust against her again, harder this time, pulling a breathless moan from her lips, making her grip his shoulders tighter. "And gods, when I saw you watching me, when your eyes darkened just so," He let out a sharp breath, his teeth grazing the sensitive skin of her jaw. "It nearly fucking ended me."

Mira exhaled shakily, her pride warring with the molten heat pooling in her belly, her hips moving in time with his. "You smiled at me," she challenged, her voice uneven but defiant. "You winked. Like you were winning."

A dark chuckle escaped him, low and breathless. "I thought I was," he admitted, shifting one hand to brace against the wall, grinding against her slowly, torturously. "I thought I had you right where I wanted you." His lips trailed down her neck, pressing hot, open-mouthed kisses against the mark he had left. "And then you walked right into his arms." His breath turned ragged, his voice dipping lower, rougher. "I saw his hands on you," he murmured, fingers pressing into her skin. "Saw the way he looked at you." But his voice wasn't anger or jealousy. It was something else, something darker, more primal. "And you didn't just turn away," he exhaled, his tone thick with heat. *"You played with me."* Mira took a slow, shuddering breath. *"You knew I was watching. Knew exactly what you were doing."* His lips brushed her ear, a voice like a heated promise. *"And I loved it."*

Her nails raked down his back, her breath uneven, her body on fire. *"Loved it so much,"* she murmured, *"that you had to run off into the gardens?"*

He let out a sharp, humorless laugh, his voice rough, breaking. *"I loved it to the point that I couldn't fucking breathe."* His hips rocked into her again, his movements slow but devastating, every shift of his body sending a shudder through her. *"I told myself I'd keep my distance. But then I saw that stunning smile directed at him, looking up at him like you..."*

He cut himself off with a groan, pressing his forehead against hers. His fingers flexed, his voice barely more than a breath. He let out a quiet curse, his head tipping back for a moment before he met her gaze again. He surged forward, capturing her lips in a bruising kiss. His hands roamed, gripping, claiming, pressing her harder against the cold stone as if he could melt into her, as if he needed to.

Mira met him with equal ferocity, her fingers tangling in his hair, her legs tightening around his waist, pulling him closer. Their bodies moved together in a fierce, intoxicating rhythm, grinding against each other, the friction sparking heat between them. Every roll of his hips sent shudders through her, pleasure pooling low in her belly, winding tighter with each deliberate movement.

He tore his lips from hers with a ragged breath. *"Mira,"* he groaned, his voice frayed, his breath uneven. His fingers dug into her skin, his restraint slipping further, his body moving against hers with more purpose, more need.

Her head fell back against the wall, her mouth parting as pleasure surged through her. He took the opportunity, his lips trailing down her chest, teeth scraping, sucking at the delicate skin, leaving more marks. She gasped, her nails raking down his back through his jacket, needing more, needing everything.

"You wanted me to break," he rasped against her neck, his voice dark, heady.

"Congratulations, Mira." He thrust against her, sharper this time, making her moan. "You win."

She clung to him, her pulse wild as she moved with him, chasing the pressure, the sensation coiling tight inside her. The heat between them was unbearable now, a fire raging, unstoppable, pushing them both closer to the edge.

She cursed and his movements turning frantic, desperate. His breath on her was hot, erratic, his hands gripping her like she was the only thing keeping him tethered to the earth.

"Mira," His voice broke, "I can't," His jaw clenched, his entire body taut.

"Don't stop," she breathed, her voice almost a plea, her nails digging into his shoulders as she rocked against him harder, faster. The coil inside her tightened, about to snap.

Pleasure crashed over them, sharp and consuming, sending a shuddering cry past her lips. He followed an instant later, a strangled groan tearing from his throat as he ground himself against her, his entire body trembling.

They stayed like that, breathing hard, wrapped up in each other, their bodies still shaking in the aftermath. He pressed a lingering kiss against her shoulder, his grip on her hips gentling, though he didn't let her go. Mira swallowed, her pulse still racing, her limbs weak. She felt his breath against her skin, still uneven, still shaken. Finally, after a heavy silence, he let out a breathless laugh, his lips brushing against her neck.

✳ ✳ ✳

Ren's voice echoed in her ears, pulling her back. "Mira…"

His forehead rested against hers, his breath unsteady, his grip on her hips gentling but not letting go. His touch still anchored her, grounding her in a moment that felt like it was slipping through her fingers. His eyes burned into hers, searching, waiting. She blinked, her pulse pounding, her mind tangled in the haze of heat, of memory, of something.

"Did I..." she hesitated, pulse thrumming as the weight of the question pressed against her ribs. Was it the way she danced with him? The way her laughter lingered too long, her body too close? The doubt curled in her stomach, sharp and rising.

"Did I make you think ... that I wanted..." Her voice faltered. "Did I use you? To get under Tharion's skin?"

Ren stilled. His expression didn't shift, but something flickered behind his eyes. Pain, maybe. Disbelief. The air between them tightened.

"Mira." He said her name like a plea.

"Tell me." Her voice came sharper this time, edged with annoyance.

Ren's jaw tightened, his throat bobbing as he swallowed. His grip on her hips flexed, but he didn't step away. Didn't let her go.

"No," Ren said quietly, but there was steel beneath the softness. "You didn't use me. I knew what I was doing." his voice steady but low.

163

A rush of relief, sharp and fleeting, before the weight of what she had just done slammed into her. Until now. A sick, twisting ache unfurled in her stomach. Mira shoved at his chest and staggered to the side. Desperate to create space between them, between the reality of what she had just let happen.

"No... what have we...?" The words slipped for her, ragged and raw. Her chest rose and fell too fast, panic threading through the haze.

Ren reached for her, his face open now, concern etched in every line. "Mira,"

"Don't!" Her voice cracked, her fingers curling into fists as rage, at herself, at him, at this entire Navigator-damned situation, burned through her like fire.

"I, " She dragged in a shuddering breath, trying to quell the sharp sting in her chest, in her ribs, in her very soul.

What had she done? She had kissed him and let him touch her. And now, she could never take it back. Her breath hitched, shallow and sharp. She turned away, pressing the heels of her hands to her eyes, trying to think, trying to breathe. The betrayal, her betrayal, coiled tight inside her, suffocating.

Tharion was still recovering. Still fevered, bruised, wounded. And she had been out here, tangled in another's hands, letting herself forget the shape of her loyalty. Of what they were to each other. She had been faithful. Even without her memories, she had been faithful.

Until tonight. A sound escaped her, something ragged and small. Shame prickled across her skin like a scorching fire. She could still feel the warmth of Ren's mouth on hers, the ghost of his hands at her waist, the touch that had once comforted now turned cruel by what it had cost.

Ren stepped around her. His hands found her face, gently, fingers trembling as though afraid she'd vanish beneath them. Mira flinched, but didn't pull away. Ren's eyes burned into hers, his breath unsteady, his jaw tight. He let her anger crash against him, let the silence stretch between them like a blade, but he did not look away. His throat bobbed, words thick behind his teeth. When they came, they were raw, stripped of anything but truth.

"He was lying there. Hurt. And I was here..." her voice cracked, then sharpened as the guilt curdled into something bitter. "With you." The words hissed out, laced with venom, not at Ren, not entirely, but at herself. Her arms wrapped around her middle like she could hold herself together. Ren's thumbs brushed her cheeks, not to wipe away tears. There were none, but to feel if she was still herself. If she still let him touch that part of her.

"I didn't come here to take anything from you," he said. "I just… I saw you slipping. I just wanted to catch you..."

Her breath caught. The lantern light from the garden flickered around them, casting soft shadows across the stones.

Ren stepped back. But he didn't let go. His fingers lingered down her neck, and arms, warm and steady, and wrapped around hers as if holding on just a little longer might change everything. He exhaled, then took a step back as he slowly, painfully, let his grip slip away. He was giving her space. Not enough for her to forget the way he had looked at her, the way he had felt. The way he wanted her.

Mira sucked in a breath like it might hold her together, then turned, too fast, too sharp, as if running before the weight of him pulled her under. Her footsteps echoed hard against the stone corridors, too fast, too loud. Her breath came in shallow bursts, sharp with panic and something else, something tangled and burning that still clung to her skin. She pushed through the side entrance to the kitchens, her heart hammering in her chest.

The cot was empty and the quilt she'd left folded at the foot of it was gone. The cup of water she'd set by his side, untouched.

"Tharion?" she called out, but the name fell too quietly into the warm clatter of morning preparations. No one looked up. The staff moved around her in polite ignorance, too used to the quiet storms that came through to ask questions.

She turned on her heel, skirt catching around her calves as she took the back stairs two at a time, ignoring the voices echoing from the courtyard, the shimmer of lanterns glowing through the tall windows. Her breath caught in her throat as she reached their quarters and threw the door open.

Tharion stood in the center of the room, dressed in his official uniform, the tailored jacket buttoned high at the collar, brass fastenings gleaming faintly in the dim light. The fabric was crisp, the deep earth-tone of it drawing out the sharp lines of his shoulders and the quiet authority he wore so naturally. His hair had been combed back, though a few strands still clung stubbornly to his brow. He looked steady on his feet, though pale. There was a hint of exhaustion in his eyes, but also clarity. Presence.

And when he turned at the sound of the door, his gaze met hers. Mira froze in the doorway, her breath still ragged, her heart still racing for reasons she couldn't yet name.

"You're awake," she said, voice barely above a whisper. Tharion tilted his head slightly, and his smile, small, tired, was not quite a question, not quite a forgiveness.

"You weren't there," he said softly, adjusting the cuff on his wrist. "So I figured I'd meet you where you were going to be.”

She swallowed hard, her throat burning. “I didn’t think you’d be up”

“I know,” he said. Mira took a step in, her hands trembling at her sides. “You should be resting.”

“I’ve done enough of that,” Tharion murmured. His eyes stayed on her, quiet, unwavering. “It’s the Festival of the Final Sun. You think I’d miss the night the court celebrates the Navigators?” He offered her the faintest smile. Tired, but real. Then he glanced to the chair by the hearth, where a folded shape of fabric rested atop a box. “A dress was delivered for you,” he said, nodding toward it. “Perrin’s handwriting.”

Mira’s gaze drifted toward the bundle. Dark silk and soft silver embroidery peeked out from between the folds. It felt too fine now. Too soft. A thing from another life, from another Mira. One who hadn’t seen hunger behind palace walls or heard the quiet desperation in Brahn’s voice. Tharion leaned forward slightly. He studied her in silence for a long moment. Not demanding. Just… watching.

“You don’t have to wear it,” he said eventually, nodding again toward the dress. “But you should. You always loved the lanterns.”

She nodded slowly, her eyes still locked on the bundle of fabric, as if it might speak first. “I’ll change,” she whispered.

Tharion leaned back, his voice even softer. “I’ll wait.”

* * *

Mira stood near the vanity, fastening the final clasp of her gown. The fabric draped over her like liquid midnight, catching in the candlelight, shimmering as if spun from the very essence of the night sky. The black silk clung to her like a whispered secret, the delicate silver embroidery curling over the bodice like constellations mapped across her skin.

The long sleeves tapered at her wrists, the metallic thread catching with every movement, gleaming like fragments of stars. The plunging neckline dipped just enough to command attention without surrendering to it, and a high slit traced one leg, subtle yet undeniably daring. Every shift of fabric left a promise, a question, a fleeting invitation. It was a masterpiece. And yet, it felt like armor.

She exhaled, pressing her palms against the cool vanity, trying to ground herself. The weight of the evening pressed down on her chest, thick and unshakable. She should feel something, pride, excitement, anticipation. But all she felt was a quiet, sinking guilt. She thought of the silk beneath her fingers. The weight of Ren's hand on her waist.

A knock at the door shattered the stillness. She turned as it opened. Tharion. He stepped inside, the warm glow of the lamps outlining his broad frame. The insignia over his chest gleamed faintly, a mark of his station, his duty. He looked at her, really looked at her. His gaze dragged over every inch of her, slow, deliberate, as if committing this version of her to memory. The silence stretched just long enough for her to feel the weight of it settle between them.

Then, at last, his lips parted. "Thank you." She blinked, the word catching her off guard with its quiet sincerity. Tharion's gaze didn't waver.

"Brahn told me you brought Cleric Perrin." Mira's breath caught. "I remember… not much," he added, softer now. "But I remember you storming out."

"Of course." She replied. The room felt too still. Too small for everything pressing at the edges of her chest.

"You look stunning." The words landed softly between

them. Softer than they should have been.

Mira swallowed. She wanted to feel something. The rush, the thrill, the pull of familiarity. She wanted his words to affect her the way they once had. But all she could think about was another pair of hands. Another voice, rough with need, murmuring her name in the dark. Another touch, stolen in a moment she could never take back.

Guilt twisted through her like a blade. She forced a small smile, dipping her chin. "Thank you." the weight of what she had done settled in her ribs like lead.

Tharion stepped forward. The scent of leather and something distinctly him, clean, sharp, familiar, drifted toward her. He held out his arm. Mira hesitated. Just for a breath. Then, moving through the ache in her chest, she placed her hand in the crook of his elbow. His warmth bled through the layers of silk and embroidery, steady and unwavering. But it also felt wrong.

For a year, they had been floating around each other, orbiting without ever quite colliding. Holding on, waiting, hoping that time would mend what had frayed between them. That if they kept pretending, if they kept trying, things would click back into place. But now she knew.

She had shattered them.

10

THE FESTIVAL OF THE FINAL SUN was in full swing, the air thick with the scent of citrus trees and blooming tahla flowers. Lanterns lined the marble pathways, casting soft, flickering gold across silk gowns and embroidered coats. Laughter and music wove together in the air like thread, a string quartet playing beneath a canopy of night- blooming vines, their notes floating gently through the garden like something sacred.

Mira and Tharion arrived just as the final lanterns were being lit. They stepped into the glow together, side by side, the picture of bonded elegance, but beneath the surface, the weight between them told a different story. His hand rested lightly at the small of her back. Familiar. Practiced. It was an echo of what had been, not a tether. His gaze swept the crowd in constant motion, always assessing, always searching. Even now, even injured, he patrolled. Mira didn't speak. She knew better than to ask if he saw threats where there were none.

Around them, the celebration unfolded with curated ease. Courtiers raised glasses of spiced wine. Attendants passed trays of sugared fruits and golden honey cakes. Children danced with woven circlets of stars in their hair. The world glowed as if the kingdom itself had remembered how to hope just for one night.

A hush fell as the lanterns were released. One by one, small paper suns floated into the dark sky, their warm light lifting into the sky with soft sighs of parchment and flame.

Hundreds of them, each inscribed with prayers and

promises, rising like a constellation reborn.

Mira tilted her head, watching the sky bloom with light. It should have felt beautiful. It used to. But tonight, she felt like the only thing not captivated by the sight. Her feet rooted to stone, her heart pulled taut with guilt and memories she couldn't touch. Beside her, Tharion watched, too, though his expression remained unreadable, carved in shadow and restraint.

A silver bell chimed across the garden, clear and bright. It rang once, a signal to the crowd. A chance. The festival's oldest tradition. If you caught a lantern before it rose beyond reach, it was said your hope whispered into the flame would come true. A game. As the bell's echo faded into the night, children scrambled from the edge of the crowd, laughter peeling through the quiet awe. Their hands stretched skyward, chasing the drifting lights with a wild devotion only youth possessed. Mira didn't move. She stood in the lantern-glow, her fingers curled loosely at her side.

Harwen darted past her, dark braid swinging as she ran barefoot across the marble. She leapt for a low-sailing lantern, laughing as it rose just out of reach. Mira watched, envy prickling somewhere deep and quiet. Not for Harwen, but for the lantern. For the weightlessness of it, the effortless glow. For the way it floated, unburdened, while she remained tethered to the ground.

She glanced at Tharion. He hadn't moved either. His arms remained crossed behind his back, his stance too formal, too stiff. He wasn't watching the lanterns. He was watching the edges again, the walls, the shadows, the guards posted in the dark. Even in this celebration, he was never truly present with her. Mira's gaze shifted skyward. Her heart felt heavier than it should in a moment, so full of beauty.

A soft flutter of wind brushed her cheek, and something flickered in her periphery. She turned just in time to see a lantern break from the cluster just above, its flame flickering unsteadily, tugged low by the breeze. It drifted down like a falling star. Closer. Slower landing in her open palms. A ripple of delighted surprise moved through the crowd, followed by a smattering of applause. Mira blinked down at it, stunned.

The paper was warm and thin beneath her fingers. She hesitated for only a breath before turning, her eyes scanning the crowd until she spotted a child near the hedge wide-eyed, frozen with awe, tiny hands half-raised as if willing the lantern to change its mind and return. Mira stepped toward her, gently kneeling as the girl's mother gasped softly. She leaned in, smiled, and extended the lantern. The little girl squealed, voice high and breathless.

"Really? For me?" Mira nodded once, her voice quiet but warm.

"It found its way to me… but I think it was meant for you." The child cradled the lantern like it was something sacred, then turned and darted back to her mother, who lifted her high into the air so she could release it again. The lantern caught the breeze and soared upward, brighter than before. More applause followed. Laughter. Joy. Mira felt none of it. She stood slowly, her expression serene. But inside, guilt was ripping her apart.

Beyond the winding garden paths, a wide, open grassy expanse stretched beneath the stars, its surface smooth and meticulously maintained for the evening's festivities. At its center, couples twirled and stepped in elegant formation, their silken garments catching the lantern light as they moved in time with the music. Around the edges, clusters of guests gathered, some watching with keen interest, others murmuring behind their jeweled goblets. A few lingered just at the boundary, waiting for the right moment to step onto the dance floor, while others, content to observe, exchanged quiet gossip and knowing glances beneath the golden glow of the festival lights.

Tharion exhaled sharply, his gaze settling on a group of advisors at the far end of the pavilion. A messenger approached, speaking in hushed tones, and Mira caught the flicker of the conversation.

"Lord Asric still hasn't delivered the requisition for Emreth. We need the ledger by morning to prepare the supply routes."

Tharion's jaw tensed. "He had it signed three days ago."

"Yes," the steward glanced nervously at Mira, "But he's… withholding. He said it was a matter best handled with a personal touch."

"Of course he did," Tharion muttered under his breath. He turned slightly, catching Mira's eye. "I'll only be a moment." Before she could reply, he was already striding across the grass with clipped precision, the movement born of too many battles and not enough patience.

Mira let out a slow breath and turned her gaze back to the dance floor. The night was just beginning. She moved through the celebration with practiced ease, the weight of silk clinging to her body like a second skin. Moving through the revelry, she let the noise wash over her, laughter spilling from wine-flushed lips, the chiming of crystal goblets, the murmur of hushed conversations woven between the music. Every gathering like this was a stage, performative. She caught snatches as she passed.

"I swear, the guest quarters get smaller every year, "

"What about Hallen's Reach? That's close enough, isn't it?"

"Will the Crowned Betrothed make an appearance tonight?"

"Did you hear? Lord Asric's looking for a new lover."

Then, something sharper, cutting through the usual courtly gossip. "Ren defended the convoy himself, can you believe it?"

Mira stopped. Not abruptly, not noticeably. Just enough to appear she had been caught by the flow of the celebration, her movements languid, effortless. She drifted toward the carved stone railing beside a lantern-lit archway, tilting her head as if admiring the glow of the floating lights in the fountain beyond. She listened.

"Surprising, isn't it?" a voice mused, rich and contemplative. "For all his reputation, he didn't hesitate."

She recognized the speaker instantly. Cleric Perrin. She stood amid a small cluster of nobles and officials, her pristine robes untouched by the warmth of the evening. The ceremonial silverwork embroidered into her sleeves shimmered faintly in the lantern light, casting subtle sigils across her silhouette. Her headdress, sheer and celestial, crowned her with quiet reverence. Her expression was mild. Measured. She spoke, as she always did, with careful precision, every word designed to seed itself in the minds of those who mattered most.

A woman scoffed lightly. "A bastard prince playing hero?"

Another noble chuckled into his drink. "He has a talent for spectacle."

Perrin only smiled. "Perhaps. But he didn't have to be in Anyerit. And yet, he was."

Mira's fingers traced along the railing. It was subtle, but she could hear it in their voices, the shift, the curiosity laced with something close to respect. The way they were speaking of him as something other than reckless, selfish, untamed. Ren had spent his life standing just outside the lines they had drawn for him. And now, it seemed, the lines were blurring.

Suddenly, she was back in Anyerit. The wind whipping against her face, the scent of sweat and steel thick in the air. Ren in front of her. They had fought with no hesitation, no space between them. His voice, sharp and commanding, his body a shield against the worst of it.

Then, another voice hushed, insistent. "And Tharion? I heard he was injured. Shot through the shoulder?"

Cleric Perrin, ever composed, offered a quiet, diplomatic smile. "He returned with the convoy."

Mira's jaw tensed. Why let Ren take the credit? He had planned with Ren to return the convoy. He had bled for their survival. And yet, here in the gardens where praise echoed, it was Ren's name on their lips, not his. Tharion had never cared for praise. But this felt different.

A familiar figure caught her eye. Draped in sapphire silk, fanning herself lazily, was Lady Elandra. She lounged alone beneath a cluster of citrus trees at the edge of the eastern garden. The trees arched gracefully overhead, their branches heavy with golden fruit, casting dappled shadows across the stone benches and soft moss beneath. Mira made her approach, slipping into the seat across from her just as Elandra's sharp eyes flicked up in recognition.

"Speaking of tragedy," she began, her voice lowering to a conspiratorial whisper as she leaned in, plucking a grape from the silver dish before her. "I hear the Crowned Betrothed is still catatonic. Not a word from him. The council is growing restless, but he delays, day after day." Elandra clicked her tongue in disdain. "How can a kingdom survive with a king who's lost his will to rule?"

Mira's fingers tightened. Her gaze drifted toward the distant fountains, where the water caught the lantern light in fractured ribbons of gold and silver.

Elandra continued, "I heard it from a reliable source. You know, they're facing down the barrel of an uprising. The people are restless, starving, and the Kharadors aren't helping matters. The advisors have begged him to take action, but he's paralyzed." She shook her head, her fan waving gently in frustration. "It's a mess, really."

Mira spoke without fully meaning to, her voice low, thoughtful. "The people in those towns… they're desperate. The hunger, the fear. They need something to believe in.

Something that gives them hope, or else…" She caught herself, the final words catching in her throat.

Elendra's eyes glinted with interest, her curiosity piqued. She purred. "Or else... what? Revolution? Fire in the streets? A charming little coup?"

Mira gave a soft, breathy laugh, too smooth, too quick. "Oh, ignore me. Too much wine..."

She collected a glass from the table and sipped, letting the sweetness mask the bitterness on her tongue. But Elendra wasn't so easily led astray.

"Mira..." she murmured, the name stretched with quiet reprimand. "You forget who you're speaking to." Elendra's gaze didn't waver. She already knew there was more. She always did. Then, with a conspirator's smile, her voice lowered, smooth as velvet over a knife. "I'll make you a trade."

Mira arched a brow, wary. "I'll tell you what Lord Asric actually wants for that degree he's withholding." Elendra let the words hang between them, lazily watching Mira's reaction. "A detail that not even your darling Tharion has pried from him yet."

Mira's heart ticked up, but her expression didn't falter. But beneath the silk of her gown and the practiced stillness of her face, guilt curled sharp and persistent. If she could fix this, if she could help him, even in this small way, maybe it would make her betrayal quieter. Maybe it would be enough to prove, if only to herself, that the way Ren had looked at her, like she was still wanted, still seen, was a mistake.

"And in return?" she asked, tone even. Elendra smiled like a cat. "You finish your sentence."

Mira blinked.

"You said, 'or else…'" Elendra repeated, tilting her head. "Finish the thought." Mira hesitated. For a breath, two, three.

Quietly, "Or else they'll turn to someone else. Someone who promises change." The words tasted like rust. She didn't name the resistance, not directly. But it hung there, plain and sharp in the silence that followed. Elendra's fan resumed its lazy flutter, but her gaze sharpened. Just slightly.

"There you go darling," she said softly, "I was wondering when you'd stop pretending you didn't see what was right in front of you."

Mira didn't respond. Couldn't. The admission felt heavier now that it had shape. Confusion twisted through her. If Elendra had already known of the uprising, then what had she paid her with? What had she truly given away?

Elendra leaned in, her voice velvet-smooth. "Lord Asric wants support in tonight's council session. That's all. A simple show of loyalty."

Mira's eyes narrowed slightly. "And what does he get out of that?" Elendra's fan paused mid-motion, then folded with a soft snap.

She smiled, but it no longer reached her eyes. "Now, Mira," she said, voice low and almost amused, "that wasn't part of our deal." She tilted her head. "You offered a truth. I offered you a secret. Don't spoil this beautiful moment by asking for more than you're owed."

Mira knew enough of Asric to know he never moved without layers, always smiling on the surface while his true intentions burrowed deeper. And Tharion… He'd never back something he didn't believe in. Not willingly. He would though, to get the decree, Mira was sure of it. The one that could secure Tharion's logistics and bring relief to the outer townships. Asric was probably holding it even now, waiting. Watching. Waiting for another piece would fall into place.

But maybe… Maybe she could find it. Get to it before Tharion was forced into something. If she was clever enough and if she moved quietly she could. A rustle of silk and the gentle clinking of crystal snapped her attention back. Elendra's flock had returned, handmaidens in feathered silks and embroidered veils, bearing silver trays laden with spiced fruits, candied almonds, chilled wine and delicate pastries shaped like petals. They drifted around their lady like orbiting moons, placing the offerings on the low marble table with rehearsed elegance. Elendra plucked a glazed fig from the tray, bit into it with casual grace.

"Ah, speaking of strategic moves, looks like the bastard prince is making quite the effort to repair his political standing tonight." Elendra's lips curved, sharp with amusement. "Shame he doesn't treat his romantic reputation with the same care." She tipped her chin toward the dance circle.

Mira turned in her seat, her gaze following Elendra's eyes. Ren. Smiling effortlessly in the middle of a waltz, his hand resting lightly on the waist of a woman wrapped in silver silk. His movements were fluid, confident, too smooth to be careless. The woman laughed, her voice light and clear, head tilted back as if the entire world had narrowed to just him.

Mira's stomach dropped. But the way his hand rested at the small of the woman's bare back, the way he looked utterly unbothered, completely present, sent a sharp pulse of jealousy through her chest. No hesitation or guilt. No trace of what had passed between them in the shadows. Maybe he'd accepted that it had meant nothing.

Guilt bloomed immediately. She had no right to feel this way. She was bound by rite and blood and memory. Even if that memory was now a ghost.

Whatever had happened with Ren, whatever she had let happen, it was a betrayal of something sacred. Of Tharion. Her throat tightened, and instinctively, her gaze swept the crowd, searching. Needing to see Tharion. To remind herself of what she owed him.

She spotted him at the far edge of the garden, half-shadowed by the golden curve of a column. His posture was stiff. He stood with one hand clenched behind his back, the other gesturing tightly as he spoke. Even from this distance, she could see the strain in his expression, the quiet fury just beneath the surface, the way his arm moved too fast, too low. It wasn't the conversation of a man enjoying a celebration. It was war, disguised as diplomacy. And he was fighting it alone. Her guilt twisted deeper.

Mira inhaled slowly, the edges of her corset pressing against the sharp rise of breath. She had stood at the center of too many moments like this. Waiting for someone else to act. Not tonight. Her gaze swept the garden until it found who she needed. Lord Asric.

He stood near the wine terrace, surrounded by a crescent of admirers, his laugh low and indulgent, fingers glittering with rings that caught the flickering lantern light. He was exactly where he thrived. At the center of attention, cloaked in charm, posturing as generous while quietly maneuvering for power. Silver hair swept back from sharp features. His allure hadn't faded with time, it had sharpened. His name lingered in court whispers, both as a strategist and a lover. Tonight, Mira had heard those murmurs louder than usual speculation about the woman who had just left him. A lover scorned. A vacancy to be filled. She could use that.

Mira rose from her seat with purpose, her gown whispering against the marble as she crossed the floor. Asric turned toward her, interest already stirring in his eyes.

"Well, Lady Solwynd," he said, bowing just enough to be courteous, never humble. "I hadn't expected the pleasure of your company tonight." She offered a honeyed smile.

"I like to keep people guessing, my lord." Her voice was low, warm, intimate enough to pique interest, not scandal. "I've heard some interesting rumors."

His eyes sharpened. "Rumors, you say? I enjoy a good story. Especially the unexpected kind."

Her fingers brushed his arm, light as a breath. He focused entirely on her now. "Then perhaps," she murmured, "you'd like to write one with me tonight." She let the suggestion hang, then tilted her head with playful boldness. "Dance with me?"

Asric's smile deepened, indulgent and intrigued. "I'd be

delighted."

They swept onto the dance floor, the crowd parting around them in a graceful ripple. The music shifted, slow, rich with strings, as if cued for something theatrical. Their bodies moved in perfect synchrony. Mira allowed herself to be led, but only just, every step calculated, every glance a weapon. Her gown whispered against his legs with each turn, a flirtation in the fabric. His hand settled at her waist, firm but respectful, though the heat beneath his touch was unmistakable.

She let her fingertips rest lightly on his shoulder, tracing the subtle seam of his jacket, sending a thrill through her own nerves as much as his. The dance became more than movement, it became a narrative, one crafted from rhythm and restraint, flirtation and fire. Their eyes locked as they turned, and in his gaze, Mira saw understanding.

They were both players. Both predators. Asric dipped her low, his breath ghosting against her ear.

"My former lover is certainly watching us now," he said, amusement woven through his voice. "But tell me, is it our Underguard Steward, whom you're trying to make jealous?"

Mira's breath caught. She let the thrill of the moment dance in her eyes, letting the intimacy of his question settle like a secret between them. She was performing now, not just for the crowd, but for him. Feeding his ego. Letting him believe he'd peeled back a layer that he'd seen through her. That he'd figured her out. Asric swept her into a turn, their bodies brushing. The music curled around them like smoke.

Mira tilted her head, lips curling. "Never mind who I'm trying to impress," she whispered. "Let's give him something to watch."

Asric chuckled, low and rich, but leaned in, playing his

part to perfection. Her fingers traced along his shoulder and down his chest as he spun her again, her touch graceful, effortless. But beneath the folds of his jacket, a subtle shift of fabric. A piece of parchment. There. The order. Her fingers drifted into his jacket, closing around the letter. Smooth. Folded tight. She moved closer to Asric, letting the moment stretch, their bodies nearly flush. The music peaking, as she slid the letter into the folds of her gown with practiced ease.

He never noticed. Their last turn was slow, deliberate, a punctuation mark at the end of their shared sentence. The music faded. Applause rose like mist around them. They bowed to one another, the tension between them still humming. Lord Asric smiled, pleased, smug, unaware. But Mira's heart thundered in her chest. The letter was hers now.

Mira stepped away, collecting a goblet of wine from a passing tray. The weight of the letter tucked safely into her gown anchored her more than the drink in her hand. She scanned the crowd with practiced ease, the soft hum of courtly chatter washing over. She lifted the goblet to her lips, savoring the sweet, floral notes of the wine. The warmth of the night pressed gently around her, and for the first time in what felt like hours, she let herself breathe. Because she'd done something that mattered. She'd helped him. Tharion might never know the cost, or the risk, but it didn't matter. The letter was theirs now.

She felt the eyes on her still, the soft stir of whispers trailing after her and Lord Asric's performance. But none of them mattered.

A hand closed around her wrist. Not harsh. Not cruel. But firm enough to send a message. Tharion. He didn't speak. Just pulled her from the edge of the crowd with practiced precision, his grip steady, his pace sure. Her glass slipped from her hand, hitting the marble floor with a sharp crack, shattering into silence-breaking pieces. Heads turned. Conversation faltered.

Mira stumbled once, startled by the suddenness of it, but she didn't resist. Eyes followed them as he led her past the dancers, past the musicians, past the stares that clung to their backs like static. He didn't stop until they were past the marble archway. He led her into the shadowed alcove of the garden, quiet, cool, and away from the stage the court had made of them. The air shifted. Lanterns flickered behind the hedges.

"Are you out of your mind?" Tharion's voice was low, not harsh, but tight with concern. A raw edge threaded through his usual calm, like a blade dulled from restraint. His expression, typically unreadable, was etched with more fear than fury.

Mira didn't speak right away. Instead, with slow, deliberate movements, she reached into the folds of her gown. Tharion's breath caught as her fingers withdrew the parchment. Smooth, warm from her skin, sealed with the sigil of the court. She held it out to him, eyes never leaving him.

His brows drew together, disbelief flickering across his features as he took it. His fingers brushed hers, and for a moment, he didn't look at the letter. He looked at her. Really looked. A muscle ticked in his jaw.

"Mira," he breathed, low and sharp. "You don't know what kind of risk you took." She arched her brow, calm, unflinching. "I knew exactly what I was doing."

He shook his head once, the letter clenched in his hand, as though it might vanish if he loosened his grip. "He could've caught you. Anyone could have. You could've…"

Her gaze sharpened. "I had one chance, Tharion. One. Before they forced your hand, before you were cornered into something you couldn't come back from." She paused, the weight of her next words falling between them like a stone. "And I took it. For you."

Tharion looked down at the letter again. Then at her. "You don't have to fight my battles," he said, the words strained, almost hollow.

"No," Mira replied, voice quiet but unshaken, "but I will." She let the silence hang for a moment, then added, "Asric was going to use it. To blackmail you."

Tharion's eyes snapped to hers. "What?"

"He wants your support at the next council meeting. He's ready to use this as leverage."

Tharion swore under his breath, already half-turning before stopping himself. "They've just called a session," he said. "An emergency meeting. Tonight."

Mira's breath caught. "Tonight?"

He nodded once, sharply, already calculating. He looked at the letter again, as if it might scorch him. "I have to go," he said, voice tightening with urgency. "I need to prepare these, send word. If I move fast, I can get ahead of whatever Asric's planning."

He turned, but then paused, just long enough to look back at her, his gaze softening once more. "Mira..."

She tilted her head, waiting. But he only shook his head, as if there weren't words for what he wanted to say. Then he was gone, his cloak catching the breeze as he vanished into the shadows, the letter clutched tightly in his hand.

Mira stood motionless, her breath caught somewhere between disbelief and fury. The tension in her chest twisted tighter by the second. She turned sharply, pacing the flagstones beneath her feet. The cool garden air did nothing to soothe the fire rising in her throat.

He'd take the risk, face the council, face Asric... but not with her at his side. It didn't matter that she had the letter. That she had made this possible. The moment it was done, he took it from her hands. Again.

Her gaze lifted to the shadowed windows above. Somewhere behind them, the council was already assembling, preparing to plot and posture behind their heavy doors and titles. She should be in that room. She needed to be in that room. Surely there would be something, a whisper, a name, a plan, to prove to the resistance that not all hope was lost. That someone within these walls hadn't forgotten them. She clenched her fists. If they wouldn't let her, she would find another way.

A rustle stirred the hedges. Mira turned, already tensing, but the flicker of motion resolved into a familiar lean silhouette, half-cast in moonlight.

Ren stepped from the shadows like he'd always belonged to them, a lazy smile curving his lips. "Well," he said, voice low and teasing, "that was quite the performance."

Mira narrowed her eyes. "How long were you watching?" "Long enough," he drawled, stepping closer.

"You really shouldn't be lurking in bushes," she said.

He tilted his head, mock-injured. "Lurking? I was strategically positioned. Watching your back, in case you needed rescuing."

"I didn't," she said, but her voice was softer. He caught that softness. A step closer, his tone dipping just slightly more sincere.

"I know you don't" he paused, "but still, sometimes it's good to know someone is at your back."

Mira folded her arms, trying to steady herself. "Did you follow me just to offer commentary?"

"No," Ren said, eyes gleaming, "I followed you because I have something you want" Mira rolled her eyes. "I can get you into the council meeting."

She blinked. "How did you know that's what I wanted?"

The grin returned, slow and sure. "I know the palace better than most. I know who's guarding which hall, which stair creaks, and which council doors are never truly locked."

She narrowed her eyes. "That's not what I asked" Ren crossed his arms over his chest. "No... It's not"

"Why would you help me?" Mira asked, her voice low, edged with distrust. "What do you get out of this?"

He shrugged, every inch the image of practiced indifference. "You need to hear what they're saying. What they're planning."

"And?" she asked, hearing the edge tucked behind his casual tone.

Ren looked down, just briefly, like he was choosing his words, then met her eyes again, his smile flickering, half-shadow and half dare. "And... after I get you in, you'll owe me a debt. I won't call it in tonight or tomorrow. But when I do, you'll do as I ask"

Her instincts bristled, but so did her curiosity. "That's a dangerous promise to make."

He leaned in slightly, not quite touching her, but close enough that her pulse quickened. "Not a promise," he said softly. "A bargain."

She studied him, every angle of that maddening, half-smiling face. There was a catch, she was sure of it. There always was. But something in his eyes, steady and unreadable, told her what her gut had already begun to accept:

he wouldn't harm her, not really. Not physically. Not intentionally. There was danger in playing his game, but there was also a strange kind of safety in the rules of playing with Ren. She didn't have time to negotiate. She needed access. And he was the only one offering it.

She nodded once, slow and deliberate. "Deal."

He extended his hand, palm open. Mira hesitated only a heartbeat before placing hers in his. His fingers curled around hers, warm and certain.

He lifted her hand slowly, deliberately, and pressed a kiss to her knuckles. It wasn't chaste. It wasn't performative. His lips lingered just long enough for her pulse to spike, for heat to ripple up her arm and settle low in her belly.

She felt his promise in his kiss.

11

MIRA MOVED LIKE A SHADOW through the upper halls of the celestial observatory, her breath tight in her chest. The vast stained-glass windows shimmered in the moonlight, casting fractured constellations across the polished marble floor. Each pane told stories of old skies, celestial beasts, and the Navigators' journey.

Above her, the domed ceiling stretched like the heavens themselves, the painted stars glinting with specks of silver leaf. The slow tick and whirl of the grand golden orrery echoed in the stillness, its rings rotating with patient precision at the observatory's center.

Shadows danced over the mosaic floor below, where the realm's five zodiac signs circled in eternal orbit. The scent of parchment, aged wood, and melted candle wax filled the air, adding to the sense of ancient wisdom steeped within these walls.

Mira didn't know this place well. She'd helped Harwen place the ceremonial candles here once. But tonight, the candles were gone, replaced by voices. Urgent, low, and echoing from below. She edged closer to the marble railing, her eyes dropping to the long table that stretched beneath the dome. The royal advisors and Crowned Betrothed, were already seated, their faces lined with stress and sleeplessness. One chair remained conspicuously empty. Torvyn's. At the far end of the table, Tharion sat, his expression hard, shoulders tight. Tonight only, he sat as more than a Steward, an invited representative of the people, at the council's behest.

And beside her, stepping silently into the alcove from the opposite side, was Ren.

"You missed that guard by seconds," he whispered near her ear, his breath warm and maddening. "You need to be careful, I'd hate to have smuggled you this far only for you to get caught leaning into a moonbeam."

Mira rolled her eyes but didn't argue. His timing, as always, was infuriatingly perfect. "I could've handled it," she muttered.

Ren smirked. "Of course. But why be careful when you can be dazzlingly reckless?"

She ignored him, focusing on the scene below. The council was already deep in discussion.

"We can't delay this conversation any longer," Lord Edric said, his voice sharp, cutting through the hum of tension. "It's been a year. His Majesty's episodes have worsened with every passing moon. We no longer have a king, we have a relic."

Lady Brenna's fingers twisted the ring on her hand, her jaw tight. "He was lucid briefly, two months ago."

"Lucid enough to mistake his steward for his father," Lord Asric said dryly. "He hasn't spoken since the last solstice. He has looked no one in the eye. That is not a ruler." Silence fell, heavy and cold.

Edric's voice was low, but it carried across the room. "We all knew this was coming. His decline was gradual. We kept hoping for recovery. But hope is not a strategy."

"And what would you have us do?" Brenna asked. "Declare the throne vacant?" Asric didn't flinch. "We need leadership. Now."

Below, murmurs broke out. Ren leaned against the stone beside Mira, arms crossed as he watched the scene unfold.

"Does anyone even know what this is?… To collapse like this, it seems like more than grief?" Mira whispered, more to herself than to him.

Ren's gaze slid sideways to her. "My father was always a sentimental man."

Asric slammed a palm onto the table below. "We need to crown a regent, or the realm will tear itself apart while we wait for a ghost to speak!"

Mira flinched, her heart pounding. Even from a distance, she could feel the desperation in the room. The way the kingdom stood on the edge of something vast and dangerous.

Mira nodded, the weight of it pressing into her ribs. "If the people saw this… if they knew the truth of what's happening behind these walls…" Ren said nothing, just waited. She swallowed hard. "There's no one steering the ship. They're just waiting."

"And he won't." Ren's voice trembled slightly. Mira turned to look at him fully now.

"They need someone who can lead. Someone who understands both sides, the palace and the people. Someone who can decide instead of watching the kingdom rot from inaction." Ren's face showed none of the usual charm, not even the sharp, knowing glint he wore like armor. He reached out, cupping her face gently in both hands. His palms were warm, calloused, trembling just slightly.

"Mira," he said, steadying himself through her. "You need to stay here." Her brows drew together. "Ren…"

"No." His voice hardened, not with anger, but with urgency. "You stay hidden. Whatever happens next, nobody can know you were here." His thumb brushed her cheekbone once, a slow, aching touch, like he wasn't sure he'd be able to do this if he let go too soon.

"I need to do this," he said. "But not if you're exposed. Not if they can use you as leverage before I can move." She searched his eyes, something rising in her chest. Fear, disbelief, maybe even pride. Ren looked down at the council before he slipped from the alcove back the way they had entered.

Below, the chamber had dissolved into noise, voices overlapping in rising waves.

Some called for a regency, others for preemptive war, and still others clung to indecision like a shield. Then the wooden door swung open with a sharp crack. Silence fell like a blade.

Heads turned as Ren entered. Not slowly, not with ceremony, but with purpose. He didn't glide or posture. He stalked forward, each step measured, grounded, utterly certain. Gone was the flirt, the provocateur, the half-smiling storm she'd always known. What walked into the room now was something else. Something inevitable. He moved not like a man with a claim, but a man with a reason. Not born into rule, destined for it. A prince.

Ren didn't wait to be acknowledged. He walked the length of the chamber and came to stand at the head of the table. The queen's seat, untouched for months. He did not hesitate. He sat. A shocked murmur rippled through the room. Ren placed both hands flat on the table. No dramatics. Just stillness, calm and cutting.

"We are fractured," he said simply. "Half of you argue for action. The rest hide behind a throne that no longer speaks." No one interrupted. "We need three things," he continued, voice steady, deliberate. "A regent to stabilize the line of succession. Reinforcements to the eastern border before Kharador grows bold. And intelligence on the uprising that's taking root within the kingdom."

He let the words settle like stones. "We move quietly. We send trusted agents to the villages, not soldiers. We listen. Find the leaders, the weak points, the truths behind the whispers. If we rush, we will make martyrs. If we wait, we invite rebellion."

Lady Brenna blinked, slow and deliberate. "And tell me, who, exactly, is meant to serve as regent?"

"I'll serve," Ren said without pause. "As steward in the father's stead, until his voice returns, or the realm decides otherwise." A few heads snapped up.

Asric's jaw tightened. "You presume much."

"I act," Ren replied coolly. "And the realm needs action." Ren leaned forward slightly, his tone colder now. "You want to call a vote? Call it. But while you debate legitimacy, our enemies organize. Choose your priorities carefully." A hush fell again. The weight of the moment pressing against every shoulder.

Then Lord Garran spoke. "And if we back you? What then?" Ren's answer came without hesitation. "Then we stand united. We quiet the unrest. We secure our borders. And we remind every corner of this kingdom that its heart still beats, even if its king cannot speak."

The room sat in stunned silence, until Asric exhaled sharply, the sound halfway between a scoff and a growl.

He rose slowly from his chair, knuckles white against the polished wood. "Of course it would come to this," he muttered. Eyes turned toward him. Asric didn't care. He was building steam now, voice growing louder, more theatrical.

"You break hearts, Ren. That's what you're good at. Whispered promises and vanishing acts. That's what you've always been, a shadow with charm and no spine for consequence."

Ren didn't move. He simply watched him with that maddening calm, unbothered by the storm brewing across the table.

Asric jabbed a finger toward him. "You are not the rulers, Bonded Betrothed. Nor are you of the late queen's line. You have no standing here. "No," Asric's voice rose, not with anger, but with incredulous flair. "No, we will not crown a bastard boy with a silver tongue and a fondness for teasing women."

Asric ignored the murmurs that followed, pressing forward, his voice gaining force. "I've served this realm for over three decades. I've outlasted two monarchs and more than a few ill-advised heirs. You want strength? Stability? A spine behind the throne while the king sleeps in silence?" His hand struck the table, fingers splayed. "Then name me regent."

That set the room alight, advisors shifting, exchanging wary glances, voices rising in uncertain murmurs. Asric raised his chin, commanding their attention like a man who already saw himself robed in authority. "If we wait, we fracture. If we placate rebellion, we embolden it. The boy wants to feed the border? I say we close it. Fortify it with steel and flame."

Asric swept his gaze across them. "We strike first. Hard. Let Kharador know that Bharalyn still has teeth. And as for the insurrection brewing within , we root it out. Public trials. Swift punishment. No whispers, no shadows."

His eyes flicked briefly toward Ren. "This is not the time for sentiment or experiments with charming illegitimate sires and poetic ideas of unity." Then back to the council. "It is the time for rule. For order."

He paused, letting his words sink in, then added, "Give me command, and within a fortnight, you'll have peace. Not the soft kind, but the kind that lasts." For a moment, no one spoke.

The room pulsed with tension. Asric remained standing, defiant, his proposal echoing in the charged silence. Ren hadn't moved, but his gaze had sharpened, fixed on the older man with quiet fire.

From the far end of the table, a chair creaked. Tharion stood. He had said little throughout the meeting, choosing to watch, to measure. But now his voice rang clear, steady as stone.

"This debate serves no purpose if it ends in argument." The murmurs faded. Even Asric turned his head. Tharion's gaze moved over the room, calm, composed, utterly unreadable.

"The king cannot speak. The realm is leaderless, and we are out of time. Two paths have been placed before us tonight." He looked to Ren, then to Asric, giving each man the full weight of his gaze.

"Then let you do what this council was made to do. Vote." A ripple of unease ran through the room. Tharion continued, voice firmer now. "Do not vote for speeches. Not for bloodlines. Vote for the regent that is best for Bharalyn. One voice to lead. One plan to follow."

Tension pressed down on the room like a storm barely held at bay. Sharp, suffocating, and heavy with consequence.

For a heartbeat, no one moved.

Then Lady Brenna exhaled and raised her hand. "Ren," she said clearly, her eyes never leaving him.

Lord Garran followed. "Ren."

Across the table, Lord Veylin leaned back, lips pursed,

then nodded once. "Asric." A pause. Then Lord Harwin. "Asric."

The room shifted. Two to Ren. Two to Asric. Lord Davin hesitated. His gaze flicked toward Asric, then to Tharion, as if searching for a safer choice that didn't exist.

His fingers tapped once against the table. "Asric," he said.

Three to two. A silence settled like ash. Mira, watching from the shadows above, felt the air catch in her lungs.

Softly, unexpectedly, Lady Nyla raised her hand. "Ren."

Three to three. All eyes turned to the last man at the table. The invited guest. Tharion. He sat motionless, gaze fixed on the space between the two men across from him.

This was why Brahn had been delayed, to force a deadlock. Tharion raised his head. His voice was low, deliberate. "Ren."

Four to three. The words struck the room like a final chime in a cathedral. Ren had won.

Above, Mira's knees nearly buckled. Her throat tightened, not from relief, but from the sudden, bone-deep understanding of what had almost happened. If she hadn't taken the letter… If Asric had still held the threat over Tharion's vote. Tharion wouldn't have been free to cast his vote. She had saved him. From being used. From being made a weapon in someone else's hand.

Silence lingered in the observatory like smoke after lightning. The vote had been cast. The regent had been chosen. Ren sat still for a moment, as though letting the weight of the decision settle into his bones.

After a moment he rose. Not abruptly. Not triumphantly. He rose like the tide, inevitable, steady, undeniable. His hands rested once more on the table, and when he spoke, his voice carried not just across the chamber, but into something deeper. The heart of the room. The heart of the realm.

"Our king can no longer rule. Whether he wakes or not, our work for the kingdom does not stop. The people do not stop needing. The enemies at our gates do not wait."

He glanced across the table. At Brenna, at Garran, at Tharion. "We reinforce the borders. Quietly. Without fanfare. We send supplies to the outer villages, not soldiers. Not yet. Let the people feel protected before they feel watched." He turned to Asric, who met his gaze with cold, begrudging silence.

"And we listen. To the unrest. To the leaders behind it. We do not crush what we do not yet understand. We learn their names. Their fears. Their reasons. And then we decide who among them can be turned and who must be stopped." A breath passed between the gathered lords and ladies. The beginning of something. The edge of unity.

Ren's voice lowered, but it grew no less steady. "There will be no purges. No open executions. No fear-driven show of force. This kingdom doesn't need a hand that crushes, it needs one that holds." He exhaled, gaze lowering slightly. "We do not restore order through terror. We restore it through truth. And through presence. The crown cannot be a myth while the realm is bleeding."

She watched as the council shifted, no longer locked in indecision but moving now, slowly, into purpose. Voices rose, quieter this time, layered with strategy rather than argument. They leaned over maps. Marked supply lines. Named outposts. Ren stood among them. His shoulders squared beneath the mantle he had taken, listening as much as he spoke. Steering, not ruling.

Mira watched it all, the shape of ruling power as it

reformed under Ren. This was what she had risked everything for. Not just a seat claimed, but the movement that followed. The ripple. The moment after a fire that might become warmth instead of ruin. All of it born from her instinct. From a dance and a letter. From a single breath held between two people in the dark.

As the hours wore on, the voices below grew more tired. Ren lifted a hand, and the murmurs faded as if pulled by a thread. "That's enough for tonight," he said, voice firm. "We have a course. You have your orders. The rest... can wait until morning."

No one argued. Chairs scraped quietly across the stone. Scrolls were gathered, glances exchanged. Even now, with the firelight flickering low and the weight of history hanging thick in the air, the council bowed to the quiet command in Ren's voice.

"Tharion…stay" That caught a few looks, but none dared linger long enough to question it.

One by one, the advisors filed out, leaving only the echo of their boots and the hush of fading tension. The great doors closed with a soft, final sound. Ren didn't speak for a moment. His hands rested lightly on the table's edge, as he looked up, not at Tharion. But at the gallery above.

"You can come down now," a half-smile tugging at the corner of his mouth. "They're gone."

Mira stepped down the spiral stairs and out from the shadows. The air below felt different, heavier, now that the council was gone. Only the soft crackle of fire and the distant creak of banners overhead remained.

Tharion watched her with the faintest furrow between his brows, but he said nothing more. Not yet. Ren stood at the head of the table, where the king's seal still pressed faintly into the candlelit wax before him. Ren didn't look tired. He looked alive, sharp, grounded, present in a way she'd never seen in him before. Then he turned to her fully.

"What do you think?" The words were simple. Unadorned. She hesitated, just a breath. He was asking her. Not as a courtesy. Not as an afterthought. As an equal. She stepped closer, her arms loose at her sides.

"You've bought yourself time," she said, voice quiet but sure. "And a narrow path forward." Ren nodded once, waiting. "But that room was full of knives, Ren." Her eyes flicked to Tharion, then back. "You'll need more than strategy. You'll need loyalty.

From people who owe you nothing."

He didn't flinch. "The decisions that are coming won't leave room for fence-sitting," he said. "And you're both tied to the resistance, so that makes things tricky."

Mira stiffened. "How did you know?"

"Clever work leaves a trace. Few could've taken down that travelling convoy and vanished." Ren's mouth curved into a smile. "And then there was Tharion's injury, followed by his sudden absence. It wasn't hard to put the pieces together."

Mira didn't deny it. She didn't need to. "I'm not here to punish you for it," Ren went on. "I actually need you to carry the word back." He looked between them now, nothing about his posture defensive. Just honest.

"No orders. No threats. I want to show them we are trying." Ren's voice softened slightly, not losing its edge, but gaining weight. "Tell them we've named no enemies. That there are no executions coming in the night. That we want to listen to them." He paused.

"But tell them I will fight. If I must. I will not let this

kingdom fall apart while we argue over its ashes." Mira met his gaze. She saw not just a man seeking power to rule but one choosing it with the people and kingdom at his core.

* * *

Mira pushed open the heavy wooden door, stepping into the lingering warmth of the castle's kitchen. The scent of roasted herbs and baked roots clung to the air, mingling with the fading smoke of the hearth.

Tonight's evening meal had long been cleared, but its ghosts remained, red wine stains on counters, a flicker of firelight across hanging pans, the hush of a place that had once been full. The space felt different now. Not just quieter, expectant.

At the long oak table, usually alive with flour-dusted hands and the thrum of knives on cutting boards, Torvyn leaned against the table's edge. His fingers tapping with a restless rhythm. Brahn stood beside him, arms crossed, his posture sharp with restrained energy. Neither wore the flush of wine or the ease of celebration. They were untouched by the revelry of the solstice night. Their tunics remained crisp, their postures rigid.

The celebrations had passed them by completely, overshadowed by duty, by war, by burdens that never lifted. Mira stepped closer, the parchment in her hand still faintly creased from where Ren had pressed it into her palm. It wasn't just a letter, it was the first ripple of the new tide. She placed it between them.

"This is the plan," she said. Her voice was steady, threaded with the weight of what she'd just seen. "Ren's first orders as regent." Torvyn looked down at the paper, shocked.

Brahn raised a brow. Not in surprise, but recognition.

"Reinforcements to the eastern border," she continued. "Quietly. No banners, no fanfare." Her gaze flicked to the letter again. "Food, medicine, repairs. He's sending aid to the outer districts before the end of summer." Brahn unfolded the parchment, scanning it in silence. Torvyn's fingers stilled.

"And the unrest?" Brahn asked.

Mira didn't hesitate. "He wants to know their names. Their reasons. No arrests. No executions." A beat passed. "He wants to listen. First."

Brahn's lips twitched, like he wasn't sure whether to scoff or smirk. Torvyn's voice cut in, "You were there. In the observatory?"

Mira met his eyes. "Yes."

"You weren't summoned?" Torvyn stared at her, eyes wide, the words escaping in a breathless mix of worry and concern.

"No," she said.

Brahn made a sound, a soft laugh of disbelief. "This is… unexpected," he said. "Though not as unexpected as your performance with Lord Asric."

Mira tilted her head, "Was it convincing?"

"Very," Brahn said, mouth curling.

"She stole the letter right off him," Torvyn muttered.

She let the silence hang, let them sit with the fact that she had moved through the highest chamber of power and come out the other side with more than information.

Brahn shook his head. "I think I'm beginning to understand why Torvyn brought you to me." Mira's brow furrowed. She glanced down at the parchment still resting between them, at the list of changes Ren had already set into motion. Aid.

Reinforcements. Restraint. She looked back up at Brahn.

"But… aren't we getting what we asked for?" The words slipped out before she could temper them. Naïve. Honest. The two men stilled. Torvyn's gaze flicked toward her, thoughtful. Brahn tilted his head, studying her like he wasn't sure if she was joking or testing him.

"We're getting part of what we asked for," Brahn said at last. "The simple part." He tapped the letter with one callused finger. "This?" he said. "This is a gesture. Good. Important. But still just a gesture."

Mira's eyes narrowed. "It's a start."

"It is a start," Brahn agreed. "But starts don't win wars. They delay them."

Torvyn's voice cut in, softer. "He's trying, Mira. That's a good step. But change doesn't stick because one person sent some supplies. It sticks when the people below have the power to demand it. Again and again."

Mira let that settle, the words turning over in her mind. She wanted to believe Ren's orders would be enough, that this could have been the moment everything shifted. And maybe, in some small way, it still was. But looking at Brahn's unwavering gaze, hearing the quiet certainty in Torvyn's voice… She saw them differently.

This wasn't doubt for doubt's sake. It wasn't cynicism. They weren't asking her to stop believing in Ren. They were asking her to understand the stakes if she believed in only him.

She exhaled, low and slow. "So what now?"

Brahn's smile curved. "Now," he said, "You wait, while we gather support."

He folded the parchment again with the same care someone might close a trap. "We'll let you know when, and where, you're needed."

12

THE SUN BORE DOWN like a judgment. Mira knelt in the dry earth of the courtyard garden, sweat slipping down her spine beneath her coarse linen shift. The soil was stubborn, cracked and sun-baked, clinging to the roots she tried to coax freely. Her palms were raw, the edges of her nails dark with grit. Every breath tasted of heat and dust and crushed rosemary.

The days had turned stifling after the solstice, as if summer, sensing its own decline, was making one last, desperate display of heat. The air hung thick, pressing down on the palace like an unseen weight. Around her, others worked in silence, sleeves rolled, heads bowed. No conversation, only the scrape of metal tines and the occasional snap of a broken root.

She wiped her brow with the back of her wrist, squinting toward the courtyard wall where the shadows stretched short. The air shimmered above the stones. Her knees ached. Her shoulders burned. Still, she stayed hunched over the stubborn patch of weeds, fingers aching.

"Mira." Perrin's voice was always kind, but it carried across the garden with authority. Mira looked up, blinking against the light. Perrin stood just inside the archway, her hands folded, her white robes catching the sun like polished bone.

She didn't step into the garden. She never did. As if she knew Mira needed the space more than the company. Perrin tilted her head, eyes searching Mira's face in that calm, unreadable way that always made Mira feel like she was being gently held rather than judged.

"You're to move to the western guest rooms," Perrin said. "Just after midday." Mira's brow furrowed.

"Why?" There was a pause. Perrin studied her a moment longer. "You've earned a reprieve out of the heat," Perrin replied.

Less than an hour later, Mira roamed the western halls. Inside, at least, there was shade. The thick stone walls held the cool of earlier hours, offering a breath of relief from the sun's relentless press outside. An unnatural quiet hung in the air of this corridor, compared to the rest of the palace. A kind of stillness that pressed against her ribs and made her footsteps sound too loud.

These rooms were rarely used. Set aside for visiting clerics, dignitaries, or those important enough to warrant privacy. But today, they belonged to no one. The doors stood closed, the air untouched. Mira paused before the first door before pushing it open slowly, the hinges sighing in protest.

Inside, a modest bed lay stripped of linens, a film of dust softening the corners of the furniture. The curtains hung stiff and untouched, their folds heavy with weeks of disuse. She moved without speaking, without hurrying. She tugged the curtains free and tied them back to let the light in, shook out the folded linens from the shelf by the door, and smoothed them over the mattress with practiced care. Dust danced in the sunlight as she swept the sill with a damp rag.

The second room was much the same. A half-burned candle still sat in a brass holder beside the bed, its wax warped from heat. Mira replaced it with a fresh one from the satchel Perrin had left for her. Window, sheets, basin, floor. Then the third. And the fourth. It became a rhythm, not unlike the garden, but cooler, quieter, less rooted in ache. Her muscles remembered the motions.

The sixth door was stuck when she tried to open it. Mira pushed harder, the wood groaning before it gave out. The room beyond was dim, the curtains drawn, the scent of ash and worn leather was thicker here than in any of the others. And something else. Cedar...

Her breath caught as she glanced over the room. Tharion lay curled on the bed, one arm thrown over his brow, the other resting against the hilt of the blade still sheathed at his hip. His tunic was creased, his hair mussed with sleep.

This room wasn't waiting for a visitor. It already had one. This was where he'd been sleeping. Not in their rooms. Here. Mira was frozen. She just stood in the doorway, the familiar ache rising in her chest as the scent of him wrapped around her, cedar and smoke, like the remnants of a fire left burning too long. Familiar. And distant. And aching.

He stirred. His eyes opened, unfocused for a breath, and then locked onto her. He didn't sit up. Didn't speak right away. Only looked at her like she was the ghost in the room.

Mira swallowed. Her fingers tightened around the linen bundle still pressed to her chest.

"I didn't know you were sleeping here," she whispered.

Tharion exhaled slowly, rubbing a hand across his face as he sat up. Mira didn't move from the doorway. She let the silence stretch. He sat fully now, planting his feet on the cool stone floor, elbows resting on his knees. He didn't look at her. Just stared down.

"I needed some space," Tharion said finally. It was barely a sentence. Mira sighed. His gaze flicked toward her. "It wasn't about you."

She smiled sadly. "It never is."

He winced, the sound hitting somewhere he hadn't armored. She knew it wasn't meant to be cruel. It was just the truth. That was the pattern, wasn't it?

She took a step into the room, then stopped herself, hovering in the half-light.

"You didn't even tell me," she said, voice low, trembling at the edges. "I wouldn't have minded... I just..." Her throat tightened. "I thought I would have been the first person you'd tell."

Tharion didn't flinch, but his silence was louder than anything he could've said. "I didn't think it would matter," he muttered.

That hurt more than any outburst. He hadn't just hidden this from her, he hadn't even considered her. Something hot flared beneath the sadness. Anger, sharp and sudden.

"You didn't think it would matter?" she repeated, voice tighter now, cracking under the weight of restraint. "I come back to an empty room every night and I'm supposed to, what? Pretend you're on patrol? That this..." she gestured faintly to the bed, the tucked-away life, "That I don't matter?"

"Mira, that's not it..." he answered, the words clipped.

The hurt settled in her chest like stones in water. Mira drew a breath and steadied her voice. Mira stood still for a breath. Then stepped into the room. The door eased shut behind her with a soft click. Tharion still sat on the bed, head bowed, hands braced on his knees. She stopped just in front of him.

"Then why?" she asked, quietly. "I don't understand Tharion?" He didn't look up. She hesitated, then knelt before him, her fingers brushing lightly against his cheek, coaxing him to meet her gaze. When he didn't pull away, she leaned in tentatively, searching for a kiss. But his hand came up, firm against her shoulder, halting her just before their mouths could meet.

"Don't," he said, voice raw, barely audible.

He finally looked at her then, and the regret in his eyes was almost worse than anger. He released her and the space between them felt wider than ever.

A murmur of voices, hushed with purpose, drifted through the stone hall beyond. They both looked to the door.

"But they want assurance. They want something, someone, to stand behind." Torvyn. She knew his voice. Steady. Measured. But there was something different in it now. Something careful.

Her brow furrowed. The second voice answered, smooth as silk, carrying a touch of amusement beneath something far colder.

"It's all planned for the Veiled Night," said Lord Asric. Torvyn and Asric? She held her breath, straining.

"That's too late," Torvyn replied, still even, still composed. Then came Asric's chuckle, soft, deliberate. A sound that didn't belong in the back corridors.

"Patience," he said. "A well-placed distraction at the right moment holds more weight than a blackmailed decision."

The Veiled Night celebration was the darkest night of the year. No moon. Just masks, music, and revelry. A perfect place to vanish. Or strike. She stood and crept forward a step, heart pounding. Tharion's hand closed around her wrist. Not rough. But firm.

Deliberate. Mira looked down at him, startled.

"Don't," he murmured, eyes locked on hers. Low. Calm. A warning.

Her mind raced. Torvyn had always been the careful one, deliberate, principled. A man who measured twice before daring to speak once. He believed in structure, in steady hands, in the quiet strength of doing what was right, even when it earned him nothing.

But now he was whispering with Asric. Asric, who wanted the regency? Asric, who wore power like perfume and wielded it like a blade. It made no sense. Not with the uprising already sneaking its way through the kingdom.

Their voices drifted down the corridor, low and urgent, until they disappeared further into the wing. Mira stood frozen, her stomach coiling tight. Her thoughts screamed at her that this was wrong, that she had to know what it meant.

Tharion moved, quick and sure, stepping in front of the doorway before she could reach it, planting himself there. "Mira don't."

She spoke firmly, her eyes sharp. "You can't stop me."

"You're not thinking clearly. If Torvyn's with Asric, this is far bigger than either of us thought."

"Exactly! We need to know what they are doing." she shot back, stepping sideways.

"That's the problem..." He shifted, keeping himself between her and the door. "We don't understand what they're capable of."

She snapped, suddenly sharp. "I can handle myself Tharion" "That's not what I'm..."

"You're trying to protect me," she said, softer, but no less fierce. "And I'm telling you, I don't need you to."

Tharion's eyes searched hers, desperate to find the right words.

"You always rush in," Mira continued, "That if you move

fast enough, you can protect everyone"

Tharion's voice dropped, hoarse. "I'm trying to keep you alive." "I can keep myself alive," Mira said, her voice steady.

"No, you can't!" he shouted, shaking his head. "If you could, we wouldn't be standing in this Navigator damned mess!"

The words hung in the air between them like a slap. He realized too late what he'd said, or maybe he'd meant it and just regretted the shape it took. Mira's expression didn't shift, not at first. Only her breath. One sharp inhale. One heartbeat's pause.

"Is that what you think?" she asked quietly. "That what happened to us, was my fault?"

"I didn't mean it like that," Tharion said quickly, but it didn't matter. The damage was already done. "You know I didn't."

She took a step back, out of his reach. Her voice didn't rise. It didn't need to. Tharion opened his mouth. Closed it again. The words wouldn't come, because there was nothing he could say to take it back. Mira turned. Her steps were sharp, unhesitating. She moved past him, through the door, not looking back.

The corridor was cool, the hush of stone swallowing her footsteps. But Tharion's voice in her head was relentless. The words echoed behind her like footsteps that refused to fade. And perhaps… he wasn't wrong.

She swallowed, her throat tight, the memory of their people dying on the road was bitter against her tongue. She had told herself it was all for them. For the people. But they were the ones who had paid the price.

Her fingers grazed the cool stone wall, searching for something solid. Something that wouldn't crack beneath her.

Is this who she had always been? The thought came unbidden, sharper than the rest. Had she always put herself above everyone else without even realizing it? Did she cause this drifting between them before the bond even dulled? Before they forgot?

Her steps slowed. The quiet wrapped around her like fog. Perhaps she and Tharion were always going to break. Maybe no one had handed her the chisel. Maybe she'd chosen to pick it up herself.

Footsteps came from behind her. Steady, measured. Never rushing. Never faltering. Of course, Tharion had followed her. He always did. Mira turned sharply, ducking behind a faded velvet tapestry that swallowed the light in its folds. She stepped inside and let the curtain fall behind her. Darkness embraced her like an old friend. The fabric gave way to a narrow stone passage. Cold and stale with the scent of old dust and mildew. An attendants' tunnel.

She pressed her back to the wall, closing her eyes. Her hands trembled, fingers curled into fists at her side.

Outside, his footsteps slowed. She could picture him searching the corridor. Cautious and patient. Her breath hitched. She tried to swallow it down, to hold it all where no one could see. A single tear slipped down her cheek. Then another. She covered her mouth with her hand, not to keep quiet, there was no one to hear, but to stop herself from breaking wider.

Maybe she hadn't meant to betray him. Ren's kiss hadn't felt like betrayal in the moment, just a fleeting escape, a breath she didn't realize she was holding. But it was. And the worst part wasn't that Tharion might never forgive her. It was that she couldn't forgive herself. Another tear traced the curve of her jaw. She didn't wipe it away. Let it fall.

Let herself feel it, just for a minute.

Mira exhaled, just a breath before pushing forward into the tunnel. The passage was unlit, narrow and humid. The arched ceiling dipped low enough that she had to duck in places, and the damp, dust-heavy air clung to her lungs. She knew where this tunnel led. The Grand Hall, the kitchens, the attendant's quarters. She let her fingers trail along the familiar curves of the stone, steadying herself as she moved. A draft stirred the stale air. This passage had always been meant for quiet, unseen movement. She'd walked this tunnel before. Dozens of times. But tonight, it felt different. Lonelier. The light filtered through narrow slits in the wall, thin beams cutting across her path like cautions she didn't have time to heed. A turn. Another.

Mira barely had time to react before she nearly collided with a broad chest. She caught the faint glint of a white apron in the dim light. Brahn. He filled the tunnel completely, arms crossed, gaze assessing. For a moment, neither of them spoke.

Then he smirked, voice dry. "Mira, most people use the actual hallways."

She let out a breath that might have been a laugh if it didn't feel so fragile. "Maybe I wanted to disappear for a minute."

Brahn tilted his head, studying her more closely now. "And did it work?" She shrugged, too tired to be clever. He shifted slightly, giving her room in the narrow space. "Mira, what's wrong?"

She didn't answer right away. But the tunnel made her too close to Brahn to lie comfortably. "I overheard something," she said at last. "Something at the nobles' dinner, Asric. He's planning something." She would never utter Torvyn's name. She would protect her brother until her dying breath.

Brahn's expression didn't change, but something in his posture did. A small straightening. A sharpening. "You're sure?"

"I'm sure," she said. "I didn't hear everything. Just enough to know something's coming."

Brahn's expression didn't change. If anything, he looked almost satisfied. "You did the right thing coming to me," he said.

Mira let out a slow breath, uncertain whether she felt relieved or uneasy. Brahn's stance softened just slightly, and for a moment, he seemed almost pleased.

"Don't worry," he assured her. "I'll handle it." A pause. Then, a shift in posture, something like approval. "But I'm glad you told me." Brahn studied her for a moment longer, then tilted his head slightly. "I have a job for you, if you're up for a distraction?"

Mira straightened, almost before she could think about it. The motion was automatic, a reflex more than a choice. She met his eyes, posture firming even as something inside her still felt hollow. Let it be dangerous, she thought. Let it be far away and anywhere but here.

"You'll need to travel with the convoy to Seacliffe. Torvyn can arrange it with Cleric Perrin. I'll be going as well … just more discreetly. He'll give you the rest of the details once we arrive."

Seacliffe. She turned the name over in her mind. There were worse-off towns to visit, but if Brahn was involved, it meant something more than just a simple errand.

Mira nodded. She didn't push for more. Brahn wouldn't give her anything else anyway. She glanced past him, toward the heavy stone walls, toward the looming unknown of Seacliffe.

The tunnel around them was narrow, barely wide enough for one to pass without brushing the rough stone walls. She moved forward, and he shifted back, pressing his shoulders into the cold rock to give her room, careful not to touch her.

Her shoulder still brushed the wall as she passed. Bootsteps echoed behind her now, but she didn't look back. The dark ahead was no less uncertain than what trailed behind.

13

MIRA AND THARION hadn't spoken since their fight. The past day had been filled with a silence that felt thick. They passed each other like ghosts. No arguments. No apologies. Just the brittle quiet of hurt and regret.

Outside, the sweltering press of summer had finally eased. The heat that clung to stone and skin was fading now, little by little, as if the world itself was exhaling. Shadows stretched longer, and the light softened. Not cool, but no longer suffocating.

Mira climbed into the carriage without hesitation, gripping the door handle with more force than was necessary. She turned, watching Tharion approach, steady, unreadable, always composed. He was dressed for travel. His usual coat was gone, abandoned to the lingering heat, leaving only a charcoal tunic with its sleeves rolled to his forearms. A deep navy cloak, thinner than the one he usually wore, hung from one shoulder, pinned with a silver clasp, a quiet nod to his rank, never more than he needed. The breeze toyed with the edge of the fabric as he walked, stirring the cloak with gentle insistence, but offering no real relief. Somehow, he looked infuriatingly composed.

She curled her fingers around the handle tighter as he reached for the carriage door. She moved, shifting just enough to block his way, planting herself between him and the carriage interior.

"Mira." Tharion didn't falter. One hand braced on the

doorframe, the other gripping the roof's edge as he stepped up toward the carriage. "We both know I'm coming."

She didn't look directly at him, but sighed. "Of course you are." Not sarcasm. Just resignation. Like the ending of a sentence she'd already heard before.

He let out a slow, weary breath, not exasperated, just tired. Measured. But it sounded too close to detachment. "Mira... ."

Her eyes flicked up to meet his. There was no fire left in them. "What?" she hissed. "Don't keep my distance before I wreck what little we haven't ruined?"

He flinched. "What I said, it wasn't fair of me," he blurted, his voice low. I didn't"

"No," she cut in, "You were right." She didn't look away. Didn't raise her voice. "What happened to our memories? Maybe that was my fault. Maybe the bond faded because I broke it. And maybe staying away from you is the kindest thing I've done in a long time."

Tharion opened his mouth, but before he could answer, she pushed his chest. Not hard. Just enough. He staggered back. She slammed the carriage door shut. The sound echoed louder than it should have. Inside the carriage, Mira didn't move. She just closed her eyes and let the silence settle. Heavy. Final. Familiar.

✳ ✳ ✳

The sound of hooves striking packed dirt filled the air as the convoy moved. The main highway to Seacliffe was well worn, stretching long and winding through the lowland plains before reaching the craggy cliffs of the coast. Merchants and nobles shared the wide road, their carriages creating slow-moving processions. Dust kicking up in thick clouds that clung to the air. Farmers led carts laden with late-season crops, their tired mules trudging forward under the weight.

The farther they traveled, the more the scenery shifted. A heavy, relentless summer heat bore down, making the air thick and shimmering where the sun hit the ground. The packed dirt road became softer, flecked with pale sand, the occasional gust of wind sending small grains swirling into the air, sticking to damp skin and settling in the creases of clothes. The air grew lighter but no cooler, carrying with it the briny tang of the ocean, the scent of salt thickening with every mile.

Heat waves rippled along the horizon, blurring the line where land met sky, making the distant dunes seem like they were shifting with every step forward. Towering inland forest trees transitioned to low, windswept pines and resilient dune grass, their forms sculpted by relentless sea breezes and scorching sun. Sunbaked wood, dry grass, and salt filled the air with a strong, clinging scent. The sunlight no longer filtered through dense foliage but stretched wide and open, searing against exposed skin, casting long, golden streaks over the rolling dunes beyond. The rhythmic crash of waves, once a distant murmur, grew louder, steady, endless. A promise of cool water that remained just out of reach.

By the time they reached the coastal stretch, the sun had set, and the road became rougher, the once-even path now riddled with stones and deep wagon ruts. The rhythmic clatter of wheels against uneven ground made the carriage rattle, and Mira braced herself against the seat to keep from jostling too much.

Through the small window, she caught the first glimpse of Seacliffe Stronghold. As the road curved toward the coast a fortress hewn directly into the cliff side itself came into view. It loomed over the town not from above, but from within, its walls rising seamlessly from the rock. As if the cliff had grown battlements and towers of its own. The entry stood level with the fishing town, an imposing iron-gated tunnel cut straight into the cliff face, flanked by towering walls that blended so seamlessly into the natural stone that, from a distance, it was nearly invisible. Far above, the fortress itself stretched back into the rock, a labyrinth of carved corridors and wind-worn chambers, their narrow windows like watchful eyes staring out at the endless sea.

Beneath it, the fishing town of Seacliffe sprawled against the shoreline, caught between the fortress and the churning waves beyond. Thatched-roof cottages and stone houses clustered together, their walls streaked white from salt spray. The streets were narrow and uneven, paved with flat, sea-smoothed stones, their surfaces slick from mist.

Fishermen hauled in their morning catch, nets heavy with writhing silver, while traders called out from stalls overflowing with dried fish, rough-woven nets, and thick coils of rope meant to withstand the might of the sea. Seagulls circled overhead, their cries sharp against the rhythmic crash of waves against the cliffs. The scent of brine and tar filled the humid air, clinging to everything.

The convoy moved slowly through the town, the weight of watchful eyes pressing in on them. Seacliffe was not a place accustomed to a convoy of visitors. Outsiders were noticed, and nobles especially, were watched. The road narrowed, funneled toward the fortress gates. The entry tunnel lay before them, its heavy iron gates groaning open as the convoy approached. The moment they passed through, the temperature shifted, the heat of the summer sun was replaced by the cool, damp chill of stone that had never known warmth.

Inside, the stronghold stretched deep into the rock, a fortress built less for comfort and more for survival. The courtyard was an open space, half-exposed to the sky above, half-shadowed beneath the overhanging rock. The surrounding walls were not just built, they were part of the cliff, reinforced by masonry where needed but still unmistakably raw stone.

Stable hands moved forward to take the horses as the convoy came to a stop, their movements quick but silent. The Seacliffe Under Guard stood at attention along the walls, their simple tabards marked with the crest of Seacliffe. A roaring sea serpent coiled around a blade.

Mira stepped down from the carriage, her boots scuffing against stone worn smooth by centuries of footsteps. She lifted her gaze, following the fortress as it climbed deeper into the cliff side, its upper levels exposed to the sky, the wind whistling through narrow towers and high parapets.

The Royal Guard had already begun unpacking the supplies from the convoy, their movements precise, methodical, as they lifted crates from wagons and checked their inventory. The murmurs of their work blended into the steady sounds of waves crashing below. Tharion was already speaking with a Seacliffe Under Guard. His posture relaxed but his voice low and clipped with authority. The lieutenant, a grizzled, broad- shouldered man, listened intently, nodding along, his sharp eyes flicking between Tharion and the newly arrived convoy. Mira moved through the courtyard, weaving between guards and attendants, unloading the last of the supplies. A voice came bright and sharp from the open kitchen path.

"Well, Navigators above, Tharion! Is that you?" A

woman bustled toward him with a linen apron tied at the waist and flour dusting her sleeves. She moved like someone who hadn't stopped working since sunrise and had no plans to stop now. Sunlight caught in the streaks of silver braided through her hair.

"Miller," Tharion greeted her, his smile bright and genuine.

"It's good to see you." She exclaimed. She reached him in a few quick strides and pulled him down into a firm hug around the shoulders, the kind that left no room for protest and no need for one.

Tharion held her back, his arms wrapping around her with something almost reverent. A breath left him, low and quiet, and his shoulders, always squared, always braced, finally dropped. For just a moment, he wasn't a steward. Not a soldier. Not bonded.

Just a boy grown too fast, in the arms of someone he obviously trusted. Miller patted his back twice before pulling away, studying him with eyes that saw far too much.

"You look thinner," she muttered, inspecting his face. "And tired."

"I'm always tired," he said with a half-smile, like it was a joke he'd told too many times to laugh at anymore.

Mira watched the exchange, her brows slightly furrowed. She had never seen him react like that to her. Even though it was clearly a maternal relationship, Tharion was still capable of warmth, of affection, just not with her. With her, he was a wall, impenetrable, unwavering. Always steady, always distant.

Miller's eyes flicked toward the carriage, sharp and expectant. "And where's your bonded? I was told she'd be coming too."

Tharion hesitated. "She's here," he murmured. Miller's gaze barely touched on Tharion before flicking toward Mira. Miller squinted, then blinked. Then she gasped.

"Oh, by the stars, Tharion, she is beautiful." Miller was already crossing the short distance, apron fluttering behind her, arms half-lifted like she might embrace Mira, but didn't want to startle her.

Mira instinctively stepped back, just a fraction. Her posture tightened, chin lifting, the way it always did when she felt eyes on her for too long. Her fingers brushed over the crease in her travel-wrinkled dress, then dropped to her sides.

"I'm Mira," she said, her voice clear but careful. Like stepping onto a floor she wasn't sure would hold.

Miller let out a soft, reverent laugh. "Welcome, Mira." Her voice dipped into something warmer. "Any bonded of Tharion is more than welcome here." Mira blinked. The words caught her off guard. They were kindness. Uncomplicated. Immediate.

Undeserved. She nodded, unsure what to say. Mira cast a glance at Tharion, who merely watched her with that infuriating mix of sadness and regret.

Miller's eyes flicked from one to the other, catching the space between them like a thread pulled too tight. But she didn't comment. She just clapped her hands once and smiled like she hadn't seen a thing.

"Well," she said, turning briskly, "Come in, both of you. The bread's still warm and I'm not reheating the stew twice in one sitting." She didn't wait for agreement, just turned and strode up the kitchen path.

Tharion, still watching Mira, lifted a hand in a quiet gesture, motioning her forward.

She didn't speak, just walked. Past him. Toward the open

door and the scent of rosemary and wood smoke. He followed close behind, boots quiet on the stone path.

* * *

The kitchen was nothing like the ones in the palace. It was narrow, long, and well-worn. Built for function, not display. Salt-stained floorboards groaned underfoot, softened by years of feet and spilled water. The wide stone counters bore the marks of knives and cleavers. Mira could see faint grooves from years of brining fish, cleaning shell- cracked crabs, and pressing herbs into oil. Nets hung near the ceiling, coiled and drying, with bunches of rosemary and sea fennel dangled beside them. The herby scent rich and sharp in the warm air. Hooks along the far wall held knives of every size and purpose, their handles smoothed from use. A wide basin, stained with sea minerals, sat beneath a window that looked out toward the dusk-brushed cliffs.

Mira paused just past the threshold. The fire in the hearth crackled with a lazy confidence, its light dancing across shelves lined with battered tin containers, jars filled with thick salt and dried citrus peels. A pot of stew rested on a over the heat, its lid askew just enough for steam to curl out, rich with thyme and slow-cooked root vegetables.

Miller was already halfway across the room, muttering to herself as she pulled thick slices of bread from a cloth-covered basket and fetched chipped ceramic bowls from a top shelf. She didn't look back to see if they were following. Mira hesitated again, her fingers brushing over the door frame before she stepped inside fully. The air was warmer here, thicker. She could still feel Tharion behind her, close enough to sense, not close enough to reach. The invisible space

221

between them followed her into the room like a second shadow.

Miller looked over her shoulder. "Sit, girl," she chided, "Don't make me ask you twice."

Mira nodded and moved toward the heavy wooden table that ran down the middle of the room. She slid into one of the mismatched chairs, her hands folding in her lap as she took in the room. Sun-warped wood, a string of garlic near the door, a cat asleep on a sack of flour in the corner. It was not her world.

Tharion sat across from her. Of course not beside her. He offered no words, just a small, tired exhale as he settled into the chair, shoulders taut as bowstrings. Mira didn't meet his gaze. She couldn't. Not yet. Miller set two bowls down with a practiced clatter, followed by a hunk of bread, a block of herb butter, and two iron spoons so old the engraving had worn away. Then, at last, she sat too, her own bowl steaming, her apron finally stilled.

Mira broke the silence first, her spoon pausing just above the bowl. "So... how do you know Tharion?"

Miller glanced up mid-chew, eyes twinkling as she swallowed. She turned to Tharion, lips curving wickedly.

"She doesn't know?" Tharion sighed like a man who knew exactly what was coming.

"Miller," she smacked his arm with the back of her hand, mock offense blooming across her face.

"You didn't tell her?" she huffed, though there was no heat in it. "Stars above, I raised this one like he was mine, and he just tosses me into the sea like a forgotten rag!"

"I didn't toss you," Tharion muttered, but there was the faintest hint of a smile behind the words.

Miller turned her gaze back to Mira, warm and full of

memory. "From the time he was thirteen," she said proudly, "I was his guardian, his teacher, and, when needed, his jailer." She shot Tharion a look, and he had the good sense to glance away. "The late Queen asked me to school him and the prince." Mira took in Miller's face before a spark of recognition.

"You were chasing them through the gardens that day." Mira said, softly.

Miller blinked, then laughed, loud and full-bodied. "Oh, that could have been any day! Navigators help me. Those boys nearly gave me heart failure on a weekly basis.

Constantly slipping past special tutors, hiding in trees, blaming each other for every stolen pastry and broken vase."

Tharion stiffened slightly in his chair, and Mira didn't miss it. She watched him for a moment, but Miller either didn't notice or chose not to comment.

"They were tricky boys," she said fondly. "Ren with his smart mouth, Tharion with his quiet schemes. One would distract you while the other vanished entirely. I don't think I ever won a full day with both of them in the classroom."

Mira smiled, letting the image settle. A younger Tharion with windblown hair and a spark in his eye, a wild Ren close behind. It fit.

"So then why are you in Seacliffe?" she asked. "How did you come to be all the way out here?"

Miller sat back, wiping her hands on her apron. "This was always home for me," she said simply. "I was born on this coast. And once the boys grew up, once they didn't need me anymore, I came back." Miller stood and gathered her bowl.

"This place doesn't change much. Salt still stings, wind still howls, and the sea always has something to say." She paused, her eyes growing distant for a breath. "But they will always be my boys. No matter how tall they get or how many swords they carry."

Miller turned back to Tharion, narrowing her eyes slightly. "And you, lad, need to visit more. I shouldn't have to hear about your goings-on through gossip and grain shipments."

Tharion raised a brow. "You hear gossip through grain shipments?"

Miller huffed. "I hear everything through something. You'd be surprised at what people say when they think no one's listening."

Mira grinned. It was the first genuine smile she'd had in days. "You and Lady Elendra would get along."

"Oh my stars, don't curse me, girl." Miller barked a laugh. "I've had my fill of court spiders." Miller moved to begin washing her bowl. The warmth of the kitchen wrapped tighter, not from the fire but from the space itself. Familiar. Lived in. Mira's fingers tapped at the edge of the table. She wasn't meant to be here, not really. But for a fleeting moment, it felt like the place had been meant for someone like her.

The kitchen door swung open with a gust of wind. Torvyn stepped inside, his boots thudding solidly against the floorboards. His usual formality was there, proper and polished, but his eyes scanned the room with a different urgency.

"Mira." Her name landed like an anchor. His voice was steady, but beneath it, just faintly, was relief.

Then his gaze shifted past her. He stilled. A pause. His brow furrowed, lips parting slightly. "Miller?"

She turned, drying her hands on her apron as she took in the tall figure in her doorway. "So you're Torvyn," she said, voice pitched with surprise. "Well, I'll be... I've heard plenty about you.”

Torvyn laughed, already striding forward, offering both hands like an old friend. “I’m guessing none of it is good. Brahn has a big mouth.”

Miller grinned and took his hands, sizing him up in one sweeping glance. “Mostly good.

Some embellishments, I’m sure. You’ve grown taller than your father ever was, and broader too. I am sure he would be proud.”

Torvyn’s expression faltered for just a breath. “Thank you,” he breathed. “That means a lot.”

Miller studied him a moment longer, then gave a firm nod. “Well, it’s about time I met you. I raised that one,” she jerked her chin toward Tharion, “and chased Ren across half the court. I knew your name, just never crossed paths before.”

“A Navigator’s small miracle,” Torvyn chuckled. “I’m sure I would’ve gotten myself into more trouble.”

“You still might,” Miller said, swatting his arm. “Especially if you keep showing up at my door without warning.”

The laughter between them eased something in the room. Mira watched the exchange with quiet interest, feeling, oddly, like an observer in a memory she hadn’t lived. But then Torvyn’s eyes drifted past Miller, to her, to Tharion. His smile didn’t vanish, but it dulled, weighed down by reality. He rubbed the back of his neck.

“As much as I’d love to stay and trade stories, I was actually sent to find you two.” Mira’s posture straightened.

Tharion narrowed his eyes. “Find us… for what, exactly?”

His gaze flicked between her and Tharion, careful. Too careful. “To escort you to your chambers.”

The words landed cold. Mira felt her stomach dip, the air catch. She'd known it was coming and had told herself to be ready. Their chambers. Tharion was across from her, still and quiet. She wouldn't, couldn't, look at him. Miller's gaze swept between them with a subtle crease forming between her brows. She didn't speak, just reached for the pot and began ladling stew into another bowl, giving them the moment without making it a spectacle.

Mira inhaled slowly, then pushed back from the table. Her chair scraped softly against the floor. "We should go, then."

No one moved right away. The kitchen, moments ago, filled with the scent of bread and the low hum of comfort, now felt suspended, held in the pause between one breath and the next. Mira's fingers tightened briefly against the edge of the table before she let go.

Across from her, Tharion shifted slightly, the movement small but sharp in her periphery.

Torvyn said nothing else, just stepped back toward the door. Mira offered Miller a faint smile and nod, gratitude tucked beneath it like a folded note. Then, without looking back, she followed her brother out into the corridor.

The walk through Seacliffe's winding halls was silent, save for the muffled echo of their footsteps against the damp stone. The air was thick with salt and the humid bite of moisture. The ever-present scent of the ocean seeping into every corner of the stronghold.

Torvyn led them up a narrow, spiraling staircase, the walls rough-hewn and slick where the sea had left its mark. Unlike the grander sections of the keep, this part of Seacliffe Stronghold was quieter, more private. Built for a purpose rather than luxury.

Finally, Torvyn stopped before a heavy wooden door, iron-banded and reinforced. Their room. He pushed it open and stepped aside. The space was small but practical, crafted with Seacliffe's usual unforgiving efficiency.

Thick wooden beams stretched across the ceiling, their surfaces smoothed by time. The walls, carved straight from the cliff side, bore faint scars from centuries of salt and wind. At the end of the room stood a single, double-sized bed, the sheets simple but clean, the blankets neatly folded at the foot. Mira's chest tightened. There was nowhere else to sleep. But before that thought could settle, her gaze drifted past the bed, to the far wall, where an arched window opened to the sea.

The room was built into the cliff, the stone hollowed out to frame a breathtaking, uninterrupted view of the horizon. Mira wandered toward it, drawn by her curiosity.

Beyond the carved ledge, the ocean stretched endlessly, its deep blue surface shifting beneath the darkening sky. The wind rushed in, carrying the tang of salt and open water against her skin. Waves rolled in steady rhythm, their white crests dissolving into the jagged rocks below. Mira closed her eyes, inhaling deeply. It felt like a memory.

Torvyn's voice broke the silence. "It's not much, but it's private. And the view's not bad." Mira forced her expression smooth as she turned back to him. He was watching, not just her, but her and Tharion. Gauging the space between them.

Then, with a flicker of earnestness, he added, "And it'll mean something for Seacliffe, too. The supplies will help. Folks have gone without longer than they should have."

"But that's not what you need her here for, is it?" Tharion's voice was low, deliberate. Mira turned to him, surprised. Of course, Torvyn had told him. He already knew that this was more than dropping off supplies. Hearing it from

Tharion, realizing how much they discussed without her, landed strangely. Not a betrayal. Just... distance. That old and familiar ache.

Torvyn straightened, shifting back to the matter at hand. "Brahn will be here in an hour." Mira caught the slight tension in his stance. That wasn't what this was about. Her stomach twisted. "But, we have wind of a Kharador officer who's infiltrated Seacliffe."

Mira froze. The words hit like a dropped blade. "What?" She didn't mean to whisper it, but it came out thin, her breath catching behind the syllables. A Kharador officer. Here. In Seacliffe. It was impossible. This coast was a world away from the Kharador border, across their kingdom. The farthest reach.

Tharion stiffened beside her. "How did he get this far across the kingdom?" His voice was low and clipped, each word edged in disbelief and alarm. His eyes cut toward Torvyn, already parsing the logistics, the implications. "This border is patrolled," he went on, jaw tight. "It's watched. Quiet. Nobody slips through unnoticed."

Tharion stared directly at Torvyn. "Unless someone let them."

Mira's memory clicked, sharp and clear. The old coastal maps, the trading routes, the jagged cliff paths and narrow coves that no longer saw merchant sails.

"He wasn't let in," she stated. "Sail around the continent. Land in Seacliffe. Then make their way back through the kingdom." The words hung there, stark and heavy.

Torvyn nodded, grim. The truth of it settled like cold iron between them. This wasn't a breach. It was a strategy. A test. Mira's pulse thudded louder in her ears. The implication hadn't been said aloud yet, but it hung in the air like smoke, thick and inescapable. Tharion had remained completely still beside her. She could feel it, the way his muscles had coiled beneath his armor, the weight of his silence.

"So you need Mira to do something to him?" he asked, voice low. Controlled. But Mira could hear the edge beneath it. The warning. Torvyn hesitated. That alone said enough.

Torvyn's voice was colder, or trying to be. His gaze shifted toward Tharion, then dropped, like he regretted even looking. "There's a bar in Seacliffe," he said, the words slow, careful. "Well-known among the sailors. It also..." He hesitated, throat working. "Also serves as a pleasure house."

Mira didn't flinch. But behind her ribs, clenched.

Torvyn cleared his throat, straightening just slightly. "This wasn't my idea, Mira. Brahn asked for you specifically. Said he was impressed by your work with Lord Asric."

Both Mira and Tharion flinched.

"We don't mean for you to sleep with him," Torvyn stammered. "Just ply him with drinks, keep him distracted, and slip the movements we need him to know into conversation." Mira stared at Torvyn. A Kharador officer. False troop movements. A pleasure house. The room felt smaller, as if the walls themselves had tightened around her.

She swallowed hard. "You can't be serious."

Torvyn sighed, his voice quieting. "Mira... Brahn has trusted no one else with this." He met her gaze, steady, unreadable. "But if you don't want to do this, I can try to convince him there's another way."

Mira didn't answer. She just stood there, eyes fixed on Torvyn like she might steady herself. Her breath came slow, deliberate, but her chest felt tight, like pressure building before a storm.

She could do this. Her voice could soften, her smile could

entice, but neither ever truly betrayed her true feelings. She knew how to use the quiet space between words like a blade, disarming, precise, deliberate. She wasn't afraid of the task. Not of the bar. Not the officer. What unsettled her, what scraped raw at the edge of her thoughts, was him. Tharion. What would this do to him? This might tear them wider apart.

Maybe that's why the Queen had taken their memories. Not to punish them, but to protect him. Maybe she'd seen the way he looked at Mira and decided it was too much for him.

Maybe it had been easier for everyone to forget. Her eyes flicked to him. He hadn't moved. His expression was faux calm, but his posture hadn't softened. Still tense. Still wound tight, like every instinct in him was telling him to protect her from this. She didn't blame him. But he was given her the choice. Like she had told him.

Even if the space between them never closed, if the bond had dimmed to a flicker. Even when her name still stirred rumors in the palace halls. They were still bonded together. That meant something.

But she could also be a weapon. She could protect others. To buy time. To tip the scales when brute force wouldn't. She drew in a slow, steadying breath. When she looked over to Torvyn, there was steel in her eyes.

"I'll do it," she said. Torvyn's relief was almost imperceptible, but she saw it in the way his shoulders eased, just slightly.

Tharion, however, moved. A sharp inhale, a shift of weight, the faintest tightening of his jaw. She didn't look at him. She already felt the way her choice cut into him.

Torvyn nodded. "We leave at midnight. The officer frequents the bar late." Mira forced herself to return the nod. Torvyn lingered for only a moment longer before stepping toward the door. He paused, his hand on the frame, and looked back at her one last time. "This will work, Mira," he said quietly. "I trust you." And then he was gone.

The door shut behind him with a dull thud. Final. Heavy. The silence that followed wasn't peaceful. It settled over the room, pressing in from all sides. She turned to face him but Tharion hadn't moved.

Slowly, without a word, he crossed the space between them. His steps were quiet, his movements unhurried, as if he were approaching something fragile. Mira watched him, his presence steady, stopping just a breath away.

Without fanfare, he wrapped his arms around her. It wasn't a sweeping gesture, it wasn't desperate. His arms folded around her back, his chest against her shoulder, and for a moment, everything else dropped away. The uprising, the officer. The silence between them. It all slipped into the background. She stood still, surprised, not by the touch, but by how familiar it felt. How easy. Like a language they hadn't forgotten. After a breath, her hand came up curled tightly around him.

And then he spoke, voice low, close to her ear. "Mira," he began, "I'm so sorry. For what I said. For how I've been."

She didn't pull back, but her shoulders tensed slightly beneath his hands.

"This isn't your fault," he murmured. "And it's not mine, either. What they did … you didn't choose any of it." He pulled back enough to meet her gaze, still holding her in place. His expression was bare. Unmasked.

"All I've ever tried to do is to keep you safe." Her breath hitched, but she didn't look away. "I don't support this." he said. "Not because I doubt you. But because it's you. If it were anyone else, I'd be talking tactics. I'd be fine with it. But it's not anyone else." He swallowed. "It's you. I'm coming with you. Not to stop you. To stand with you." A beat passed. "And if anything happens, if he crosses a line, if you so much as look like you want out, I'll help you No hesitation."

Mira let the silence settle again. Not tense. Just full. Then, softly as she smiled, "You always do that."

Tharion frowned. "Do what?"

Her gaze didn't waver. "Make it hard to be angry with you."

Tharion's expression softened, and then, slowly, he smiled. Not wide. Just enough for her to see it was real. "Good," he said. "I was starting to worry I'd lost the knack."

She stepped back, just enough to breathe. "I'll get ready," she said. "You should too." She turned, quietly, and moved toward the small adjoining room.

✳ ✳ ✳

Mira let out a slow breath as she stepped away from the waterfall's steady cascade, the warm droplets rolling down her skin one last time before she reached for a towel. The water had cooled her, washing away the salt, the sweat, the exhaustion clinging to her like a second skin.

She wrapped the simple linen towel around herself, tucking it securely. Then, a knock. Her head snapped toward the door, muscles instinctively tensing. A pause. Tharion's voice was low and composed.

"Mira." She inhaled slowly, exhaling just as carefully.

"Yes?" The door cracked open just enough for her to see a sliver of him, a glimpse of his broad shoulders.

"May I come in?" His voice was careful, measured. A flicker of something passed through her, hesitation, awareness, something more tangled.

She shifted her grip on the towel, then sighed. "Go ahead."

The door swung open a fraction more, just enough for him to step inside without intruding. She blinked at the sight before her. In his hands, a folded set of clothes. A small cosmetics kit. And resting atop them, a sealed note. Mira frowned.

Tharion stepped closer, extending the bundle toward her. "Instructions, they were just delivered"

Her stomach twisted. She reached out, taking the items from him, her fingers brushing the edge of the note before flipping it over. Brahn's handwriting. Her pulse ticked faster. She opened the letter.

> *The officer's name is Captain Dren Solvar. He's been stationed along Kharador's western front for a few years. Experienced, smart, but reckless. He doesn't always follow orders. He operates well under pressure. And he's willing to take risks if it means securing an advantage. Tell him we are going to be passing through Harrow's Hollow in three day's time. He prefers dark-haired women. Burn this note.*

She glanced at the cosmetics kit, and her auburn hair on her shoulder. The implication sinking in. Change your face. Change your hair. Become the woman he'd notice.

Tharion cleared his throat, drawing her gaze back to him. His expression was tense. She lifted the garments that were delivered, the fabric shifting like liquid between her fingers. It was an exquisite ivory corset and undergarment set, crafted from shadowlace, thin enough to see through in parts, yet snug enough to mold to her skin.

Mira was no stranger to bare skin, to dressing for appearances, but this, this was different. Alongside was a dark, floor-length robe, its fabric soft yet deceptively heavy, meant to conceal and reveal in equal measure. She met Tharion's gaze once more.

"I'm going to need some time." His jaw tensed, but he only nodded. Without another word, he stepped back and shut the door.

14

THE STREETS OF SEACLIFFE stretched before them, alive with lantern glow and the hum of voices. Torvyn and Tharion moved beside her, their hoods pulled low, their faces half- hidden in the flickering torchlight.

Mira, however, looked nothing like herself. Her hair, now a deep dark hue, fell in loose, glossy waves over her shoulders. The transformation was uncanny, unnatural, like stepping into someone else's skin. Kohl rimmed her eyes, the dark pigment sharp against her now-pale complexion. Her lashes, long, feathered, framed her gaze with an otherworldly allure. Even her lips, glossed and plump, whispered of mystery, of temptation. Her robe fluttered around her as they moved, the airy fabric tugged gently by the breeze, its hem weighted just enough to keep it grounded. Shadows clung to their frames, making them just another trio of nameless figures navigating the narrow streets.

But beneath it… Mira felt exposed. The exquisite corset and shadowlace undergarments clung to her, thin, revealing, leaving little to the imagination. A second skin, one meant to be seen, to be noticed. Every step made her hyperaware of how little she truly wore underneath. She lifted her chin, adjusting the way the robe settled over her shoulders, forcing herself into the role she had to play.

The alley behind the pleasure house was narrow, dimly lit, the scent of spiced smoke, ale, and perfume thick in the humid air. The faint hum of laughter and music seeped through the walls, a distant promise of indulgence and secrecy.

Mira forced herself to keep her steps steady. Ahead, Torvyn knocked once, twice, sharp and deliberate. A moment later, a metal eye slot scraped open, revealing nothing but a pair of sharp, assessing eyes. Torvyn and Tharion stepped aside. Mira lifted her chin. A pause, then the clunk of an iron latch. The heavy wooden door groaned open, revealing a broad-shouldered man with dark, inked skin, his forearms wrapped in leather bindings. His eyes flicked over Mira first, slow, deliberate, before shifting to Torvyn and Tharion, suspicion curling at the edge of his mouth.

"You're almost too late. We've been sending girls to tease him all night." His voice was gravel-thick, laced with impatience. Clearly down by too many nights in the haze of this place. "I think he's almost done." Without another word, he stepped aside, motioning them forward.

Inside, the backroom was warm, suffocating, thick with the scent of burning incense, old wine, and bodies pressed too close. The walls were draped in rich, deep-colored fabrics, muffling the sounds of music beyond. Plush seating, velvet cushions thrown over low wooden lounges lined the space.

In the far corner, a half-curtained doorway led deeper into the pleasure house, where the true indulgences waited.

Torvyn moved first, leading them toward the far side of the room, where a small, private alcove had been set aside. And there, waiting with an air of effortless control, was Brahn. He lounged in one of the well-kept chairs, boots planted firmly on the floor, a glass of something dark and amber-rich resting loosely in his hand.

His sharp gaze flicked up as they approached, assessing, calculating. At his booth sat a young woman, arms folded, her expression cool. Mira studied her high cheekbones, keen dark eyes, and a confidence that spoke of someone who understood the power of this place. Her dress was simple but effective, the fabric clinging in a way that suggested purpose rather than accident.

She met Mira's gaze before looking at Brahn. "This is her, then?" Brahn nodded, setting his glass down. "Mira, and..."

His brows lifted just slightly. Anger crossed Brahn's features, as though Tharion's presence had not been accounted for. A flick of his eyes toward Torvyn. The message is clear. This intrusion will be dealt with later. Mira caught it, caught the silent exchange between the two men, but before she could comment, Brahn leaned back in his chair, resting his elbow lazily against the armrest.

Brahn's eyes flicked between them, something knowing, calculating, settling behind his gaze. But he didn't push. Instead, he gestured between them and the young woman. "This is Aelynn." A pause. Then, with the faintest hint of amusement, he added, "My cousin."

Mira blinked, glancing between them. Aelynn gave a slow, knowing smile, tilting her head. "Surprised?"

Mira barely let her expression shift. "You don't look like family." Aelynn laughed, a low, smoky laugh. "Good."

Aelynn's gaze drifted down, scanning the robe Mira wore, as if she could see through it, straight to what lay beneath.

She turned to Brahn. "He's expecting another drink. And something better than the last girl."

Mira lifted her chin. "I had better get out there then."

Mira moved toward the curtain, steady, deliberate. Behind her, she heard Tharion shift, felt the weight of his presence at her back. Before he could follow, Aelynn stepped smoothly into his path, cutting him off with effortless grace.

One brow arched, she murmured, voice like silk laced with steel, "If you come out of that curtain, you may as well declare yourself for sale."

The words hung between them, sharp and edged. Mira stilled, glancing back just in time to see Tharion's jaw tighten. Aelynn, utterly unbothered, turned her attention back to Mira, amusement glinting in her dark eyes.

"Might be best if your boy enters through the front door instead. That way, he can keep an eye on you without ruining the illusion."

Mira inhaled slowly. Aelynn was right. If Tharion followed her through, it would shatter the role she had to play before it even began. She held his gaze, waiting.

"She's not wrong," Mira said gently. "If you follow me out, the illusion breaks."

Tharion's fists curled just slightly at his sides, not in anger, not in protest, but in restraint. With a stiff nod, he stepped back. Mira turned to the curtain once more. And without another word, she stepped through.

The bar stretched long and lush, its polished mahogany counter gleaming under the low, golden light of the chandeliers above. Bottles of deep amber liquors and exotic elixirs lined the shelves behind it, their glass catching the flickering candlelight, casting warm glows across the room.

Men and women tended the bar, their attire scandalously minimal, designed more for allure than function. Bare skin, silk ribbons, corsets meant to be loosened. They moved with an effortless grace, their smiles lazy. Practiced predators as much as they were entertainers.

The room itself was draped in decadence, red velvet

seating wrapped around the space, alcoves darkened by heavy, silk curtains, meant for sensual moments whispered away from prying eyes. Smoke curled lazily in the air, carrying the scent of sandalwood, wine, and something richer, headier.

At the center, a small stage stood elevated, designed for performances meant to entertain and entice. Tonight, it sat empty, but the air still hummed with the ghosts of laughter, of music, of promises exchanged in the haze of pleasure.

Mira moved toward the bar, forcing her movements to be unhurried, practiced, like she belonged. She leaned against the counter, fingers trailing along its polished surface. The woman behind the bar, a striking beauty wrapped in only crimson silk, blonde curls falling over bare shoulders, paused in pouring a drink, her gaze flicking toward Mira with knowing amusement.

"You must be our special entertainment for Dren." Mira didn't blink. "Am I that obvious?"

"The dark hair, the robe just waiting to be unwrapped. Absolutely," she said, lips curving as she leaned against the bar. "He likes that, though." She tilted her chin toward the far corner of the room. "He's been watching the girls all night, but he didn't touch them. He was told you were just for him."

Mira followed her gaze. There. Tall, broad-shouldered, with windswept brown hair and sun-bronzed skin, the unmistakable look of a man hardened by years at sea. He sat alone in a shadowed corner, one hand lazily curled around his glass, the other resting against the armrest with confidence. And yet, the moment their eyes met, his confidence wavered. Mira saw it, the flicker of surprise, of intrigue. His mouth parted slightly, his grip tightening around his glass.

Her pulse beat steady and slow. Good. She let her lashes

flutter just slightly, tilting her head, letting a slow, shy smile curve her lips. Play the game. She had meant to ease into it, take her time, let him look, let him want. But the way his expression shifted, fascinated, ensnared, hungry, made her push a little harder than she'd intended.

Mira picked up the drink meant for him, wrapping her fingers around the glass as she moved across the room, her steps unhurried, deliberate. The weight of his gaze dragged over her as she approached, his eyes darkening with interest. She stopped in front of him, holding out the drink.

"This is for you," she said softly, her voice barely above the hum of the room. Then, after a slight pause, she bit her lip. Dren leaned forward and took it from her hand, his fingers brushing against hers, lingering a second too long.

His lips moved into a slow smile as he studied her, head tilting slightly. "They told me I'd be pleased with someone special tonight."

Mira's stomach twisted. A flicker of panic shot through her. But before the moment could spiral, Dren exhaled, lifting the glass to his lips. "They didn't tell me I'd be looking at something damn near divine."

Mira's pulse steadied. The panic faded, replaced by quiet confidence. She let her lashes lower, exhaling softly as she sat beside him, just slightly closer than politeness allowed. Her voice dipping into something playful, teasing. "Careful, you don't want to anger the Navigators."

Dren's smile deepened. He didn't hesitate, didn't even pretend to hold back. He shifted closer, his presence wrapping around her like a slow, deliberate snare. His arm draped over her shoulders, possessive, as though he'd already claimed her.

His breath was warm against her ear as he murmured,

"For a night with you, I would."

He drained his glass in one slow pull, then clicked his fingers for another. The bartender moved without question.

Dren leaned in again, his lips curving with something dark, something wanting. "What's your name?"

Mira didn't even blink. "Selene.", She smiled effortlessly, the lie rolling off her tongue like silk.

He smirked, tilting his head. "Stunning"

The fresh drink was placed before him, but he didn't reach for it. Mira's gaze flicked to the blonde bartender, who lingered just within reach waiting, for the next order, for the next command.

Without breaking his gaze from Mira, his voice came low, smooth, certain. "We'll need a private booth. Just me and Selene."

The bartender nodded once, a flicker of something, approval, amusement, maybe even curiosity, flashing in her eyes as she set down the drink, before she turned to make the arrangements.

Dren finally lifted his glass, taking a slow sip, his smirk deepening as he watched Mira over the rim. "Let's find out just how divine you really are."

Dren took her hand, his grip firm but effortless, as if guiding her was his natural right. Mira let him, let herself be led, her steps smooth, practiced, every movement calculated. He drew back the curtain.

The private booth was dimly lit, the cushions plush along the edges of the wall and along the floor, the air thick with the scent of spiced wine and burning oil. Mira's gaze caught on something beyond the veil of candlelight. Tharion. Coming through the front door. Their eyes locked.

Tharion's fear was unmistakable. It was in the way he

stiffened, the flicker of tension barely contained beneath his ever-controlled exterior. Fear. She batted her lashes at him, the smallest smile tugging at her mouth, the unspoken message clear. *I'm fine.*

Without hesitation, she stepped inside. The heavy fabric swung shut behind them, sealing her off from the world outside. From anything that wasn't this moment, this game.

Dren lounged back against the pillows on the seat, his body sinking into the lush cushions, one arm draped lazily along the backrest. He lifted his glass to his lips, but his attention was on drinking her in far more than the liquor in his hand. Mira let the silence stretch, let him look.

After a moment, with slow ease, she undid the ties of her robe, just enough for the heavy fabric to slip from her shoulders, revealing the smooth curve of her collarbone, the barest hint of lace beneath. Dren's smile sharpened, knowing, like a predator recognizing easy prey.

"Tell me," she murmured, tilting her head slightly, letting her fingers ghost along the edge of her robe, "what is it you do, exactly?"

He exhaled a soft chuckle, watching her as if he knew exactly what she was doing, but was in no rush to stop her. He tipped his glass back, draining the last of the liquid before pouring himself another from the private reserve, swallowing half in a single sip.

"I command," he said simply, rolling his glass between his fingers. "I've served for years, at sea, at war."

Mira forced a look of impressed curiosity, but inside, she scoffed. He was inflating his importance, playing up his influence the way men like him always did. She knew the type, a soldier, perhaps seasoned, but not a leader. No one truly reported to him. At best, he was a blunt instrument for someone else's orders. Still, she played along.

"You've been in battle?" Her voice was light, curious, her fingers toying with the edge of her robe. Dren nodded, watching as the fabric inched just a little lower with every breath she took.

"More than most," he said, his voice dropping into something rougher, something edged. "You learn quickly what it takes to survive in battle. What it takes to win."

Mira let the words linger, let them settle. Then, ever so slowly, she let the robe slide lower over her chest. The candlelight flickered over her skin, the delicate ivory lace catching the glow, whispering of everything that remained hidden. She let the robe fall completely.

Dren drained the rest of his glass in one swallow, setting it down with a quiet thud. Mira lowered herself onto the cushions at his feet, tilting her head up to look at him, eyes wide, innocent.

"So, you command fleets, then?" She shifted subtly, her hips rolling in slow, hypnotic circles, moving with the rhythm of the music.

Dren chuckled, running a hand along her neck, his fingers dragging slowly along the sensitive skin beneath her jaw. "Among other things." Mira tilted her head into his touch, feigning comfort.

"And what does a man like you command?" She glanced up through her lashes, brushing her fingers lightly against his thigh. "Just ships, or do you have men willing to follow you into battle?"

Dren's smirk deepened. "Both." He exhaled, his thumb brushing over her pulse, pressing just slightly. "The sea doesn't forgive weakness, and neither do I." Mira parted her lips slightly, as if fascinated, her fingers tracing delicate circles along his leg.

"It must take a certain type of man to do what you do," she murmured, shifting just slightly so that her ribs brushed against his knee.

"To know when to strike. When to hold back." Dren's gaze flicked downward, to the curve of her body, to the subtle shift of lace against her skin. "That's the difference between winning and losing."

She pretended to falter, just slightly. "And how do you know?"

Dren leaned in, his hand trailing up her throat, his breath warm against her skin. "Instinct. Experience." His lips hovered close to hers. "I trust my gut. And my gut tells me exactly what I want."

Mira smiled, slow and knowing. "And what does your gut say about me?"

Dren's fingers tightened slightly at her throat. His eyes locked onto hers. He leaned closer. Mira felt the shift, felt the moment closing in on her. She would have to kiss him. Disgust curled in her stomach, a sharp, suffocating thing. But she swallowed it down.

Let herself stay in the role in the game. Just as their lips were about to meet, Dren exhaled and whispered. "My gut says there's more to you than an easy fuck, Selene."

Mira froze. Just for a fraction of a second. Then she smiled, tilting her head in faux confusion. Dren smirked, his thumb brushing along her lower lip. He thought she wanted him. That she was just as ensnared by the game as he was. Inside, revulsion curled in her stomach.

He was a pig, a man so steeped in his own ego he couldn't fathom that she might not want him, that this was just a job to her. But Mira played along. She leaned into his touch, exhaling softly, letting her lips part ever so slightly, as if indulging in the moment. That was when he pressed his thumb into her mouth. The taste of him flooded her senses, masculine, with the tang of spiced liquor, but underneath it… something else.

Sour. A faint bite of sweat and salt, of indulgence, gone stale.

Her stomach churned. She resisted the urge to recoil, to bite down, to pull away. Instead, she let her tongue flick against the tip of his thumb, playing the part, feigning submission. Dren's satisfaction flickering across his sharp features.

"You must be surrounded by high-ranking officials here, seeing as they hide you away until someone important comes along." He drawled.

The words were too smooth. Too intentional. Her stomach tensed. Of course. He wasn't just playing, he was trying to get information out of her. It was too perfect. He wanted something from her just as much as he thought she wanted something from him. Her fingers trailed up his leg lazily, a slow, teasing touch. She let out a soft, muffled sound around his thumb, a low hum of affirmation. Dren chuckled, shifting closer, and before she could brace herself, he dragged her fully between his legs. The movement was firm, deliberate. His thumb remained in her mouth, pressing just slightly deeper, as though testing her obedience, as though daring her to resist. She wanted to gag. Wanted to rip his hand away, wipe the taste of him off her tongue. Instead, she lowered her lashes, letting the game play out.

"Because a woman like you doesn't go unnoticed," Dren murmured, voice low, amused. His other hand traced along her jaw. "Men like me take notice." Mira tilted her head slightly before she slowly pulled away, rising onto her knees. His thumb left her mouth and she suppressed another gag. Mira dragged a hand up his chest, over his shoulders, her fingertips grazing along the tension hidden beneath his layers of silk and leather.

"And what is it you want me to notice, Commander?" Her voice softened into something sultry, teasing. He groaned, his grip on her tightening just slightly, not enough to hurt, just enough to remind her he thought he was in control.

"Tell me something worth my while…" he murmured, his fingers pressing firmly into her neck. "And then we can play together." Mira feigned a thought, letting the silence stretch just long enough before finally meeting his eyes.

"I overheard an interesting conversation earlier." The shift was immediate. Dren's smirk faltered just slightly, replaced with interest. Hooked. Mira leaned in, her lips just a breath away from his ear.

"I heard a royal guard complaining yesterday," she whispered. She felt his grip flex, his body going still, listening. She let the words drip from her lips, slow, deliberate. "They're marching through Harrow's Hollow in four days. Well, three now I guess." Dren's smirk returned, slow and pleased, the glint of satisfaction flickering in his dark gaze.

"Good girl," he murmured, fingers tracing the line of her throat.

She saw the way his gaze dipped to her lips, the way his hand slid from her throat to the nape, drawing her closer. His breath ghosted against her skin, his lips nearly on hers.

Disgust curdled in her stomach. Mira braced herself. The curtain flew open.

"Get your hands off her." Mira barely had time to register the words before Tharion stepped into the room. His voice wasn't loud. It didn't need to be. A command, not a request. The atmosphere shifted like a sudden drop in temperature. His presence swallowed the space whole, shoulders squared, jaw locked, every movement controlled, deliberate.

Dren froze. The weight of Tharion's gaze pinned him in place, sharp and assessing. Too still. Tharion didn't yell or draw his weapon. His presence alone radiated, making him the most dangerous thing in the room. Dren's hand slipped back from Mira slowly, hesitantly. He swallowed hard, the smirk he wore moments ago faltering as unease crept into his expression.

"I didn't know she had a bodyguard," he muttered, voice thin, brittle.

Tharion didn't blink. He stepped forward once, just once, and Dren shrunk back, hands half-raised in a gesture of surrender as his eyes flicked toward the exit.

Tharion's voice came again, quieter now. "No," he said. "You didn't."

Dren's smirk had vanished. His face paled, realization dawning a second too late. His breath hitched, panic flickering in his eyes as his body instinctively tensed to bolt. He had his information. He wasn't about to risk more.

"Easy now," he muttered, trying to mask his unease with bravado. "No need to start a fight over a whore."

Tharion bared his teeth and stepped forward, a low growl curling from his throat. "What did you call her?"

Dren bolted. He crashed through the curtain, shoving past onlookers, knocking a drink from someone's hand in his frantic scramble to escape.

Mira stared at the space where Dren had disappeared, her breath still caught in her chest, her pulse thrumming like war drums in her ears.

Tharion's dry voice interrupted, "Come on, we're leaving."

She blinked, grounding herself. Her hands moved automatically, adjusting the robe and re-tightening the sash at her waist. When she finally looked up, met Tharion's eyes, the emotion in her eyes was quiet but clear. Gratitude. Not loud. Not spoken. But it was there.

He exhaled sharply, before taking a step back. He turned on his heel, shoving past the curtain without another word. Mira lingered just a second longer before following.

∗ ∗ ∗

Outside, the night had settled deep over Seacliffe. The streets were still alive with murmured voices, flickering lanterns, the distant sound of waves against stone. By the time they reached their room, the air between them was still thick, unspoken, heavy.

Mira pulled the door shut, the latch clicking into place, sealing them inside. Tharion barely spared her a glance as he leaned against the wall, rolling his shoulders before pulling down his hood.

Tharion finally spoke. "I sent word to Brahn. He knows the message was delivered."

Before exhaustion could settle in her bones, Mira turned, her eyes finding Tharion from across the room. "How did you know about the pleasure house?"

He paused, rolling up the sleeves of his tunic, his expression unreadable in that way she knew meant he was choosing his words carefully.

Then, with a quiet exhale, he shrugged. "Ren and I used to come here," he said. "Back in our… less disciplined days."

Mira blinked. That was not what she'd expected to hear. "You? In a pleasure house?" she echoed, more amused than anything else. There was no trace of jealousy in her voice, just curiosity, and maybe a bit of disbelief.

A flicker of amusement, tugged at the corner of his mouth. But he didn't rise to the bait.

He was already moving past her, reaching for his flask of water like the question had been purely hypothetical. She watched him for a moment, then asked, more quietly, "Why did you stop him?" Tharion drank, wiped his mouth on the back of his hand, and finally met her eyes.

"You'd done the job," he said simply. A beat. "You needed an exit."

Mira frowned slightly, studying him. "You might have ruined it," she said, a brow lifting. "If I hadn't already told him what I wanted him to believe."

Tharion didn't flinch. "I was just outside," he replied, calm. "I waited for the right moment."

Her breath caught "You were listening," she breathed. "Of course I was," he said. "I said I'd be there."

She let out a slow breath. "Thank you."

Tharion didn't speak. He just nodded once, already moving toward the bed with quiet familiarity.

Mira turned away, heading into the washroom. The door clicked shut behind her, muffling the sounds of the city still humming outside the window.

She washed the disguise from her body and donned a simple nightgown. The cotton slip was loose against her skin, a stark contrast to the silk and shadowlace she'd worn hours earlier. No pretense. No performance. Tharion had removed his boots and lay stretched on his side of the bed, one arm tucked beneath his head. His breathing was steady, slow.

Asleep, or close enough.

Mira hesitated. There had been a time when sharing a bed with him was effortless. Those moments felt far away now, dulled at the edges, unreachable. But not gone. She wasn't sure if they could ever get back to what they had been. But as she stood there, watching him sleep in the soft hush of the room, she knew. She would try. Because he was worth the effort.

She climbed in beside him quietly. The mattress dipped under her weight as she settled under the cover. For a moment, she simply listened to the waves, to the steady rhythm of Tharion's breath. She let the exhaustion pull her under, the night folding around them like the tide.

15

THE MORNING SUN BROKE through the lingering mist in beams, casting a golden glow over the cliff side paths below Seacliffe. The tide had drawn back just far enough to reveal a stretch of black-stone pools and salt-slicked rock. Each pool held tiny reflections of the sky, glimmering mirrors nestled in stone.

Mira adjusted the shawl over her shoulders as the wind swept up from the sea. The temperature had dropped overnight. Not enough to bite, but enough to make her skin prickle. Summer had ended. Autumn had crept in on swift silent feet, brushing the air with its cooler breath.

She inhaled deeply, filling her lungs with the scent of salt and seaweed and something deeper, older, the damp, briny smell of earth meeting the ocean.

Below the cliffs, she spotted movement. Tharion crouched near one of the larger tide pools, fingers skimming just above the surface. Not touching. Just observing. She made her way down the narrow path toward him, boots crunching softly over worn stone and sea-glass fragments. The closer she got, the more the noise of Seacliffe faded.

Tharion didn't look up as she approached, but his voice carried over the soft hiss of waves. "This was my favorite place," he said. "When I was a boy."

Mira stopped beside him, letting her eyes fall to the tide pool. Tiny fish darted between shadows. A crab scuttled backward into a crack in the rock. Water shimmered, touched by gold. "Ren hated the cold," Tharion continued, "but he came anyway. I'd stay out here for hours. Just... watching."

He shifted slightly to the side, making room for her. She knelt next to him, her shawl slipping down her arm as she reached to trace the edge of a barnacled stone. "Still remember what most of these are called," he said, quieter now.

They moved from one rock pool to the next, unhurried. Mira pointed out the faint glimmer of a sea snail clinging to stone. Tharion nodded. She found a starfish in another pool, pale pink and curled tight. For a moment, they just watched it, the sea lapping gently in and out around their boots. There was peace here, not perfect, not complete, but real. Mira glanced over at him. The lines in his brow had softened. He wasn't smiling, exactly. But he looked... lighter.

"We should come back here more often," she said, voice soft, breaking the stillness. Tharion didn't hesitate. "Yeah," he said. "We should."

A familiar voice echoed from above. "Mira!" Torvyn's shout carried over the wind, roughened by the sea air.

She turned to see him standing farther up the bluff, hands cupped around his mouth, his silhouette framed against the pale sky. He waved an arm, motioning them up the path. Tharion exhaled through his nose, just shy of a laugh.

"That would be your brother," he muttered, already heading up the path.

Mira moved to follow, but something caught her eye, a gleam of color hidden beneath a tangle of sea grapes at the edge of a tide pool. She crouched, brushing the slippery greenery aside. There, half-buried in wet sand and stone, was a piece of sea glass. Not the pale green she usually found, but a deep, striking blue. The blue of ocean depths. It was just larger than her palm, smooth to the touch, and as she lifted it into the light, it shimmered faintly, just for a moment, as if it had caught something more than just the sun.

Mira blinked. The shimmer faded. Just glass again. But she held it for a long second before slipping it into the folds of her shawl. She turned, climbing after Tharion toward the sound of her brother's voice, the wind tugging at her cloak.

* * *

Brahn and Torvyn walked together, their voices low but firm, deep in conversation. Brahn's stride was measured, steady, arms crossed over his chest as he listened. Torvyn gestured with sharp precision, speaking in the clipped tones of a man who had long since run out of patience for bureaucracy. Mira caught only fragments. Trade disputes.

Fragile alliances. The upcoming council session.

She wasn't listening. Not really. Her eyes were on the streets. Worn, uneven stone. People thinner than they should be, wrapped in patched clothes that had seen too many winters. Children sat on doorsteps, their eyes curious. A woman sold dried fish and bread from a near-empty stall. Seacliffe had been built to endure. That didn't mean it wasn't struggling. Tharion stepped quietly into place beside her, his gaze moving with hers. He saw it too. The poverty. The quiet strain.

After a long moment, he spoke. "Seacliffe wasn't built to thrive."

Mira turned to him. "What do you mean?"

Tharion slid his hands into the pockets. "This place was never meant to be a jewel of the kingdom. It was a stronghold first, a city second. A last line of defense carved into the cliffs."

She glanced toward the towering stone walls, the fortress etched into the rock. "A city meant to survive."

Tharion nodded. "Exactly." His voice dropped. "Centuries ago, Seacliffe was just an outpost. A place for ships to take shelter in storms. The people here… they're not here to prosper, Mira." His gaze swept across the market, across the faces worn thin with endurance. "They're here to hold the line."

Mira's heart clenched. Seacliffe wasn't simply forgotten. It was expected to suffer. To be the place left behind while the rest of the kingdom moved on. And yet, the people remained. They endured. Her fingers brushed the worn stone of a nearby wall as she walked, letting the texture ground her thoughts.

Ahead, Brahn and Torvyn pressed on, their voices now indistinct. They came to a small, weathered house. Its roof sagged at the corners, stone dark with salt and age. The door was gray and splintered, hanging askew on rusted hinges. A single window, warped and dull, caught the pale sky. Outside stood Miller, shaking out a thin, patched quilt. Dust drifted in the breeze. The house was holding, but only just. Mira's heart clenched. She had known Seacliffe was struggling. But seeing it affect Miller. It was heartbreaking.

Tharion was already moving before the thought fully formed. "Miller..."

The older woman turned, and her expression softened at once. "Oh hush, boy," she said, wiping her hands on her apron. "No need to look like that."

Tharion's gaze took in the sagging roof, the threadbare dress, the thinner frame. "Miller… why didn't you tell me?" he whispered.

Miller blinked, then gave a soft, dismissive laugh. "Tell you what, lad?" She gestured around them. "This is Seacliffe. This is just how things are."

"It shouldn't be. I could send you.." Tharion's offer died in his throat as Miller gave him a long look. Warm. Steady. The kind a mother gives to her naive son. "And what would that do for everyone else?"

Tharion didn't answer. He looked down, his jaw tightening as he took in the ground beneath their feet, the broken fence, the creeping vines, the dust still clinging to the quilt in Miller's hands. Then, slowly, his gaze lifted again, meeting hers with a steadiness that hadn't been there the last time he was in this place.

"I'd do whatever it takes," he said, voice low. Miller's lips pressed into something like a smile. Faint. Sad. Proud.

"You always were a stubborn one," she murmured, folding the quilt over her arm. Tharion didn't speak, but something shifted in his eyes, grief and love wrapped into one quiet breath.

"And he's not the only one," Brahn said, voice firm. "You won't have to weather this alone anymore."

Miller gave him a look, grateful, cautious, amused all at once. "Careful, young man. You talk like that and we might start believing you."

Torvyn lifted his chin. "Good."

The wind stirred around them, catching the edge of Miller's quilt and lifting the scent of salt and hearth smoke into the air. She looked between the four of them and something softened in her expression. Not quite surrender, but acceptance. Like she'd seen enough of the world to know when a promise was more than just words.

"Well then," she said, tucking the quilt under her arm,

"you'd better come in." he turned without waiting for an answer, pushing open the warped door with her shoulder. It creaked like it hadn't been used in years, though Mira knew it had. The air inside was thick with the scent of old wood, damp stone, and the faint, lingering warmth of a long-doused fire. The floorboards, warped with age, creaked beneath their feet, and cobwebs clung to the exposed rafters, trembling in the dim light.

Despite its neglect, the house still held a sense of warmth. A patchwork of mismatched rugs covered the worn floor, and a battered wooden table stood at the center of the room, surrounded by chairs that wobbled precariously with every shift. A threadbare quilt was draped over a lumpy armchair near the hearth, where embers smoldered weakly in the soot-blackened fireplace.

But it was the people who made the house feel alive. They were everywhere, grouped near the fire, perched on benches, leaning against the sagging walls. Their faces were a mix of worry and relief, eyes flickering toward them with expectation. Some whispered among themselves, others watched in silence, their expressions unreadable. Whatever had brought them all together, it was clear they had been waiting.

Brahn stepped through the doorway, his presence commanding even in the dim light. He didn't hesitate, didn't take a moment to gather his thoughts. He simply began, his voice steady and sure, cutting through the indistinct murmurs in the room.

"This isn't where our story ends. Not if we refuse to let it." His dark eyes swept over the gathered faces, his tone as firm as the tide. "We are not just trying to stay afloat, we are fighting to take back what was stolen. To rebuild stronger than before. To prove that what they tried to sink was never theirs to drown."

Mira stood at the edge of the room, her fingers tightening around the worn wood of the doorframe. She had heard these words before. Not just their meaning, not just the conviction behind them, but these very words. In Anyerit, she had thought she was witnessing a transformation, the moment Brahn stepped into himself, found his voice. But now, watching the way his presence filled the space, how his words moved through the room like a current drawing everyone in, she understood the truth. He hadn't changed. He hadn't risen to meet this moment. He was the moment. This wasn't something he had just become. It was something he had always been. She just hadn't seen it clearly until now.

"Look around you," he continued, his voice unwavering. "This is one town, one harbor among many, but the story is the same. The raids come like rising waves, each one pulling more from us, leaving us with less than before. And yet those who claim to rule us sit safe in their gilded halls, letting us weather the storm alone."

A murmur of agreement rolled through the room, quietly at first but growing, swelling like an oncoming tide.

Brahn's voice deepened, quiet yet ironclad. "We are not wreckage, scattered and broken. We are not lost sailors clinging to the driftwood of what once was. We are the tide that will rise. We are the storm they should have feared." His gaze flicked toward the children in the room. His tone softened, but the strength remained. "We fight for them. For the chance to give them a world where the sea is a promise, not a threat. For a tomorrow where they can dream of more than survival."

The hush in the room was no longer the silence of despair.

It was hope, exactly the same and in Anyerit.

Brahn straightened, his presence filling the space as he finished. "This is where we set sail once more, like Bharas did. We will step in the footprints of the navigators before us." A ripple of murmurs passed through the crowd. "For our freedom." he murmured, his voice raw with emotion.

The mantra spread, catching like wildfire, sweeping through the room until it became a chorus. Mira exhaled, her chest tightening. She had seen this before. Had felt this before. And yet, even knowing that, even knowing this was not the first time Brahn had stood in a room like this and turned fear into fury, turned despair into purpose, she still felt the pull of it. The pull of hope.

* * *

The morning chill had never quite lifted, and as the sun dipped lower, the air grew even cooler, the scent of brine and damp earth seeping through the carriage windows. Mira sat next to Tharion whose legs stretched out across the cabin. She could still hear the echo of Miller's voice, the weight of her words settling into her chest like a stone. The carriage rocked gently, the rhythm of the wheels against the dirt road steady, almost soothing. Tharion watched out the window, his mind likely working through his own calculations, his own thoughts.

Mira exhaled, shifting slightly, pulling her shawl tighter around her shoulders. The weight of the last few days pressed down on her, heavy, unrelenting.

Tharion must have noticed because his eyes flicked to hers. "You should rest."

The warmth of the carriage, the rocking motion, the faint

sound of horses' hooves against the road, it pulled at her like a tide. Slowly, Mira shifted, settling close to him, but not too close. Tharion didn't move. Didn't shift away. He adjusted just enough to make sure she had room.

Mira didn't mean to let her head tilt just slightly onto his shoulder, but the weight of exhaustion dragged her down.

∗ ∗ ∗

The cold didn't bite so much as melt around her, softened by the hush of snow and pine. Winter had laid its weight over the forest, quiet and deep, but it barely touched her. Not with his hand in hers. Warm. Familiar. Anchoring her even as the world grew surreal.

Mira moved through the trees like she was half-remembering the path, guiding them forward, breath silvering in the air. Each step felt softer than the last, like walking through the pages of a memory, unfolding with each heartbeat.

"We're almost there," she murmured, though she wasn't sure how she knew. The trees parted all at once.

Steam curled from the earth, thick and silken, rising off water that shimmered with faint, impossible light. The hidden springs. Moonlight kissed the surface, and the snow glowed around it like frost-laced glass. Mira turned to him, something slow and knowing pulling at her lips.

"Still think I was lying?" she teased.

He didn't answer with words. Only with a look. Like he saw her entirely and had no idea what to do with the truth of it. She let her cloak fall, fabric spilling into the snow without sound. The cold touched her skin. The forest held its breath. She glanced back at him, that familiar dare behind her eyes.

259

Her fingers found the straps of her dress, sliding them down her shoulders like un-spooling silk. Her skin caught the moonlight and her heartbeat drummed slow and steady, like it was echoing from the trees themselves.

She paused again. Let him feel it. Let herself feel it. The moment stretched, timeless and fragile.

"Something wrong?" she asked, voice like the ripple of water. "You're stalling," came his reply, half-laugh, half-prayer.

She smiled, letting the dress fall. The air caught it and carried it into the snow. She stepped into the water, slow and weightless, like slipping into a dream. It wrapped around her, welcoming her.

"You coming in?" she called over her shoulder. "Or just going to watch me disappear?"

The sound of footsteps. Fabric hitting snow. The hush of water stirred. Then he was there. Not close enough to touch, but close enough to feel. Like a second current beneath the surface. Mira turned, and the world narrowed. "Not bad, is it?" she said, voice softer now, more breath than sound.

His answer came slowly, like it had traveled far.

"The view's...captivating." She floated toward him. The water licked at her skin, steam curling over her shoulders. When she reached him, she didn't touch him, just stopped, inches apart.

"You're staring again." His hand brushed against her thigh. "Can't help it." He murmured.

"You should stop looking at me like that," she whispered. "Like what?" he teased.

"Like you're going to devour me." The air shifted. And then his hands were on her waist, pulling her in, grounding her with impossible gentleness. The kiss came like a slow tide,

warm, enveloping, undoing. She folded into it.

Her arms wrapped around his neck, her legs around his waist, bodies moving as if they'd always belonged to this rhythm, this heat, this moment suspended in silence. He groaned against her lips, low and reverent, his hands dragging across her skin like he was memorizing her by feel alone.

"Reckless," she breathed. His reply was a whisper against her jaw.

"With you... always." She shivered. The world disappeared into steam. There was only water and warmth and the echo of breath. The hush of the trees. The Navigators above.

✳ ✳ ✳

Mira barely stirred as the carriage rolled to a stop. The distant creak of wheels, the muffled voices beyond the door, they all felt far away, submerged in the heavy warmth of sleep. Steady arms lifted her. A scent wrapped around her, familiar even through the haze. She shifted slightly, her cheek brushing against his shoulder, but exhaustion kept her limbs heavy, her body pliant in his hold.

She was carried through the palace corridors, his steps steady, unhurried. She drifted in and out, slipping between the waking world and the remnants of her dream, whispers of steam, the press of lips against skin, the taste of something forbidden lingering on her lips. A door opened. Cool air touched her skin.

Her bed met her body, sheets soft beneath her, and she exhaled a slow breath. A weight lingered beside her for a moment. A hand brushed her hair back from her face.

Then, warmth receded. She sank deeper into sleep, the echoes of a dream calling her in.

* * *

Mira shifted in her bed, the sheet tangled around her legs. She could swear she heard something, stone against glass. She sat up, blinking against the dim glow of moonlight.

Then another sound. Just a soft clink. She crossed to the window, heart already rising in her throat before she even saw him. There he was. Standing beneath her balcony, hood pushed back, a stone in his hand, his eyes already locked on hers. Warmth bloomed behind her ribs.

"You're early," she whispered, barely able to breathe. He grinned up at her, crooked, boyish, reckless.

"The convoy arrives tomorrow," he said, his voice like gravel and starlight. "I couldn't wait."

She pressed her hand to the railing, leaning out, moonlight catching on her nightgown, on her hair, on the quick rise and fall of her chest. Navigators, she had missed him.

"You're reckless," she whispered, eyes shining. "You climbed the walls for me?" His grin deepened. "Would you rather I knocked?"

"No," she said without thinking, her smile tipping into mischief. "I'd rather something more dramatic."

She saw the shift in his eyes, sudden and dangerous and beautiful. And then he was climbing. Her breath caught. He moved fast, fingers gripping the ivy, boots scraping the stone. She could feel it, his need, his thrill, his longing threading into hers like a second heartbeat. She stepped back just as he crested the ledge, and the second his boots hit the balcony, she threw herself into his arms.

He caught her easily. Like he always did. Her arms wrapped around his neck, face pressed into his shoulder, the scent of him familiar and wild and safe, stealing the air from her lungs.

"You're real," she breathed, the words trembling. "You're really here."

"I'm real," he murmured, his mouth brushing her temple. His hands slid to her waist, pulling her tighter.

She leaned back just enough to look at him, her fingers grazing the stubble on his jaw, needing contact. Needing to prove to herself he wasn't something her heart had conjured in sleep. "I thought I was dreaming you again." Her voice cracked. And then she smiled. Slow. Devastating.

He kissed her. Heat spilled through her like lightning, slow and sharp and impossible to contain. Her fingers tangled in his hair, her body pressing closer, melting into him as if the space between them had never existed. The kiss was messy, aching, desperate, everything she hadn't said, everything she'd needed. She whimpered against his mouth, and he swallowed the sound like it was sacred.

"Come with me," he said against her lips.

She hesitated, but only for a breath. Her hands slid to his chest, the heat of him soaking through her fingers.

"I don't know…" she teased, her voice in faux fear.

A dark laugh rumbled in his chest. "Cruel," he said, kissing her again, slower this time, deeper. "Come with me."

She exhaled, nodding without realising.

Before she could pull away, before she could grab a cloak or remember the how far down the world below was, he lifted her. Mira gasped, laughter spilling out of her as her legs wrapped instinctively around his waist.

"What are you…?"

"Stealing you," he whispered, his grin wicked and full of promise. Her arms locked around his shoulders as he stepped onto the ledge, the wind tugging at her hair, the scent of spring thick in her lungs.

16

THE ROOM WAS DIM, washed in the muted grey of an autumn morning. Shadows stretched softly across the floor. The kind that blurred at the edges, like half-forgotten memories. Mira blinked slowly, the weight of sleep still clinging to her lashes. Her dream was already slipping away. The warmth of a hand. The brush of lips. Laughter echoing through the moonlight. A promise, maybe. Or a memory.

She reached for it, but it dissolved between blinks. Her fingers curled into the bedding, still faintly warm where her body had been curled through the night. The dress she'd fallen asleep in was wrinkled, the fabric creased and familiar. Mira exhaled, sitting up with a quiet groan, the soft stretch of her spine grounding her in the waking world. She remembered the way the carriage rocked, the cool weight of the evening air.

She remembered Tharion's arms. He'd carried her back. She was sure of it. She could still feel the ghost, the way her body had leaned into his without thought, her head against his shoulder, his steady breath close. But when she had woken in the early hours, the room was empty. He hadn't stayed. That was okay. It had to be. What was broken didn't mend overnight. They would need time. She wanted to give him that time. Still… she had missed his presence beside her like the night before.

Mira stood, her bare feet brushing the cool floor. She crossed to the bathing chamber where steam was already curling from the deep basin, scented with citrus and stone. The warmth of the water wrapped around her like a cloak as she stepped in, her muscles easing slowly into the heat. She closed her eyes, tried again to find the dream. But only impressions remained. A laugh. A kiss. The feeling of falling and not being afraid.

By the time she rose from the water, her skin glowed with warmth, and her thoughts had quieted. She dressed simply, an earth-toned dress, soft and worn, layered with a cardigan that settled gently over her shoulders. The air wasn't cold, just cool enough.

She pulled her hair down, combed through it with her fingers, and moved to the door.

Outside, the palace had stirred, soft voices, footsteps echoing over marble, the metallic rhythm of daily life rising like a tide. The corridor beyond was still touched by the morning hush. The light through the tall windows glowed pale and gold, and the scent of autumn drifted in, dried leaves, sun-warmed stone, something faintly sweet. She stepped into the hall.

The corridor curved away from the main palace like a vein, quieter, narrower, the scent of damp stone mixing with traces of burnt oil and cold air. Mira hadn't meant this far from the altar room, but her feet had wandered. She liked the quiet of the south wing, the way it felt older than the rest. Like the palace had tried to forget it.

She rounded the corner and stopped short. Voices echoed ahead, low and clipped, the low, deliberate murmur of a weighty conversation. Three advisors in deep conversation, their backs to her. And in the middle, was Ren. He stood with his arms crossed, dressed in deep navy, his posture a quiet command. His voice was calm, direct.

"We'll increase the guards presence in the west wing. If the Queen of Myrdathis arrives early, she will have her own guard, but we won't risk appearing unprepared."

The men murmured in agreement. She should have turned away. Should have taken the side hall like she had meant to. But the sight of him, her breath caught, her pulse quickened. Low and traitorous. And as if summoned by the thought, his head lifted. His eyes traced the length of the hall until they found her. The conversation continued around him. His expression shifted a little in his eyes. Warmth and longing. Ren's gaze held hers for a breath longer before he turned slightly, his voice lifting just enough to reach the others.

"Thank you, all of you. That'll be all for now. Head back through the east hall. I'll catch up shortly."

There was no tension in the dismissal, just calm authority and a trace of gratitude. The men nodded, murmuring acknowledgments as they turned away from Mira, their backs never once glancing in her direction. One of them chuckled softly at something the others said, their voices already fading as they disappeared around the corner.

Ren didn't move right away. He waited a second longer, listening to their footsteps recede completely before facing her. With that same quiet certainty, he closed the distance between them.

"You shouldn't be here," he said softly, but his voice held no reprimand. Mira held his gaze, the quiet between them pulling tighter, like a string drawn taut.

She shifted slightly, her hand brushing the edge of her sleeve, needing something to do with the weight in her chest. "I didn't mean to interrupt."

"You didn't," he said, voice even. "You never do" His eyes flicked briefly down the corridor where the advisors had gone. "I didn't think I would get to see you."

Mira glanced past him, toward the end of the hall she should've taken, the one that would've kept her from this. But something in her, stubborn, curious, maybe foolish, had stopped her feet before her mind could catch up.

Ren looked down at her , his voice low, "I heard about Seacliffe… " Mira blinked, her spine straightening slightly. "Did you?"

Ren stepped closer, the sharp edges of his usual bravado softened now. "Officers. Troop movements. A pleasure house." He let the words hang for a moment, thoughtful.

She watched him carefully. "Tharion told you?"

Ren nodded, slow and quiet. "Not the kind of maneuver you'd attempt without knowing what you're doing."

Mira tilted her head slightly, watching him. "You sound surprised."

"I'm not," he said. "I'm impressed." She felt the pride bloom in her chest, and Ren's gaze sharpened. "But I'm also furious."

Her brows lifted. "Oh?"

He hesitated, "You shouldn't have had to risk everything while the rest of us sat in council rooms pretending strategy and protocol were enough."

Mira's lips curved faintly. "Not an official presence. Wasn't that your plan?"

He exhaled slowly, jaw tight. "I agreed to subtle. I didn't agree to you playing bait for some preening Kharadorian."

The air between them shifted. The words weren't biting, but they carried an edge. Controlled. Calculated. Jealous. Mira felt it like a spark against skin, sharp and sudden. That edge in his voice, the fire he was trying to mask with formality, it lit a dark satisfaction low and undeniable in her.

Part of her recognized the fire in him and didn't look away. Ren saw it. The flicker in her eyes. The slight, involuntary catch of her breath. And for a moment, the mask he wore cracked just enough to show the fire underneath.

His voice dropped, a low, dark rumble that seemed to vibrate more than speak. "How many eyes followed you in there?"

Mira raised an eyebrow, amused. "Only the necessary ones."

His eyes narrowed slightly. "Necessary," he echoed, then looked away for a heartbeat.

There was a beat of silence between them. Then softer "I just…" he stopped, jaw tightening, then added more quietly, "If I'd been there… I could've played the part. Backed your play."

Mira's heart caught, just for a moment. She didn't move. And Navigators help her, this was what she had waited for. Not permission. Not pity. But this, someone who saw the weight of what she'd done and wanted to carry it with her. Who would have stood beside her, played his part, not to take control but to make her stronger. Not Tharion's cold logic. Not the council's approval. Just this.

Ren met her gaze, and this time, the fire in his eyes burned hot with jealousy, regret, longing, and a fierce kind of admiration.

"Careful," she warned. "You sound jealous."

Ren glanced down the corridor where the advisors had quietly dispersed, then shifted. His hand came up, bracing against the wall just above her shoulder. He leaned in, not close enough to touch, but close enough for the air to shift between them. His eyes met hers, steady. Unreadable.

"Would you care if I was?" The silence stretched, taut as

wire. Mira's breath caught. She could feel her heart beating in her throat, too loud, too fast. She didn't blink. Didn't drop her gaze.

"Yes," she breathed. It was only a whisper. But Ren exhaled, like he'd been holding his breath for days. His hand pressed firmer to the wall above her, as if steadying himself. As if stopping himself from reaching for her entirely.

"You have no idea what it felt like, do you?" he said, voice rough around the edges. "Rumours started trickling in, and I couldn't think straight. Hearing what you were doing out there. What you were risking." His eyes never left hers. Mira's breath hitched. With a slow, deliberate movement, Ren leaned in, almost close enough to kiss. His voice dropped to a murmur, intimate and dangerous.

"And all I could think about was riding to Seacliffe myself, walking into that place, into that room, and showing him exactly how impossible you are to resist..."

A darker part of her thrilled at the way he tensed. She couldn't help it, it was too easy, too delicious, drawing that fire from him. For a heartbeat, she pictured it...

Seacliffe, the room heavy with perfume and pretense, and Ren stepping through the door. No hesitation. No questions. His hand would settle low at her back, fingers spreading with the kind of ease that suggested long-held intimacy, the kind that didn't need explanation. Then he'd lean in, slow and deliberate, mouth brushing the edge of her ear, lips close enough to graze but never quite touch. Ren wasn't just claiming her. He was offering the illusion of a challenge. She's not yours yet, it whispered. But maybe she could be, if you were bold enough to take her.

Mira knew she shouldn't toy with him like this, but she

couldn't help it. Her voice was low, almost a purr. "I wonder… how would you have played the part, Ren? Kissed me like I was yours?"

His jaw clenched. "I wanted to see you in that shadowlace," The words hung between them, electric and heavy and painfully honest. "undoing it, piece by piece, with my teeth."

Mira's breath caught, sharp and quiet. Heat licked up her spine, pooling somewhere low and molten. The image he painted struck with brutal precision, too vivid, too real, and she felt her grip on control fray at the edges. There was no manipulation here, no staged seduction. Just Ren.

He leaned in, close enough that his breath stirred the curve of her neck, and whispered against her ear. "I wanted him to watch. To see what it looked like when you weren't pretending."

Her eyes fluttered shut for a heartbeat. She could taste the want in his voice. Rough and aching and it curled around her like smoke. Whatever game they'd started, it was no longer clear who held the reins.

Her breath caught, trembling in her chest like a secret she'd tried too long to bury. Every inch of her ached to close the distance. To give in. To let it all burn. But she didn't have the chance.

Ren stepped back, not far, but enough. Enough to draw breath between them. Enough to reclaim the space before either of them crossed a line that couldn't be uncrossed. He exhaled. A slow, deliberate release. The heat didn't vanish, but it cooled. Contained now, drawn back like a blade into its sheath.

"You were right Mira, we can't keep circling." he said, voice thick but steady. Mira opened her mouth, but he held up a hand, not in anger, but finality. His jaw was tight, but not cruel.

"But you need to know something, Mira." His voice dipped, rough with the weight of it. "You're it for me. And if the memory of these moments, of you, is all I ever get, I'll take it. Gladly." He paused, the fire still there, but tempered now. "But I won't chase you… but you need to choose."

For a heartbeat, she couldn't breathe. The ache in Ren's voice, the truth in his eyes. It tugged at something deep and ancient inside her. But then she thought of Tharion. Of the bond between them. Real, rooted, chosen. Even if the memories still sat just out of reach, she had seen a spark of him in Seacliffe. The man he used to be. The one who had once held her heart with quiet strength. And despite everything, he had stayed. Suffered. Waited. They deserved the chance to rebuild what they had lost.

"I'm sorry Ren, I..." she said, her voice barely above a whisper, but unwavering.

Ren gave a slight shake of his head, just enough to stop her. "You don't owe me anything. I knew what this was." A pause. His eyes burned, but the fire wasn't wild anymore. Just steady. Focused. Her heart twisted as she looked up at Ren.

"You love him," he said. Not a question. A truth he was making peace with. Something shattered in Ren's eyes, but then he blinked, and what was left was hardened resolve.

"And so you should," he added, softer. "If I were Tharion, I'd want you to choose me too..."

Her lips parted, the beginning of a question she didn't know how to ask. But with one last look at her, he turned and walked away.

She stood there for a long moment after he left. Not moving. Not breathing, really. The air still hummed with the echo of his words, and something deep in her chest ached, sharp and silent. Her heart felt bruised. Like pressure pressed into a soft place she hadn't protected.

* * *

She slipped into the altar, the crowd of attendants parted slightly as Cleric Perrin stood at the center. Her robe dragging over the floor as she moved to the raised step where offerings were once laid.

"She's coming herself," Perrin announced, her voice low but clear. "The Queen of Myrdathis has agreed to meet with the advisory council and newly appointed Regent one week from today."

Gasps stirred the circle. Mira stiffened. Myrdathis. Their queens did not travel. They sent dreams. Declarations. Seers. Never the Queen herself.

"The wisdom of the Seers has shaped our kingdoms for generations," Perrin continued. "And Queen Danlea brings more than that. She brings a vision of what is coming for our kingdom".

The word sent a shiver down Mira's spine. She exhaled, slowly, letting the chill settle. She didn't notice the hush until it folded into silence again.

"Mira," Perrin's voice called her back. "You and Nerra will prepare the Queen's chambers. Come with me."

Mira's legs moved before her thoughts caught up. Nerra joined her silently, though Mira noticed the quick flash of surprise, maybe even excitement. They followed the cleric through a narrow arch into the rear sanctum of the altar room. The ceilings dropped low, heavy with soot and time. The scent of rosemary clung to the air, mixing with old smoke and something almost sweet beneath it, like blood long dried.

As they stepped into the quiet of the chamber, Perrin paused and turned to face them, her expression sharper now, edged with warning.

"You must both be respectful," she said, her voice low, each word weighted. "No girlish squeals, no whispered speculation, no foolish excitement. You are not meeting a court beauty. You are serving a sovereign who walks with visions of the future."

"Yes, Cleric," Nerra replied quickly, ducking her head. Mira didn't miss the slight grimace that followed. The rebuke had struck home. Perrin's eyes lingered on her a moment longer before continuing forward, the rustle of her robes brushing the stone floor like a whisper of wind through old trees. Mira caught Nerra's eyes, a small shrug of embarrassment in her expression. Mira only offered a slight nod in return.

The sanctum was lined with tomes and glass jars, all aged and labeled in delicate script. A single iron candle flickered in the far sconce, casting uneasy shadows that stretched like fingers across the floor.

"You are to speak of none of this," Perrin said quietly. "The Queen's needs are... private." Mira's mouth was dry. She only nodded. Perrin's eyes sharpened. "Her chamber in the western wing must be completely blacked out. Every crack is sealed.

Every curtain is heavy. No sunlight." Mira's brow pinched. But she said nothing. "There is a salve. Crushed leaves on a wrap over the eyes. The wrap must be placed with care. No deviations. No questions."

Beside her, Nerra murmured agreement. Mira managed the same. But her thoughts were already tangled. Why complete darkness? Why the eyes?

Perrin moved to the back table and gestured. "Watch carefully." They did. Mira's fingers memorized each motion. The slow crush of dried leaves, the spiral of oil folded into them, the careful smear across the cloth. She watched Nerra apply the wrap to her, the way the ointment stung first, then spread its warmth like a hush beneath her skin.

When it was her turn, her fingers trembled. She steadied them, but her mind wandered.

To this Queen, cloaked in secrecy and shadows, asking to be tended by night, veiled in a chamber with no light.

Mira jumped at Perrin's stern voice. "That oil is spiraling the wrong direction. Again." Mira obeyed.

* * *

The week that followed Perrin's instructions passed in a blur of heavy fabric and quiet tension. Mira's days became a pattern of muted steps and measured movements, of sealing away every stray thread of light from the Queen's appointed chamber. She layered thick black drapes over the narrow windows until the sun could no longer touch the stone. Nerra stitched dark cloth into every seam, wedging it into the cracks where the sun might still sneak through. By the third day, the room felt more like a tomb than a place meant for sleep. Cool, hushed, airless. Like it was holding its breath.

Each morning, she and Nerra repeated the ritual with the ointment and the tonic. The routine grew precise, quiet. Mira found comfort in the rhythm, the grinding of dried herbs into fine powder, the slow pour of warmed oil, the careful wrapping of cloth across closed eyes. They remained silent, not out of reluctance, but because it felt like the respectful thing to do. Even in privacy, it felt as if something in the room listened. Even after the final salve had been smoothed and the Queen's chambers sealed in shadow. But it was the moments in-between her work that weighed on Mira most. The empty corridors, the long walks back to her quarters, the absence of notes from Brahn.

She ate with Tharion most nights, just the two of them, tucked away in quiet corners of the palace. The conversation was soft. Comfortable, even. He laughed sometimes, and so did she. There was warmth there. Familiarity. A rebuilding, slow but real. But when the meal was done, when the tea cooled in their cups and her eyes grew heavy, Tharion would thank her, and leave. He never stayed. He hadn't since the night in Seacliffe. She told herself it was okay. That space was what they needed. That healing wasn't supposed to feel perfect. But some nights, she didn't sleep. A quiet war plagued her, between the safety she found with Tharion and the wildfire memory of Ren. When she was with Tharion, she felt them mending. But with Ren, she had burned.

She didn't see Ren. He was buried behind doors now, council rooms thick with maps and murmuring voices. War tables scattered with parchment and ink, always surrounded, always busy. The weight of his Regency clung to him.

She had turned a corner and there he was, mid-conversation with an advisor. So achingly reminiscent of that moment in the hall. His hair was pulled back, slightly tousled from a long morning. The scent of him hit her before he even reached her. A warm, familiar blend of cedar and clean linen, touched with the faintest trace of ink and smoke. Navigators, it made her heart clench. With Ren, it wasn't an echo of almost memories. It wasn't imagined. It was unmistakably him.

And then he passed her. He didn't even glance in her direction. His eyes moved across the hallway as though she weren't there. As if she were part of the stone. Mira stood still, the breath tight in her chest, the sunlight warming her face but not her skin.

She told herself it was for the best. That rebuilding with Tharion was her choice. She had made this choice. But Mira felt her heart and chest burst into flame at that moment.

This was what the court meant when they called him a heartbreaker. The way he could walk by her with that same quiet intensity, like she no longer reached him at all. As he disappeared down the corridor, swallowed by gold light and the rustle of robes, the fire bloomed wide in her chest. Even though she had made her choice, somehow, it still felt like she was the one being left behind.

The evening of the Queen's arrival settled heavily over the palace, the last light of the sun fading to a deep wash of indigo across the sky. Lanterns had been lit in every corridor, their glow flickering softly against the stone walls. Outside, the wind was cool, the kind that whispered of omens and turning tides. Everyone had gathered in the great hall, pressed close beneath the vaulted ceiling. A sense of anticipation thick in the air.

Mira stood at the front, Tharion beside her, his steady presence anchoring her in place. His hand brushed hers only briefly, a silent reassurance.

At the dais, Ren stood next to the seated Caelric, framed

in the golden light of sconces. He slumped in his throne. A silhouette carved in stillness, but beside the Betrothed's hollow form, Ren radiated life. He wore the formal attire of a blood-borne prince.

Deep navy regalia, almost black, with silver thread tracing the lapels and cuffs in patterns that curled like rivers or smoke. His hair was combed back in that familiar wave, softening the stern lines of his face, though the short stubble across his jaw defied the court's expectation of polished tradition.

Mira's gaze lingered, helpless to look away. There was no smile on his face, only stillness and a tension she recognized as apprehension. The tower bell rang. A deep and resonant, echoing through the hall. Mira felt it in her bones. The great doors at the end of the hall creaked open.

She appeared in the threshold, bathed in the lantern light. The Queen of Myrdathis. Tall and lithe, she moved with a grace that defied age or time. Her hair spilled down her back in a sheet of white silk, catching the glow of the torches shimmering like starlight. She wore a gown of silver and soft blue, translucent veils drifting around her like mist edged with silver so fine it looked like frost. With every step, her robes whispered against the polished floor.

Behind her came only a handful of attendants. No grand entourage, no gilded procession. Just three footmen cloaked in dusk-grey, and one silent woman in a veil of pale blue. That was all. The hall seemed to bend around her as if a thousand had entered. Her presence filled every space, every breath. Like gravity or prophecy. A circlet of silver vines, set with pale stones that didn't simply reflect light, sat atop her head.

Mira watched as she approached. The queen's eyes were what silenced the breath in Mira's throat. Milky white.

Unfocused and yet all-seeing. And in the center of each one, a pinprick of glimmering light, like the last star before dawn. A ripple moved through the crowd. Awe and fear. The Queen passed down the aisle between the lines of attendants and guards, her gaze never faltering, though she looked at no one directly.

As she passed the line of clerics, Mira caught the slight dip of Cleric Perrin's head in a gesture of reverent greeting. Behind her, the acolytes mirrored the motion, bowing in practiced unison. Not a word passed between them, but the gesture spoke volumes.

Recognition. Respect.

At the dais, the Queen paused. Ren stepped forward, and Mira noted the subtle shift in him. The way he bowed low, every movement precise and reverent. Only the Crowned Betrothed stayed motionless, his eyes vacant, his body unmoving. A figurehead on a throne, alive in flesh, but hollow in soul.

Ren straightened and offered his hand. The Queen took it. Her pale fingers slipped into his without hesitation, and Mira's chest tightened. A flicker of heat. Irrational.

Immediate. A spike of jealousy was so sharp it surprised her. Because of the way Ren's head bowed slightly when their fingers met, the care in the gesture, the quiet gravity of it. Mira forced her shoulders still, her breath steady. Jealousy bloomed low and mean behind her ribs as she watched Ren guide the Queen forward into the firelight.

For a heartbeat, her eyes met his, just over the Queen's shoulder. It hit her like lightning. Sharp and blinding, curling beneath her ribs and stealing the air from her lungs. Her heart stuttered, and in the flickering hush of the firelight, she watched as a smallest smile flashed across his face. Just as quickly, it vanished. He steeled himself, gaze shuttering, expression returning to its practiced calm.

Queen Danlea released him, then stepped into the center alone. Her gaze moved across the crowd, not skimming but seeing. As if every soul stood bare before her. When her eyes swept past Mira, it felt like being seen by something ancient.

"I am rarely among you," she said, her voice a soft thread woven with stillness. It was not loud. It didn't need to be. "My place has long been with the seers, with the threads of fate that guide all kingdoms. I have stood apart, offering wisdom when asked, but rarely stepping beyond the borders of Myrdathis. But now, that must change."

A murmur swept through the room, but it didn't last long. Her voice carried over it, a winter wind.

"Kharador has tested you. They have cast a shadow upon Bharalyn, upon all the kingdoms.. their ambitions are a threat too great, a slight too large to be ignored." Her tone deepened. "Myrdathis Seers are visionaries and advisors. Our sight is not only for far-off dreams of men but also for the future of all our kingdoms. We will not stand idle while this darkness spreads. We will lend our wisdom and guidance to Bharalyn." The words didn't echo. They settled. Heavy. Permanent.

Ren stepped forward again, his voice cutting through the silence. "Your words are a beacon in the shadows," he said, his tone rich and steady. "We are grateful for your wisdom and support. Our kingdoms have long stood as allies, but today, you have shown us that our friendship is rooted in more than tradition." Mira watched him speak, pride blooming quietly in her chest. He turned to the gathered crowd, his voice still strong.

"Her Majesty, Queen Danela will meet with the advisory

council to deliberate on our path forward. There is much to consider, and we must ensure every step is measured and true. In one week's time, we will continue with the veiled night celebrations, not as two kingdoms shrouded in darkness, but as allies who embrace the dawn."

A ripple of anticipation swept through the masses. Murmurs of excitement interwoven with nods of agreement. Though uncertainty lingered at the edges, the promise of celebration and unity cast a warm, undeniable glow over the gathering. And yet, beneath it all, a quiet knot tightened in Mira's chest.

What if it wasn't enough?

17

THE PALACE HALLS WERE still in the hours before dawn. Mira and Nerra moved quietly through the dim corridors, their steps hushed against the stone, softened further by the worn rugs beneath their feet.

The Queen's private wing loomed ahead, veiled in shadow and stillness. A fresh, crisp coldness filled the air. A cold that woke the skin rather than numbed it, threaded through the hallways. When they opened the chamber door, it did so soundlessly, revealing a room washed in the faintest silver light. Not from the moon. That had long since set. The glow came from candle flames that shimmered without flickering, suspended in tall glass sconces like starlight caught in crystal. Their light wavered softly across the stone walls, creating shifting, dreamlike patterns that didn't quite stay still.

The Queen stood at the center of the chamber. She was barefoot on the cold floor, her long white hair loose down her back. She wore only a simple robe over her nightdress. Translucent at the edges, trimmed in fine silver thread that caught the strange light and held it. Incense coiled around her, slow and deliberate, the scent of something ancient and herbal, sweet and sharp all at once.

"Come closer, I've been waiting on you both" the Queen said. Her voice was barely more than breath, but it filled the room.

She didn't look at them directly. Her gaze lingered somewhere else, just beyond them, as though she was watching something they couldn't see. Mira stepped forward first, Nerra just behind, their movements instinctively careful. No command passed the Queen's lips, yet silence settled with ease. It wasn't fear that stilled them, but something subtler. The way the air shifted around her, as if drawn to her presence, like it had in the great hall. In her stillness, the room itself seemed to breathe differently.

She lifted her arms with a slow, fluid grace, her long sleeves falling away like mist as she signaled Mira and Nerra forward. They approached in silence, hands practiced, careful. Mira reached for the silken wrap, the fabric catching the candlelight in soft waves. It was nearly weightless, a gossamer veil threaded with pale silver that shimmered like moonlight on water.

Nerra took the small dish of dried herbs from the table, her grip steady as she passed it to Mira. Mira crushed the leaves between her fingers, releasing their scent, rich, earthy, and faintly floral. She scattered the crumbled pieces onto the veil, Nerra poured the warmed oil letting them settle into the weave of the cloth.

"In Myrdathis," the Queen said, her voice quiet and steady, "we slumber beneath the sun and rise beneath the moon. The stars chart our course. Night unveils what day would rather hide." Her words drifted through the room like a lullaby.

Nerra stepped closer, arms outstretched, holding one end of the veil. Mira mirrored her, the wrap suspended between them like the beginning of something sacred. The Queen lowered her head, her long hair spilling forward like strands of silver thread. Together, they raised the cloth, letting the scented fabric pass over her face, covering her eyes.

Mira tied it gently at the back of the Queen's head, careful not to disturb the curtain of hair.

Nerra hesitated, her voice soft but curious. "Does that mean you can never walk in the sun?"

The Queen lifted her head. Her wrap shimmered faintly in the candlelight, silver threads catching every flicker.

"No," she said, "but it is more difficult for us than most. Light distracts. It scatters what is true. The sun can burn away illusions, but it also blinds. In the shadows, things can be clearer. More honest." Mira glanced at Nerra, catching the quiet furrow of her brow, the way she absorbed every word.

Mira looked back at the Queen, "Is that what the wrap is for?" she asked quietly. "To make sure you aren't blinded?"

"In part," the Queen replied, her voice calm but offering no more.

Mira hesitated, sensing the boundary in her tone. She didn't press further. Some truths, it seemed, weren't meant to be shared all at once.

"The stars have always spoken to us," the Queen said. Her head tilted slightly, as though listening to something only she could hear. "Each constellation holds a story. Each shadow, a whisper. We honor them by keeping our eyes open to the night and our hearts attuned to what lies just beyond."

Mira watched Nerra as she hesitated before asking. Her voice quiet, careful. "Does everyone in Myrdathis see what you do, Your Grace? Are all your people... gifted?"

The Queen's lips curved, a soft expression that seemed both warm and far away. "Please," she said, her voice drifting like smoke. "Call me Danlea. Titles build walls, and I do not need to distance myself from either of you."

Mira and Nerra exchanged a glance, both nodding, though the shift unsettled them. There was something intimate about it, something disarming.

Danlea turned back to the veiled candlelight. "To answer

you Nerra, No," she continued, her tone even and precise. "The gift of true sight is rare. Some are born with a flicker, a dream, a fleeting echo. Others see nothing at all. But those who are chosen," her fingers traced a slow arc through the air, "carry the weight of that vision for a lifetime."

She paused. The silence stretched. Her hands moved gently, sketching shapes as if threading unseen constellations between them.

"In Myrdathis, we do not choose our royalty through lineage or courtly favor. A vision comes. A knowing. It may be a name spoken in sleep, or a face seen through the veil of time. And when the stars demand it, the mantle passes."

Nerra furrowed her brow, trying to process the meaning. But Mira, watching the way Danlea navigated through silence like it was her native language, she felt something shift.

"You already know who will succeed you," Mira said softly, almost to herself. Danlea turned slightly away from her.

The candlelight caught the gleam in her strange, opalescent eyes. "The stars have shown me many things, Mira," she said. "But the future is not a single road. It bends, it branches. To see is not to know with certainty, but to hold a candle to the mist."

Her words hung in the air, weighty and delicate. Mira felt a chill slide down her spine, as if something ancient had reached out to brush against her skin. The candle flames shivered, their light dancing on the walls, and for a heartbeat, it seemed as if the entire room breathed with them. Nerra's eyes flicked to the shifting shapes, her confusion deepening, but Mira remained still.

"Are you... uncertain of the vision?" Nerra asked

hesitantly. Danlea's smile softened, a trace of sorrow pulling at the corners of her mouth.

"Truth is never whole without uncertainty beside it," she said. "Even the brightest star is veiled by clouds from time to time." The Queen's head tilted slightly, the curve of her neck graceful and exposed. "I know the staging of what is to come, but the pieces shift, just as shadows do. Like standing in a doorway with one foot in each room, never fully in one or the other." Danlea looked at Nerra. "You would understand that, being raised at the border."

Nerra's hands stilled, the scent of crushed herbs still clung to her fingers. "Yes," she whispered. "Where Bharalyn, Kharador, and Lyren meet. My family traded between the lands."

A soft hum rose from Danlea, deep and knowing. "You are a child of three. Each one in your bones, each one whispering something different." The Queen tilted her head slightly, the silver threads of her wrap catching the flickering light. "It is a good thing. They will help you know where to stand in the days coming." The Queen sighed, a breath that seemed to carry the weight of dreams. Nerra's brow furrowed, but she said nothing.

Mira's hands fell to her sides, the ritual complete, yet something in her chest whispered they had only just brushed the edge of understanding. And they had only glimpsed what lay beneath.

"Thank you," Danlea whispered. Whether it was meant for them or for the silent forces that filled the chamber, Mira could not tell. "You may go now. I need a few moments of sleep to adjust to walking in the light."

They withdrew in silence, the door clicking shut behind them with a sound that felt more like a seal than a dismissal.

The cool air of the corridor met them like a breath of reality. Mira felt the stone beneath her shoes. It was too solid, too cold. The palace was too bright, even cloaked in the early shadows of dawn.

The corridor had warmed slightly with the stirring breath of morning. Lanterns guttered low on their hooks as the palace slowly came to life around them, the hush of candlelight giving way to the distant clatter of kitchens and the rustle of attendants beginning their rounds.

Mira and Nerra retraced their steps through the winding hall that led to the altar chamber. The stone beneath their feet felt less cold now, the path familiar, though the memory of Danlea's strange, starlit presence still clung to their skin like smoke.

"What is she?" Nerra asked. Her voice carried not just curiosity, but awe and fear. Mira reached out, brushing her fingertips against the smooth wall beside them.

"I don't know," she said slowly. "She's a queen, but something in her feels older than that. Something Ancient"

Nerra turned slightly, her expression unreadable, the flickering torchlight catching in her eyes. " But how does someone come to be like that? To know so much without being told?"

Mira's lips parted. She let the silence stretch a moment longer before answering. "I don't know..." They reached a quiet fork in the hallway. Mira paused. The moment pressed at her chest, the weight of Danlea's presence still lingering.

Nerra shivered, her hands tucked into her sleeves. "Do you think she sees us?" she asked. "Not just the surface, but... deeper?"

"Yes," Mira said. And she meant it. "And not just who we are. What the kingdoms might become."

The words landed gently between them. Nerra's breath caught, and her hand drifted free of her cloak. Mira took it, fingers warm against the cool of the corridor, anchoring them both.

The sanctum was quieter than usual, steeped in the soft haze of early morning light. Mira and Nerra stepped back into its cool embrace, the scent of lavender and old incense still lingering in the air. Streaks of rose and gold filtered through the narrow stained-glass windows, painting the stone floor in fractured hues as the sky outside slowly lightened.

Cleric Perrin stood at the center of the room, her white robes motionless, as if she had been standing there since before dawn. She turned at the sound of their footsteps, her eyes as calm and sharp as ever, her veil catching a glint of light from the altar candles.

"How did you fare?" she said simply, then let her gaze rest on Nerra for a breath longer than necessary.

Nerra straightened instinctively, hands clasping before her. "Well. I didn't speak out of turn."

Perrin's lips curved, just barely. "Good. She is not a spectacle." Nerra nodded again, more earnestly this time, understanding the correction had been both a reminder and a kindness.

Perrin's attention shifted to Mira. "And you?"

Mira gave a measured nod. "The rites were performed without error. The wrap was successful. The Queen seemed… satisfied."

Perrin studied her for a moment, then nodded. Well done, both of you" With the briefest of gestures, she motioned for Nerra. "You're to assist the kitchens this morning," she said, voice low but clear. "Check the spice stores. Some of the imported stock has turned, and we can't recover it.”

“Yes, Cleric,” Nerra replied quickly.

Perrin gave a brief smile, almost approving, then turned to Mira. “You, Mira, will begin cataloguing the oldest of our texts. The archives need restructuring, and I expect you to find the errors no one else has bothered to correct.”

Mira inclined her head. “Of course, Cleric.”

“Off with you then,” Perrin said, already turning back to her prayers, her robes trailing across the floor.

Mira and Nerra exchanged a glance. Nerra offered a small, grateful smile before slipping from the sanctum toward the kitchens. Mira lingered only a second longer before making her way to the library, the scent of incense still clinging to her skin.

✳ ✳ ✳

Mira spent the rest of her day in the library, the cool, dusty air a welcome contrast to the heat of her thoughts. The high shelves loomed over her, their spines worn and gilded, a forest of stories and secrets.

She moved between them with quiet steps, her fingers grazing the leather-bound tomes, but her mind was miles away. Mira tried to focus on the pages in front of her, but the words blurred, slipping through her thoughts like mist. She searched for the book Ren had once shown her, the one filled with myths and visions of the Navigators, but it remained elusive, tucked away or spirited into some deeper corner.

The sound of light footsteps interrupted her thoughts.

“I got sent to the kitchens first,” Harwen said, brushing flour from her sleeve. “Apparently I’m terrible at slicing turnips."

Mira let out a quiet breath of laughter. "Seems you're better suited to ink than knives, then."

Harwen's smile lingered for a moment, then faded. She glanced around the dim library, taking in the towering shelves, the thin sunlight filtering through the tall windows. They fell into companionable silence for a while, sorting scrolls, cataloguing spines, documenting fading names with careful and precise lettering.

After a time, Harwen spoke again, her voice quieter, more deliberate. "My sister lives near the southern cliffs. Just beyond Seacliffe."

Mira looked up. Harwen didn't meet her gaze. She kept her eyes on the stack of books between them, her fingers absently smoothing a crease in the parchment.

"She's got two little ones. Bright-eyed, always hungry, always laughing. Their father... he didn't come home from the water last spring." Mira's heart ached for Harwen's family.

"I told her I'd found work. Said I was hired on as a governess to a merchant family." Harwen's mouth curled, wry and tired. "Safe. Quiet. She thinks I'm somewhere warm, teaching arithmetic by a fire with a cat in my lap." She hesitated, then added softly, "But it was Brahn who brought me here."

Mira stilled. Harwen's voice remained steady, but there was something fierce beneath it now. "I wanted to do more. To fight for something better than scraps. For them. For my nephews. I thought… maybe here, I could help shape the world they'll grow up in."

Mira caught Harwen's eye. "You did what you could, Harwen. That's more than most and sometimes, that's exactly what starts the change."

18

THE ALTAR CHAMBER WAS not as she remembered it. It pulsed with wrongness, a thick, humming silence beneath a sky that was not a sky at all. The windows were tall and arched, but outside, there was no light, only a wall of shifting gray, as if the world had been erased. Dust hung in the air like ash, unmoving, as though even time had forgotten how to pass.

The murals above had changed. The Navigators were smeared beyond recognition, eyes gouged out, mouths frozen mid-scream. One raised a hand. She wasn't alone. The door had closed behind her, not with sound, but with a sensation. Like bone splintering in water.

She turned, but there was no door anymore, only stone. Ahead, a figure stood at the altar, tall and unmoving, cloaked in shadow. His face was obscured, a blur of familiarity.

"You came," he said. The words were not spoken. They arrived in her head, heavy and cold.

She tried to speak, but her tongue was heavy with soot. He raised a hand. She followed. Down a corridor that bent where it shouldn't. The walls throbbed with power.

Books lined the shelves, whispering in languages she did not know, their spines shifting each time she tried to read them. Her name rippled across a thousand covers.

A pedestal waited in the center. The book atop it was bound in blackened leather, stitched shut with gold thread. A heartbeat-like pulse throbbed in its spine. The thread unraveled. Pages opened of their own accord.

"You will restore this," the voice echoed in her head. *"Don't"* she whispered, though she didn't know when she'd started crying.

He stepped closer. His eyes caught fire. The flames leapt to hers. She screamed, but the sound never reached her ears. Her lungs filled with smoke. The book snapped shut with a sound like thunder. The light fractured, and the ground gave way.

* * *

Grass beneath her fingers. Cold dew on her bare feet. Mira sat up with a sharp gasp and the dream shattered like glass around her. Her chest rose and fell in frantic bursts, her skin slick with sweat despite the chill in the air. Her lungs ached as she tried to draw a breath that didn't taste of ash.

But there was no fire here. Only the garden. Wide and quiet. The soft hush of early dawn lay over it like a blanket, the trees touched with silver-blue light. The scent of wet earth and morning jasmine filled her lungs, and it steadied her, little by little. Her fingers clenched against the damp grass. Real. Cool. Alive. She was outside. The palace loomed behind her, cloaked in shadow.

She didn't remember walking here. Her nightdress clung to her legs, soaked from the grass and sweat. Her hands trembled, but she could feel them now. Feel the tremor and not just the terror. Above, the sky stretched wide and velvet-dark, stitched with stars. The moon hung low, a silver arc caught between the palace spires.

Mira stood slowly, her knees unsteady, her breath still uneven. She crossed her arms around herself, holding the heat of her own skin. The silence wrapped around her like fog. But the garden was not empty. Queen Danlea sat alone beneath a tree, the branches clawing gently at the sky. She rested on a stone bench, posture relaxed but regal, a figure untouched by fear or night. A velvet cloak spilled around her, dark as the sky, its silver embroidery gleaming faintly in the starlight. She did not look over, but her voice drifted through the hush, calm and sure.

"You'll catch your death, standing there like that." Danlea turned slightly, lifting one side of her cloak and holding it open with a quiet invitation. "Come sit with me. There is enough warmth for two."

Mira hesitated, her breath fogging in the air. But then her feet moved, slowly. She stepped into the clearing and lowered herself onto the bench.

The cloak fell around her shoulders, and it was warmer than she'd expected. The scent of orchids and old parchment wrapped around her. They sat in silence for a while, the hush between them filled only with the soft rustle of leaves and the distant coo of a morning bird somewhere in the trees. The palace behind them remained still, its looming shadow forgotten under the soft weight of dawn.

Danlea's voice came again, low and level, but not unkind. "Do you need clarity?"

Mira's fingers curled into the velvet. She stared at the crushed grass between her bare feet, the dew like cold silver threading over her skin. The words hovered just behind her teeth, sharp and trembling, begging to be released. But what if speaking them made them real? What if, once they left her mouth, they couldn't be taken back?

Mira swallowed, then said, almost too quietly, "I had a dream..."

Danlea gaze was still on the trees, on the pale streaks of

light curling over the palace eaves.

"It was the altar chamber," Mira said. Danlea turned her head a fraction. "But it wasn't how I remember it. Everything was… wrong. Her voice dropped. "There was something waiting for me." Mira looked down at her hands. "What if it wasn't a dream? What if it was a memory? And if it was…?" Then, gently, Danlea took Mira's cheek and turned her face toward her, careful, deliberate, her milky eyes penetrating her soul.

"Why do you question your choices?"

Mira swallowed, her throat dry despite the cool air. The weight of that gaze made it impossible to lie, even to herself.

"Sometimes it feels like I'm not choosing at all," she said. "Like I'm just… drifting. Pushed forward because I can't remember why I started. Why I said yes. Why I would have."

The Queen's presence was a strange contradiction, calm and quiet, yet impossibly vast. There was no judgment in her voice, no pressure in her stillness. Only space. And in that space, Mira felt something soften in her chest. She realized, suddenly, how easy it was to speak with her.

Danlea didn't look away. "Then trust who you are now," she said softly. "Even if the past is unclear. Even if the reasons haven't come back yet."

Mira's lip trembled. Danlea's expression didn't change, but her posture shifted. Her shoulders dipped slightly, a subtle uncoiling, as though she, too, had once known that feeling. The garden remained still, the hush of dawn stretching out between words like threads waiting to be woven.

"You don't need every memory to know yourself," Danlea said. "You're still choosing. Every moment of who you are now."

Mira closed her eyes. Let the words settle. Let the cloak

hold her steady. And for the first time in what felt like days, she let herself lean. Just a little. Just enough to feel the warmth of another person beside her.

They walked back through the quiet corridors in silence, the hush of early morning pressing gently around them like fog. The palace had not fully woken yet, its torches dimmed and windows silvered with the last traces of dawn. Mira's footsteps were soft against the stones, the hem of her damp nightdress catching slightly at her ankles.

Beside her, the Queen moved with quiet grace, the sweep of her cloak around Mira's shoulders whispering with every step. Mira had been in awe that previous morning, intimidated, uncertain, every word she spoke measured twice. And yet now, walking in silence beside her, wrapped in the Queen's warmth, she felt… safe. At ease. It confused her, this sudden comfort, this quiet trust blooming in the space between them. But she wasn't ungrateful for it. Just unsure how something so soft had settled into her chest so quickly. Danlea did not press her. She did not demand it. She simply walked, steady and unshaken, like someone who had already seen the road ahead and knew there was time.

They reached Danlea's chambers just as the palace began to stir. Nerra was waiting inside, already at the small preparation table, laying out the wrap and herbal dish with practiced hands. She looked up as the door opened, her eyes widening slightly at the sight of the Queen beside Mira, but she dipped her head without question. Danlea stepped aside, allowing Mira to cross the room.

Together, they finished the ritual in silence. Mira lifted the softened cloth, infused with the crushed herbs and oils and Nerra gently guided the Queen to sit. With deft, careful fingers, Mira wrapped the veil over Danlea's eyes, letting the scent of sage and ashwood bloom gently through the air.

Danlea leaned back slightly. "You are learning, both of you. You needn't judge yourselves so harshly. " she said softly. Mira felt those simple words settle inside her like warmth in her chest.

"I'll leave you to rest," she murmured.

Nerra stepped forward before Mira could gather the cloth. "I'll clean up," she offered, her voice quiet but steady.

Mira gave her a small, grateful nod, then slipped from the room, the heavy door closing with a quiet click behind her. For a moment, the hush of the garden still clung to her, like the last breath of a dream not yet gone. The velvet warmth of the Queen's cloak still ghosted her shoulders. As she turned toward the corridor, she felt her bare feet felt the cold stone. The damp fabric clinging to her calves. She froze, heart stuttering.

The hallway ahead was empty, but sunlight was creeping in through the tall windows, gilding the stone floor in pale gold. Light enough to reveal her. Light enough that if anyone came around the corner now... embarrassment rushed to her face, a flush rising from her neck to her cheeks. Navigators. She'd left her chambers like this.

Wandered the palace halls in nothing but her nightdress, barefoot. She wrapped her arms around herself, shoulders hunching slightly as she turned down a quieter passage, keeping close to the wall. Each footstep felt like a shout now. The silence didn't feel gentle anymore, it felt watchful.

Tharion's rooms were closer. Her feet moved before she thought, her hand rising to knock against the carved wood. The sound was soft, but the door opened almost immediately.

He stood, bleary-eyed, shirt half-laced, dark hair still

tousled from sleep. Whatever greeting he'd meant to offer died the moment his gaze dropped, then jerked away just as fast. He turned his head sharply, jaw tightening, the tips of his ears flushing dark.

"Mira," his voice caught. He cleared his throat, staring hard at the door frame. "What... what are you doing out like that?"

She opened her mouth, then shut it again. He avoided looking at her. Disappointment flared low in her chest.

"I didn't mean to," she muttered, arms folding tighter around herself. "I woke up outside. Near the garden. It... it wasn't on purpose."

Tharion nodded, still not meeting her eyes. "It's early. Most of the halls will be empty. Just hold on."

He stepped back inside, returning with a thick robe draped over one arm. Soft wool, lined in dark velvet. He held it out to her without looking, keeping his gaze turned. She slipped it on quickly, grateful for the warmth, though it didn't soften the embarrassment fully.

"Thank you." At that, he finally looked at her. Just a glance, quick and cautious. "Come on," he said, stepping into the hall. "I'll walk you back." They walked in silence. His steps were careful beside hers, protective in the way she remembered from Anyerit and Seacliffe. He didn't ask what had woken her. And she didn't offer.

As they rounded the final corridor toward her wing, Mira heard the low murmur of voices ahead. Footsteps, measured and deliberate, the scrape of boots on polished stone. She stiffened before she even saw them. Tharion sensed it too, because he shifted subtly, stepping just half a pace in front of her. Protective. Not possessive. But enough to shield.

A group of advisors turned the corner. Ren walked at the

center. A scroll half-unfurled in his hand, his voice calm and clipped as he spoke. He was dressed for court, for duty. He stopped walking the moment he saw her. The words died in his throat. His gaze flicked over her, Tharion's robe around her, the mess of her hair, the faint smudge of dreaming still lingering across her face.

Mira felt the flush rise, hot and immediate. She didn't need a mirror to know what she looked like. Tharion didn't break stride. He simply moved a fraction faster than her, his shoulder angling to block Ren's view as if by accident. But it was too late. Ren was already looking. Not with judgment. Not even with surprise. Just that unbearable, unmistakable heartbreak. Like gravity had decided she was the center of his orbit after all, but she was already gone.

Longing twisted in her stomach, but something else stirred beneath it. An almost irresistible pull, old and sharp and terribly familiar. Sunlight streamed through a high, colored window, casting fractured golds and reds across the floor. The warmth wrapped around her like a balm, brushing against the chill still clinging to her skin, and Mira straightened without meaning to. She didn't look back. Didn't give Ren the satisfaction of another glance. Instead, she walked the rest of the way to her door beside Tharion, chin lifted. Inside her chest, her heart thundered like a secret. And behind her, she felt Ren's stare linger like a touch.

✳ ✳ ✳

As they reached her door, Tharion paused beside her, his eyes sweeping the corridor out of habit, ever watchful. The morning sun caught the edge of his profile, gilding the soft edges of his tired expression. She turned toward him, her hand resting lightly on the doorframe.

"Thank you," she said quietly, voice just above a whisper.

Tharion gave a small shrug, one corner of his mouth tipping up. "You'd do the same for me."

"I am sure that I have, even if we can't remember," she teased, the hint of a smile breaking through the lingering haze of her dream.

For a moment, they just stood there. Not in silence exactly, but in a kind of calm. The kind only shared by people who had faced worse things together and walked through it still standing. He looked down at her, his gaze steady, not searching, not asking for anything more. Just... seeing her. For what she was in that moment. Rumpled, shaken, barefoot.

"Sleepwalking?" he said, voice lighter now. "That's a new one   you're okay now?" he said. Not quite a question. Not quite a statement.

Mira nodded, fingers resting lightly over the robe's lapels. "I'm alright." His expression softened. He gave a small nod, then stepped back into the hallway.

As she slipped inside and closed the door, she let her forehead rest against the cool wood for a heartbeat longer. The quiet of her chambers folded around her like a blanket, dim and still, the morning light just beginning to warm the stone floors. She leaned against the door, the robe still wrapped around her, fingers curled in the thick wool as if it could anchor her there at this moment. In this choice. If it was a choice.

Tharion had come when she needed him. He always did. He was steady, kind, patient in ways that soothed the frayed edges of her. A calm she hadn't known she was starved for. It made sense to be with him. She could picture a future. A safe one. But as she stood there, the warmth of his presence already fading, a quiet tug crept back into her chest.

She peeled away the robe and nightdress, folding them neatly despite her distraction. Her bare feet padded across the stone to the warm bathing pool, steam curling up in soft tendrils beckoning her in. She slipped beneath the surface slowly, the heat enveloping her like a second skin. It eased the tightness in her muscles, smoothed the raw edges of the night. She sank lower until only her face remained above the surface, eyes staring up at the carved stone ceiling. Her heart beat steadily beneath the water, but her mind wouldn't quiet.

Tharion offered her something safe, something dependable. But Ren was fire. She didn't want him to be but even when she turned away, the spark of him never quite went out.

She hated herself for it. How her thoughts still lingered on the sound of his voice, the weight of his gaze, the way her pulse leapt when they had locked eyes in the great hall.

She dried off, dressed quickly. A simple dark green dress. Her hands moved with quiet purpose. By the time she stepped out into the hall, the palace hummed with activity. The day was already moving. Mira walked forward, but her heart remained behind, caught somewhere between the comfort of what could be, and the fire of what still might.

Hallways echoed with the sound of moving feet and low conversations, banners catching the wind from open windows. Mira made her way toward the altar, weaving through the growing rhythm of the day. She found Cleric Perrin at her worktable, surrounded by scrolls, half-used ink pots, and several open books. Her sleeves were rolled, her hair tied back in a loose knot, and she looked up through her veil only briefly when Mira approached.

"You're earlier than I expected," Perrin remarked, though her tone held no annoyance, only surprise.

"Nerra cleaned up for me." Mira said simply.

Perrin studied her for a moment, then nodded to herself and returned to scribbling something into a ledger.

"Good. The gardens need attention." Mira blinked. "The gardens?"

"Specifically the reflecting pool," Perrin clarified, not looking up. "The leaves are clogging the stone beds, and the water's begun to scum over." Mira nodded. "I understand."

"Good," Perrin murmured, already moving on to the next line of script. "Take the gloves from the lower hooks. And Mira." She paused, finally lifting her eyes. "Don't rush."

Mira nodded her head, then turned toward the door. The stone hallway felt cooler somehow, the weight of the morning settling around her shoulders like the memory of velvet. And outside, the light continued to rise.

✳ ✳ ✳

Mira's hands had been wrist-deep in the cold waters all day. The last water-lilies of the season brushed her fingers, fragile as breath, as she trimmed back into the overgrowth. Silverleaf vines coiled like serpents across the shallows, their roots tangling in the stone beds. The day had been crisp with a hint of autumn's chill, but as the sun began to set, its last rays still gently warmed her neck and the backs of her hands. The air smelled of damp leaves and mint, the sweet decline of fading summer buried beneath it. She moved methodically, letting the sounds of the palace stir around her, boots scuffing stone, the soft clatter of buckets, voices rising and falling in the rhythm of routine. It was the background. Noise she had long since learned to ignore. Until a name cleaved through it.

"Hallen…" someone whispered.

Mira froze. Her fingers curled involuntarily around a lily, crushing the petals. White bruised into pink. The bloom floated free in the rippling surface, a small, broken thing drifting on the water.

"The Kharador's came in the night," said Harwen, voice hushed and frayed, as though speaking it too loud might summon the same fate. Her sleeves were pushed to her elbows, arms dusted with flour. "Fires. Screams. The whole town's gone." Mira didn't move.

"They slipped through like smoke," Garrick added, stooping beside a cart of mulch, his gnarled hands stained with earth. "No alarm. No warning. Just... gone."

The name thudded in Mira's chest again, and this time it dragged something with it. A memory. The Festival of the Final Sun. Velvet and wine and laughter sharp as crystal. She hadn't paid attention. A noble's bored murmur. Her mind twisted around the edges of the memory, fingers searching for the seams.

A whisper, half-drowned by music and clinking glasses. Someone had mentioned the Hollow, offhand, careless. She couldn't place the voice, not clearly, but it had been male. Sharp. Familiar. A laugh edged in cruelty. She felt the cold of realization crawling up her spine. If someone had fed the Kharador information, if someone had marked Hallen's Reach for ruin, then it had come from within the palace. She stood, water dripping from her hands, her breath shallow.

She moved fast, weaving between the hedgerows and

garden walls, her damp hands leaving ghostly prints on sun-warmed stone. Her pulse beat too loud. She reached the palace doors just as a pair of guards passed her, but neither stopped her. The cold marble of the hallway hit her like a slap. She paused, just for a breath.

She should warn someone. Ren flickered at the edge of her thoughts. A gnawing unease settled. Ren, who stood at council tables. Voice calm, eyes sharper than steel. Ren, who had always asked the right questions. The kind that left no doubt. The kind that carved the truth out of silence. But what if that wasn't all he carved? A Regent bore the weight of choices that protected the many not the few.

Her breath snagged in her throat as the thought formed fully. What if Hallen hadn't fallen? What if it had been strategically unprotected? Mira rushed through the halls, the cold marble under her feet echoing the drumbeat of her heart. Past the carved pillars, past the tapestries, past the whispers that clung to the edges of the halls like smoke.

Brahn had told her to speak to Dren, the Kharador officer. He'd told her what to wear. What to say. Tell him we'll be in Harrow's Hollow. Harrows Hollow, the nearest trade route to Hallen. Her mouth went dry.

Not they. We. Mira stopped short in the middle of the corridor. She hadn't given Dren a lie, she hadn't fed him misdirection. She'd confirmed a plan. Brahn's plan. He hadn't needed to tell her more. He'd counted on her not to ask. On her loyalty. On her belief in him. He'd used her voice like a knife, her body like a lure. Dren had taken the bait, and Mira had smiled while he swallowed it.

And Hallen had burned. She gripped the edge of a stone archway, fingers digging into the carved sigils like they could anchor her to this moment, to this realization that bloomed sharp and hot behind her ribs. Brahn had set her up.

19

MIRA FOUND BRAHN in the kitchens, past the quiet corridor where the scent of morning bread and spice masked tension better than any soldier's steel. He was already speaking low to a pair of cloaked couriers. Sharp-eyed men who blended into stone and shadow too easily. One accepted a scroll, nodded once, and slipped through the side door. The other moved past her without a word.

Brahn looked up when he saw her. Not surprised. Not cautious. Just calm. As if he had expected her.

"You heard," he said simply. Mira nodded, her face carefully composed.

"Harrow's Hollow." Her voice held just the right amount of shaken, just the right breathlessness.

Brahn nodded once, sleeves rolled to the elbow, forearms dusted with flour. "We've already sent people. Quiet ones. They'll move the survivors. Shelter beyond the river." He didn't look up from the dough he was folding. "Kharador hit harder than expected. But they didn't stay. Just swept through."

Mira stepped closer, letting the fire's warmth brush her skin, but the chill inside her had nothing to do with the cold.

"I know who attacked," she said softly. "That's not what I'm here for." Brahn turned his head to look at her. Carefully. Measured.

She met his gaze, steady as she could. "Who told them Hallen would be undefended?" The pause was slight, but it was there.

Brahn's mouth pulled tight. "I don't know." Too fast. Too even.

Mira tilted her head, softening her tone. Feigning uncertainty. "But you have guesses."

"Of course I do," he snapped, heat rising just enough to mask the deflection. "Someone let the Kharador through. Someone who knew how to cover their tracks. And you think it's not from inside? You think it's not someone who walks these halls?"

He turned, pacing now, not toward her, but away, so she wouldn't see his face. Because that slip, that moment, it was enough. It was too smooth. Too practiced. She schooled her expression, watching him carefully from the corner of her eye as he continued his tirade.

"We've got a court full of silk-draped snakes," he muttered, fists clenched. "And a Regent too blind to see them. And the Betrothed? Decorative. He's practically an Ornamental." A bitter scoff. "If either of them had done more than pose for paintings, Hallen might still be standing right now."

Mira's anger flared hot and tight in her chest. He had known. Not just known. Expected. He wasn't upset that Hallen had fallen. He was angry it had fallen too soon. And that meant he had planned for it to fall. Mira stayed quiet. Let him talk. Let him reveal himself.

"This didn't happen by accident," he said, voice low and burning. "Someone made a deal. Someone traded lives for favor. And unless we find out who, more villages will burn."

Mira almost flinched. He was still pretending. Still playing both sides, still casting himself as the vigilant hero, the only one willing to fight fire with fire. And all the while, he was the one holding the match. The kitchen door creaked open. Torvyn rushed in like the shifting of a tide, quiet and inevitable. His gaze landed on Brahn instantly, a sharp read, the kind that didn't need words.

"Enough," he said, cool and precise. "These walls are not soundproof. We lose more than a village if you can't keep quiet." Brahn stilled. Mira watched the shift in him like a blade slipping into its sheath. Not cooled. Controlled.

His next words were smoother, tailored. "We've already begun. Quiet rescues. No banners. No approval needed." Brahn turned back to her, a gleam in his eyes like polished brass. And Mira saw him, truly saw it. There was no guilt in his eyes. No mask at all. He wasn't hiding because he didn't think he had to. He thought she didn't know.

She swallowed hard, and looked to Torvyn. He didn't know. She was sure of it now. He didn't know what Brahn had done, what he had allowed. What he had planned.

He was still standing in the dark, thinking they were on the same side. She couldn't tell him. Torvyn had always believed in people like Brahn. He believed in loyalty. In love. If she told him now, if she stripped that belief away too quickly, she would be the one he blamed. Mira didn't know if she could be the one to break his heart.

"Discretion is survival," Torvyn said, folding his cloak over a chair. Brahn nodded. "The people will remember who helped them. Not who waited for permission."

Mira kept her expression neutral. Her fingers curled around the edge of the long prep table, steadying herself as her chest tightened. He thought she was still a part of it. Still his tool.

Brahn stepped closer, lowering his voice like a conspirator. "Smile for them. Sit in their circles. Someone betrayed us, Mira. But they're not in the shadows. They're right in front of us."

Mira's heart slammed in her chest. She let out a soft breath, like a sigh of agreement and nodded. Let him believe she was still caught in his game.

Mira left the kitchens with her pulse thudding in her ears, Brahn's voice still hot in her mind. His certainty. His strategy. His ambition masked as duty. It coiled around her ribs like a snare. But even knowing Brahn had wanted Hallen to fall, it had still fallen early. If someone had given Hallen to the Kharadorians ahead of Brahn's plan, then it had come from someone in power. She needed to know it wasn't Ren.

Her steps quickened through the palace's corridors. The sunlight through the stained- glass windows cast fractured colors across the stone. She followed it upward, toward the observatory. If Ren had given the order, then   Mira pushed the thought down. He wouldn't have.

✳ ✳ ✳

Mira hesitated at the arched doorway, her fingers brushing the cool stone as she peered inside. The observatory was dimly lit, a hush settling over the space like a held breath. The mechanical orrery stood like a sentinel in the center of room, and amidst moved a familiar figure in flowing white robes, each step a study in grace and precision.

"Cleric Perrin," Mira called softly. She turned. Her pale eyes, sharp and unwavering, settled on her.

"Mira?" she said, quiet surprise threading her voice. "You are supposed to be at the reflecting pool?"

Mira stepped inside, the stone cool beneath her feet, the air thick with the faint scent of old parchment and polished brass. "I was... I" Mira fumbled, grasping for something. "I was hoping to find Torvyn."

Perrin's expression remained measured, though the edges of her veil shifted slightly as she tilted her head toward a brass astrolabe. Her fingers, gloved and steady, brushed a fine layer of dust from its etched rings.

"He was here. But the council has since adjourned for the Veiled Night Celebrations tomorrow." Her voice carried no judgment, but Mira could hear the suspicion.

Mira nodded, her pulse a steady thrum in her ears. Ren's quarters were in the north wing, close to the council chamber. If he had returned there, she needed to find him before he attended the Celebrations.

"Thank you, Cleric Perrin." Mira turned toward the door, the faintest echo of her footsteps swallowed by the thick stone walls. But before she could cross the threshold, Perrin's voice stopped her.

"Mira." Her tone was softer now, almost laced with curiosity, but never without control. "Is something wrong?"

Mira hesitated, her hand grazing the cold frame of the door. Perrin had been a mentor once. A friend, maybe. But now? She wasn't sure where she stood, or who she could trust. The truth hovered, unspoken.

Instead, she offered a smile. Thin. Measured. "Everything is fine. I just...need to see him." Perrin's pale eyes lingered on her a moment longer, veiled and unreadable. Then she dipped her head, graceful and composed.

"Very well." She didn't press, but Mira felt the weight of her gaze even after she'd turned away. It wasn't a lie. She was looking for someone.

The halls stretched before her, narrow and winding, the sconces casting long fingers of shadow along the stone. Her boots whispered over the polished floors, and with every step, her heart beat harder against her ribs. She felt the pull of urgency, a thread winding tighter, drawing her toward Ren's quarters.

Mira reached the double doors and paused. The dark wood was carved with intricate patterns, vines and Tahla leaves entwined around the frame. She reached for the handle, but the faint echo of footsteps caused her to snap back, her instincts pulling her into the alcove just beyond the archway to hide.

She pressed herself against the wall, breath shallow, eyes half-closed as the sounds drew closer. The cool stone bit into her back, grounding her as her pulse thundered in her ears. She hadn't meant to eavesdrop. She'd followed the echo of familiar voices by instinct, by need. But now, rooted in place, she couldn't move.

Ren's voice cut through the quiet first, a low murmur that sent a shiver down her spine. "You think she knows?"

"Not yet," Tharion replied, his voice steady but edged with something she couldn't name. "But she's getting close."

The words dropped like stones into still water, sending Mira's thoughts scattering in every direction. She, they were talking about her. A flicker of anger sparked behind her ribs, low and hot. Her? Like she was a threat.

"You were supposed to protect her," Ren continued, his voice dropping to a low, urgent whisper that lost none of its intensity. "Not let her stumble blindly into the jaws of this."

Her breath caught.

"I've done what I can. Do you think it's easy? She has her own mind, Ren. She always has." Tharion's muttered.

"Don't you think I know that? Her mind is not the point," Ren hissed.

Mira's stomach twisted. The words were wrong in his mouth, like chains wrapped in velvet. Her mind. Her choices. When had she become a burden to manage?

Tharion's voice strained "I thought you wanted her to remember."

Mira bit down on the inside of her cheek, the sharp sting of pain anchoring her to the moment. Blood bloomed on her tongue, copper and salt. Silence stretched between the men, thick and suffocating. She could almost see them through the wall, Ren's fists clenched at his sides, Tharion's jaw tight with frustration. The air around them burned with tension.

"She made her choice," Ren said finally. His voice was quieter now, but no less absolute. "In the end, it should be her to choose..."

Mira's thoughts spun, untethered. Choose what? Choose to remember? Choose to restore whatever her dream meant? To choose him? The weight of their words pressed against her lungs. They were keeping this from her. Something dangerous. She could feel it, like the edge of a blade sliding under her skin.

"Trust takes time to rebuild and we're not there yet," Tharion admitted, voice rough. "Not after... everything."

"That's on you." Ren snapped.

Mira's fists curled at her sides. The heat of her fury built slowly, creeping up her spine. Why was Ren giving Tharion orders about her?

"You think this is all on me?" Tharion said, voice low. "You've been playing your own game with her since the start of this." Ren didn't answer.

Mira heard Tharion take a step forward, "You keep talking about what she should choose, but everything you do pushes her toward the outcome you want." Ren's breath hitched.

His voice came out hoarse, barely more than a whisper but sharp with feeling. "Of course I am."

His words bloomed in Mira's chest. Sudden and bright, like warmth catching flame in a cold room.

Ren continued, "Because it's my fault. All of it. And if I don't guide her... if I don't try to protect her, she'll get hurt again."

A rush of something fierce and breathless surged through Mira. Relief, maybe, at hearing him speak with such raw protectiveness. But it twisted almost instantly, turning sour. They were going inside now. She heard the door creak, their voices dimming as it shut behind them. Still talking. Still deciding. About her. Without her. Like she was something to manage, to protect, to control. Her hands trembled.

It was Ren's fault. The words landed like a blow, sharp and staggering. He'd said it himself. Not just guilt, responsibility. Her thoughts spun, crashing into one another. What had he done? What had he broken? Had all of this, their stolen memories, the dreams, the Kharadors, started with him?

Her pulse pounded, furious and erratic. And Tharion? Had he known? Had he been helping him, guiding her down a path they'd laid out together? Her stomach turned. The weight of their secrets pressed down on her chest, thick and suffocating.

And yet, Ren's voice still echoed in her head. That quiet, cracked confession. It hadn't sounded like manipulation. It had sounded like a man trying not to shatter. That sliver of doubt, of something softer, dug in like a thorn.

Mira drew a breath, the cold air slicing through her like a blade. There would be no answers here in the shadows. She knocked on the heavy double doors, the sound sharp in the quiet corridor. She did not wait for a response. Her hand found the cool metal of the latch, and she pushed it open, the door swinging inward with a soft groan of old hinges.

20

REN'S ROOMS ENVELOPED HER. It was a world of deep greens and muted golds. An echo of the palace's grandeur, but shaped by his own hand.

The walls were a dark wood, carved with motifs of twisted vines and delicate leaves. Heavy drapes of green velvet framed tall, arched windows, the fabric woven with bronze threads that caught the dim light.

Nature touched everything. Delicate glass terrariums sat on the mantle, each a miniature world of moss and ferns, their glass panes fogged with condensation. The rug underfoot was a tapestry of roots and leaves, soft beneath her boots. Light filtered through fixtures shaped like winding branches, their metal leaves casting gentle, swaying shadows over the ceiling.

As her eyes adjusted to the low light, she saw what lay beneath, something still, untouched as if frozen in time. A vanity stood against the far wall, its mirror clouded with dust. The delicate glass bottles of perfume were lined up in perfect rows, neatly arranged, untouched. A brush the bristles stiff with age.

Mira moved further into the room, her fingers trailing over the vanity's edge. Dustmotes floated up, a soft gray film stained her fingertips.

She glanced into the bedroom beyond, where the bed lay half-shadowed. The deep green coverlet was neatly arranged, but only on one side. The other side showed clear signs of use. Blankets rumpled, a pillow slightly dented, the sheets creased and pulled back. The second pillow remained untouched, its surface smooth, undented.

Two of everything, but only one life being lived here. She felt the room close in around her, the stillness pressing against her skin. Whoever had once shared this room was gone, absent for longer than dust alone could explain.

"Is there something you needed, Mira?"

She spun, heart slamming against her ribs. Ren stood in the doorway to the adjoining study, his silhouette outlined in the amber glow of low-burning sconces behind him. He looked taller there, broader somehow, the light casting sharp angles across his face. His face was unreadable, controlled, the flicker of emotion held behind the glint of eyes that didn't soften when they met hers.

Behind him, Tharion. Arms crossed, posture guarded, his eyes were ice. Watchful. Calculated.

"I…" Mira's voice faltered. She'd meant to demand answers, to confront them about the things they were keeping from her—but now, standing in front of them, the certainty drained from her. Her mouth went dry. She swallowed hard and forced the words out, thin and brittle "I needed to speak with you. Both of you."

She steadied herself, brushing the dust from her palms as though it could rid her of the weight pressing into her chest. The stillness in the room felt unnatural, stretched too tightly around them. Mira drew in a slow breath, quieting the tremor in her hands.

"There's been a raid," she said, her voice finally steady, though soft. She stepped deeper into the room and lifted her gaze to meet Ren's again.

But the man she found staring back wasn't the one she remembered from moonlit corridors and whispered laughter.

This wasn't the Ren who had stolen a moment in the garden. This was Bharalyn's Regent. Sharp, measured, with his focus was entirely on her.

And it struck her harder than she cared to admit. It wasn't fear. It was desire. It hit her like a flush of heat, a treacherous, undeniable pulse that slid low and sudden through her stomach. Longing curled quiet and hot beneath the composure she fought to keep in place.

"Hallen is gone." She whispered "The Kharadors struck without warning. It was too clean. Too targeted. Someone led them there."

Ren didn't react. No shock. No outburst. Just a subtle darkening behind his eyes. He stepped into the room. Tharion followed, his body tense, every movement coiled with alertness.

"Mira....who told you that?" Ren asked. His voice was low, laced with iron. Her name clung to the edge of it, quiet but deliberate. Mira. He said it like she meant something to him. She swallowed, pulse thrumming in her ears.

"The attendants. Whispers in the gardens. Some of the survivors are here I think."

Ren didn't speak. His eyes stayed locked on hers, sharp and unblinking, as if trying to read more in her words than she was saying. The weight of his attention pressed against her, fierce and undivided.

She forced herself to keep going. "Garrick said whatever they came for, they either took or burned."

Tharion's gaze flicked toward Ren. His jaw worked once before he spoke. "And you think someone inside pointed the Kharadors to it?"

"I know someone did." Mira said.

She crossed her arms, not in retreat but in defiance, her

fingers tightening around the coarse fabric of her sleeves like a tether. Anything to keep her focus, to anchor herself against the heat that rose under Ren's gaze.

"There was a moment at the Summer Solstice Ball. Names. I thought it was just court gossip but now…" She hesitated, her voice lowering. "With the Veiled Night Celebrations tomorrow, and the conversations we overheard … it feels coordinated. Like someone's setting the stage."

Ren's jaw flexed. His face remained still, but tension rolled off him like smoke. His hands stayed at his sides, but his fingers twitched, once, then again, before curling into restrained fists.

"What conversations?" Ren asked, his voice low and directed at Tharion, but his eyes never left Mira. His focus stayed fixed on her, as if watching for the truth beneath her silence.

Tharion stood like stone beside him, unreadable but not innocent. He hadn't told Ren. A sliver of hope stirred. Maybe there was still something left to mend between her and Tharion. A thread not entirely severed.

Her eyes flicked back to Ren. And the rest of it vanished. His gaze remained on her, fierce and unblinking. That tug she tried so hard to resist threatened to drag her under.

No matter how tightly she crossed her arms, she couldn't block it out. She inhaled slowly.

"In the west hall, I heard Asric speaking with someone. He said their next move comes at Veiled Night..." Ren didn't flinch, but his jaw tightened, frustration flashing in his eyes.

She chose her words carefully. Tharion told you about Seacliffe," she said, voice taut. "But not this?"

Ren nodded once. Her gaze darted to Tharion, still silent at Ren's side. Of course. Tharion had been feeding Ren more than what they had done. He'd passed on the Kharadors' movements to Ren. Her chest tightened, the sting of betrayal burning hot behind her ribs.

She stared at Tharion "Did you lead the Kharadors to Hallen?"

"Yes," Ren said, finally. His voice was low. Frustrated. Unapologetic. Mira's stomach churned.

"But not before we got them out," Tharion added. "Every single person we could reach. We pulled them from their homes before Kharador crossed the ridge. Ren gave the order to evacuate while we were in Seacliffe."

Her voice rose. "So you handed it to them? You just gave it up?"

"No," Ren growled, his frustration flaring just beneath the surface. "I made a choice. The kind rulers are supposed to make. I put Bharalyn people above land."

Mira shook her head. "You let it burn."

"I saved what mattered," Ren snapped, his voice cutting through her anger like ice. "You think I wanted this? You think I've slept at all, knowing what was coming? But it was either evacuate them quietly, or let them stay and die screaming."

Tharion's jaw tightened as he looked away, retreating a fraction.

"Do you know what happens if we try to defend every inch?" Ren asked, softer now. His voice no longer sharp, but heavy with exhaustion. "We lose. Slowly, completely."

Ren lifted a hand, palm open, not pleading, exposed. The gesture hovered in the air for a moment, then fell as he took a slow step toward her.

"You think I don't hate it?" he continued. "That I don't ache with guilt over what I've had to sign off on? But there's no glory in dying for stones and smoke."

Another step. Closer now.

"I made sure we didn't lose them," he said, eyes locked to hers. "The land can be taken back. People can't."

Mira's breath caught. Her fury wavered, but the ache didn't fade. It only shifted, lower in her chest, heavier.

"You're not the only one who's trying to help them," Her voice didn't waver. She looked between Ren and Tharion. "But I can't do that if I'm always chasing shadows. If I'm always the last to know."

Ren's mouth pressed into a line. Mira stepped forward, closing the last of the distance between her and Ren, until they stood almost chest to chest. She could feel the heat of him, the tension thrumming beneath his stillness. Neither of them moved, the air between them drawn tight, sharp as wire. Ren's gaze faltered, just for a moment. He glanced at Tharion. And Tharion, for the first time, looked uncertain.

Mira didn't let the moment pass. "I know there's something more you're not telling me, something about my memories. And Tharion's."

The silence that followed was not hesitation. It was a precipice. Mira felt it in her bones, the shift in air, the bracing before a fall. Neither man moved, but the air shifted. Something final exchanged in silence, no glance required. A line being crossed. A door opening that could not be closed again.

Tharion spoke. "Tell her," he murmured. "Or I will."

Ren spun around to face him. The flicker of betrayal lit in his expression, raw and sudden. His jaw tensed, and his hands curled into fists at his sides.

"You don't get to decide this Tharion." His voice flared, raw and incendiary.

Tharion didn't flinch. "But it is hers to know. You've waited too long already. You're not protecting her by keeping her in the dark."

Mira stood between them, her breath came in shallow bursts, each second stretching into forever. She looked between them, watching the way neither would yield. Whatever had been silent before was now boiling to the surface.

Ren's posture shifted. The fight washed out of him. His head dropped slightly, as if the weight of the world had found his shoulders all at once. He inhaled once, deep and slow and turned, and when he opened his eyes again, the fire was gone. Only ash and truth remained.

"I am the blood-born son of the Crowned Betrothed," he sighed. Mira stared. Then scoffed. "The whole court knows that."

Ren didn't blink. "Then tell me," he said quietly, "what do you know of the Queen when she found out about my impending birth?"

Mira blinked, caught off-guard. Her lips parted before her mind could catch up.

"The story?" she asked, tone flat with disbelief. "She withdrew. Wouldn't hold court for months." Mira glanced toward Tharion, confusion flickering in her eyes, but he didn't look at her. His gaze stayed fixed on the ground.

"No one saw her, but a few." Mira continued, slower now. "My father for one. The Crowned Betrothed. They ruled in her place while she recovered." Ren didn't speak.

Tharion shifted, the wooden floor groaning beneath his boots.

Her mind reached back, fast and trembling, like fingers brushing against something half- forgotten. She caught it.

And this time, it didn't slip away.

* * *

The outer chamber of the Great Hall pressed in around her, all stone and silence, its walls heavy with portraits that had watched generations come and go. Mira slowed, her steps faltering beside Ren, her eyes drawn to the towering canvases that lined the chamber like sentinels.

Gilded frames caught the flickering torchlight, their painted faces ageless and serene. A dynasty laid bare in oil and pigment, each expression carved from legacy.

She felt the weight of it as she always had. That oppressive sense of lineage, of stories told too often to question. And yet, something was different this time.

Ren stopped before one portrait. She followed the line of his gaze. King Caelric and Queen Sarelle. The familiar, untouchable image.

Caelric, a picture of nobility, stood draped in dark blue and gold, his eyes calm and unwavering. And beside him, Sarelle. Crimson silk wrapped around her like flame, her eyes poised and unreadable. Her beauty had always been regal in a way that always felt a little otherworldly.

Mira studied the painting, a flicker of unease rising in her chest. Ren's silence made her skin prickle.

"Compare me to my father," Ren asked.

She turned to him in surprise, but said what seemed obvious. "You look exactly like him."

Ren said nothing. Just waited. Her gaze returned to the portrait, her focus narrowing. She scanned Caelric's face. The square jaw, the slope of his cheekbones, the arch of his brow. All mirrored in Ren's.

Ren nodded, barely.

Her head snapped toward the painting. Sarelle's gaze stared back at her, calm and quiet. Her chest tightened. She took a step back, the world shifting beneath her feet.

Ren, always on the periphery. A noble, not royal. Not quite. Because they hadn't let him be. Because the truth had been hidden. Because... Mira's eyes met Ren's, and in that moment, everything in her stilled.

The secret crashed into her like cold water. A prince hidden in plain sight. Sarelle's son. The rightful heir.

* * *

Her voice cracked when she spoke.

"You're her son." She took a step back, her hand searching for the wall. She didn't feel the stone. Only the door. "You're Sarelle's son," she said again, softer now. The truth split the room wide open. It lay between them like a blade on the table, impossible to ignore and just as deadly.

Ren didn't move. "Yes,"

Her breath came fast and sharp, as if she had been pulled through icy water. The warmth of the memory evaporated, leaving only the chill of betrayal seeping into her bones. Ren stood before her, his posture taut, every muscle drawn tight as if bracing for impact.

His face remained a careful mask, but the tremor in his voice betrayed him. "Mira "

"I knew... that's why she..." The words tore from her, raw and jagged. Her hands shook, and she pressed them against the door handle, desperate for something solid, something real.

Ren stepped forward, worry etched across his face. The

regent was gone. In his place stood a man weighed down by guilt, his eyes fixed on her like he was afraid she might break.

"Mira," he began, voice catching on the weight of her name. "I wanted to tell you. I meant to. But every time I reached for the words, I saw what it did to you, what it could cost you again, and I."

She stared at him, fury and disbelief twisted tight behind her ribs. "That wasn't your choice to make," she said, her voice low.

Tharion shifted beside her, then stepped closer, a quiet attempt at comfort. But she barely noticed. Her entire being was locked onto Ren.

"You say it was to protect us," she continued, voice measured but cutting. "But this wasn't protection, it was control. You made sure we couldn't move, couldn't question, because we didn't know enough to act."

"That's not true," Ren said, desperation thickening in his voice. "You were the only person I wanted to tell. Navigators, Mira, I wanted you to know more than anyone."

He reached for her hand, fingers brushing against hers. She pulled hers away. "But the moment I let you in, you became leverage. You know what this court is, what they'd do if they knew."

His eyes flicked to Tharion. A single glance. Quick. Reflexive. She saw the shift. Her breath caught in her throat. She turned to Tharion slowly, deliberately, as though the movement itself might hold her together.

"You knew." Her voice was quiet, brittle as cracked glass. Tharion opened his mouth, then closed it. His silence said everything.

Ren's voice broke. "Tharion knew. He's known since he was a boy. He was brought here to protect me. But you..." His voice cracked, raw and frayed. "They couldn't trust you..."

Mira blinked. The pieces clicked into place. Her lips parted, but no sound came. The realization, slow and final. It had been only her. She was the one who had been erased. The Queen had taken her memories. Not Tharion's. Hers. To protect Ren.

Every strange glance, every hesitation, every shard of distance she'd blamed on Tharion's and her fractured past. It had never been that. It had just been space. Chosen. Maintained.

She took a breath, and it didn't reach her lungs. The room seemed to close in on her, the shadows thickening, the air too thin.

She pushed the door handle, "I... I can't... I don't..."

Her vision blurred, the world narrowing to the two men before her, one pleading, the other a sentinel. Ren's face was a storm of grief and desperation as he continued to talk. Tharion remained still, the weight of his own choices etched into every hard line of his body.

Tharion's voice was soft, almost a whisper. "We thought we were protecting you, but you deserve the truth, Mira. You deserved it then, and you deserve it now,"

"I can't be here," Mira breathed.

She shoved the door open with more force than intended, the impact echoing through the space. Her breath caught as she stumbled backward through the threshold, barely holding herself upright. She didn't look back. She couldn't.

21

MIRA RUSHED THROUGH the palace's corridors. Her steps were fast and uneven, like she wasn't fully connected to the floor beneath her. She should have returned to her quarters, shut the door. But the thought of silence, true silence, was too much. Too sharp. Too final.

Her feet turned, familiar with the path even as her mind spun. She found herself at Torvyn's door. He had always been her rock, even when everything else was falling apart. The door creaked open at her touch. Empty. His cloak was missing, the hearth unlit. Only the faint scent of rosewood lingered. She blinked hard against the sting in her eyes and turned. If he wasn't here, he was likely in the library.

The library candles burned low in their sconces, soft pools of amber light. She stepped between them, her fingers grazing the worn spines, letting their presence ground her. She found Torvyn by the arched window, slouched in a familiar velvet-backed chair, a book resting forgotten on his lap. His eyes were closed, snoring.

"Torvyn," she said. It came out more breath than word. His eyes flew open and he lifted his head at once. As soon as he saw her, his expression changed, weariness gave way to worry.

"Mira?" He stood quickly, the book sliding to the floor. "What's wrong?"

She wanted to answer, but her voice caught. The words didn't know how to shape what she was feeling. Instead, she stepped into him. Her fingers clutched the front of his shirt as the tears came, silent and hot. He pulled her close without hesitation. One arm wrapped tight around her shoulders, the other hand smoothing down her back. His presence steadied her, but it couldn't quiet the ache beneath her ribs.

"I've got you," he murmured.

She let herself breathe against him, jaw clenched as her mind spun with too many truths she couldn't say out loud. She had trusted him, believed in Tharion. In them. That was the worst of it. She had trusted his steadiness, his quiet strength. She had believed in the version of them that chose love over duty. But he had lied. Over and over. And now all that belief felt like a wound she'd given herself.

Torvyn held her as the sob built low in her chest. She didn't let it out. She wouldn't give it that much space, not when she was the one who had let her guard down.

"What happened?" he asked, voice quiet but laced with steel. "Mira, if someone..."

She shook her head, cutting him off. "It's not like that." Her voice was raw. "It's just... I should've this seen coming. Things I should've known better than to hope for." Torvyn leaned back enough to see her face, his brows drawn in concern.

"I thought I could trust them," she whispered. Torvyn said nothing, just pulled her closer, arms tightening around her.

A bitter breath escaped her. "I feel so stupid..."

He didn't flinch. "You feel stupid because of who you trusted," he said softly. "But trust isn't a mistake, Mira. They just weren't worthy of it."

She swallowed hard. "I should've seen it. He had no interest in me. I just didn't want to believe it."

Torvyn brushed a thumb beneath her eye, wiping away a tear. "Sometimes we see what we need to. And sometimes people are better at hiding than we think."

Her gaze dropped to the floor. Torvyn was quiet for a long moment. Mira just leaned into the warmth of him, grateful for the steadiness she had never questioned. His comfort didn't erase the hurt, but it gave it a place to rest.

"Stay here tonight, Brahn is away tonight, so I was going to stay here anyway" he said. "You don't have to be alone." She nodded, her throat too tight to speak.

He guided her to the settee and draped a blanket around her shoulders, then moved to fetch another for himself. He settled beside her. A fire somewhere nearby crackled softly. The silence between them was thick, but gentle. Safe.

Mira curled deeper into the blanket and beside her, Torvyn read in silence. The steady rustle of pages the only sound. She leaned into him, her head resting against his shoulder. He didn't stop reading, but she felt the subtle shift as he adjusted to hold her weight as she fell asleep.

✳ ✳ ✳

Mira sat on the cold stone bench outside Queen Danlea's chambers, her hands folded in her lap as she stared straight ahead. The air was still, caught in that breathless space between night and dawn. A faint chill pressed through the thin fabric of her dress, raising goosebumps along her arms.

She had tried to sleep, tried to close her eyes and find peace, but dreams came fractured and strange, threaded with voices that didn't belong to her and accusations that echoed long after she jolted awake. Quietly, she left the library, leaving Torvyn sleeping, his hand on an open book. She hadn't woken him. Only whispered a silent apology and crept into the night-dimmed halls, her footsteps barely a murmur on the stone.

Now she waited. The door to Danlea's chambers stood closed before her, ornate and unmoved. When she'd knocked earlier, lightly, uncertainly, there'd been no answer.

Mira leaned her head back against the wall. The stone was cool against her head, a small, steadying relief.

She couldn't stop retracing the past few months, every conversation, every withheld truth. The lies she'd told Tharion. The truths he'd never given her. Ren's lineage, hidden in plain sight. And above it all, the stolen memories, once dismissed as mere consequence, now stood clear in her mind as something else entirely. Not chance. Not punishment. A calculated theft.

The door opened. A sliver of light spilled into the corridor. Queen Danlea stepped into the threshold, framed in the glow of flickering candles. Her silver hair shimmered like frost, and her eyes, milky and unreadable, settled on Mira with calm intent.

"Mira," she said, her voice gentle and unwavering. "Come in." Mira rose slowly, her bones aching in a way that had nothing to do with sleep.

"What about Nerra?" she asked, her voice hushed but even. "She is not needed today," Danlea replied.

Inside, the room was cloaked in quiet. Candles flickered in their glass bowls, their silver flames muted, casting a gentle luminescence over the room. Mira stepped in and closed the door behind her, leaning back against the wood as if she needed it to hold her upright. Her heart beat too loud in her ears. The world was too quiet, too still. Her eyes adjusted slowly, herbs arranged on the table, a small ceremonial blade catching the candlelight.

She moved toward the table, reaching for the herbs. But before she could touch it, a hand closed over hers. Cool. Steady. Final. Mira flinched at the touch, drawing her hand back with more force than she intended. The herbs scattered across the table, spilling into a mess of dried petals and crushed stems.

"There's no need for that," Danlea said softly.

"Then what do you want me to do?" Her voice cracked, sharp and brittle. "You asked for help with the preparations?" Danlea didn't move. Her expression was as still as the candles, but her presence filled the room like a tide.

"I said what I needed to..." she replied, "to ensure you would be here." Mira blinked, stunned. The anger surged too quickly to catch.

"To bring me here?" she repeated, voice low and shaking. "Why?" She stepped back, her heel catching on the edge of a rug. Mira steadied herself, eyes falling to the floor.

Danlea regarded her, calm and composed, but the stillness in her gaze only stoked the fury burning in Mira's chest. "There are many paths, Mira," she whispered. "You chose one lined with thorns. I wanted to make sure you had what you needed for what's ahead."

Mira let out a sharp, bitter laugh. "Meant to? I needed this?" Her voice cracked as it rose. "You think I needed to be lied to? To be betrayed? To fumble around in the dark?"

Danlea didn't flinch. Instead, she watched Mira with an unreadable calm, as if waiting for something to pass. It didn't. The silence stretched until Mira couldn't bear it any longer.

"Say something," she snapped, though her voice faltered at the end. "Tell me why."

Danlea moved to the bed, her pale hair catching in the

candlelight like strands of moonlight.

"You needed to grow roots strong enough to hold through the storm. Not for what's passed, but for what's still coming. You'll need that strength. And you'll need those who can stand beside you." Mira opened her mouth, but the instinctive answer died on her tongue. A hollow ache bloomed in her chest.

Danlea's voice gentled, barely above a breath. "Mira… you've been fighting so long, you don't know how to stop." Mira looked away, jaw clenched. But Danlea stepped closer, slow and unthreatening.

"This isn't another battle. Not here. Not with me." Mira's shoulders trembled. Her breath caught.

"I didn't bring you here to test you," Danlea said. "I brought you here to rest." Danlea reached out, brushing a strand of hair behind Mira's ear. The gesture was light, reverent.

"Rest with me a while longer," she said.

Mira hesitated, her heart still heavy with betrayal, but she nodded. She hated how exposed she felt, how easily Danlea's quiet kindness cracked through the armor she'd built around herself. Part of her still burned with resentment, a voice in her mind screaming not to let this go so easily, not to forget the lies, the manipulation. But another part, the one too tired to keep bleeding, ached for the solace Danlea offered.

A single tear traced the curve of her cheek.Danlea's gaze softened further. She gestured to a nearby chair, draped in forest-green velvet. Mira's body moved before her mind caught up. She sank into the chair, folding in on herself, her arms hugging her sides as if to hold herself together.

Danlea crossed the room with a slow elegance. She poured tea into a delicate cup, the fragrant steam curling with lavender and chamomile. When she placed it in Mira's hands, the warmth of it startled her. Real. Steadying.

"Drink," the Queen whispered. "This will help."

Mira lifted the cup to her lips. The tea was soft, floral, grounding. A deep breath followed, steadier than the last. Across from her, Danlea folded herself into her seat, graceful and unhurried. The Queen smiled, cradled her own teacup in both hands and closed her eyes for a moment.

Danlea's voice broke the quiet, low and reverent, as if reciting something sacred from memory. "Kharad was a slave in the darkened halls of the Ironhold. His days were a symphony of iron against stone, his nights filled with the weight of chains and the cold bite of a world that did not remember kindness."

She wasn't looking at Mira as she spoke, her gaze distant, fixed somewhere beyond the room. The flicker of candlelight caught in her eyes, turning them to liquid gold. The words fell from her lips like an old prayer.

"The masters of the Ironhold were as cruel as the mountains they mined, and they sought to break him, to turn his spirit to dust beneath their heels."

Mira didn't move. Something in Danlea's tone held her still. She felt suspended, as if the air had thickened around them. The pain in her chest hadn't vanished, but it dulled under Danlea's voice, like waves smoothing jagged stone.

"But within Kharad burned the spirit of a storm. One evening, as the sun sank beneath ash-colored clouds, he saw his chance. His chains, once his prison, became his weapon. He shattered them against the rock, the iron breaking with a sound like thunder. His strength, forged through years of backbreaking labor, became his sword."

The silver-blue firelight flickered softly, casting long

shadows against the stone walls. As Danlea spoke, the flames seemed to shape themselves around the story. Iron chains snapped and danced in silhouette. A figure rose, tall and defiant, the tremble of the flames turning his movement into myth. Behind him, other shadows followed, smaller but growing, like hope taking root in darkness.

"The path to freedom was not kind," Danlea continued "The roads were twisted, the thorns sharp, and the rivers rose to swallow them whole. But Kharad never faltered. When the waters rose, he tore trees from the earth to build bridges. When wolves circled, his roar alone sent them fleeing. His strength was not only in his arms but in his heart, in the way he refused to abandon hope."

"When Kharad and his people reached the sea, they found the Navigators. Together, they crafted ships, weaving wood and willpower into vessels that could carry them beyond the horizon. The sea rose to challenge him, the storms testing his resolve, but he stood at the helm, unyielding. His strength became a shield, his voice the wind in their sails."

Her voice dipped, the words slowing, each one placed with care. "And when they reached the new lands, it was Kharad who set the first stone on their new home. He did not build from iron and rock alone but from the strength he had earned, and the freedom he had claimed."

Silence settled over them, the story hanging in the air like mist. Mira's tea had cooled, but the warmth lingered, a small ember in the dark.

Danlea leaned forward, her milky eyes gentle, luminous in the firelight. "You're standing at the edge of the sea, Mira. Behind you lie the mines, the chains of everything you once believed was unchangeable. But ahead... ahead is open water. You can build your ship and set sail, not because the sea is safe, but because you've grown strong enough to face its storms. The roots you've planted will hold, even when the wind howls."

Mira's lips parted, the air sharp against her teeth. "But what if I can't? What if I break?"

Danlea reached out, her cool fingers brushing gently against Mira's. "There are many paths ahead, Mira. And if you break… then it will be your breaking that makes space for something new. Even ruin can be fertile ground. What falls apart may yet become the foundation for something stronger, truer. That too is part of the journey. That too is strength."

The room seemed to shift with her words, the firelight steadying, the silver glow at the windows sharpening into clarity. A hush fell, thick and absolute.

Mira opened her mouth to speak, but the words didn't come. Her limbs felt suddenly heavy, her thoughts blurred. It was as if the weight of everything. Her anger, the ache, the sheer exhaustion, finally collapsed inward.

Her eyes fluttered once, then closed. She slumped gently against the cushions before she even realized she was falling, sleep crashing over her like a wave. The world vanished in an instant, pulled from her grasp like a thread slipping through fingers.

Danlea remained still beside her, watching, silent as the flame.

22

DANLEA'S FINGERS, cool and steady, brushed gently against Mira's temple. The touch was light, yet it pulled her from the soft edges of sleep with the precision of purpose.

"It's time," the Queen murmured, her voice a low ripple across the stillness.

Mira stirred, the lingering haze of dreams slipping from her shoulders as her eyes fluttered open. The room was dimly lit, kissed by the silvery glow of early evening that seeped through the narrow cracks in the curtains. She was wrapped in a soft blanket.

The dregs of cold tea in a delicate cup rested on the table beside her.

She hadn't meant to sleep. But now, waking slowly, Mira realized the tea was what had drawn her under, warm, quiet, and carefully laced. For once, there had been no dreams. No nightmares clawing at the edges of her mind. Just silence. Rest. She blinked up at the low light, her voice still hoarse with sleep. Danlea's hand lingered for a breath longer. Grounding. Comforting.

Another presence shifted nearby, one she had not registered before. From the far side of the room, where the curtain had been drawn back slightly, Cleric Perrin stepped into view. She wore her ceremonial veil, sheer and dignified, embroidered in silver sigils that caught the candlelight. Her white robes moved in soft folds, her hands folded in front of her.

"You rested well," Perrin said, her voice quiet but assured. "It was needed."

Mira sat up more fully, her gaze flicking between the two women. "How long have I?" she asked, her voice low, sharp at the edges.

"Long enough," Perrin replied gently.

Mira's jaw clenched. "You gave me something," She swung her legs out from under her body, the sudden movement making her dizzy. "Without asking."

Neither woman answered right away. Danlea's eyes remained on the fire, unreadable. "It was not to harm you, it was only to help you rest" Perrin said softly.

The silence that followed was thick, but not ashamed. Not apologetic. Danlea didn't move.

Mira's eyes narrowed slightly. "How did you know I was here?"

"Your bonded called for me," Perrin replied, her tone soft and sincere. "He was concerned about your sleepwalking."

Danlea gestured toward the washroom with a slight tilt of her head. There was no command in it, only understanding. An invitation. A moment to center. Mira rose, her limbs stiff, and made her way to the adjoining chamber.

Inside, warmth enveloped her. The soft scent of dried lavender and lemon balm hung in the air. Lamps flickered gently. As she lowered herself into the steaming bath, Mira let the water draw out the tension in her limbs. Her thoughts were quiet.

She considered the secrets she'd uncovered, the memories beginning to take shape, and the revelation that the truth she had once believed, were now fractured. Losing her memory had been as much a political maneuver as it had been an act of protection. Sarelle had taken them, not out of cruelty, but out of desperation. To protect Ren. But protect him from what?

When she emerged, a robe lay draped across the vanity. She slipped the plush fabric over her skin with deliberate care. Her reflection in the mirror, illuminated by the silver light.

A gentle knock sounded at the door. Before she could answer, Perrin stepped inside without waiting, already holding a steaming cup of tea in her hands. Wordlessly, she crossed the room and set it down beside the combs and powder on the vanity.

"You have questions," she said simply.

Mira gave a small nod, toward the cup, not Perrin.

"Will this one make me sleep too?" Her voice was calm, but there was steel threaded through it.

Danlea crossed the room and stood behind Mira, fingers already combing through her hair.

"Tonight marks a turning," Danlea said softly, her fingers steady as she worked. Danlea's hands never faltered. She began to gently curl Mira's hair with steam and quiet reverence.

"What do you remember?" Danlea asked. "Of your moments that were hidden from you?"

Mira tensed under Danlea's touch. Her guiding hands, the gentle positioning, it all made her feel managed, like a child dressed for a ceremony she didn't ask to attend. She nearly pulled away.

But Danlea's presence was steady, unhurried. There was no force behind her actions, only care. A quiet rhythm that spoke of patience, of purpose. Like water smoothing stone. Mira's breath eased.

"Fragments," Mira whispered. "Like the dream of

someone else's life."

Perrin stepped forward. "They're yours. Memory doesn't always return as a storm. Sometimes it comes like mist."

Mira's gaze flicked to the mirror, her reflection watching back, wary and worn.

Danlea picked up the porcelain cup and held it out. Mira took it but didn't drink. "You can drink or not. One offers clarity, the other shelter. But both carry a cost."

Silence settled around them. Mira stared down at the cup, steam curling like breath into the air.

"I'm tired of being protected," she said at last. "I want to know what I am being protected from."

Danlea met her eyes in the mirror. "Then drink. Knowing that this is a choice freely made."

Mira drank. The tea was hot and bitter, and she coughed once, the taste unfamiliar, grounding. She heard Perrin's voice echo around the room. "It will open the way."

Danlea's eyes were clouded and pale, but deeper than sight. The room seemed to still, the air softening, shadows melting into stone.

Mira's pulse slowed, the thunder in her ears fading to a soft rhythm, like the lull of waves against the shore. Her limbs felt light, as if the burdens of truth and lies, of rebellion and loyalty, had been lifted from her shoulders.

Danlea's face remained the only anchor, her expression filled with understanding, with an unspoken promise. Mira's balance wavered. But it was not a violent collapse. She sank back into someone's hands. Gentle, careful, cradling her as she was lowered.

✳ ✳ ✳

338

A vast nothingness that pressed against her skin seeped into her bones. She drifted within it, weightless and unmoored. The world was not solid here. It breathed, shifting like mist caught in the wind.

Shapes emerged.

At first, faint smudges against the black, little more than whispers of color and light.

Then, clarity. A hall. The Great Hall. But not as she remembered it. The towering banners of Bharalyn, once rich with gold and deep crimson, were torn, their fabric curling like dying embers.

Dark veins, like creeping vines, cracked the polished marble floors, once mirrors of the heavens. The air smelled of smoke and something older, something wrong. At the center of it all, the throne. Mira knew, before she even saw him.

Brahn. He sat there, draped in midnight blue and silver, a crown glinting atop golden hair, his posture as relaxed as a man who had always known he would win. The throne fit him too well, as if it had been shaped for him long before he ever reached for it. His hands rested on the armrests, fingers tapping a slow, patient rhythm.

A king in waiting. A king who had already claimed his prize. The sight of him sent a wave of nausea through Mira, an aching, twisting sickness that clawed at her insides. This wasn't how it was supposed to be.

She took a step forward and the world rippled.

A woman stood before her. A queen. Sarelle. Her dark hair was a river of moonlight, her eyes piercing. Tears streaked her face, though she held herself with the stillness of someone who had long since learned not to tremble. She stood in a chamber that felt eerily familiar. The scent of aged paper, candle wax, and something sweet, pear maybe, filled the air. Sarelle's lips moved, but the sound was distant, blurred by time, as though the moment was struggling to reach her.

Mira leaned forward, straining,   then another voice. Ren. She turned. He stood behind her. A younger Ren, not more than seventeen. He looked softer, his dark hair falling over his brow, his eyes uncertain. His hands were clenched into fists at his sides, fire curling around his wrists like bindings.

Sarelle reached out, her fingers brushing his cheek. He flinched. Not in fear. In grief. "Blood of my blood."

The words sent a shiver through her, sinking into her bones, nestling into the hollow spaces of her memory. Sarelle's touch was not that of a queen. It was my mother's.

Mira's breath caught in her throat. Truth coiled in the pit of her stomach like a snake awakening from slumber.

The moment fractured.

Fire spread and burned through, folding over itself. The heat of the room melted into something cooler. The floor beneath Mira's feet faded, replaced by a surface that seemed to glow from within, like moonlight captured beneath glass. The fire dissipated to mist and pulled back, revealing a familiar figure standing at the center of this dreamscape. Queen Danlea. The mist cleared to show her stood beneath a canopy of stars, her dark gown woven with threads of twilight.

The veil over her eyes was gone, revealing soft, silver irises that held no blindness. Her expression was calm, lips curved in a gentle smile, and her presence washed over Mira like a warm breeze, a stark contrast to the jagged edges of the previous vision.

"You are safe, Mira," Danlea said, her voice a melody.

Mira's thoughts spun, confusion knotting with the remnants of fear. Danlea moved closer, her bare feet silent against the light-filled ground.

"The strongest among my kingdom can share our visions. And what you saw now is what I saw when I looked at the succession of your kingdom." Danlea's expression saddened, shadows passing over her features. "The usurper stands upon the precipice of a throne not meant for him. But what you have seen is not an ultimate future, but a thread of what may come."

"What do I do?" Mira's voice wavered, caught between the fear of what she had seen and the quiet comfort of Danlea's presence.

"I do not know," Danlea said, her eyes full of sorrow. "I never know. The future is not a set path but a sea, ever-changing. I can show you the waves, the pull of the tides, but only you can decide which way to steer."

Danlea pointed to Mira's feet. Mira looked down to see a boat rocking gently beneath her. Its polished wooden hull dipping with the rhythm of unseen waves. But there was no sea, no horizon, only an endless sky stretching in every direction. The stars were not above them, they were below, within the waves.

The boat drifted through a sea of constellations, their golden threads weaving intricate, shifting paths. Mira gripped the edges of the vessel as she leaned over the side. The stars pulsed, their glow piercing through dark waters that were not waters at all, but light.

"This…" Mira whispered, voice hushed with awe. "This is what the Navigators must have felt like."

Danlea sat across from her, the folds of her gown

pooling around her feet like mist.

She smiled, dipping a single finger into the glowing water beside them. Ripples spread. The constellations twisted, their threads unweaving and rewinding, into the same patterns. The boat rocked slightly as Danlea lifted her hand, pointing toward a particular place among the tangle of stars across the waters, a convergence.

Mira's gaze followed, landing on the glowing knot of threads where many constellations met. Unlike the others this one did not pulse. It waited. Mira swallowed, a strange weight settling in her chest. It glowed beneath them, a golden heartbeat beneath the sea of night. Mira looked across the waters and saw others like it. They seem uncommon, and this was the closest one.

Mira reached forward, hesitating. The moment her fingers brushed the waters, warmth flooded her. A deep, resounding pull, like the tide changing direction, like she had been caught in a current too strong to fight.

Her voice was barely a breath. "What is it?"

Danlea let the boat drift closer, its wooden frame groaning softly as the water of stars lapped at its sides. Then, finally, she spoke.

"This, Mira" she murmured, "is your choice."

Mira's fingers hovered over the golden convergence, her pulse matching the slow, steady rhythm of the lines around it. The warmth from the water seeped into her skin, curling into the marrow of her bones. It was unlike anything she had ever felt, not just power, not just knowledge, but something more. Something alive.

The boat rocked gently beneath her, carrying them forward, though there was no wind, no current, only motion. Danlea sat in perfect stillness, watching, waiting.

Mira swallowed hard, her voice barely above the whisper of waves against the wooden hull. "What... am I choosing?"

Danlea's silver eyes reflected the constellations around them, as though the stars themselves bent to her presence. "Your path." Her voice was as steady as the sea beneath them, as the stars that lit their way. "The choice is yours, which way to steer."

Mira's chest tensed, her breath shallow and strained. Steer. She had spent her whole life moving between both, and even more so since her memories were stolen, grasping not for survival, not for the greater good, but for the simple, radical act of choosing.

Of claiming something for herself. This moment, this felt like her choice entirely. No one was guiding her hand, no manipulation shaping her path. It was hers. And it terrified her. Mira tore her gaze away from it, from the unspoken promise tangled within its threads. She turned to Danlea instead.

"What happens if I refuse?" she demanded. Her voice cracked against the silence of the star-filled void.

Danlea did not flinch. She simply tilted her head, unshaken by the venom in Mira's words. "To let the boat drift is also a choice."

Beneath them, the golden threads throbbed, causing the boat to sway. The sea of stars whispered. Danlea leaned forward, just slightly. Enough that the space between them lessened, enough that her words came low, careful, deliberate. Then, gently, "This is the bargain you made with them."

Mira's breath hitched. The word curled through her mind like a ghost, pressing against something distant, something buried deep. "With who?" she whispered.

"I can not tell you, you will know this in your own time" Danlea's voice was as smooth as water lapping against the sides of their boat. "Soon."

The stars under them pulsed faster, and she felt the pull of waking. Queen Danlea's form wavered, the delicate strands of her gown unraveling into mist. Her edges blurred, as if the dream itself was pulling her away, strand by strand. Yet her expression remained serene.

Mira's vision blurred as she heard a whisper, "Wake now, Mira"

The stars folded inward. The sea of light turned dark. Soft mist swallowed the constellations one by one. The boat faded. The warmth receded and Mira fell.

✳ ✳ ✳

She blinked, breath caught in her chest, the scent of lavender grounding her in reality. Her thoughts stirred sluggishly, but gradually, the room came back into focus. Someone, gentle yet steady, held her back in silent support. She lifted her eyes and met Perrin's.

Her veiled face hovered close, her white robes a curtain of softness and sanctuary. Mira's head rested against the Cleric's shoulder, as if she had been there for hours.

Danlea knelt beside them, her gown pooling like moonlight on the floor. Her milky eyes studied Mira with an intensity.

"Do you understand?" Danlea asked. The question pressed like a tide pulling at Mira. She closed her eyes.

The cracked marble of the Great Hall. Brahn seated where he never should have been. The stars. Sarelle. Ren. The flicker of truth that danced just beyond her reach. And that final golden convergence, waiting for her. Her choice. Not yet made.

Mira opened her eyes. The room was soft with silver candlelight. Her throat ached, but her voice was steady when she finally spoke. "I understand.".

Danlea nodded. Perrin shifted only slightly beneath her, but her voice was quiet and warm, a hum beneath Mira's bones.

"Come. The Veiled Night approaches, and you must be ready."

23

M IRA ENTERED THE grand foyer, arm linked with Danlea as the gentle hum of conversation and the delicate clink of crystal welcomed her. The room buzzed with life. Courtiers and nobles draped in velvets and silks moved in a vibrant tapestry of color and sound, while jewels caught the candlelight to scatter fractured rainbows across stone walls and gilded frames.

Although Danlea exchanged pleasantries, Mira remained vigilant. Her fingers brushed the waist of her corset. The champagne bodice clung to her torso, its navy constellations embroidered along the boning, catching the soft glow of the chandeliers overhead. The garment cinched her waist and lifted her chest, cascading down like a waterfall of starlight. Danlea insisted she wear the gown.

Beyond them, towering oak doors stood firmly shut, their heavy panels carved with the likenesses of past rulers and adorned with gilded flourishes that danced in the dim corridor light. They blocked the lively foyer from the great hall and the opulent spectacle waiting beyond.

Mira could feel the anticipation in the air. The polite laughter, and the clink of fine silverware and crystal goblets. Guests glided across marble floors in rustling silks and brocade, their steps echoing as they waited for the grand reveal. Every year the secretive theme of the night would be known only at the moment the doors swung open.

Mira frowned. Lord Asric was this year's patron. Whatever waited behind those doors it would be a performance of ambition and peril. And Torvyn? Navigators only knew what Asric had manipulated him into.

The corridor hushed as deliberate footsteps echoed through the marble halls. Lord Asric moved with the quiet authority of a man who owned the room. The candlelight cast flickering shadows over his deep crimson coat, which was adorned with gold embroidery, curling along the edges like flickering flames. His dark vest, gleaming buttons, neatly arranged silk cravat, and a sharply tilted black hat all spoke of elegance intertwined with mischief.

He paused briefly before Queen Danlea. Asric bowed low.

"Your Majesty," he said smoothly. There was a respectfulness to his tone, almost fond.

Mira felt the undercurrent, the performance beneath the words. His eyes tracked along Mira as he stood. He turned and continued down the foyer until stopping at the towering doors. With a flourish, he swept his arms wide and addressed the assembled crowd.

"Welcome, my friends, to the Veiled Night celebrations!" A murmur of intrigue rippled through the gathering as silks rustled and eyes leaned in.

His smile widened as he continued, "Tonight, the wonders of the Enchanted Faire have been brought forth. Marvels, mystery, entertainment unlike any you have ever seen."

At his snap, the towering doors groaned open to reveal a transformed Grand Hall. Long tables, set with gleaming silver flatware and crystal goblets, stretched from end to end, each place marked with a delicately scripted name card.

But the true marvel was the living performances woven throughout the space. Above, aerialists soared on silken ribbons, their bodies twisting like celestial dancers, their shimmering costumes catching the glow of enchanted lanterns. Off to one side, a shadow puppeteer animated entire stories with the flick of his nimble hands, painting tales of lost kings, daring thieves, and forbidden loves against a stretched canvas. Fire breathers strode confidently through the aisles, their bursts of flame painting the air in gold and crimson.

Everywhere Mira looked, the hall exuded an otherworldly charm, both chaotic and mesmerizing. But this was no mere display of excess, it was a deliberate illusion meant to entertain and to distract. Slowly, she drew in a steady breath, straightened her shoulders, and, together with Danlea, stepped further into the den of wonder and intrigue.

* * *

The Enchanted Faire was not merely spectacle, it was pure indulgence. Each detail had been meticulously designed, curated, and controlled. The deeper she moved into the hall, the more clear it became.

The overhead lanterns burned lower, casting warmer, flickering pools of light. Deep reds and golds wove through the fabrics draped along the walls, shadows playing across them like whispers. Performers meandered between the tables, women in beaded silks that clung like a second skin, skirts slit high along their thighs. Men adorned in loose, open-chested tunics, the fabric decadent against their skin. Gold cuffs at their wrists, chains draped over collarbones.

Every movement was deliberate. A hand grazing an arm. A mouth too close to an ear. The barely there touch of a dancer whose fingers lingered too long before slipping into the next moment. Music curled through the space, low and pulsing, strings plucked with teasing slowness, a drumbeat that thrummed like a heartbeat beneath it all.

Mira exhaled slowly through her nose, steadying herself as she absorbed the charged atmosphere. Lord Asric's intent was unmistakable. This was no ordinary Enchanted Faire. It was a night of seduction, where temptation was cloaked in layers of carefully spun illusion.

"Let's find our seats," Queen Danlea murmured, as she guided them toward the arranged tables.

Each name was written in silver ink, each curve precise, a testament to the careful planning behind the evening's event. As they approached, Danlea's eyes flitted to her placecard, already affixed to the center of a place setting.

With a graceful turn, she leaned toward a nearby performer and requested an additional seat for Mira. The performer spun a silver coin across his fingers, the metal catching the warm glow of the lanterns. He offered her a slow, knowing smile, his lips curving with a secret only he understood.

He inclined his head respectfully. "Of course, Your Majesty."

As the extra chair was set by their side, Danlea turned back to Mira with a smile. They settled into the newly cleared space, and Danlea leaned in with a conspiratorial tone. "For now, you can sit here beside me."

Mira's eyes met hers, a mixture of relief and anticipation mingling in the shared glance. Around them, the hall buzzed with a curious energy as guests settled into their seats.

Some lounged back with laughter, others exchanged secretive smiles, as if shedding their usual constraints. The air shimmered with a sense of liberation; inhibitions seemed to melt away under the spell of the evening.

Mira reached for the goblet that had been set before her, its delicate stem catching the candlelight. As she took a careful sip of the sweet berry wine, as she absorbed the spectacle around her. Noble faces softened into expressions of joyful abandon, the clink of crystal punctuating the murmurs of a crowd unafraid to revel in the night's seductive promise.

The first course arrived, a delicate pastry, golden and flaky. Mira watched as it was placed before her. She carefully lifted it, tearing off a small piece and bringing it to her lips. The pastry melted on her tongue; its crisp layers gave way to a warm, decadent filling that was savory and rich, with just a hint of spice lingering long after the bite.

Mira looked up and found Tharion standing and staring at her from across the table. "Mira" he exhaled, his voice low and awestruck.

He wore his best uniform. A sharply tailored black ensemble adorned with intricate silver embroidery, the edges immaculate and precise. The silver clasp at his shoulder, polished to a gleam, bore the unmistakable mark of his station. In that unguarded second, Mira caught a glimpse of the man he used to be. The surprise in his eyes, when they landed on her, was fleeting but real.

"You look… stunning," Tharion murmured.

His words sent a mixture of pride and irritation through Mira. Tharion took a stumbling step forward, nearly reaching for her as he placed a hand on the table.

"Where… where did you get your dress?" he continued, his brow furrowing as he searched her face for answers.

Mira wanted to ignore him. But before she could find the words, Danlea leaned in, placing a gentle hand on her arm. At that silent touch, Mira turned and met the queen's milky eyes. For a moment, it was as if two paths opened before her.

Mira rose gracefully, smoothing her dress with deliberate care, and approached him with a steady gaze.

"Will you dance?" she asked.

Tharion looked away, distracted by something across the room. But when his eyes returned to hers, they held a trace of reluctant agreement. A slight nod confirmed his acceptance.

✳ ✳ ✳

As Mira and Tharion approached the dance floor, she felt the familiar pulse of music, soft, sweeping notes that filled the air. She extended her hand to him. He took it without words, his grip warm but unsteady. For a moment, they simply stood there, an uncomfortable stillness settling over them. Then, Tharion led her into the waltz.

Their feet found the rhythm together, moving in practiced arcs. The music swelled around them, creating a quiet sanctuary despite the crowded floor. But Tharion, ever the picture of control, missed a beat. The smooth, confident rhythm of his dancing gave way to faltering steps, as if his body had forgotten. Mira adjusted instinctively, matching his hesitations as best she could. Still, she felt the struggle in him with every shift, every stumble.

His gaze wandered, out of focus, scanning the crowd around them. Each flicker of attention that left her tightened the knot forming in her chest.

"I'm sorry," she said, her voice barely above the music. "For storming off. I shouldn't have."

Tharion didn't respond. His grip didn't tighten. His eyes didn't flick to hers. Mira kept her gaze on his shoulder, pretending it didn't hurt. "I think I made the wrong choice before" she said quietly, more to herself now than to him. "I want to help. You. Ren. All of it. I just… I need you to let me."

His hand tightened around hers, but only for a brief moment before once again his gaze slipped away, his shoulders tense. They collided with another dancing couple. The graceful movement of their steps shifted abruptly as skirts and trousers brushed against each other. Mira's eyes widened in surprise, and she instinctively pulled back a step.

"I'm so sorry," she murmured, her voice soft with genuine regret. But the couple they had disturbed barely glanced their way, lost in their own dance. Their smiles and quiet laughter dismissed the interruption as nothing more than a fleeting misstep in the night.

Mira turned to Tharion, her brows knitting with concern. "Are you okay?" He didn't respond. His gaze was somewhere far off, trapped behind his own storm-clouded eyes. She reached out, her fingers brushing against his sleeve. "Tharion? Are you okay?"

His head snapped toward her, the sharpness in his expression catching her off guard. "He's blinded to what this is doing to him". He bit out, the words raw and unpolished, scraping against the air between them.

Mira blinked "Tharion…"

Before she could say more, his hand found hers again, rough yet deliberate, pulling her back into the waltz. The music swelled around them. His steps were precise, a little too fast. He spun her, the world blurring around her in a sweep of soft lights and murmured laughter. His fingers slipped away, the ghost of his touch vanishing as he melted into the crowd.

Mira stumbled, unmoored, the room a sea of whirling couples and shifting shadows. Strong arms around her waist caught her. Ren's face came into focus, his expression a raw canvas of yearning. His arms tightened around her, not just to steady her but to claim. Without a word, he pulled her into another waltz, their bodies finding the rhythm. They moved together, as if by memory.

His breath ghosted over her temple as he leaned down, his lips brushing the air just above her ear. She felt him inhale, the warmth of his breath threading through the strands of her hair.

"Mira..." he murmured, her name slipping from his lips like a secret.

Her pulse quickened, the sound of her name on his tongue both an anchor and a current, pulling her towards Ren. Her breath hitched, heat flashing through her like wildfire. For one suspended second, the world narrowed to the space between them. Just them.

Clarity struck her, hard and unforgiving. Mira shoved him back, the movement sharp and sudden, instinct more than thought. The force of it surprised them both. His hand shot out, fingers curling around her arm, firm but not painful. His expression flashed with confusion and desperation, but before either of them could speak, a voice boomed over the music.

"Ladies and gentlemen," Lord Asric's voice rang out from the front of the hall.

The hum of conversation died down, every gaze redirected. Mira's eyes snapped to the dais, the gilded platform where Asric stood. Ren didn't let go. He moved behind her, pulling her back against his chest. His arm slid around her waist, the warmth of his palm flattening against her. His other hand rose, gentle but unyielding, fingers brushing against the curve of her hip. He rested his chin on her shoulder, his breath hot against the skin of her neck.

Her body betrayed her, a shiver running through her despite the layers of silk and lace between them. She liked the way his presence enveloped her. The intensity of his hold of her, how her body seemed to mold against his as if they were carved from the same stone. It felt dangerous and familiar all at once.

Asric spread his arms wide, grinning. "You all know I have never been one for bonding, but pleasure? Secrets? Now that… I do appreciate." Soft laughter rippled through the crowd, goblets raised in amusement.

Ren exhaled against her neck, his lips brushing skin. Mira's breath came in shallow pulls, her fingers curling around Ren's arm.

Asric continued, "And tonight, I have procured something very...special." Lord Asric's voice unfurled through the hall, smooth as velvet and just as dark. As his arm swept in a grand gesture, hundreds of small, light with a pop, glimmering flames lined the walls, their light waltzing with the shadows.

Mira didn't recognise the scent. Spiced, warm and heady. It curled around her senses, a whisper of something forbidden. She inhaled again, and the scent deepened, unfurling in her mind like smoke. It was like desire made tangible, soft and consuming.

Asric's gaze landed directly on her and Ren as he announced "Emberbane Candles, for your enjoyment and your deniability."

24

Her stomach dropped. Mira had heard of these before. Candles not merely for ambiance, but alchemical wonders designed to erode the edges of control. The smoke was slow burning, threading through the senses, lowering inhibitions, peeling back layers of propriety, and leaving nothing but raw, unvarnished truth.

Ren groaned softly against her ear, his lips brushing her skin. It was rough, a rasp that slid through her like silk over a blade. Mira's breath hitched, the realization crashing into her with brutal clarity. The fluttering in her chest, the warmth of Ren's arms around her, the pulse of need that hummed beneath her skin.It was undeniably her desire intensified, drawn out by the Emberbane's pull. Yet unmistakably her own.

Each inhale of the spiced, sweet air chipped away at her restraint, fanning the embers of her desire into a flame. Her gaze darted around the hall. What had been a refined, elegant gathering was rapidly descending into chaos and debauchery. People whispered secrets between touches, fingers slipping beneath the folds of skirts, hands tracing skin in darkened corners. Eyes half-lidded, mouths parted, movements fluid and languid as if the entire room were submerged in warm water.

But amid the slow descent of decorum, Mira felt the oddity of her own senses. Yes, she felt the Emberbane's pull, the way it smudged the lines of her desire, but it wasn't an all-consuming fog. Her thoughts still had edges, and beneath the heat, she felt the solidity of self-control. It was as if the candle's magic could bend her but not break her.

Her eyes snagged on Danlea. The Queen was rising from her seat with an elegance that cut through the haze. Her expression remained cool, composed, untouched by the smoke. Danlea met Mira's gaze, a spark of recognition passing between them. With a subtle nod towards the door, Danlea began to weave her way to the exit. Her movement deliberate and unhurried, as if to avoid drawing attention.

Ren's arm around her waist tightened, drawing her back into him. His lips skimmed her temple, a whisper of warmth.

"Mira..." he murmured, and there was something wounded in his voice, a crack beneath the desire. She spun sharply in his arms. His pupils, wide and ravenous, locked onto her.

The realization struck her. This wasn't just about indulgence. Nobles would speak too freely, revealing alliances and ambitions they would normally guard. Jealousy, hunger for power, whispered manipulations. Tonight, under the haze of these candles, restraint would crumble. This night of indulgence wasn't just chance, wasn't just theatrics, this was carefully crafted, designed to make people lose themselves.

She heard Lord Asric's voice rise again, splintering the moment. "Enjoy, my friends. Tonight, I want to see nothing but desire and truth."

Mira brought her hands up pressing against his chest.

"Ren..." she said, meant it as a warning, a call back to sense, but his name came out low, fragile. Aching like a confession she hadn't meant to make.

Ren's hands hadn't moved, but the space between them had grown dangerous. Her pulse fluttered beneath her skin. She should step back. She should say something sharp and sobering.

Mira could almost feel him. The desire and unguarded need. They way his arms curled around her like he didn't trust the world to keep her safe, like letting go might break something in both of them. And beneath that heat, beneath the hunger, there was regret as if he already knew what this would cost them.

Her body leaned closer caught in the current of the moment she didn't want to resist. He lowered his head, gently, reverently, his nose grazing hers. A silent plea. Mira closed the distance.

It was a desperate kiss, fierce and unsteady. His hands tangled in her hair, pulling her closer as if he could fuse them together. His touch was heat and urgency, and each brush of his mouth against hers was a promise. Raw and unguarded, the unspoken words he couldn't find the voice to say.

The weight of the room, the tangle of bodies and secrets, melted away until there was only Ren, the warmth of his breath, the solid press of his chest, the steady, frantic beat of his heart beneath her palms. Her senses sharpened, each detail etching itself into her memory. The way his fingers tightened in her hair, not enough to hurt but enough to hold her still, to ground her in this moment.

The taste of him, familiar, like the first sip of dark wine, heady and lingering. Time seemed to stutter, and the world moved in slow, molten drips. His hands slid down, fingers grazing her neck, tracing the line of her jaw as if discovering her skin. Each touch left sparks in its wake, tiny embers that smoldered beneath her surface.

She gasped into his mouth, and the sound seemed to encourage him. Her fingers found their way into his hair, winding through the strands, tugging just enough to draw a breathless sound from him. His lips left hers, trailing the delicate skin beneath her ear. Each brush of his mouth was a flame against her, melting through layers of caution and restraint.

He pulled back, and pressed his forehead against her temple, his breath ragged, and Mira felt the shape of his words in her before he spoke them.

"Mira…" His voice was rough, a whisper ground against stone. "Don't leave me again. I can't survive it "

She shivered, the ache in his voice a mirror of her own. But even as he spoke, reality crept back in, a cold wind against the heat of their embrace.

She could feel the room around them, the slow, insidious unraveling of decorum. The Emberbane twisted through the air, a reminder that this moment, no matter what real emotions it was based on, was laced with magic, with manipulation. The court whispered and moved, secrets spilled between kisses, ambitions laid bare between touches. Mira pulled back, she still caught the flicker of confusion and hurt in his expression.

Her eyes shifted to Caelric, the Crowned Betrothed, seated upon the throne. His expression was still distant, as if he were not fully present, his mind drifting. Asric leaned close to him, every inch of his posture a serpentine coil of satisfaction. His lips moved quickly, words flowing into Caelric's ear, but his expression told the story, eager, victorious, dangerous.

Her heart twisted. She turned sharply, searching for familiar faces. Someone to help her. Tharion stood in an alcove, his hands gesturing sharply as he argued with Torvyn and Brahn. Torvyn's face was flushed, his jaw tight with fury, and their exchange crackled with the threat of violence. Whatever they were saying was drowned out by the noise, but the tension between them was obvious.

Mira reached for Ren's hand, threading her fingers through his. She couldn't walk away, not after the way he'd looked at her, not after his silent plea. Without a word, she pulled him with her, slipping between bodies and into the crowd.

Mira pushed forward, between bodies. She ignored the hands that grasped, the lips that brushed against her as she moved. She felt Ren behind her, his hand a steady presence in hers, grounding her as they wove through the crowd. His touch never left her, not for a heartbeat. His fingers flexed, occasionally gripping her tighter.

Each step felt like wading through honey, the Emberbane's smoke dragging at her senses, pulling her into the warmth, into the want. Hands grazed her skin, seeking warmth and connection. Lips brushed against her shoulder, strangers drawn by the candle's call. She bit down on the urge to recoil, swallowing the rising tide of unease.

Ren shifted closer to her, his arm slipping around her again, drawing her against him, his body a barrier between her and the hungry touch of the crowd.

His breath was hot against her ear, his voice a raw edge. "Mine..."

The single word rippled through her, a shiver of possession and protection. It threaded through the fog of the Emberbane. His arm tightened around her waist, and she let herself lean into him, their bodies moving as one as he carved a path through the crowd.

They reached Tharion and Torvyn and Mira's voice rose, sharp and clear, cutting through the room's fog.

"Tharion!" Neither of them turned.

Tharion's eyes were glassy, his pupils blown wide. His movements had lost their precision, his usually controlled gestures now wild arcs, reckless and unmoored.

Torvyn fared no better, his entire body trembled, as if the magic in the air had turned his blood to molten metal.

Brahn leant against a pillar, arms crossed. "You always think you know best, Tharion"

Tharion's expression twisted in anger. " You don't understand, Torvyn." Tharion's hands flexed at his sides, the tendons in his neck pulled taut.

A muscle in Torvyn's jaw jumped. His knuckles turned white where his fists clenched at his sides. "Don't," he warned, the word drawn through his teeth.

"I've done what I had to, I can't see any other way" Tharion said, his voice rough.

Brahn's eyes caught Miras, before his voice cut through the haze, edged with something bitter. "Do you think she knows, Tharion? Does she feel it, the way you flinch when she touches you? The way you close your eyes and..."

Tharion's fist connected with Brahn's face with a sickening thud. The force of the blow sent Brahn stumbling back, blood blooming at the corner of his mouth. He straightened slowly, a smear of crimson on his lips, and laughed, a hollow, fractured sound. A dark echo in the room, winding through the Emberbane smoke like a serpent.

Brahn lunged, his body a blur of motion. His shoulder crashed into Tharion's chest, and they tumbled to the marble floor, a mess of fists and snarls. The sharp crack of bone against bone filled the air, and the surrounding crowd hardly noticed, too lost in their own whispered truths and tangled limbs.

Torvyn moved to intervene, his hands grasping at Tharion's arm, trying to pull him back. But his voice was lost, swallowed by the chaos, and soon he was dragged into the fray. Brahn's elbow caught him in the ribs.

Mira felt the room closing in around her, the swell of voices rising as the court began to lose itself to Emberbane's influence. The four men around her were too far gone, their emotions no longer their own. Her eyes snapped to the throne. Caelric sat at its center, his expression a mask of detachment, but then, his gaze flickered. Sharp and searching, darting from face to face. Not dazed. Not lost. A moment of clarity. He was awake. If only for an instant, the fog had parted. The Crowned Betrothed saw everything.

Mira tore free of Ren's grasp. His hand fell away, and she felt the shift in him immediately. His breath caught a broken, keening sound, and when she glanced back, his face was a twisted mask of pain and panic.

"Mira!" His voice was a rasp, dark and desperate.

He launched toward her with a speed she had not expected. His movements were not graceful but driven by a force beyond reason, beyond restraint. She bolted, her feet slipping slightly against the polished floor. Ren stumbled and fell to the ground.

She had to reach Caelric before Asric got what he needed. The Crowned Betrothed eyes remained open, his lips moving in a slow, silent murmur as he leaned toward Asric. The lord hovered by his side, his posture casual, but there was a razor's edge to his smile, a serpent's coil in the curve of his spine. Asric's hand rested lightly on Caelric's shoulder, fingers digging in, a grip both possessive and guiding.

The crowd pressed in, their bodies a suffocating wall, but she pushed through, slipping between limbs and silk, ducking beneath outstretched hands. Her heart pounded, a wild rhythm in her ears, drowning out the room's murmur. Caelric's eyes flickered across the faces, his lips parting as if to speak, but the words died, his voice caught in the thorns of uncertainty.

Behind her, Mira felt the heat of Ren's approach, a storm brewing at her back. His footsteps were swift, each one a thunderclap against the cold stone. She could hear the sharp rustle of fabric, the startled gasps. He was shoving his way through the throng without hesitation.

She didn't dare look back. She couldn't. If she did, she knew she'd be lost, caught in his gravity, pulled into his orbit. She forced herself forward, every step a struggle against the tide of need bearing down on her. She reached the throne just as Ren lost sight of her in the crush of bodies. His voice cut through the air. A sharp, frantic cry of her name. Asric turned at the sound, his gaze finding Ren.

"Caelric, you need to get out," she breathed, her voice thin, stretched between reality and the dreamlike haze of the room.

Caelric blinked slowly, his pupils blown wide, "Mira?"

Her vision blurred. Her body swayed, her feet numb against the marble, and before she could catch herself, she was falling.

✳ ✳ ✳

"Why are you telling me this?" Mira asked.

Caelric exhaled slowly. "I had hoped you would understand Mira, that you would see what must be done. That you would submit."

Mira lifted her chin. "Submit?" she echoed, voice razor-

sharp.

Caelric moved before she could react. Fire. It seared into her skull. A burning so deep, so all-consuming, that she barely had time to scream before everything vanished.

✳ ✳ ✳

Mira blinked back, but before she could answer, Ren barreled into her, his momentum throwing her forward. His arms wrapped around her waist, ironclad and unyielding.

The breath whooshed from her lungs as he dragged her back. Ren growled toward Caelric, "Don't touch her."

Ren's lips brushed against her temple, his breath hot and uneven. His grip tightened, the fabric of her dress pulling taut beneath his fist. She could feel his desperation, the way it twisted through him, a coil of raw fear mixed with desire. Mira's feet barely touched the ground as he hauled her against him, his arm a band across her waist, the other hand across her shoulders. She twisted, struggling to find her footing, but the Emberbane's influence and Ren's overpowering strength turned every movement sluggish, dreamlike.

A shadow slipped into view, and Asric's voice cut through the air, cool and sharp.

"Well, this is... unexpected." His lips curled into a thin, amused smile. "How very interesting." His eyes moved over them, a predator assessing prey, curiosity gleaming beneath his controlled exterior.

Mira's swallowed, a small sound swallowed by the heavy air. Asric took a step forward, but Ren reacted instantly. His body shifted, angling away, pulling her deeper into his embrace. His fingers dug into her waist, a warning and a promise. A low growl rumbled through Ren's chest, vibrating against her spine. The sound was raw, unpolished, more beast than man.

"Don't come near her." The word slipped from him, a harsh rasp, his voice frayed at the edges.

Asric's smile widened, a dark bloom of victory. "The Emberbane has many uses, but I must admit, its influence over desire is my favorite. It's amazing, isn't it? How it can strip away the façade of control, leaving nothing but truth."

His gaze over to Mira, and his expression shifted, curiosity knitting with suspicion. "And yet, you… You seem far more lucid than I expected." Asric's eyes narrowed. "How is it, Mira, that you remain clear while everyone around you drowns?"

A tremor of fear coiled deep in her stomach, but she refused to let it show. "Is that what you think?" she said, her voice a careful, velvety drawl. "Perhaps I'm simply better at hiding what I truly want." Asric's brows lifted, amusement slipping over his suspicion.

"Perhaps," Asric murmured, his voice a silken thread weaving through the dimly lit room.

Asric's hand moved with a practiced grace, slipping into the folds of his cloak. When it emerged, he held a small leather pouch, worn and unassuming except for the faint, pulsing glow that seeped through its seams. With a flick of his wrist, he loosened the drawstring. The bag opened, and the powder within shimmered, a deep, iridescent hue. The air around it rippled, a distortion that made the room tilt at the edges.

Mira's vision swam, the walls stretching and bending as if caught in a dream. He stepped closer, each movement a slow, deliberate promise. Ren took a step back, tension coiling through his frame. Asric held his ground.

"Tell me, Mira," he said, his voice a low hum that resonated through her bones. "What is it you truly desire?"

A sly smile curved his lips as he brought the pouch to his lips and blew. The Emberbane dust billowed out, a cloud of ethereal smoke that engulfed her face in an instant. Cool and soft, it coated her skin, slipping into every breath. Her knees buckled.

Her lips parted, but the answer tangled in her throat. Desire. The word pulsed through her, an insistent drumbeat that blurred the line between truth and illusion. She felt weightless, untethered, as if the floor had vanished beneath her feet. She gasped, the world spinning, and Ren's hold became all she could think about.

His arms were iron bands around her waist, his chest a solid wall against her back. His breath was hot against her neck, each exhale a gust of fevered air. The world beyond him blurred, reduced to nothing but a backdrop to his presence.

Her own thoughts twisted, slippery and malleable. She couldn't grasp them, couldn't hold on to anything but the sensation of Ren's hands, the press of his body, the weight of his need.

His voice whispered through the haze, a low hum against her ear. "Stay with me," he murmured, the words looping, a gentle snare. "Mine. Always mine." Mira groaned, the sound torn from her before she blinked into a memory.

✳ ✳ ✳

Warmth. The press of strong hands on her thighs. A sharp inhale, a quiet groan. Candlelight flickering, throwing gold across bare skin. Shadows stretch long, shifting as bodies move. Her hands pressing down, steadying herself on a firm chest, feeling muscles shift beneath her palms. A slow roll of her hips. A sharp, broken sound from the man beneath her. His fingers twitched where they rested against her skin, as if waiting, straining, holding back.

"Be patient." The words left her lips, soft, teasing, meant to provoke.

A pause. A sharp inhale. His eyes, bright green, wild, burning, snapped back to hers, dark and demanding. Then, a voice, low, wrecked, frayed at the edges.

"Patience is for men who don't know what they want."

A haze of heat. He surged up, kissed her, hands to her hips, flipping her beneath him in one swift, fluid motion. A gasp. A shudder. The weight of him above her. His breath hot at her throat, his lips just a whisper away. A sharp, helpless cry tore from her lips, swallowed by his mouth as he kissed her, as he pressed deeper, filling every part of her.

She felt him, the tension in his body, the way his breath turned ragged, the way his rhythm faltered, shaking, frantic. A low, wrecked groan tore from his throat, his body tensing, shuddering, as he spilled into her, filling her, claiming her.

* * *

Ren's hold tightened, his fingers digging into her waist, anchoring her to him as reality splintered.

"Come back to me.." his voice was a whisper edged with desperation. His hands slid upwards, one arm turning her to face him, the other curling into her hair, fingers tangling in the strands. Her vision filled with him, dark eyes, shadows and fire, every sharp line of his face. He paused for a heartbeat, searching her eyes.

His lips found hers in a heartbeat, a clash of heat and need. The kiss was fierce, claiming. His mouth moved against hers, a rhythm that was all-consuming, drawing the breath from her lungs. The growl that rumbled through him sent a shiver down her spine, a sound that vibrated against her lips, slipped into her, and curled tight around her heart.

Her hands found his chest, nails scraping against the fabric, a desperate attempt to find balance when the floor felt as though it had disappeared beneath her. His heartbeat pounded under her palms, a wild tempo that matched her own. Ren's mouth moved, tracing the curve of her jaw, the line of her throat, before returning to her lips. His breaths were harsh, mingling with hers, a dance of warmth and urgency. He kissed her like he couldn't bear to stop, like every brush of their lips was a promise neither of them dared to voice.

The room spun around them, shadows and smoke stretching and twisting, but she couldn't focus on anything but him. His hands in her hair, his body pressed against hers. The hunger in his eyes matched the ache in her chest. His grip tightened, and she felt the tremor in his hands, the fine edge of control slipping away.

"Ren..." she whispered. The word barely more than a breath and the moment it left her lips, something in him snapped.

With a swift, practiced motion, he snatched her up and slung her over his shoulder. The world flipped, her view shifting to the ground. She gasped, but it was lost in the noise of the hall. His hand pressed against the back of her thigh, holding her steady as he turned, his stride long and purposeful. Her heart thundered, a wild staccato that echoed through her.

She could feel the strength in him, every muscle coiled

and ready, the tension beneath his skin palpable. The heavy double doors crashed open, a rush of cool air slamming into her as he charged into the palace gardens. The world spun with every step, her view an erratic mix of rain-soaked stone paths and the blurred canopy of storm clouds above.

His shoulder dug into her stomach, solid and unyielding, as he carried her. Rain soaked through her hair, plastering it to her face, and every inhale brought the sharp, earthy scent of wet leaves and fresh rain. She felt the cold seep through her, the chill a stark contrast to the heat of his skin against her. Her world had narrowed to the sway of his steps, the drum of the rain, and the press of his hand against her leg.

They reached the edge of the garden, slipping through a narrow archway shrouded in ivy. The world shifted, the sharp sting of rain giving way to the dim warmth of the palace interior. He moved through an attendant's corridor, the carpet muffling his footsteps. Candlelight licked the stone walls, as the corridors curved around them.

Shadows danced along the stone walls, and with every step, the intensity between them simmered, a heat that wrapped around them both. Ren's breaths, harsh and fast, began to slow, each exhale a little steadier than the last.

His grip on her thigh loosened, just slightly, his fingers flexing against her skin as if he was trying to ground himself. His pace eased into something more measured, his boots striking the stone with quiet deliberation.

"Mira?" he murmured her name.

She could hear the change in his voice, the raw edge smoothing, the heat cooling into something softer, questioning. Ren placed her on the ground and his steps faltered. His shoulders tightened, a ripple of tension that ran through him.

The hallway was quiet, the distant sound of voices reduced to a muffled hum. His eyes found hers, wide and dark, the lingering effects of the Emberbane curling around her senses. The room still spun, the world softened at the edges, and every nerve felt as if it had been set alight.

His concern was written across his face, but it barely registered. The need inside her was burning. Hot, relentless, impossible to silence.

"You didn't hurt me, Ren." she breathed, but the word came out husky.

"I wasn't, I didn't mean..." His hands raked through his hair, the movement frantic. "The Emberbane... it, " His breath came out in a shudder.

Mira moved. Her hands pressed against his chest, firm and insistent, and he staggered back, his shoulders hitting the cold stonewall. His breath rushed out in a sharp exhale, his eyes widening as she stepped into him, closing the space between them.

Her hands fisting in the fabric of his shirt. The Emberbane twisted through her, a thread of heat and need that tightened with every heartbeat. Her body pressed against his, his thigh slipping between her legs, the friction sparking something dangerous and undeniable.

"Mira..." his voice was hoarse, the sound scraping against the quiet of the corridor. His hands hovered at her waist, not pulling her closer, not pushing her away. "I need to think, "

"I don't want you to think..." she admitted, her forehead resting against his throat. Her breath came in quick, shallow bursts, every inhale pulling him deeper into her senses, the smoke and spice of him, the warmth of his skin. A shudder ran through him, his fingers finally curling into her waist, an anchor as much for him as for her.

"It's the Emberbane," he said, though his voice lacked conviction.

"Then help me..." Her hips moved, a slow, intentional roll, and his breath shivered running through him. Mira felt him flexing under her. His grip tightened, and his head fell back against the wall with a quiet thud.

"Mira," he groaned, the sound rich with need and struggle.

Slowly, he opened his eyes, and the darkness in them had softened, the shadows gentled. He looked fragile and unguarded. His hands moved, a quiet invitation, and he pulled her closer, their foreheads touching, their breaths mingling.

His voice was a murmur, a brush of warmth against her skin. "I can't say no to you..."

He slid his hand into hers, their fingers interlocking. The world around them seemed to hold its breath as he pulled her along, their steps fast and echoing.

25

THEY REACHED MIRA'S QUARTERS, the corridor hushed save for the hurried rhythm of their footsteps echoing off the stone. Candlelight flickered wildly along the high walls, shadows leaping with every breath. Ren's hand pressed at the small of her back, his touch firm, grounding her, but beneath it pulsed something deeper, something hot, reckless.

Mira didn't hesitate. Her fingers closed around the handle, shoving the door open with a sharp click, and they stumbled inside. The room was warm, thick with the scent of tahla and sandalwood. The steam from the untouched bath still hung in the air. But the heat that licked at her spine wasn't from the room. The Emberbane curled through her blood like smoke, coaxing, daring, demanding. She didn't step away. She couldn't. The fire in her veins begged for more.

"Ren... " she whispered, his name a fragile plea, breathless and raw.

Mira turned and pulled him down to her. Their mouths collided, in a searing kiss. A kiss that left no space for breath, only hunger. His lips broke from hers just long enough to whisper, voice rough with need.

"I need to hear you," he murmured, voice rough with restraint. "Say it again." Her throat tightened, the heat rising fast, flushing her skin as she leaned in, lips close enough to brush his.

"Ren please" she begged, steadier this time, but no less aching.

His eyes shut, his forehead dropping to hers, their breath tangled. He slowly pressed her back against the door, caging her in, his body flush with hers, his breath ragged, his eyes dark with need. But even through the haze, he stilled, just enough to meet her gaze.

Pressed against him, she could feel the hard, unmistakable proof of his desire through the thin barrier of her dress.

His voice was rough, low, almost reverent. "Tell me you want this. Not the Emberbane. Not the magic. You."

Mira's breath hitched. The fire in her veins burned, the Emberbane a constant thrum beneath her skin, but this... It wasn't the powder or smoke guiding her, it was her choice. She saw the boat of stars, the tangled threads of fate Danlea had shown her. The choice waiting beneath the surface, glowing and golden, pulsing with possibility. And this wasn't a mistake. Not a stolen moment. This was her choice.

Ren's gaze searched hers, something almost broken in the way he waited, braced for rejection. But she didn't pull away.

"I choose this," Mira said, voice sure, even as the heat licked at her spine. "I choose you."

He let out a shaky breath, a sound of relief. Ren's mouth crashed against hers, hot and demanding, a collision of hunger and restraint unraveling all at once. Mira melted into him, her fingers curling into his hair, nails dragging lightly along his scalp as she tilted her head, deepening the kiss.

He groaned, the sound raw and guttural, his hands gripping her waist before sliding up, tracing the curve of her spine, the dip of her lower back. His touch was everywhere, roaming without hesitation, like he needed to feel every inch of her at once. Her hips pressed flush against the door as he pinned her there. His tongue flicked against hers, teasing, consuming, and a soft moan escaped her lips.

Ren shuddered against her, his breath ragged as he pulled back just enough to let his lips brush down her jaw, to the curve of her throat. He lingered there, pressing hot, open-mouthed kisses along her skin, teeth grazing lightly before soothing the spot with his tongue. Her fingers fisted in his shirt, pulling at the fabric, needing more.

"Off," she murmured against his lips, her voice thick, breathless. He smirked against her skin.

"Impatient?" Mira let her nails scrape down his chest, feeling the ridges of muscle beneath.

"I know what I want." she breathed.

In one swift motion, he grabbed the back of his shirt and tugged it over his head, tossing it aside. Mira barely had a moment to take him in before his mouth was on hers again, desperate, consuming, as if he couldn't stand the distance for even a second. Ren braced his hands on either side of her head, caging her against the door, his bare chest rising and falling in uneven breaths. He pulled back, His eyes burned into hers, dark, searching, waiting.

His voice, thick with restraint, dropped to a husky whisper. "Tell me what you need, Mira."

She arched against him, her breath catching as the Emberbane thrummed beneath her skin, its pulse quickening with every touch.

Her fingers skimmed over Ren's shoulders, tracing the hard lines of him. "I want you inside me."

Ren groaned, his head dipping forward, his lips just brushing hers. His hands clenched against the door like it was the only thing keeping him from losing himself completely. His voice was rough, hoarse, edged with restraint.

"When I'm inside you, Mira, we won't have the

Emberbane." His forehead rested against her shoulder, his breath ragged. His words sent a shudder through her, not a warning, a vow. The Emberbane pulsed in her blood, "I'll give you anything else you want."

Mira writhed beneath him, her fingers tightening on his shoulders. "That's all I can think about."

Ren stood, and a slow, smoldering recognition sparked in Ren's eyes, deep and deliberate. He hummed, slow and deep, his lips curling into a smirk that sent heat spiraling low in her stomach.

"I have an idea..." he murmured, voice dripping with promise.

Mira's pulse pounded wildly in her throat as anticipation licked up her spine. Her body leaned toward him instinctively, drawn by the tease in his tone that made her ache with need. The Emberbane pulsed through her like liquid fire, stoking the hunger already coiled tight in her belly. Her lips parted, a soft sound escaping, half gasp, half invitation. Mira wanted every word, every touch, every wicked thought that danced behind those eyes.

His hands left the door, skimming down her sides, slow, deliberate. Mira sucked in a breath as his grip tightened on her thighs. Carefully, he gathered the layers of her dress, pulling them up, exposing her skin. He pressed her hand to the fabric, an invitation to hold it in place.

Slowly, he sank to his knees before her, eyes never leaving hers as he eased her underlace down her legs. The soft brush of his breath against her bare skin sent a shudder through her. Ren's lips traced her thigh, slow and deliberate as he placed her leg on his shoulder. Her heart hammering in anticipation.

"Stay with me," he breathed into her skin. A whisper

meant as much for himself as for her, fragile with need. Then, his mouth was on her.

Mira gasped, her head thudding back against the door as his tongue teased, slow and agonizing. He savored every second, slow and unhurried, dragging out every moment with a patience that had her trembling. She cursed, her fingers winding into his hair. Ren groaned, the sound vibrating against her, making her whimper.

His voice was dark, sinful, drenched in satisfaction. "Let me hear you." Mira couldn't help herself. She moved against him, her hips finding a faster rhythm.

He laughed softly against her, "Tell me what you need." His finger tips drifted up her thigh, hot, deliberate, teasing.

"More," Mira breathed, the word slipping out before she could temper it. Ren stilled, just for a moment. His gaze lifted to hers.

"That," he murmured, voice like silk over flame, "I can do." Before easing into her in a way that had her entire body clenching around him. Mira cried out, her hips jerking. Ren exhaled a growl, deep and husky, before burying his face in her.

Her fingers dug into Ren's head, anchoring herself as waves of pleasure crested and broke through her, relentless and consuming. The world narrowed to heat and pleasure and the ragged rhythm of her breath.

Ren groaned, deep and low, his tongue flicking, curling, pressing against her. His other hand gripped her thigh tighter, encouraging, demanding more. The pressure inside her built, unbearable, relentless.

Pleasure crashed through her, white-hot and blinding, her body trembling, her breath coming in sharp, broken gasps, his tongue and fingers never relenting, dragging it out until she was shaking, barely able to stand.

Ren sat back on his heels, his hands a brand against her thighs, his breath ragged, his lips slick from her. Tension rippled through him, his body coiled tight, like he was fighting every instinct not to lose himself in her.

Mira dropped to her knees, eyes locked on his, and pushed him onto his back. Her hands skimmed his chest as she climbed over him, her thighs sliding over his hips as she straddled him.

The shift in control was immediate, intentional. Something in Mira craved the feel of him beneath her. Wanted to guide him, to savor him, to own him for this moment.

His eyes widened, just for a blink, before that spark turned molten, dark with restraint and want. It wasn't fear. It was surrender. Willing. Eager. The Emberbane still pulsed beneath her skin, a warm, electric current that sang through her blood, but it wasn't clouding her. It was clarifying. Amplifying what she already felt. Ren's hands gripped her hips, steadying but not guiding, his body taut beneath her, his restraint visible in every corded muscle and ragged breath. But he didn't take control back. He waited. Let her lead.

"Mira," His voice was rough, pleading. "You don't have to."

She smirked, shifting lower, her hands dragging over his chest, nails scraping lightly along the ridges of muscle. Her lips brushed the center of his stomach before flicking her tongue against his skin, copying what he had done to her. Mira hummed, her fingers toying with the waistband of his trousers, her mouth hovering just above his navel. Her fingers making quick work of the belt at his waist.

Ren's hands flew to her face, his grip rough, demanding

she look at him. Lust had swallowed the color of his eyes, his breath uneven, his chest rising and falling with barely leashed restraint.

Mira smiled up at him, "I know what I want Kalren"

She knew exactly what using his full name did to him, how it stripped away the last of his control. That was the point.

"Fuck… Mira." It was a growl now desperate.

Ren's restraint burned away in a flash and he lost his mind. In a single, fluid motion, Ren moved. He pushed up and hauled her against him with a force that made her gasp. His hands were firm, unrelenting as he lifted her with ease, carrying her across the room. Mira barely had time to react before he tossed her onto the bed, her body bouncing slightly against the plush sheets.

He stood at the foot of the bed. Mira saw how he'd pulled himself back from the edge, his posture rigid with restraint, his eyes burning with everything he wasn't allowing himself to do.

"We shouldn't" he rasped, his voice strained, held together by the thinnest thread.

Mira stepped off the bed with a quiet, deliberate grace, her gaze locked on his. She reached behind her, loosening the laces of her corset with practiced ease.

"I won't be able to let you go. Not again. And the Emberbane, it's still…" His words faltered as she let the fabric slip from her shoulders and fall to the floor. Ren's breath left him in a harsh exhale.

Mira stood there, bare before him, her skin glowing in the dim light, her chest rising and falling in slow, deliberate breaths. In an instant, he was on her, his mouth crashing against hers, hands gripping her waist as he pushed her back onto the bed. His body covered hers, heat radiating from him, his need pressing into her, undeniable, unrelenting.

He pulled back but his grip on her wrists was possessive, pinning them above her head. His jaw clenched tight, his entire body vibrating with raw hunger. Mira arched beneath him, breathless, the ember of her want fanned into a blaze. Every nerve was alive, reaching for him, aching for more.

The feeling of his body against hers wasn't just pleasure, it felt inevitable, like gravity, like truth. Her pulse thundered as she met his gaze, no fear in her eyes, only desire, sharp and sure. She wanted this, wanted him, with a clarity that outshone the Emberbane's fire. This wasn't just craving, it was conviction. Her choice. Every stolen moment, each flirty remark, every undeniable pull had led them here.

With a slow, deliberate roll of her hips, she reversed their positions, her body sliding over his as she pinned him beneath her.

"Gods, Mira." he groaned, as he watched her. A growl of approval rumbling deep in his chest.

Slowly and deliberate, she crawled down his body. Her lips trailing heat against his skin. Ren shuddered, his hands twitching above his head, his body taut with anticipation. She met his gaze, sultry and certain, her smirk curling like smoke.

"Mira" His voice was tight, almost a plea.

Her only answer was removing the final barrier between them. Mira moaned, quiet and breathless, as her eyes roamed over him. Over the unmistakable evidence of the effect she had on him. Ren choked on a breath, his entire body jolting as her tongue dragged along the length of him, slow and teasing.

"Fuck," he groaned, his head pressing back against the pillows.

Mira took her time, teasing, tasting, torturing him as

her mouth worked him. Her tongue flicked, curled, dragging over the sensitive tip. She could hear Ren's moans and gasps as she explored him.

She hollowed her cheeks, taking him deeper. Ren gasped, his hips bucking slightly. Ren's breath hitched, raw and uneven, and he drove his fist into the sheets. An attempt to ground himself.

"Don't stop," he begged against a moan.

She hummed in response, the vibration sending a sharp pulse of pleasure through him. His hands flew to her hair, his fingers tangling in the strands, guiding her as his breath came in sharp, uneven gasps.

"Yes…" he groaned, his voice a growl, his control slipping. "You feel so fucking good." Mira moaned against him, taking him deeper, swallowing around him.

His entire body was shaking, his grip in her hair tightening. His muscles tensed, his breath coming in sharp, broken gasps as he tried to hold on, to prolong. Mira moved her mouth lower, slow and deep, her tongue flicking just over the base.

A raw, wrecked groan tore from his throat as his pleasure surged, his entire body trembling beneath her. She swallowed every last drop, her mouth working him through it, milking him until he was spent, his breath coming in ragged pants. Mira pulled back, wiping the corner of her mouth as she smirked up at him.

Ren lay there, utterly wrecked, his chest heaving, his head still pressed against the pillows, his hands still tangled in her hair. Slowly, lazily, he cracked one eye open, his lips curving into a dark, dangerous smile. Mira barely had the strength to move, the warmth of satisfaction settling deep in her limbs. The rush of fire that had burned so hot between them, was slowly ebbing, leaving her body heavy, her mind drifting.

She sighed, her lashes fluttering as exhaustion started to creep in. Slowly, she crawled up the length of his body, pressing herself against his side, her cheek resting against his chest. His skin was warm beneath her, his heartbeat still rapid. Ren hummed, his arm sliding around her, pulling her close, his fingers tracing slow, absentminded circles along her spine.

"It's the Emberbane," he murmured, his voice lower now, softer. "The crash is hard." Mira's lashes fluttered, her head tilting slightly to look up at him. She felt safe, wrapped in his warmth, lulled by the steady rise and fall of his chest.

"Sleep, Mira." She hummed in response, her body already giving in, already drifting. Ren pressed a slow kiss to the top of her head, his fingers still moving in lazy strokes down her back. And as Mira slipped into sleep, the last thing she heard was his voice, low, deep, almost distant. A whisper against her hair, a promise she wasn't quite awake enough to grasp.

✳ ✳ ✳

Only a few hours passed before Mira stirred. Shadows stretching longer across the walls. The air had cooled slightly, clinging damp against her skin, but the lingering scent of tahla and sandalwood still hung in the silence. She blinked against the low light.

Ren's arm lay draped over her waist, heavy with sleep, his breath warm at the back of her neck.

For a moment, she didn't move. She listened, to the stillness, to the quiet hum of her thoughts, to the way the Emberbane no longer howled, only murmured beneath her skin.

She slipped free from the bed with care. The room welcomed her with its hush. The bath still waited, the water still warm and fragrant, the petals bobbing lazily at the surface. Mira padded across the stone floor, the cold touching her bare feet like a whisper. She stepped into the bath with a soft sigh, the warmth embracing her. For a heartbeat, she simply stood in the water, watching the petals shift around her. Then, with a slow exhale, she sank down.

She dipped her head beneath the surface and the world went quiet. Mira opened her eyes. Beneath the water, everything was muted, the light, the sounds. The Emberbane's grip on her mind slackened, its claws retreating until all that remained was a quiet echo at the edges of her consciousness.

Ren had been a choice, her first choice. The first thing she had done purely for herself. Not for survival. Not for duty. But because she simply wanted him. And yet, beneath the water, the vision Danlea had shown her stirred.

The boat drifting through stars. The glowing knot of threads, golden and waiting. The convergence that pulsed with consequence. Mira had the sense that the real choice was still ahead looming, inevitable. Mira blinked the vision away. Her heart beat, slow and deliberate. She exhaled beneath the surface, bubbles rising fast from her mouth.

Slowly, Mira broke through the water, drawing breath into her lungs. Water lapped gently at the rim of the bath. Droplets clung to her lashes as she pushed her hair back. She leaned back against the smooth curve of the bathing pool, letting the warmth settle around her like a second skin.

The soft sound of footsteps broke the quiet Ren stood just within the threshold, the light from the firelight silhouetting him. Mira saw the tightness in his jaw, the tension in his posture as he moved through the room. The water rippled as he stepped into the bath, slow, almost tentative, until it reached his waist. He stilled. "Mira," he said softly.

She met his gaze, and in the silence that followed, he searched her face like he was trying to find the edge of a storm. His voice was careful, stripped of its usual charm, and laid bare.

"I know what tonight was. I know what the Emberbane can do. But what we did... what I said..." His throat worked. "I meant it. Every word. But if it wasn't real for you... if it was only the fire"

"It wasn't," she interrupted, "I wanted you." His breath left him in a slow exhale.

Mira met his eyes, "I choose you, Ren."

Ren closed the space between them, moving through the water with a quiet urgency. He reached her, his arms slipping around her waist beneath the surface, drawing her against his chest. Mira let herself fall into the embrace, into the warmth of him. His hand cradled her, his body molding to hers like it had always known how.

"Mira," he began, voice rough at the edges.

His thumb moved along her spine, a small, rhythmic motion as if the words needed coaxing. "I'm so sorry. For everything."

Her brow furrowed slightly, a question ghosting across her features, but Ren continued, his voice a low, steady.

"For the memories you lost because of me. For the choices I made. I really thought I was protecting you." His voice caught, and he swallowed, the motion sharp and visible, as if every word scraped against something raw inside him. "I was wrong."

The admission seemed to pull something from him, a

weight he had carried too long. His shoulders dropped, and for a moment, he simply looked at her, his gaze a quiet, open plea.

The candlelight cast soft shadows across his face, etching the vulnerability into every line, every curve. Mira let the silence stretch between them, the gentle slosh of water a soft undertone that filled the space with a rhythmic calm. She reached up, her fingers feeling the warmth of his cheek.

"I know." Her voice was soft, but each word settled with purpose, solid and unyielding.

Her thumb brushed against his jaw, feeling the faint tremor beneath his skin, the unspoken fragility he rarely showed. A shiver ran through him, a barely there motion, and his eyes closed. The weight of her acceptance sinking into him like a stone finding its place at the bottom of a still pond.

"I never wanted to hurt you," he whispered, the words rough and broken. "I just want you, Mira."

The air between them seemed to hum, charged with the gravity of his confession. The water cradled them, warm and still, a sanctuary.

"Every single part of you," he murmured. "I want your your mind, your heart, every scar, every guarded corner. " He pressed a soft kiss to her shoulder. His fingers slid into her hair, slow, reverent.

"I want your strength, your softness, your rage, your silence. I want the way you move, the way you dream, the way you doubt. There's not a single part of you I don't want to know, to hold, to fight for."

His forehead pressed to hers, his voice lowering, raw and trembling. "I want to stand beside you. In every storm. In every battle. I want you to look at me and know I'm yours, because you chose me. Because I choose you."

Mira closed her eyes. The warmth of Ren's words lingered on her skin, but underneath, a thread pulled taut through her chest. Mira felt the pull of him, the ache, the beauty of it, a promise wrapped in longing, in forgiveness and in devotion. Tharion's face flickered in her mind, Solid. Steady. His presence had been a shield. A constant. Their bond forged in quiet loyalty and shaped by hardship, not fire. What she and Tharion had was different than this. It was duty.

Her chest tightened. Grief and guilt pricked at the edges of this moment like a cold wind slipping through warm water. She wanted to hold it all at once, who she had chosen, and who she had not yet let go.

"I..." The word caught in her throat.

For a heartbeat, silence stretched between them. The only sound was the slow ripple of water and the faint crackle from the hearth. Ren's fingers brushed gently along her jaw. His eyes searched hers, not for proof, not for permission, but for truth. Then he nodded, just once before a genuine smile filled his face.

"You don't have to say anything, Mira," he said, voice thick but sure. "Just being with you is enough for me." His forehead touched hers again. It felt like devotion. Adoration. Love. "I'll wait," he murmured. "However long it takes."

Mira let herself breathe into the quiet between them. Ren lingered there with her, their foreheads pressed together, breath shared in the hush. His arms tightened around her, not with urgency, but with care. And then, slowly, deliberately, he shifted.

"Come on," he murmured, pressing a kiss to her temple.

The water lapped gently around them as he moved, keeping one arm secure around her waist. Mira let herself be guided, her limbs loose, pliant from heat and emotion. He helped her step from the bath, the cool air kissing her damp skin. Ren reached for a thick towel first, wrapping it around her shoulders before grabbing one for himself. He dried her slowly, his hands moving with patient gentleness. Sweeping over her arms, down her back, across the lines of her shoulders. Mira watched him in the low light, his hair black with water, his skin glistening beneath the soft sheen of hearth light. Once she was dry, he paused, and toweled off quickly.

When he met her eyes again, there was no pressure, only a warmth that settled deep.

They walked back into the main chamber, bare feet soft against the stone. Ren pulled back the covers of the bed and climbed in first, his arm outstretched in silent invitation.

Mira slipped in beside him, nestling into the space that had been waiting for her. He pulled her close without a word, her head resting back against his chest, their legs tangling beneath the blankets. His heartbeat thudded steady beneath her cheek. One of his hands moved lazily through her hair, fingers trailing.

The scent of him surrounded her, wood-smoke and warmth, like the memory of a fire long after it had burned low. It clung to her skin, to the sheets, to the air between them, grounding her more deeply than anything else could have.

Mira breathed him in, the scent wrapping around her like a blanket, settling into the hollow places where worry used to live. It was steady. Familiar. Him. Ren shifted just slightly, his hold tightening for a heartbeat before relaxing again, as if even in sleep, he didn't want to let her go.

And wrapped in the scent of wood-smoke, cradled by the quiet strength of his embrace, Mira finally let herself drift into sleep.

26

S UNLIGHT STREAMED THROUGH the windows, spilling across the bed in ribbons of light. The dawn was soft and unhurried, the world holding its breath in the hush that followed the storm of the night before. Ren's fingers traced slow, aimless patterns along Mira's bare back, his touch warm, grounding, a quiet invitation back to the waking world.

She stirred beneath the sheets, the coolness of linen kissing her skin as her eyes fluttered open. A sleepy smile pulled at the corners of her mouth before her gaze found his. He was already watching her, his head propped against one hand, dark hair tousled, eyes soft and still heavy with sleep.

"Good morning," he murmured.

Mira's smile widened, and she stretched languidly, the movement drawing a content sigh from her lips. He leaned in, brushing a kiss across her shoulder. But even as they lay wrapped in warmth and shared stillness, a flicker of concern crept into his features. He exhaled, slow and reluctant.

"Last night…" Ren's hand slid from her back to rest against her waist, fingers flexing gently, as if the act of touching her helped settle the words.

"He saw us, Mira. At the height of it. You and me. Together. In front of the entire court." Her smile faded. "Asric."

Ren gave a small nod, jaw tight.

"He saw. And he'll use it. Maybe not today. Maybe not openly. But that man doesn't forget things like that. That was the game last night. Collect enough secrets, enough leverage."

Mira pushed herself up slightly, propped on one elbow, the sheet clinging to her skin. Her pulse beat harder in her throat. Her stomach twisted, fear flickering low in her gut, but it wasn't fear of what he might do to her. It was fear of what he might try to do to Ren as the Regent.

Her voice was soft, but firm. "You don't have to protect me from this. We face it together. I won't be the weakness someone uses against you."

The fear hadn't vanished. It still sat there, coiled and waiting. She had spent too long being protected, being sheltered behind the choices of others. Not this time. She wouldn't be hidden. She wouldn't be a pawn in someone else's game. Not even for him. Ren's gaze searched hers, his fingers brushing a strand of damp hair from her cheek.

"You were never a weakness." he said quietly, Mira inhaled, steadying herself.

"I'm with you, Ren." She hesitated, "Brahn and Torvyn don't see that yet. They still think I need to be managed. I can help you."

They lingered in the quiet after that, wrapped in a stillness. His fingers resumed their path along her spine, soft and slow. But even as they lay wrapped in warmth and shared stillness, a flicker of responsibility crept into his features. He exhaled, reluctant.

"I have to go," he said, pressing a soft kiss to her temple. "Council meeting. Early and infuriating."

She groaned, muffling the sound against her pillows. Ren dropped his head to meet her eyes.

"Do you remember the first council meeting in the observatory?"

Her eyes opened, still fogged with sleep, but she nodded faintly. Ren smiled.

"I wasn't ready to rule," he said with a quiet laugh, turning to face her. "Not even close." He paused.

"Everyone down there talked like power was owed. Inherited. But you made it feel like it was chosen, like I could choose to help."

Her voice was quiet, almost teasing. "Wasn't it yours, anyway?"

He looked at her. "It wasn't my blood that convinced me to take the Regency." he said, voice low. "It was you."

The words hung there, tender and unshaken. Mira reached out, brushing a thumb along his jaw, memorizing the soft stubble, the curve of his mouth as he smiled. She adored everything about him in that moment, the sleepy husk of his voice, the way his gaze lingered on her like she was the only thing that steadied him.

He rose, finally, slowly, with the stiffness of a man who didn't want to leave. Mira watched him dress, taking in every familiar motion, the stretch of his arms as he pulled on his shirt, the quiet hum he didn't know he made.

When he reached the door, he turned back to her. "I'll find you later."

Mira stretched beneath the sheets, her bare leg sliding against the warmth he'd left behind. "Not if I can convince you to stay..."

He laughed, low and genuine. He paused, her words lingering in the air like a challenge wrapped in silk. Without a word, he crossed the room towards her, each step sure, inevitable. Mira propped herself up on one elbow, watching him with lazy delight as he reached the edge of the bed.

He leaned down, bracing one hand beside her, the other

curling gently under her jaw.

"If I could stay here between your legs I would," he murmured, voice barely above a whisper, "but I'll remember your taste all Navigators damned day."

He kissed her. It wasn't hurried, or teasing, or even entirely sweet. It was deep and slow and full of all the things he hadn't said when he'd dressed in silence.

His thumb brushed along her cheekbone as their lips met, and the warmth of him poured into her like sunlight. When he pulled back, it was with a reluctant sigh, his forehead pressing briefly to hers.

"I'll find you as soon as I am done" he whispered, and then he was gone.

Mira lay still in the quiet hours that followed, the ghost of his touch lingering. Her mind was clear. She had made her choice and now, it was time to face the consequences.

* * *

Mira found Tharion in the guard barracks, his back to her, adjusting the buckles on his armor. The room smelled of steel and sweat, the sharp tang of polish clinging to the air. The sounds of clashing blades and shouted orders drifted in from the training yard, but Tharion remained focused, his movements precise, controlled.

She hesitated for half a breath before stepping forward. "Tharion."

He turned at the sound of her voice. His eyes flickered over her, taking her in, searching, but for what, she didn't know.

He exhaled, the tension in his posture shifting, though not disappearing. "Mira."

A fresh bruise bloomed along his hand. Her chest tightened, the image of him hitting Brahn still sharp in her mind.

Her voice was fragile. "Are you okay?"

"I'll be fine." He offered a half-smile, but it didn't reach his eyes.

Her fingers itched to reach out, to brush against the mark on his skin, to offer some comfort, but she held herself still. She wasn't sure if he would accept it, or if she even had the right to offer it. Instead, she extended her hand, palm up, the simple gesture a quiet bridge over the chasm between them.

"Walk with me?" A beat of silence stretched between them.

With a slow nod, he tightened the last strap of his bracer, rolling his shoulders, and took her hand. Together, they stepped out into the open air.

The gardens stretched before them, a wild contrast to the barracks' rigid order. Sunlight streamed through the leaves, creating dappled shadows on the stone paths below. The breeze carried the scents of rain-soaked earth and roses from last night's storm.

They walked in silence. Not tense, but thick with apprehension, like the hush before a storm neither of them wanted to name. The crunch of gravel beneath their boots was the only sound between them for a long while, both of them lost in their own thoughts.

A memory stirred. Unbidden, insistent, pulling Mira back to what they had been, and the fragile, shifting shape of what they were now.

✳ ✳ ✳

The training ring lay half-buried beneath a thin crust of snow, the frost-cracked earth beneath Mira's boots as hard as stone. Each breath hung in the air, a cloud of white against the slate-gray sky. The winter chill gnawed through her layers, but she hardly felt it, not when the dagger in her hand was cold steel and the hulking figure across the ring wore a grin that didn't quite reach his eyes.

Tharion stood with his arms crossed, a mountain draped in worn leather and frost- kissed furs. His brown hair was a tangle of strands, and his breath plumed around him, a pale cloud that drifted away too quickly. He moved slowly, purposefully, the snow crunching beneath his heavy boots as if he were careful not to break the world beneath him.

"Are you going to keep staring me down, or actually take a swing?" His voice was a rumbling challenge, a warm ember against the encroaching cold.

Mira rolled her shoulders, the weight of the dagger familiar, the smooth hilt worn by years of practice. Nothing too big, he'd told her once, back when the snow was fresh, and the sky wasn't so heavy.

"You've got to learn to slip the blade in, not just shoot an arrow through their head."

She slid her boot against the snow, finding her stance. "I'm just waiting for you to blink," she shot back, her breath puffing out in small, white clouds.

"Oh, she has teeth." Tharion raised his own dagger, the blade looking almost comically small in his massive hand. He twirled it with surprising finesse, the metal catching the dull winter light. "Come on, then. Show me."

She moved, quick as a hare, her feet a soft whisper against the frozen ground. She closed the distance between them, dagger low, her body a coil of potential energy.

Tharion's eyes tracked her, sharp and bright, but there was something else there too, a shadow behind the light, a weight that neither of them spoke of.

She feigned left, her dagger darting toward his side, but he pivoted smoothly, his large frame a wall of muscle and fur. He caught her wrist, twisting just enough to make her drop the blade, and in the same fluid motion, he pulled her off balance. She hit the snow with a soft thud, the cold biting through her clothes, the impact rattling something loose inside her.

"Too slow," he said, his tone more fond than mocking. Mira huffed, her breath scattering snowflakes.

"You're like a damn tree," she muttered, "and I'm supposed to chop you down with a toothpick."

Tharion's laughter was a warm, rolling sound, but it faded too quickly. He crouched beside her, the snow crunching under his weight.

"Then stop swinging like a lumberjack." He held out her dagger, the blade nestled in his massive palm. "Fight smarter. You're quick, use it. Get in close, under their guard."

She took the dagger, the cold metal grounding her. "And if I can't get close?"

"Then you make me come to you." He stood, offering her a hand. She took it, her small fingers engulfed in his, and he hauled her to her feet with ease. "Lead me where you want. You're not here to overpower, you're here to out think."

Mira dusted the snow from her clothes, her cheeks burning from more than the cold. "Fine," she said, setting her stance again. "One more round."

He moved back into position, dagger at the ready. They circled each other, boots crunching on the frostbitten ground. Tharion's strikes were quick and controlled, his broad frame moving with a grace that belied his size. Mira darted around him, slipping through his defenses with a mix of speed and intuition. Their blades clashed, the metal ringing in the winter air, and each exchange held a blend of challenge and camaraderie, but also something more, something unspoken.

Mira feinted left, drawing his guard high, and then dropped low, sweeping her leg out to catch his ankle. Tharion's balance wavered, and with a twist and a push, she drove him back. His boots slid over the ice-packed ground, and he landed hard on his back, snow puffing up around him. Tharion grinned up at her, his expression caught somewhere between amusement and something else, something almost wistful.

Before she could react, his hands shot up, large and calloused. He gripped her waist, rolling sharply to the side. Snow and sky blurred together, and a surprised yelp escaped her lips as the world flipped. The next thing she knew, her back hit the snow, the cold biting through her layers, and Tharion was next to her, his dagger resting gently against her collarbone. Mira let out a breathless laugh, her cheeks flushed from the cold and the tumble. He pulled back, offering her a hand, and she took it, their fingers cold and tight. He pulled her to her feet, snow clinging to their clothes.

He threw his arm around her shoulders, guiding her back toward the keep. "Come on…"

✳ ✳ ✳

Mira blinked and the garden unfolded around her in perfect, aching clarity Finally, after several paces, Mira broke the silence. "I'm sorry."

Tharion's stride didn't falter, but his breath did. He exhaled, slow and measured, like he was choosing his words with care.

"Me too," Tharion admitted, no anger in it.

Mira nodded, swallowing against the tightness in her throat. An ache that had been lodged there for months, maybe longer.

"I don't want to force this with you anymore." Mira admitted, eyes downcast.

Tharion's jaw clenched, a flicker of something crossing his face, regret, grief, resignation. She squeezed his hand.

The quiet stretched between them. It wasn't peaceful. It was the kind that came when something was crumbling, when two people had already let go but hadn't dared to say the words yet.

The wind rustled the orange and yellowing leaves above them, the decaying scent of leaves and rain hanging thick in the air. It felt like mourning.

Mira slowed her steps, turning slightly toward him, studying his face. She remembered the features she had once memorized through shared laughter and stolen moments of joy. The crinkle at the corner of his eyes, the way his lips quirked into an almost-boyish grin.

But now, they were unreadable. His gaze remained fixed ahead, his lips pressed into a firm line, as if looking at her would be too much. As if acknowledging what was missing between them would make it real.

She hesitated, but the question was already forming on her lips. "What was your Emberbane desire last night?"

Tharion's stride faltered. A muscle in his jaw jumped. His fingers curled at his sides, his shoulders tightening as though bracing for impact. His breath shallowed, but he didn't answer. The silence stretched between them, raw and unrelenting.

Mira inhaled sharply, the truth sinking like a stone in her chest. "It wasn't me,"

He stiffened, his entire body locking up. The air between them turned brittle, sharp enough to cut. She swallowed, her voice quieter now but no less certain.

"And you weren't mine." The words landed softly, yet their weight pressed down on the space between them. The silence stretched, thin and delicate, as if a single breath could shatter it.

Tharion's eyes found hers, steady despite the tremor in her chest. Tharion's throat bobbed. She thought, for a fleeting moment, that he might deny it. That he might force a smile, tell her she was wrong, ease the jagged edges of what they both already knew. But he didn't. He just stood there. Silent.

Mira nodded once, "It's okay," she murmured, holding his hand with both of hers. "You don't have to tell me."

Tharion exhaled sharply, running a hand down his face before dropping his gaze to the ground. The silence stretched between them, a thin, frayed thread threatening to snap. Tharion's breath misted in the cold air, each exhale shallow and uneven.

Mira held his hand, her grip firm yet gentle, as if her touch alone could bridge the widening chasm between them. Mira let go of his hand slowly, her fingers trailing over his knuckles until there was nothing but the autumn air between them. Her arms wrapped around herself, as if she could hold the pieces of her heart.

Her voice broke the quiet, a fragile whisper that barely

rose above the soft rustle of leaves. "I know you care," she said gently, each word measured, careful. "But…this isn't good…for either of us."

Tharion stilled, his broad frame quiet against the gold-and-crimson blur of the autumn garden. Leaves drifted slowly through the air, catching on his shoulders and hair like they, too, weren't sure where to land.

"I don't feel like this is what you want. What either of us want…" she added, voice quieter now. There was no accusation. Only the soft ache of truth, of something slipping quietly apart beneath a sky. The admission gutted her, made her feel exposed in a way she hadn't expected. But it also lifted something deep inside, a weight loosening in her chest, even as it broke her.

Tharion stood, staring at the ground. After what felt like an eternity, he exhaled again, slower this time. His shoulders sagged, and when he lifted his gaze, there was a weight in his eyes that made her heart clench.

"I agree, Mira." he murmured, his voice hoarse and rough around the edges. "I'm sorry…"

In that single admission, Mira realized she had been waiting for something that would never come. She had braced herself for the truth, told herself she was ready, that she needed to hear it. But the reality of his words, the finality of them, slipped beneath her skin, sharp and unyielding. It was not a clean break, not a swift release, but a slow and aching of everything she had held together. The sharp edges of his confession pressed against wounds she had spent months trying to ignore, pushing deeper into the soft, bruised parts of her heart.

But, underneath the hurt, there was something else. Relief. For both of them. It crept in quiet and unbidden, like breath after being held too long. She saw it in the softening of his features, in the way he no longer looked at her like she was his duty.

There was peace in the honesty. In the release. But even as that freedom settled in her bones, Mira mourned. Not just the bond, but the version of them she had clung to. That love had once been waiting in the space between them. She had built her future out of that hope, sketched dreams around a love that had never quite arrived. Her breath shuddered, and she forced herself to nod, to acknowledge the truth, even as it cracked her open.

"I know," she whispered, barely more than a breath. "I think… we've both known for a while." A single tear slipped down her cheek, but she didn't move to wipe it away. She let it fall. Let it be a mark of everything they had been, and everything they couldn't be anymore.

Mira drew in a slow breath, the cool air brushing her lungs like a reminder that there was still more to say. She couldn't lie to him again.

"There's something else," she murmured, her voice barely more than a tremor. Tharion looked up at her again, his eyes tired but open, waiting.

"I was with Ren last night." The words didn't come sharp or defensive. Just quiet. Steady. "It wasn't the Emberbane. It wasn't an impulse. It was a choice. My choice."

Tharion didn't flinch. Didn't look surprised. His eyes searched hers, and for a long moment, he said nothing. Mira pressed on, needing him to understand. Not to approve, but to know.

"I need to be honest with you. You deserve that. We both do." She swallowed. "And I need you to know I still care about you. I don't want to lose you completely. Not as a friend." She looked down at the ground. "But if that's not what you want I would understand."

A wind stirred through the trees, scattering a shower of golden leaves between them.

"I want you to be happy, Tharion," she said, softer now. "Truly. Even if it's not with me."

His shoulders rose and fell with a slow breath, and then, quietly, unexpectedly, he smiled. It was small and weary, but it was real.

She blinked. "You're not upset?"

He shook his head. "How could I be? He's my brother in arms, Mira. And you…" He met her eyes again, and there was no bitterness there. Just warmth, and maybe something like relief. "You deserve someone who sees you. Who chooses you." his small smile widened "I'm glad you chose him."

Emotion swelled in her throat, and she had no words for the gratitude that settled like sunlight in her chest. She stepped forward, and Tharion opened his arms without hesitation. She folded into his embrace, her hands pressing gently against his back as she rested her cheek against his chest.

His heartbeat was steady, a quiet rhythm that anchored her to the moment. He rested his chin lightly atop her head, his breath brushing through her hair as he exhaled.

They stood there, bound not by the promises they couldn't keep, but by the friendship they could still hold on to. For all the love she had lost, for all the dreams that had crumbled between them, Tharion was still him. Still the boy who had always stood by her side.

For the moment, they simply stood in the autumn light, surrounded by falling leaves and the echo of something that had ended. Tharion pulled back just enough to meet her eyes, a smile ghosting across his lips, tired, knowing.

"Well," he said, voice low and edged with something that wasn't quite amusing, " I guess Ren's your problem now."

Mira huffed a soft laugh, the sound catching in her throat. "I think he'd say the same about me."

Tharion's smile turned lopsided, a flash of old warmth in the autumn light. "He would never."

She touched his arm briefly, grounding the moment, then stepped back. "Perrin will think I celebrated too much last night if I don't show up soon."

He gave a half-hearted mock bow. Mira smiled as she turned away.

* * *

The altar chamber was quiet, still recovering in the night's celebrations. The soft amber glow of sunlight spilled in through the high stained-glass windows. Dust motes danced in the slanted light, drifting lazily between the shafts of color that fell across the smooth stone floor.

Mira's steps echoed softly as she approached the altar she had attended each morning since her relegation began. The ritual had become more than penance. It had become a rhythm. She had grown familiar with the hush of the chamber, the weight of its stillness, the sacred ache it asked her to carry.

Cleric Perrin was already there. She stood at the base of the altar in full ceremonial robes, her veil removed, hair catching the morning light. Her hands were folded, her expression unreadable but calm, as always. Mira slowed, unease curling in her chest like a whispered warning.

"I thought I'd begin before the morning prayers," Mira

said. Her voice was quieter than she meant it to be.

Perrin turned to her fully. "That is unnecessary." Mira's brow furrowed. Something shifted in her chest. "You've been released from relegation." Perrin stated.

The words hit her like a bell in the silence, sharp and soft all at once. Mira blinked, unsure she'd heard correctly. "What?"

"You've done what was asked of you. And more." Perrin stepped closer, her voice low and certain "Your duties for me are complete. You've given your silence, your service, your time. You are no longer relegated, Lady Solwynd. You may return to the activities your station demands of you."

For a moment, Mira didn't move. Didn't speak. She had carried the weight of her relegation and had woven itself into her bones. To be freed from it felt untethering. Like stepping onto a ship just as the moorings were cut.

"I don't understand." Her voice was softer now, the stillness of the chamber wrapping tightly around her, as though it were bracing too.

Perrin studied her. For a heartbeat, Mira saw something in the cleric's expression that looked almost like sadness. Or reverence. Or both.

"I have a feeling the next chapter of our kingdom will require all of your attention." She murmured.

The words struck a chord deep within Mira. The memory of Danlea's vision surged forward. The boat of stars. The golden knot of threads. The glowing convergence that pulsed like a second heartbeat beneath her skin. She wasn't just being released. She was being prepared.

Perrin reached out, touching two fingers lightly to Mira's temple. The gesture was familiar now, but this time it felt final. Sacred.

"Go with clarity and walk in purpose." Mira stood still, the air suddenly charged around her like the breath before a storm.

Emotion swelled in her chest. Relief, apprehension, purpose. All pulling in different directions. She looked up at the altar one last time. The candles were lit. The offerings cleared. The floor swept.

There was no need for her here.

27

THE HEAVY OAK DOORS of the library loomed before her. Mira's hand curled around the worn iron handle, cool beneath her fingers, and she paused, not out of hesitation, but to savor the moment.

For the first time since her punishment, the day was hers. No duty to shoulder. Her relegation was over. She pushed open the door. The hinges groaned, but even that sound felt comforting now, familiar. The scent of old parchment and ink greeted her like an old friend. Her heart swelled in her chest. She hadn't realized how much she'd missed this, the hush of the library, the stillness. A quiet invitation to lose herself in stories, just for the joy of it.

The mid-morning light filtered through the high arched windows, turning the dust motes into flecks of gold. They floated lazily in the air, caught in sunbeams like suspended stars. Mira stepped inside, letting the door swing quietly shut behind her.

She didn't rush. Her feet knew the way, guiding her down familiar aisles, past towering shelves and ancient spines. Her fingers trailed along the books as she passed, touching each one like a small blessing.

Ren would be deep in council matters. That whole hall would be knotted with politics and tension. And Tharion... Tharion needed his own space after their confessions. Just as she did. Mira knew she couldn't hold the weight of that closeness right now, not when her heart was still mending from the truths they had finally spoken. No, the library was all she needed.

She rounded a corner into the back alcove, her favorite. The oldest texts lived here, wrapped in leather and time, their pages softened by generations of hands. Mira's breath deepened, and something inside her settled.

She scanned the shelf until her gaze caught on a familiar title, Legends of the Navigators. Her pulse leapt. The same book Ren had shown her, back when everything between them had been uncertain and delicate. The one with soft illustrations and myth drawn with reverence, not certainty.

Her fingers brushed the spine, but the leather was too smooth. The gold leaf, too sharp. She pulled it from the shelf and opened it carefully. The pages were uniform, pristine. A newer edition. Not the one he'd shown her.

Still, she lowered herself onto the cushioned window seat, cradling the book in her lap. It wasn't the one she remembered, but it was close. Sunlight streamed in, warming the side of her face. Mira tilted her head back and closed her eyes for a moment, breathing in the silence.

Mira opened the book slowly, the spine creaking faintly in her hands. The parchment was smooth, untouched, the ink still crisp. She flipped past the prologue, past the familiar names she'd seen a dozen times before. The illustrations were gone, replaced by precise columns of text.

Each legend felt flattened, its wildness trimmed away, its edges dulled by order and clarity. The silence of the library seemed to echo with it, the absence of wonder humming too loud in the stillness. And then, tucked between the lines of catalogued myths and navigators, she saw a title.

Lyren of the Tide-Worn Shore.

They say he was born beneath storm light, his first breath drawn as thunder broke, waves striking stone like a war drum's call, salt on his skin before air touched his lungs.

He was not loud, not the strongest. But stillness lived in his bones, His hands knew sail and tiller, his voice rarely used, but when it rose, it carried the hush of deep waters, a calm that felt like knowing.

They fled in silence across black waves, leaving smoke and chains behind. The boats, unsteady. The stars above watched, but the sea below grew restless. The wind soured.

The currents turned. Rain fell sharp as teeth, and the sea demanded something. Not possessions. Not gold. A deeper sacrifice.

The boats began to struggle. Oars snapped. The horizon vanished in mist. Despair crept in with every rising swell.

Until Lyren rose. He stood upon the railing, his figure small against the dark sky and rising waves. The seas had named its price.

Lyren, born against the waves and storms, was taken in payment. Dragged down by the ocean's cold, closing hand.

He drowned so others might continue. His name was not lost, but kept in the mouths of the ancestors. A lullaby beneath the waves.

Mira sat in the pool of quiet sunlight, the book still open on her lap. The final lines of Lyren's story echoing softly in her mind.

Lyren had given himself over not with fury or fight, but with quiet resolve. He had been taken into the sea knowing it would kill him, knowing that his voice would be carried beneath the surface so others might rise. It was a story passed down to remind them not just of sacrifice, but of grace. Of power that lived in surrender.

Mira's hand hovered over the page, fingertips brushing the page like she might absorb more if she just stayed a little longer. The ache in her chest wasn't sadness. Not exactly. It was recognition. A resonance that ran deeper than memory.

She saw herself, in the hush of Lyren's steps, in the weight of his quiet. She wasn't drowning, but she understood the feeling of being carried by currents she hadn't chosen. She had given up parts of herself to silence and duty. To bonds that had frayed, to false truths.

That was what the Navigators' stories had always been. Not perfect histories. Not bright fables with happy endings. But mirrors. Ways to see themselves in the shadows of the past. Mira traced the final line again with her thumb.

Footsteps. Sharp. Hurried. They echoed against the stone like strikes of iron. Mira stilled. She was tucked into the shadowed alcove between two shelves, hidden by centuries of dusty pages and stained glass light. But the voices carried. Brahn and Torvyn.

"You think keeping me in the dark makes you right?" Torvyn's voice came sharp and sudden.

Mira pressed herself deeper into the chair's worn curve, heart thudding loud in her chest.

"You are reckless. You move without my orders, make choices that put all of us at risk." Brahn spoke quietly, but the anger in his voice was unmistakable.

His boots struck the floor hard, measured. Cold. "Your little stunt last night was the last straw, Torvyn. I needed everything in place. And now?"

Mira's stomach twisted. That tone, Brahn didn't sound like a man worried for allies or the kingdom. He sounded like someone who had been denied a prize. Someone used to control, furious at its loss.

"In place? You mean beaten down and ripe for the taking?" Torvyn barked a bitter laugh. "I've helped you,

Brahn."

And suddenly Mira wasn't in the library at all. She was back in Danlea's vision. The throne room in ruin. The banners of Bharalyn torn and curling like embers. Brahn at the center, crowned in silver and blue, seated on a throne. Like it had been waiting. Like he had always known. The smile that did not reach his eyes. The way his fingers tapped, slow and patient. As if every moment had unfolded according to plan.

"We're bonded, which makes your recklessness mine to deal with" Brahn muttered.

The door creaked. She heard Brahn's steps retreating, clipped and smooth. Torvyn followed, slower. The door thudded shut and the lock clicked into place. Only then did Mira breathe.

She looked down at the book still resting in her lap. Lyren's sacrifice. Brahn was moving pieces into place and Torvyn was caught in the current. She needed to warn Ren. Mira rose from the alcove, setting the book aside. She stepped into the afternoon light and slipped from the library.

✳ ✳ ✳

The corridors stretched endlessly before Mira, each step weighed down by the burden of what she had overheard. She quickened her pace, her pulse a steady drumbeat in her ears as she approached Ren's quarters.

The door was shut, the room beyond eerily silent. She knocked once. No answer. A second time. Nothing. The emptiness on the other side sent unease crawling up her spine. The stillness felt wrong, thick with tension, with waiting. The observatory. If the council was still in session, he would be there.

She had barely made it halfway when the first warning bell shattered the afternoon. A deep, resonant chime rolled through the halls, reverberating through stone. Then another. And another. Mira had never heard the bell before, but she knew, deep down, what it warned. The palace stood on the brink of an attack.

Mira turned a corner, barely processing what she saw before she collided. A pair of steady hands caught her just in time. When she looked up, Ren's gaze met hers, dark and urgent. Outside the open corridor windows, the sun had begun its descent, streaked with the first embers of sunlit amber, swallowed by rolling clouds.

"Mira?" His brows furrowed in surprise. "I was looking for you," she breathed, catching her balance.

"I heard the bell, "

He cut in, "There's no time," his voice firm but not unkind. "Kharadors have crossed the border"

The words struck like a blade to the chest. Her fingers curled into fists, nails biting into her palms as she swallowed the tremor rising in her throat. Ren's eyes flicked down the corridor, scanning. Then, in a heartbeat, he turned back to her and pulled her close.

His hands cupped her face first, reverent, his thumbs brushing along her cheekbones like he was trying to memorize her. His lips met hers in a kiss that held all the things neither of them had the luxury of saying: love, longing, the quiet desperation of two souls caught in the storm.Mira's fingers curled into the fabric of his coat, gripping tight and anchoring herself. Her hands trembled slightly. Ren moved his hand from her face to her back and pulled her in.

He held her like he'd done it a hundred times in dreams.

It was as if his body had been molded to meet hers. She felt the rise and fall of his chest against hers, the shallow breaths uneven and syncing to her own. His heartbeat thundered beneath her hand, pressed flat against his ribs, fast and unhidden.

Despite the cold seeping through the archways, his warmth enveloped her. There was no barrier at that moment. Not war. Not history. Not the silence they had once let stretch too far. Just them, reaching, orbiting, pulled in by something inevitable.

Too soon, he pulled away. His forehead brushed hers for the briefest second, grounding them both for one heartbeat more.

"You're the best aim we've got. Meet me at the palace steps as soon as you can."

She nodded once, sure and silent, and then she ran. Mira wanted to stop him. To tell him about the vision, but the warning bells rang through the corridors, low and relentless, urgency carving out every second.

When Mira pushed open the door to her quarters, she found Tharion already inside. He turned as she entered, a bundle in his hands, her leather armor from Brahn and her crossbow.

"I figured you'd come back here first," he said simply, stepping aside to make space for her.

Mira nodded, closing the door behind her. "Good guess."

She moved toward him, taking the items without ceremony, her fingers brushing his in passing. The touch didn't spark tension the way it might have weeks ago. Whatever weight had once stretched between them had shifted into something simpler. Friendship. "Thank you," she added, almost as an afterthought.

Tharion only nodded, already turning away to shrug off his outer layers. She tossed her crossbow onto a nearby chair as they dressed in silence.

"The resistance is mobilizing and marching on the palace" Tharion said as he strapped the leather to his forearms. "Scouts say we've got less than an hour."

Mira paused, her hand halfway to the buckle on her vambrace. The words didn't sit right. Cold slipped down her spine like a premonition.

"No," she murmured, half to herself. "That's not who this is." Tharion looked over, frowning. "What?"

She shook her head, finishing the strap with more force than necessary. "It's not the resistance. It's the Kharadors."

Tharion adjusted the last strap. "Are you sure?"

Mira met his eyes, "They've crossed the border." His brows drew together, sharp and uncertain.

When she moved to retrieve her crossbow, his voice came again, quiet but firm. "I'll go with you."

Mira slung the strap over her shoulder, turning toward him. "I don't need a bodyguard."

Tharion gave a smile. "I wasn't offering to be one." She blinked. "I'm offering an ally," he added, voice steady. "I'll watch your back, if you watch mine."

She held his gaze for a beat longer as she tucked a knife into her belt. Then she offered her hand. Tharion clasped it without hesitation.

"Deal." she said quietly.

There was warmth in her tone, trust, quiet and steady. They stood in the center of the room, the setting sun slanting through the windows, catching on the worn edges of their leather armor. Not friends clinging to the past.

Not lovers mourning what might have been. Just two warriors, standing side by side, ready to face whatever came next, together.

Mira let out a breath, low and even. "Let's go."

28

THE STEPS OF THE PALACE were alive with movement, soldiers tightening armor, sharpening blades, preparing for what was to come. The air was thick with the scent of steel and sweat, with the tension of those who knew the next few hours would shape the fate of the kingdom.

Carved from ancient stone, the grand staircase leading to the palace was wide enough for an army to ascend in formation. Its edges were lined with statues of past rulers, their marble visages watching over the city as they had for centuries. Though time had worn down the sharp details of their faces, their presence remained, silent witnesses to the rise and fall of kings.

The palace walls, carved from pale stone and inlaid with veins of lapis and quartz, glowed as if they had captured the last remnants of daylight, pristine, whole, unscathed by the suffering that festered just beyond their reach.

Mira and Tharion arrived just as Ren's voice rose above the murmurs of the gathered royal guard.

"…we fight for our people, for our home, for every life that stands behind these walls!" His voice carried, steady and unyielding, cutting through the crisp evening air.

"The Khadradors think they will take what is ours, that we will falter. But we will not! We do not yield. We make our stand, and they will know that Bharalyn is not theirs to claim!"

A roar of approval swept through the assembled warriors, the clatter of weapons and pounding of fists against armor ringing in unison. Mira felt the fire of his words stir something deep in her chest.

Ren's gaze swept over the crowd, searching, until it landed on her. The noise faded away. His eyes locked onto hers, steady and fierce, and in them, she swore she could hear him. It was almost as if he had spoken aloud.

Strike true, be safe.

Her heart tightened, but she did not look away. She answered.

Don't die.

Something flickered across his face. Then, his attention shifted, his regency settling over him as he turned back to the assembled royal guard. A hush fell over the steps Ren's voice rose, his presence commanding.

"We fight for each other. For our families. For the streets where we were raised, for the rivers that carved this kingdom long before these walls ever stood. We fight for the people who have waited, too long, for someone to protect them."

The crowd shifted. This was not just another speech, this was a call to something deeper.

Ren's jaw tightened. "We fight because this is our home. And we will not let it be stolen."

A roar went up from the gathered soldiers, fists slamming against breastplates, boots stomping against the stone. Mira pulled her gaze from Ren and surveyed the scene around her.

The royal guard stood in formation, their armor catching the last light of the setting sun, their weapons gleaming with sharpened edges. Among them were soldiers and townsmen, their expressions a mixture of hardened resolve and barely concealed fear. Some clutched their swords with white-knuckled grips, others adjusted their armor with practiced efficiency.

Mira's eyes lifted to the palace itself, to the towering spires that speared into the sky. From here, she could see the tallest of them, its narrow balcony jutting over the edge of the palace roof, overlooking the city below. It was the perfect vantage point.

She turned to Tharion. "I'll see more from up there."

She nodded toward the spire, already making her calculations. A high position meant she could direct shots with her bow, call out enemy movements before they reached the gates. It was a risk, but a necessary one. Tharion followed her gaze, his expression unreadable for a moment. Then he let out a quiet exhale and nodded his head.

"Guess I'll watch my own back." He clapped a firm hand on her shoulder, his grip warm and familiar.

His voice softened, but the weight of his words remained. "Be careful, Mira." She nodded, stepping away, already moving toward the palace entrance.

Mira took the stairs two at a time, her breath steady despite the adrenaline coursing through her veins. The weight of her crossbow pressed against her back, familiar and grounding, as she climbed higher and higher, away from the growing tide of soldiers preparing for a fight.

The halls of the palace were eerily quiet. The muffled clamor from the courtyard below seemed distant, a world away from the silent corridors she moved through now. The towering stone walls stretched high above her, bathed in the fading light of the evening.

She passed through the grand library, her footsteps barely a whisper against the polished marble floor. Shelves loomed around her, stretching to the ceiling, filled with books that had survived generations of rulers, histories written and rewritten with each shifting power. Mira reached the arched opening that led to the balcony. A gust of wind rushed past her, cold against her skin, whipping her auburn hair around her face as she stepped forward, bracing herself against the stone railing.

The vantage point was perfect. From here, she could see everything. The winding path that led to the palace gates, the distant tree line that rimmed the outer town, and the vast, open land beyond it, quiet but heavy with anticipation. Mira moved with ease, below the stone ledge of the balcony.

She unslung her crossbow, the wooden grip warm and familiar beneath her fingers, and pulled an arrow from her quiver. The act steadied her. She placed the arrow, the hum of tension running through her arms like a heartbeat. Something shifted. It was subtle, against the wind. She froze.

Across the balcony, half-obscured by the curve of the balcony, she saw him. Another archer. Cloaked, crouched, too focused on the horizon to notice her. His gaze flicked sideways and met hers. His reaction was instant. He fired. The arrow hissed past her cheek, close enough that she felt its breath against her skin. Her own crossbow jerked from her hands, knocked aside by the impact of the shot. The weapon clattered to the floor, spinning uselessly out of reach. Mira launched forward.

They collided with the force of two storms meeting. Her momentum knocked him back into the stone. He grunted, twisted, and tried to recover, his elbow catching her side hard, but she was faster.

They grappled, limbs tangling, her knee catching his thigh. He rolled and slammed her against the ground, fingers searching for his blade, but her elbow found his jaw, snapping his head to the side. She drove her fist into the side of his head, just beneath the ear. His eyes rolled back and his body crumpled.

Mira shoved him off her, and stood over him. Her chest heaving, every nerve alight. She did not hesitate, retrieving her crossbow and checked the ledge again, scanning for others. There were none. But the presence of one was concerning enough.

She crouched low beside the fallen archer, catching her breath. His hood had fallen away in the scuffle, revealing a young face, barely more than a boy. Mira's eyes moved down his frame, to the rough stitching on his shoulder, the mismatched pieces of leather and wool that made up his armor. Patchwork. Not palace guard. Not Kharadorian.

She didn't recognize him. Not his face, not the worn crest sewn into the side of his collar, faded but unmistakable. Her stomach turned, cold and uncertain. The resistance. But why would they be here now? Why would they send a boy so young?

The scent of smoke cut into her thoughts. Sharp. Bitter. She turned toward the horizon. The sun had dipped low, casting a golden haze across the landscape. The smoke didn't blur with that glow. It rose thick and purposeful, curling skyward in dark columns from just beyond the treeline.

Mira narrowed her eyes. Something was wrong. She had read about battle fires. How Khadrador used them to drive enemies from the brush, to signal movement across terrain. To scare their opponents. But this wasn't the frantic curl of confusion. It was controlled. Staged.

Her fingers clenched tighter around the crossbow. The placement was central, deliberate. It wasn't the remnants of a razed village or a warning fire. It was a beacon. A bonfire.

Her breath caught in her throat as realization slammed into her like a physical force. A distraction. Mira jerked forward, gripping the railing. Her pulse roared in her ears as her gaze snapped back to the courtyard below.

Ren. He stood among the ranks of soldiers, his presence commanding, his dark blue cloak shifting in the wind. His voice rang out as he gave orders. Mira felt her heart scream at him. Unaware, unaware. Mira leaned over the balcony, the wind stealing the breath from her lungs before she could speak.

Ren whipped his head to her, his sharp eyes locking onto hers in an instant. Confusion flickered across his face, a split-second hesitation, just as archers atop the gates and palace walls loosed a deadly volley. Chaos erupted in an instant.

The first wave of arrows struck true, piercing through armor, finding their marks before the soldiers below even registered what was happening. The palace guard reeled, caught in the open, their formation crumbling under the ambush.

Some fell where they stood, others barely managing to raise their shields before another volley descended upon them. Blood dripped onto the stone steps, the banners of Bharalyn whipping in the wind. Cries of pain rang through the air as their defense fell, some crumpling to the ground before they could even draw their weapons.

Mira didn't hesitate. She dropped to one knee, bracing her crossbow against the edge of the balcony. Her fingers moved with precision. Load, aim, fire. The bolt shot downward, whistling through the air, but missing her target. She reloaded. Another shot. Another fall.

Her vantage gave her sight but not reach. Her angle was

too high, the gap too wide. She couldn't protect them from here. She cursed, yanking another bolt from her quiver and slamming it into place. Her heart pounded.

Her eyes locked on Ren, who had thrown himself toward the steps, dragging a fallen soldier aside as chaos exploded around him. She fired again, but the bolt went wide, pinging harmlessly against the stone. Useless. Too high. Too slow. Too late.

Mira rose, wrenching her crossbow back over her shoulder. The trap had been set. And now it was springing shut.

"Fall back!" Ren's voice cut through the fray, sharp and commanding. "Get inside the palace, now!"

The guards moved as one, breaking formation, retreating toward the grand entrance. Their boots pounded against the stone steps, shields raised against the onslaught of arrows. As the first soldier reached the palace doors, he skidded to a stop. They didn't budge. He threw his weight against them, panic creeping into his movements.

Another soldier joined him, then another, heaving, pounding, desperate. Ren's sword was still in his grip as he darted out, his sharp eyes scanning the battlefield, calculating. Searching. Another way. As if drawn by instinct alone, his gaze lifted. Straight to her.

She knew exactly what he was asking.

Get those doors open.

Mira had no hesitation. She turned and ran.

29

THE STONE CORRIDORS blurred as she moved, her boots striking hard against the marble floors. She took the winding staircase two steps at a time, gripping the railing to propel herself faster. The great hall loomed ahead, its towering pillars casting long, shifting shadows in the dim torchlight. Mira rounded a corner, and her stomach dropped.

Pouring out from the narrow passageways of the attendants' tunnels, their armor mismatches, their weapons gleaming. The Resistance, around seventy warriors. She didn't recognize a single face. Mira pressed herself into the shadows of a carved alcove, her breath shallow, her body coiled tight.

Her mind raced as she watched them move, swift, efficient, like a tide sweeping through the palace. They weren't breaking in. They weren't forcing their way through the defenses. Their steps were sure, their formation tight, too disciplined, too coordinated. No hesitation, no uncertainty. These weren't desperate rebels fighting for survival. A pit formed in her stomach.

A voice, cutting through the quiet, carrying that same arrogant lilt it had the last time she heard him talk. That smug, boasting edge.

"I swear to the Navigators above, easiest thing I've ever done," Dren's voice carried through the stone halls, casual, amused. "Some little whore I met in Seacliffe, just desperate to be fucked properly."

Mira's blood ran cold. He was talking about her. A few of the soldiers near him chuckled. Mira's pulse hammered against her ribs. This wasn't the resistance, these were Kharadors. Dren laughed, dark and cruel.

"Didn't even have to try. She practically begged for it, and in the end?" A pause. A smirk in his voice. "Told me everything I needed to know. Troop movements, patrol schedules, just spread her legs and handed it over."

More muffled laughter. A few muttered curses about the stupidity of some women.

"Poor thing didn't even realize what she'd done." He chuckled, shaking his head. "Just lay there, looking so damn grateful afterward. I almost felt bad for her." Another pause.

Mira heard the grin in his voice. "Almost."

Her fingers curled slowly around the hilt of the knife tucked at her hip, her pulse thundering in her ears. Mira forced herself to stay still. Forced herself to breathe. She had to be smart. She had to be calm. Not because she didn't want to bury this dagger into his lying throat right then and there. But because if she made a single mistake, if she gave herself away, she wouldn't be able to get the doors open.

If she didn't get the doors open, Ren and the palace guard would be trapped and continue to be slaughtered. She swallowed the rage clawing up her throat and forced herself to focus. Her fingers itched toward the blade, but she tightened them into a fist.

* * *

She kept close to the walls, pressing herself into alcoves and blind corners whenever soldiers passed. The air inside the palace had changed, filled with a new kind of tension, shifting beneath the surface, as if the bricks themselves knew they had been betrayed. Who was commanding this army? This wasn't a skirmish. It wasn't even an ambush. This was a coordinated strike. Someone had been waiting for it.

She moved silently, slipping past the great hall's entrance. The doors stood wide open, spilling golden light across the marble floors. She hesitated only a moment before pressing herself against the outer arch, peering inside. The hall was crawling with soldiers. They stood not in disarray, but in orderly lines. Waiting. And there, on the dais, standing above them, was their commander.

Mira's breath turned to ice in her lungs. His voice rang through the hall, thick with conviction, with purpose.

"And you, our Kharador cousins, you are free."

Torvyn's voice carried, reverberating off the towering stone walls, filling every corner of the chamber. Mira gritted her teeth, bile rising in her throat as she listened.

"Free to choose your own path," Torvyn continued, pacing along the dais like a man delivering fate itself. "You have a crown that sees you as more than a means to an end." He spread his arms wide. "You serve a ruler who will never silence you, never turn his back on you. A king who will provide for you, fight beside you, bleed beside you."

A roar of approval and stamping feet thundered through the hall, shaking the floors beneath her like the pulse of something ancient and irreversible.

Mira's breath caught, her heart hammering in her chest. She had expected a betrayal, had braced for it, but not this. Not him, standing tall beneath the carved sigils of their ancestors. Her brother. Torvyn.

Her pulse surged, nausea twisting in her gut. How had she not seen it? How had she spent her life believing they had been fighting together, believing he was beside her, not quietly laying the stones of this path beneath her feet? She had told herself he was being manipulated, controlled, caught in Brahn's web. But this wasn't coercion. Torvyn hadn't been pulled into someone else's plan. He had crafted it. Led it.

With every quiet meeting, every veiled word, every sidelong glance, he had chosen this. And the worst part was the way he stood there now, face calm, eyes bright with conviction. Not shame. Not hesitation. As if this had always been the only future he could see.

Mira stood frozen in the shadowed corridor, the cheers still echoing like thunder.

"You all know the story of the Navigators," Torvyn began, his voice smooth and resonant, rolling through the vaulted hall like smoke. "Their rebellion. Their sacrifices."

Mira stayed hidden. Something in his tone set her on edge. It had shifted, softened. Almost reverent.

"But let me tell you another story." Her pulse stumbled. "The Throne's Wrath." The words cracked like thunder across the marble.

Torvyn paced the edge of the dais, his hands open as if in offering, but his words were sharpened glass wrapped in velvet. There was no warmth in his voice. Only a careful performance of it.

"A family torn apart," he said, letting just enough grief bleed into his words to draw the crowd close. "A father exiled, not for treason, not for crime, but because a queen willed it so."

Mira's blood froze. A cold dread coiled low in her belly.

"The Queen sought to punish not just him," Torvyn continued, "but all of us. Because of her insatiable hunger for control, an entire family was scandalized. Not because of betrayal. But because one of them chose to love.”

Mira’s heart slammed against her ribs. This wasn’t just any fable. She gripped the edge of the arch beside her, knuckles pale, the stone cool against her clammy skin. Her thoughts spun, bile rising in her throat. He was telling her story, twisted, reframed, and held up for judgment like a bloodied relic.

But he wasn’t finished. “Here in Bharalyn, we lose fathers. We lose brothers,” Torvyn said, his voice growing louder, more forceful. “We watch as a crown, distant and indifferent, dictates our lives. Our grief.”

The crowd murmured, stirred like wind moving through dry grass.

“And while this queen ruled,” he went on, “while she sat high in her throne, she did more than exile.”

Mira braced herself.

“She erased. She rewrote history to fit her whims. To protect her power.”

The room shifted. The air became heavy. Mira could feel the change like a stormfront rolling in, tension swelling to the point of rupture.

“And when someone challenged her,” Torvyn said, his voice dropping low, dangerous, “when a young girl dared to love beyond the boundaries she dictated…”

His eyes flicked toward the edge of the hall. Mira ducked further into the shadows, but her breath seized in her throat. He meant her. Mira’s heart cracked open.

Rage and grief warred in her chest. Every memory, every piece of herself she had reclaimed from her lost memories, was now being paraded as propaganda.

“She made this young girl and her love forget,” Torvyn said, voice heavy with accusation.

Mira's vision blurred. Her stolen memories, the nights she awoke gasping, with something just beyond her reach, twisted into a spectacle for the masses.

She glanced back at Torvyn. The curve of his shoulders. The stiffness of his jaw. His hands, fisted tightly at his sides, no longer open and easy. This was his wound too. His father, exiled. His name, tarnished. His family, shattered. He had carried that burden in silence, just as she had. She had been too busy surviving her own fracture to see how deeply it had cut him too.

His words rose, sharp and searing. "Tell me, does that sound like a ruling class fit to lead?"

The crowd roared, a wildfire of fury.

"And that," he finished, stepping to the edge of the dais, his voice a dagger now, "is why we poisoned Queen Sarelle."

Mira gasped. The crowd exploded. Cheering, chanting, feet pounding. And still, Torvyn stood tall, letting the echo of his words settle like dust over a battlefield. His gaze swept the crowd, jaw set, shoulders squared beneath the weight of his confession. A declaration. He believed every twisted word of it. Mira pressed back into the stone, her whole body trembling.

Torvyn's voice carried through the vaulted chamber, clear and resolute. "But tonight, we give Bharalyn a leader with purpose, a ruler who will care for this kingdom, who will work with the King of Kharador, but as an equal."

He lifted his chin, his eyes sweeping the hall, daring anyone to meet them. "A ruler born not only of the blood of the people."

He stepped aside with the gravity of a herald making a proclamation. And through the haze of golden torchlight, Brahn emerged onto the dais. Draped in deep blue robes trimmed in gold. The fabric whispered behind him, echoing the colors of Bharalyn's banners, but twisted, made new, a mockery of royal legacy recast in his image. A crown rested on his brow, dark iron, heavy and bare. Not delicate, not regal, but brutal. A crown made for conquest.

The vision she saw struck Mira in a flash, vivid, undeniable. The shattered throne room. The torn banners. Smoke curling through cracked marble. And now here Brahn was, in the shape of that nightmare.

Brahn stood tall, his shoulders squared, his chin lifted. His expression was proud, until his gaze swept the crowd and landed on her. He smiled. A slow, deliberate smirk. Not joy.

Not triumph. Certainty.

The crowd's cheer increased. Stomping feet and raised fists thundered through the chamber. They chanted Brahn's name, echoing around the stone pillars. Mira's stomach twisted.

This was never about justice. Never about liberation. It had always been a coup, careful and precise, engineered to place Brahn on the throne of Bharalyn. Not to raise the people up from poverty. But to rule them.

Mira didn't bother being quiet, she just ran. The roar of the crowd in the great hall rang in her ears, but it was drowned out by a deeper, more urgent sound, the pounding against the wooden door.

The great doors swung open with a resounding boom, the force rattling through the marble floors. Soldiers and townsmen stormed inside, their banners whipping in the chaos, their armour already wet with the blood of those who had fallen outside.

And in an instant, the hall was in battle.

30

IRA BARELY HAD TIME to duck as a blade whistled past her head, slicing through the air where her throat had been moments before. She pivoted sharply, bringing up her dagger just in time to deflect the strike. The impact rattled up her arm, steel screeching against steel.

She held her ground, shoving back hard enough to send her attacker stumbling. The next blow came before she could even catch her breath. A soldier barreled into her from the side, forcing her to twist at the last second, her feet sliding on the blood-slicked stone. She used their momentum, guiding them past her with a sharp step and redirecting them into another combatant.

There was no pause. No moment to breathe. Steel clashed in a violent symphony, echoing through the marble corridors like thunder. She looked like a Kharadorian. When the palace doors had opened, she was on the wrong side of the fight.

There was no time for explanation, no time to shout above the carnage. Only the glint of weapons and the blunt force of survival. So she fought, not to kill. To disarm or wound.

Another came at her from behind. She ducked low, turned, avoiding their dagger. Bodies slammed into one another, armor scraping, swords ringing against shields.

Ren's forces fought with desperation. The ambush had stripped them of coordination, leaving only instinct and desperation. Outnumbered but unyielding, their movements sharp. They weren't trained for a battle like this.

Torvyn's forces retaliated with ruthless efficiency. Mira twisted, barely avoiding a wild swing from a soldier in Kharadorian leathers. She dropped low, rolling beneath his arm, knocking his balance off with a sharp elbow to his ribs. He grunted in pain, staggering sideways into another fighter, and Mira used the distraction to keep moving. Her bow remained in her hands, its weight solid, grounding.

Another soldier lunged. Mira barely got her bow up in time, blocking the incoming blow with the wood. The force sent her skidding backward, boots struggling for grip on the marble. She adjusted her hold, swinging the bow outward, clipping the man's shoulder just hard enough to send him reeling back.

Another strike, this time from behind. She grunted and spun, catching a charging soldier off-guard, grabbing the front of his armor and yanking him down into her knee. The air left his lungs in a ragged gasp, but he didn't go down. Another hand grabbed her wrist, trying to wrench her dagger away. Mira yanked free, twisting under the grip, her body moving on muscle memory alone.

She ducked a sword, shoved past a pair of clashing soldiers, barely avoiding the press of bodies that threatened to swallow her whole.

The heat of the battle stretched the seconds into eternity. She lost count of how many times she dodged, parried, deflected. She had no sense of where the battle began or where it would end. There was no way to tell who was who.

Someone shoved her backwards, her spine hitting a pillar hard enough to knock the breath from her lungs. She ducked just in time, an axe cleaving into the stone where her neck had been. The force cracked through the air, and Mira rolled away, coming back up to face yet another opponent.

She did not kill. She couldn't. She didn't know if the person swinging at her had once been an ally, a friend, someone she had trusted. Didn't know if the soldier in front of her now had once stood at Ren's side, or Torvyn's.

She could only fight to survive. She stole a glance toward the dais, heart hammering, just in time to see Brahn standing above the carnage, watching it unfold like a man admiring his own masterpiece. Mira's stomach turned. The battle raged on, but Brahn did not move.

Torvyn was still there, blade drawn, protecting his bonded. Mira's hands tightened around her weapons. A blur of movement in her periphery, a towering figure, coming fast.

She barely had time to pivot before a heavy arm crashed toward her, the sheer force of the strike rattling up her arms as she threw her bow up to block. She slammed her free hand against his chest and shoved, using his own momentum against him as she twisted herself loose. He stumbled back a step but recovered too slowly.

Mira saw the opening and took it. She twisted low, planting her weight before hooking her leg behind his and yanking. He toppled. It happened so fast, his armor crashed against the stone with a brutal impact, the wind knocked from his lungs. Mira surged forward, "Mira...?"

Her breath caught. The voice. Familiar. Rough. Desperate. Her heart stopped. Tharion. Mira froze, her pulse hammering as she looked down at the man beneath her.

Battered, breathing hard, eyes searching hers. Tharion. Not just another soldier. Not just an enemy in the chaos. Tharion. Her friend. Mira's grip loosened on her dagger.

She hesitated only a breath before reaching down,

grabbing his wrist in a firm, unwavering grip. Tharion took it. In a flash, he was on his feet, already pivoting to block an incoming strike. Mira moved with him, their bodies falling into rhythm, the muscle memory of training together taking over.

They fought like they were one. Where he was strength, she was speed. Where he held the line, she wove through the chaos. Firelight from fallen lanterns danced across the blood-slicked stone, casting long shadows that leapt and twisted with every clash.

The battle lit around them like a storm of sparks and smoke, the flickering glow painting them in gold and scarlet. A soldier lunged at her, sword swinging wide.

Mira ducked, spinning behind Tharion as he blocked the blow, their movements seamless. She used his back as leverage, leaping up and kicking the attacker square in the chest. Tharion didn't even flinch. He pivoted, catching an axe on his bracers, twisting the weapon from his opponent's grasp before slamming his fist into their gut.

Another enemy charged, Mira yanked an arrow from her quiver and drove it into the gap in their armor, not a fatal blow, but enough to send them stumbling back. More came.

More fell back. They moved together, unstoppable.

Tharion's sword arced through the air, a blur of steel and precision. Mira ducked under his arm, using his momentum to vault over an incoming attack. Their backs hit for a brief second, grounding each other. Then they kept going. Fighting. Dodging. Blocking.

Moving.

Tharion sent a soldier staggering, Mira swept their legs out from under them before they could recover. A strike nearly caught her from behind, Tharion deflected it with brutal efficiency, shoving the attacker away with a sharp twist of his blade. Mira staggered, breath coming in sharp gasps, her muscles screaming from the endless motion.

She tore her eyes away, looking instead at Tharion. He was already looking back. For a single slowed moment, they just stood there. Breathless. Bloody. Knowing. She felt it, the weight of him, of everything that had led them here. They had failed as lovers.

Failed as bonded. But not as fighters. And never as friends.

She gave a single, sharp nod. A soldier was on her. She staggered back, just enough to avoid the fatal strike, the edge of the steel skimming her leathers as she brought up her bow to block the next attack.

The soldier lunged. Mira pivoted. Step, shift, counter. Another charged. She sidestepped, knocking them off balance with a sharp elbow, using their weight against them. Then, another attack. This time from behind. Before Mira could react, Tharion was there intercepting the strike meant for her spine with a brutal swipe of his sword.

A clash of steel. A grunt from Tharion as he shoved his opponent back. She moved instinctively. The fighter stumbled, just long enough for Tharion to slam the hilt of his sword into their helmet, sending them sprawling.

But there was no chance to recover. More were coming. Two. Three. Four. Mira twisted, blocking a strike with her bow while Tharion parried two swords at once, his blade a blur of silver. One soldier lunged at her, she pivoted, knocking their arm aside with the solid wood of her bow before Tharion swept in from the side, kicking them hard in the ribs, sending them flying.

Another charged him, Mira was already moving. She

grabbed a discarded shield, swinging it up just in time to deflect a strike aimed at Tharion's side. He used the opening, driving the pommel of his sword into their face. They fought back-to-back, covering each other, moving as one.

A sharp, white-hot pain ripped through her side. A brutal twist of the blade as it cut through leather, through flesh, through muscle. The world blurred. Her knees buckled. Tharion roared. He was there in an instant, shoving the attacker away from her, sending them crashing to the ground.

A sudden, vicious spike of panic tore through her, sharp and suffocating. She had missed the third attacker. Tharion's voice couldn't penetrate through the haze, hands grabbing her arms, holding her upright. Mira gritted her teeth, blinking hard, forcing herself to stay standing.

The wound wasn't deep. Not fatal. She'd survive. But the blood was warm, pooling beneath her armor, soaking into her leathers. She met Tharion's gaze.

They were going to lose. Bharalyn was crumbling. The Kharadors were too precise, too calm. A force of trained warriors cutting through the hall with ruthless efficiency. While her people fought desperately, blindly, trying to keep hold of a kingdom already slipping through their fingers.

Mira turned, gaze sweeping through the chaos, past the bodies, past the screaming, until she found Torvyn. Barely fighting. He stood on the dais, like a man simply waiting for time to catch up with his plan. Every movement measured, every step deliberate. Beside him, Brahn. Lounging on the throne like it had been his all along. Mira's chest tightened. Her fingers curled around the grip of her crossbow, her knuckles white.

A horn sounded. Deep. Commanding. Not Bharalyn. The sound cut through the chaos, ringing over the clash of steel, over the cries of the dying. The fighting slowed. Just long enough for heads to turn toward the massive doors of the hall. Mira forced herself to look, her vision swimming, heart pounding, legs still unsteady beneath her.

Marching in disciplined ranks, their formation unbroken was an army. Lavender purple flags flying high above them. Myrdathis soldiers were surging into the hall, past the broken doors, through the destroyed great hall.

For one brief, terrible second, Mira thought it was over. That Myrdathis had come to take Bharalyn for themselves. That this was a second enemy, coming to finish what the Kharadors had started.

Through the crush of bodies, through the dust and smoke, she saw her. Danlea. Atop a white horse, its silver mane catching the torchlight, its hooves clattering against the stone. Her hair streamed behind her, wild and free, a river of white silk.

She wasn't clad in armor, but in her usual flowing dress, unbothered by the ruin around her. But there was steel in her milky eyes. Power radiated from her, as though the battle itself had bent around her arrival.

The Myrdath soldiers charged forward. Blades met blades. The battle erupted anew, but now, for the first time since the fighting began, Mira saw a shift. Ren's army fought alongside the Myrdathis, pushing back the Kharadorians who had stormed their home.

Hope slammed into her chest, sharp and disorienting. They weren't alone. They still had a chance. Mira's hand tightened around her bow. Tharion exhaled beside her, bracing himself, his sword held ready, his body coiled.

He could hold the line. She had another purpose. She moved. No longer trapped, no longer drowning beneath endless waves of enemies. Mira broke away, her path clear. A single target burned in her vision. Brahn.

She fought to get to him. A soldier lunged, she twisted past. Another came at her, sword high, slashing downward, she ducked, rolling under the strike, the steel barely missing her.

She rose fluidly, bow flashing as she brought it up like a staff, smashing it across a fighter's chest, sending them stumbling. She kept moving. Step. Shift. Counter. Someone grabbed at her, she wrenched free.

The hall blurred around her, nothing but a rush of movement, of instinct, of breath and muscle memory. Her focus zeroed in on the throne, on the man who had stolen it. Brahn, now fighting alongside Torvyn. Her fingers tightened around her crossbow.

Mira stopped running. She planted her feet. The battlefield raged around her, and she felt Tharion fighting at her back. Screams, metal on metal, bodies falling, dust and blood thick in the air.

To Mira, there was nothing else. Nothing but the crossbow in her hands. Nothing but Brahn, his back to her, unaware. She lifted the bow, her grip steady, her muscles taut.

Breathed out. The chaos dimmed. Mira braced, the crossbow humming with tension, the bolt already locked in place. Her fingers curled around the trigger, steady.

A shot like this, she'd taken it a hundred times before. Her heart didn't race. She breathed in. Her breath didn't falter. The bolt knew its path. She just had to release it. Her fingers squeezed.

The snap of the shot cracked through the air, sharp and final. She heard someone yell. Brahn's eyes flicked up. He dodged, just barely, but not fast enough. The bolt struck high in his shoulder.

Torvyn turned toward Brahn as crumpled with a harsh, guttural sound. Blood seeped quickly into Brahn's robe dark beneath the deep sapphire fabric.

Mira's eyes looked over Torvyn's shoulder.

A Myrdath soldier. Sword raised. Intent clear as the blade drove straight through Torvyn's chest.

31

Four Years Ago

MIRA HAD NEVER DONE it to be cruel, or to upset him. But Navigators, it was so easy to annoy him. Torvyn had always been protective, always hovering over her like a second shadow, making sure she didn't get into trouble, making sure no one bothered her.

Which meant his friends were entirely off-limits. And that just made it all the more fun. The first time she had batted her lashes at one of them, he had nearly choked on his wine. The second time, she had laughed a little too sweetly at some dumb joke, and Torvyn had dragged her away by the arm so fast she nearly tripped.

"Stop that." His voice had been low, warning, his grip tight around her wrist. She had only grinned up at him, all innocence. "Stop what?"

His glare had been thunderous. "You know exactly what."

Mira had tilted her head, feigning confusion. "You mean talking to your friends?" Torvyn's jaw had locked. "You don't need to talk to them like that."

Like that. As if he could dictate how she smiled, how she laughed, how she teased. As if she were still his little sister to shield from the world.

Mira had narrowed her eyes. "What exactly do you think I'm going to do? Fall in love with one of them? Navigators forbid I actually enjoy their company."

Torvyn had run a hand down his face, clearly trying to keep his patience intact. "They're idiots. They only like the idea of you, Mira."

That had made her blood boil. She had stepped closer, arms crossed. "You mean they only like the idea of their friend's sister?"

Torvyn had grimaced. "That's not what I... "

But she had already shoved past him. "Maybe I like the idea of them." He had cursed under his breath, catching her wrist before she could stalk off.

"You don't." His voice had been frustrated, tired, something almost pleading beneath it.

She didn't. Maybe she had only done it to annoy him. To remind him that she wasn't a child anymore. But she had still yanked her hand free. Still glanced back at him with a smirk.

"Watch me."

✳ ✳ ✳

Seven Years Ago

Mira had hated dancing. Hated the stiff posture, the rigid steps, the way the tutors clicked their tongues in disapproval whenever she got something wrong.

But Torvyn? Torvyn had excelled. Every movement had been measured, poised, flawless. Mira had stumbled through every lesson, her feet too fast, her patience too thin. Until one afternoon.

The tutors had given up on her. Torvyn had stayed behind. She had watched as he crossed the ballroom, his expression exasperated. Then, he offered her his hand.

"Try again," he had said simply.

She had scowled. "You're not my teacher."

"No," he had agreed. "I'm your brother. And I refuse to let you embarrass me at court."

She had smacked his shoulder. He sighed and took her hand. They danced. No tutors, no expectations. Just him leading, and adjusting to her mistakes. Both of them moving with the music, the way they were supposed to.

By the time they had stopped, her feet ached, but she had been smiling. "So you're not a lost cause," Torvyn had told her, grinning.

She had shoved him. But after that, she didn't dread dancing again.

* * *

Eleven Years Ago

She had called it. Fair and clear. Everyone knew calling it first meant it was yours. So when Mira walked into their rooms and saw Torvyn lounging in her chair, legs kicked out, book open, looking completely smug, she nearly choked on her own breath.

"That's my chair," she said, glaring.

Torvyn didn't even glance up from the page. "Doesn't have your name on it." "I called it, Torvyn." He hummed, casually turning a page.

"I don't think calling it counts if no one else agrees to the rules."

Mira scowled. "Everyone agrees to the rules. That's why they're the rules."

He didn't move. Didn't blink. Didn't even pretend to care. She did the only reasonable thing. She marched across the room, grabbed the back of the chair, and tipped it.

Torvyn yelped as he tumbled to the floor, limbs and book flying in every direction.

Mira stepped over the mess, flopped into the chair, and opened her book with great satisfaction. "Called it."

Torvyn groaned from the floor, rubbing the back of his head. "You're a menace." She didn't even look up. "And you're in my spot."

✳ ✳ ✳

Eighteen Years Ago

Mira didn't understand. She had stood in the grand hall, small and confused, as the murmurs of courtiers swelled around her.

Someone had whispered, Lady Solwynd is gone. Torvyn had stood beside her, rigid and silent.

She had tugged at his sleeve, searching his face, searching for answers. "Torvyn...?"

He had looked wrong. Too still. Too quiet. When he finally turned toward her, his eyes were red, like he was holding something inside his chest that he refused to let spill. But his hands shook. And when he stood in front of her, grasping her shoulders, his fingers trembled against her skin.

"Don't cry," he had whispered. "They'll watch if you cry."

Mira hadn't cried. Not then. Not until much later. Not until the hall was empty. Until Torvyn had taken her hand and led them back to their quarters, closed the door, and let himself crumble.

She had held his hand. Tight.

32

MIRA WAS FROZEN. Her body wouldn't move. Wouldn't breathe. Wouldn't blink. All she could do was watch.

The blade withdrew from Torvyn's body. Slow. Merciless. Slick with his blood, gleaming as if proud of what it had done. Torvyn's knees buckled. The strength drained from him as his body gave out. He crumpled. His hands grasped at nothing, reaching for something, for someone, before they fell limp against the stone.

A sound ripped from her chest, raw and impossible, tearing through the battlefield. A scream. A sound that didn't just come from her voice, but from her soul. Ragged.

Violent. Shattering. It ripped through the hall, cut through the clash of steel, the roars of war, the dying gasps of men.

For just a moment, the battle paused. Warriors turned. Soldiers hesitated. Because they felt it too. Felt the sound crawl under their skin, felt the weight of it press down on their bones, twisting through their marrow. A scream of loss. A scream of grief. A scream that did not just mourn the man who had fallen, but mourned the brother she thought had.

Mira moved before she could think. She let loose, her hands steady despite the shaking in her chest. She released an arrow. And another. And another. Torvyn's murderer staggered back, forced to parry the relentless onslaught of her arrows.

She moved forward, swift and deadly, her body cutting through the throng of people. Her breath tore through her lungs as she pushed past fallen bodies, boots slipping in blood-slick dust.

She needed to be there. To see him. To make sure he wasn't alone. Torvyn. Her brother. The one she had fought with. Cursed at. Clung to. The one she had hated in this moment and never stopped loving.

She was almost there. Just a few more steps. A few more breaths. Her knees hit the blood-soaked stone, hands grasping, desperate, searching, but there was nothing to find.

Torvyn's body lay still. Lifeless. The warmth already fading from his skin, the blood pooling around him in thick, glistening rivers. Her hands trembled as she touched his face, as if she could shake him from this, as if she could live back into him.

He was gone. She was too late. Her fingers curled into his tunic, into the red fabric, as if holding him tighter could tether him back to her. Her chest heaved, a sob, a shudder, a sound ripped from the deepest part of her.

He had died alone.

✳ ✳ ✳

Mira wasn't sure how long she stayed there. Seconds. Minutes. A lifetime. The world around her blurred, faded into something distant and unreal. The battle raged on.

Somewhere, warriors fought and died. Somewhere, steel clashed, boots thundered, voices shouted commands. But here, at this moment, there was only Torvyn. Only the weight of him in her arms. Only the way his body did not stir, the way his chest did not rise, did not fall. His body would never move again.

Someone gave an order. His forces hesitated, only for a breath. Then they moved. Quick. Silent. Like ghosts vanishing into the mist. They peeled away from the fight, breaking into the tunnels, slipping from the palace like they had never been there at all.

She didn't listen to the last of the retreating footsteps. She only held on to what was left of her brother. Her hands pressed against his head, his face, his chest. She just needed a moment longer with him. But there was nothing left to hold on to. Mira lay her head down on his chest. Willing. Begging. For his heart to beat. For him to wake up. But the silence was deafening.

❊ ❊ ❊

Time slipped. There was only the weight of Torvyn's chest beneath her head and the unbearable stillness where his breath should have been.

Someone reached for her. Hands. Holding her. Pulling her from Torvyn. Anchoring. Arms wrapped around her, firm but careful. She fought anyway. Wild. Desperate.

She kicked, lashed out, trying to wrench herself free, her breath coming in ragged sobs. But the grip didn't falter. A second set of hands warmer, surer, pressed against her shoulders, meant to comfort, meant to hold her together when she was already shattering.

A voice, low, urgent. She didn't hear it. Didn't care. She twisted violently, a sob tearing from her throat, raw and shattered, clawing, desperate. Back to Torvyn. Her feet scraped against stone slick with blood as she dug her heels in, her chest heaving, fingers reaching, reaching. But they held her too tight. Not in restraint, but in something like protection. As if keeping her from him now would somehow hurt her less.

A voice. Sharp. Cold. The arms around her tensed. A choked gasp broke from her lips as the hands held her too tight. Footsteps. More voices. She only knew the warmth of her brother was already fading. Torvyn was still on the floor. Still bleeding.

With a violent jerk, she threw her head back, felt the sickening crack of bone against bone as her skull collided with the person behind her. A sharp gasp of pain, the hands on her loosened. She wrenched herself free, stumbling, nearly falling, but she didn't stop. Didn't think. Didn't breathe.

She crawled to him, hands shaking as she reached for him.

"Torvyn..." His name was a whisper, a prayer, a plea, but there was no answer.

She curled against him. Holding on. As if she could keep him from slipping further away. As if, by sheer will, she could bring him back.

The voices around her blurred into noise. Distant. Meaningless. Arguing. Shouting. More hands reaching for her. She shrugged them off, her breath ragged, her hands clawing at Torvyn's tunic, fingers twisting in the fabric.

A shadow shifted above her. A face. Tharion. Mira blinked, her vision swimming, her chest aching, tearing. He was covered in blood and sweat, his tunic torn,his chest heaving. He yelled something. His lips moved, his voice urgent, his eyes soft, pained, pleading. She didn't hear him. Didn't care. She closed her eyes.

✳ ✳ ✳

A whisper. Something slipping through her, curling into the

hollowness inside her. She opened her eyes. Ren.

He was battered and bleeding, scratches along his arms, his hair clinging to his sweat-dampened skin, his tunic torn, his nose split open at the bridge. And still, His eyes found hers.

He lay beside her. Eye to eye with her. Watching. Waiting. His voice came low, steady, shaken. "Mira..."

Her throat burned, raw and tight. Her chest ached, hollow and splintering. Ren shifted closer, still lying beside her, still watching. Soft. Gentle.

"Let me hold you..." A plea, not a command.

Mira squeezed her eyes shut, her breath shuddering, hot tears slipping down her cheeks. Her fingers tightened in Torvyn's tunic.

"I... " her voice cracked. "I can't leave him alone." Ren exhaled, something soft and breaking inside him too.

"He's not alone, we'll be right here" His voice was so sure, so steady.

A sob tore through her. And another. Her body shook with each one. Ren didn't move. Didn't push. Didn't tell her to stop. He just waited.

Mira exhaled a ragged breath, her chest heaving, her body trembling as she slowly turned, shifted her gaze to Torvyn's pale face. Someone had closed his eyes. The finality of it clawed through her.

Her fingers trembled as she reached out, barely brushing his cheek. But he was so still. Unmoving. Gone.

Slowly, she crawled to Ren. He opened his arms without hesitation. And the moment she reached him, she collapsed into him. Ren held her tight. Mira clung to him, her body shaking, sobs tearing through her, relentless and raw. Breaking her apart.

He didn't speak. Ren's hand slid through her hair, slow and careful. His heartbeat thudded steady against her ear. Her grip on his tunic loosened. Her body gave in, slumping against him. Her breath deepened. The weight of sleep pulled her under.

✳ ✳ ✳

The world returned in fragments. A dull ache in her limbs. The warmth of steady arms around her. The slow, rhythmic thud of a heartbeat against her ear. Mira stirred, her body reluctant, unwilling to return to waking. But the cold, the absence, dragged her awake.

Her eyelids fluttered open. The faint glow of lantern light. The heavy hush of the palace, thick with the echoes of battle. And Torvyn. The breath she had been holding left her in a silent shudder.

He lay where she had last seen him, his body still, his face a mask of unnatural peace. His skin had turned pale, the warmth long gone, stolen. Mira swallowed against the lump in her throat. It did nothing to ease the raw, splintering ache in her chest.

Ren stirred beneath her, his grip on her tightening as if he had felt the shift in her breathing. She inhaled sharply, blinking against the blur of unshed tears. She shifted slightly, enough to turn her face up to Ren's. She saw the exhaustion lining his features, the dried blood along his temple, the bruises forming beneath his skin.

Mira's gaze drifted past him, back to Torvyn. She needed to look at him. Needed to see him, even though every second that passed made it harder to recognize the warmth, the life, the fire that had once burned so fiercely within him.

443

Her fingers trembled as she reached out. He was stiff, already drying with blood. His blood. Her lips parted, but the words barely came.

"I need to bury him." Her voice was barely a whisper.

The words sat heavy in the air, pressing down, suffocating. A finality she hadn't spoken before, hadn't dared to acknowledge. Ren hesitated. He sat up, pulling her with him, keeping his arms firm around her, as if he could shield her from the truth.

Another figure stepped forward. A shadow darkened the pool of candlelight near Torvyn's body. Cleric Perrin. She wore robes of deep ivory, embroidered with silver thread, her veil drawn back to reveal her face carved with quiet sorrow. Her hands moved with intention, shaped by years of ceremony, of loss, of memory carried like a second skin.

She knelt beside Torvyn's head, fingers resting briefly against his brow. "I will complete his rites personally." she said gently.

Mira nodded, but the movement felt detached, as if her body was answering without her. Her brother, her only family, was being prepared for the rites of the Navigators.

The thought twisted something deep inside her, curling into an ache that felt like it would swallow her whole.

"I don't want him to be alone." Ren's arms tightened around her.

"He won't be," he murmured, voice steady despite the storm breaking inside of him too.

We're here. We'll take care of him." His grip was an anchor, and yet she still felt adrift. Beyond the circle of candlelight, her eyes caught a glint of red across the floor, a dark river staining the marble beneath the dais.

Blood. A trail that led away, smeared and dragged.

Brahn. Someone had pulled him from where he'd fallen. Mira didn't know where he had been taken, or if he still breathed, but Navigators above, she hoped he was dead.

Mira barely registered Perrin stepping back, her presence no less commanding for its stillness. She nodded to someone outside Mira's field of vision.

"Tharion." Ren called his name softly, and for a moment, nothing happened.

Mira turned to look. Then a shudder. Tharion was kneeling, his back to Torvyn. But his sword lay discarded at his side, forgotten. His chest rose and fell in uneven, ragged breaths. He did not move.

His grief had rooted him to the spot, as if stepping away would make it real.

Mira's voice barely found her. "Tharion...". His breath hitched and turned to look at her. Tears carved silent tracks through the blood and grime on his face.

He blinked, his gaze flickering from Torvyn's still face to hers, as if seeing her for the first time. He exhaled, slowly, carefully and moved. Ren shifted. Mira felt the strength of his arms tighten briefly before he gently eased her from his lap, his movements slow, tender.

He set her beside him with care, as if afraid she might splinter apart if handled too roughly. Then, with a quiet breath, Ren shuffled forward. Tharion approached Torvyn's body and sank to his knees opposite Ren, his head bowed.

They worked in silence, with rags soaked in warm water, wiping the blood from his face. Every motion was an impossible kindness for a man who had attacked their home. Cleric Perrin knelt again at Torvyn's head, whispering words in an ancient language.

The language of the Navigators, old and reverent. The same words spoken over those lost to sea, to time, to war.

Mira could barely breathe through it. When the rites were done, Perrin raised her gaze, her face shadowed with the weight of the moment.

"Where is his final resting place?" The question shattered something inside her.

Mira closed her eyes, as her tears fell. Torvyn had been many things, a brother, a traitor, a leader. But Mira has no doubt, he would rest where he belonged. In their family crypt.

"With our mother." The words left her lips like a vow.

As the silence settled once more, Ren stepped back and stood at her side. She felt the brush of his hand against hers, grounding.

A moment later, Tharion joined them. Together, the three of them stood, shoulder to shoulder.

Perrin nodded once, solemn. Only the rustle of fabric, the careful gathering of limbs. Mira watched Perrin's acolytes filed in. And as they lifted him, something inside Mira shattered.

Her chest clenched with unbearable pain, and the sobs tore from her throat, raw and unrelenting. Tears streamed down her face as Torvyn was carried away, each step a cruel echo, toward the place where he would rest forever.

33

ONE MOMENT, SHE had been standing in the empty space where Torvyn had been. The next, she was here, walking through the door, stepping into the quiet warmth of Ren's quarters.

She didn't remember climbing the stairs. Didn't remember the halls passing by. The door clicked shut behind them, sealing them in the stillness. None of them spoke.

Tharion stood stiffly just inside the threshold, his posture carved from stone. His fingers twitched at his sides like he wanted to reach for something, but there was nothing left to hold. Nothing left to fight.

Mira felt it in herself, too. The exhaustion that went deeper than her bones, the weight of grief pressing down like a tide with no shore.

Ren said nothing. He guided Mira forward, his touch careful, as if she might break apart beneath it. But she was already broken. She barely noticed when he led her toward the bathing chamber, her feet moving without thought.

She caught a glimpse of herself in the mirror as she passed. Blood. Her leathers were stiff with it, darkened, dried, clinging to her skin like a second layer. Her arms, her hands, stained. Some of it was hers. But most of it, most of it was Torvyn's.

Her stomach twisted. A wave of nausea swelled in her chest. She swayed on her feet, her vision tilting. Ren snaked a hand around her. Steadying her before she could collapse. Mira barely registered his touch, barely felt the way he braced her against him, keeping her upright.

Steam curled from the deep bathing pool sunk into the floor, swirling like mist in the dim candlelight. The water rippled with the heat, dark and inviting, the scent of oils hanging in the air, clinging to the stone.

Ren's hands found the buckles of her leathers first, fingers gentle as they worked. Unbuckling. Peeling away. Mira didn't move to help him. Didn't stop him, either. Just stood there, motionless, as the layers fell away, piece by piece, the last remnants of battle stripped from her.

Her tunic clung to her skin, damp with sweat and blood. Ren hesitated, looking up at her. She nodded. Carefully, he tugged the fabric over her head. Slow. Deliberate. She barely felt the warm air hit her skin. Ren's breath hitched.

The bruises had already begun to bloom, deep purples and sickly yellows, painted across her ribs, her arms, her shoulders. A dark map of the fight she had survived.

But Ren's focus landed on something else. The stab wound. Just beneath her ribs, an angry slash of red, the edges inflamed and tender. Ren's jaw tightened.

His fingers hovered over it, careful, assessing. Mira didn't react, she barely felt the sting of his touch. Her body was too worn, too hollowed out for fresh pain.

"This will need to be stitched," he murmured, mostly to himself.

As he guided her into the pool, his movements stayed carefully deliberate. Even as the warmth seeped into her bones, the blood stayed. She sank into the water, as the heat wrapped around her, pulling her under. Ren followed alongside her at the pool's edge, rolling up his sleeves, kneeling beside her.

His hands found hers. Gently, he cupped her fingers,

dipping them into the water. Mira stared at the surface of the water, at the way it swirled, the blood unfurling like smoke.

Ren reached for a cloth, soaked it, and pressed it to her shoulder first. Careful. Soft. Wiping away the dried sweat, the filth of battle. He worked in silence, trailing the cloth down her arms, over her bruised ribs, up to the curve of her neck.

Ren's hand dipped into the water again, dragging the cloth over her collarbone, washing away what was left of the night. Mira swallowed hard, staring at the ripples spreading out across the water, at the deep red that still swirled in lazy, dissolving patterns before vanishing beneath the surface.

Some things could be washed away. Some things couldn't. Ren exhaled, his hand stilling just over her wrist. His voice was low, gentle. Careful.

"Will you be alright in here for a moment?" She blinked.

The words took a second to settle, to push through the fog in her mind. Would she? Mira let out a slow breath and nodded.

Ren studied her, his dark eyes searching, but he didn't press. Didn't make her say anything more. He just gave a small, almost imperceptible nod in return. Then, he rose, as he took a step away from the pool.

She stayed in the water, staring at the surface of the water.

The door creaked open. Tharion stepped inside. Mira lifted her head and looked over her shoulder, watching him. He looked awful. Worse than she had ever seen him.

His leathers were gone, but the dried blood still clung to his skin in places, streaked along his forearms, his collarbone. His hair was a mess, strands stiff with sweat and grime. His eyes, red-rimmed, hollowed-out.

Mira swallowed hard, gripping the edge of the bathing pool as if it could steady the weight pressing down on her chest. Tharion stood in the doorway, lost in the dim candlelight, looking like a man who had survived a battle only to realize the war had already been lost.

Her eyes flicked past him, toward Ren, who was moving behind him with slow, careful steps.

"It's okay, go on." Ren murmured.

Tharion hesitated. Just for a breath. Just long enough that Mira saw the war waging inside him, the resistance, the stubborn refusal to let himself be taken care of when everything inside him was screaming that he didn't deserve it.

But then he exhaled. And let Ren guide him forward. Mira turned away, giving them the space. She stared at the water instead, at the way the ripples distorted her reflection.

But she still heard them. The rustle of fabric as Ren helped Tharion out of what remained of his clothing.

"I should've been there." His voice was raw.

Mira's hands curled into fists beneath the water. Ren didn't answer right away. She heard the splash of water, the sound of Tharion lowering himself into the pool.

Mira didn't turn, didn't look. But she felt it, the way the grief settled between them, thick and inescapable.

"You couldn't have stopped it," Ren said, steady, even. "You know that." A ragged breath from Tharion. Then, lower, "But I could have been there."

Mira closed her eyes, a tear slipping. Ren didn't push. She heard the sound of water shifting, Ren's quiet movements. Then the damp cloth being drawn over Tharion's skin, Ren washing away the remnants of blood and battle.

For a long time, no one spoke. The water lapped gently against the edge of the pool, the steam curling around them like something sacred, something fragile. Ren waded in, slow and careful. Closer now. His hand settled gently on Mira's shoulder, his warmth steady against her.

Tharion's voice was quiet, "I don't... I don't know how to do this without him."

In that single, fractured confession pulled all the pieces into place. She had tried to make it something more, love, or at least the shadow of it. But now she saw the truth. Their bond wasn't made for romance. It was built on loyalty, trust, and friendship.

Mira turned towards him, meeting his gaze. There was no room for embarrassment, no space for modesty. They had seen each other bloodied, broken.

Their eyes met, and for a moment, Tharion looked like he might break. His jaw was clenched, brow furrowed, eyes shining with the weight of words left unsaid. Regret clung to him, raw, unspoken.

Tharion's throat worked as he tried to swallow the weight behind his silence. "I should have told you," he rasped. "I wanted to. I just... didn't know how." Mira gave a sad smile and shook her head, not in dismissal, but acceptance. "It's okay... I understand..."

His shoulders dropped, just slightly, like he'd been holding something for far too long, and had finally let it go.

Ren washed himself quickly, his movements efficient. He turned to her. His hands were steady as he guided Mira toward the edge of the bath, his grip firm but gentle.

The warmth had settled deep in her muscles, easing the tension coiled within her, but the moment the cool air met her damp skin, she shivered.

Without hesitation, Ren wrapped her in a thick towel, securing it around her shoulders with careful hands before tugging another around his hips. He crouched in front of her, the flickering light catching on the damp strands of his hair, casting his features in shifting shadow.

His eyes dropped to the deep red bloom beneath the towel, just beneath her ribs. Gently, he reached forward, fingers brushing against the edge of the fabric.

"Let me see," he said, low and steady.

Mira didn't resist. He peeled the towel back slowly, exposing the jagged tear in her side, the skin around it flushed and raw. The blood had slowed, but not stopped, and Ren's jaw clenched at the sight of it. His fingers hovered for a moment before pressing gently along the skin, checking the depth, the spread.

"This needs tending," he murmured, though the weight in his voice betrayed the quiet edge of fear threaded underneath.

Mira didn't argue. She was too tired, too wrung out to protest as Ren carefully dabbed at the wound, his movements practiced and efficient. He worked in silence, save for the occasional exhale, his fingers gentle against the bruised, battered skin.

She watched him, her vision hazy with exhaustion. He was meticulous. Purposeful. As if this, tending to her, was the only thing in the world that mattered in this moment.

Tharion stood still in the water, his arms braced at his sides. He hadn't moved. Hadn't spoken. He just breathed, slow and deep, as if he were trying to hold himself together one breath at a time.

Ren finished dressing the wound and helped Mira to her feet. A new towel placed snug around her as he led her out of the washroom and into the dimly lit bedchamber.

Waiting on the bed were three neatly folded sets of clothes. Loose pants. Soft, oversized shirts. Ren's. She let out a slow breath, fingers brushing over the fabric. It was familiar. Safe.

Ren didn't say a word as he turned away, giving her space to change. Mira let the towel slip from her shoulders and reached for the clothes. The fabric was worn and soft, the scent of wood smoke, distinctly Ren, clinging to it.

She pulled on the loose pants first, tying them at the waist before slipping the oversized shirt over her head. When she turned back, Ren was watching her from the doorway in his towel. Not in a way that made her feel self-conscious, but in the way someone watches over something fragile. Something breaking.

He turned away as she crawled beneath the blankets, the soft fabric cool against her battered skin. She barely had the energy to pull them up over her shoulders, exhaustion pressing her deep into the mattress.

She heard him move back to the washroom, the soft shuffle of his footsteps against the floor. A murmur of voices. Then the sound of water sloshing as Tharion was helped out of the bath.

Mira closed her eyes, not out of sleepiness, but to steady herself against the quiet weight of grief in the air. She listened. To the rustle of fabric as Tharion dressed. To the steady, measured pace of Ren's movements. To the heavy silence that stretched between them all. Then footsteps. She heard Tharion move toward the door, hesitation in his steps. He was leaving.

But before he could go, Ren's voice cut through the quiet. "You're staying in here, Tharion."

The bed dipped beside her as Ren slid beneath the blankets. The warmth of him radiated through the space behind her. On the opposite side of Ren, another weight.

Tharion. He hesitated only for a breath before settling in, silent, exhausted.

Mira exhaled slowly, the tension in her limbs loosening just slightly. No one spoke. No one needed to. They had survived the night. And for now, for just a moment, none of them had to be alone.

* * *

Mira stirred in the haze of sleep, the world soft and blurred around the edges. Dawn's first light filtered through the window, flickering across the room in shifting patterns. The warmth around her was steady, solid, Ren's arm wrapped tightly around her waist, his breath slow and even, buried in her hair. She barely had the strength to open her eyes, barely had the will to pull herself from the quiet comfort of it. His grip, even in sleep, was firm, like some part of him feared she might slip away if he let go.

Through the haze, she caught movement. Tharion. Standing by the window, his silhouette framed against the soft gold of the rising sun. His arms were crossed, his posture still and quiet, gaze locked on the horizon where night bled into morning.

The light flickered over his face, tracing the exhaustion carved deep into his features. Mira watched, or maybe only dreamed she did. The weight of sleep pulled at her again, the warmth of Ren's embrace, the hush of the morning.

She let herself sink back into it, closing her eyes, slipping once more into the depths of sleep.

34

A GENTLE TOUCH brushed against her shoulder. Mira stirred, sleep clinging to her like mist, thick and unrelenting. The warmth of it wrapped around her, heavy, pulling her back down.

But the fingers against her arm were patient, careful, coaxing her toward waking. "Mira." Ren's voice, low, quiet.

She blinked, the golden light of morning filtering through her lashes. The space behind her was empty. The warmth of the night had long since faded, leaving only the cool imprint of where Ren had been.

Her fingers brushed over the sheets, finding them cold, untouched. He sat at the edge of the bed, already dressed. The deep green of his shirt caught the morning light as he ran a hand through his hair, his shoulders tense, his posture weighted with something unspoken.

Mira sat up slowly, her body aching in places she hadn't noticed before, exhaustion still dragging at her limbs.

She hadn't seen the room last night, had barely noticed anything beyond the grief and weariness that had swallowed her whole. But now, with the morning sun filtering through the heavy velvet drapes, she took it in.

The room enveloped her in deep greens and muted golds, warm and rich, like the rest of Ren's quarters. The walls were carved dark wood, etched with twisting vines and delicate leaves, a reflection of the palace's grandeur, but softened by his own touch. The tall, arched windows framed the light in long golden beams, casting a quiet glow over the heavy drapes, green velvet woven with bronze threads that shimmered with the movement of the breeze.

Nature touched everything. The fixtures above, shaped like winding branches, cast shifting shadows across the ceiling, swaying gently with the morning light. But beneath the beauty, there was something still. Untouched. She exhaled slowly, dragging her gaze back to Ren.

Mira looked at Ren's face. A tiredness she knew hadn't come from sleep alone was all over him.

"Did you sleep more than a few hours last night?" Mira asked.

Ren gave a small, sad smile but didn't answer. Instead, he shifted slightly. His fingers brushed gently along her temple, tucking a stray lock of hair behind her ear with absent care.

Then his hand lingered for a breath longer than it should have. His gaze held hers. "I'm so sorry, Mira," he said, voice low and raw.

The words undid something in her. The tears came again, fresh and silent. Ren pulled her into him without hesitation, his arms wrapping around her as though trying to hold the pieces together himself. She buried her face into his shoulder.

He said nothing. Just held her. One hand moved slowly along her back, his touch steady, anchoring. He didn't speak, didn't rush her. He simply stayed, silent and solid, until her breathing slowed and the storm inside her began to quiet.

Only then did he speak softly, as if afraid to disturb the fragile calm. "The council is meeting this morning. They're gathering to discuss the attack."

Mira nodded slowly, the words settling in her mind like stones sinking into water. "Of course, I'll be okay on my own." Ren paused before grimacing.

"You're required to attend." He said it quietly, but the weight of those words landed like a blow.

Mira froze. She turned to him, brows furrowing. Ren's gaze had dropped. But the tension in his jaw, the way his shoulders squared as if bracing for impact, told her this wasn't just some formality.

"We need a Solwynd on the council." he said softly, his gaze lifting to meet hers with quiet weight.

There was no pressure in the words. The only surviving representative. She hadn't noticed the ring in his palm until now, a simple silver ring darkened with age, engraved into the surface like a quiet vow, guiding stars. Their points stretching outward, reaching, searching. A solemn reminder of the family that had represented before her.

Slowly, he took her right hand, his fingers steady as he slid the ring onto her fourth finger. She swallowed hard, her chest tightening, her thoughts dragging her back, to the blood-soaked ground, to the weight of Torvyn's body in her arms, to the moment everything had shattered.

Ren must have seen the shift in her expression because his voice softened. "Mira..."

But she didn't let him finish. "I'll meet you there," she said, the words distant. "I just...I need some time alone..." She turned away before he could say anything else, before he had to see the pain that flickered behind his eyes.

Ren nodded, "I collected some of your dresses from your quarters," he said quietly. "They're in the closet."

Mira hesitated for only a second before nodding. She didn't move as Ren stepped closer. He paused beside her, then bent down and pressed a gentle kiss to the top of her head. She closed her eyes as he stepped into the hall.

The room was silent. She crawled beneath the blankets,

pulling the covers over her head as if they could shield her from the weight of the world.

And there, in the stillness, she let it come. The sobs hit her in waves. Quiet at first, then shaking her shoulders as the pain broke free. For Torvyn. Her brother. Gone. She buried her face into the pillow and wept.

* * *

Mira stepped into the celestial observatory, her head high, her shoulders squared despite the weight pressing against her ribs. The vast stained-glass windows shimmered with the morning light, casting shifting patterns of color across the polished marble floor.

The last time she had been here, she had stood on the upper landing, concealed in the darkness, listening as the council debated war. That night, Torvyn's chair had also sat empty. Now, it belonged to her.

Mira barely had time to steel herself before she felt Ren's presence beside her. He met her just inside, his gaze sweeping over her as if ensuring she was whole, steady. Saying nothing, he extended his arm to her in quiet solidarity.

She hesitated for only a breath before placing her hand in the crook of his elbow. The moment they stepped forward, the hum of voices quieted. Eyes turned to her, watching, measuring. Some were blank, impassive. Others held the weight of expectation. A few, skepticism. She didn't waver. Ren walked her to her seat.

To her right sat Lady Brenna Helmard. Her silver hair was twisted into a sleek coil at the nape of her neck, her deep emerald gown embroidered with the silver falcon of her house. She regarded Mira with quiet kindness.

To her left sat Lord Varian, an older man draped in deep blue robes, his red hair neatly combed back. There was a weight to his presence, not unkind, but patient, as if waiting to see whether Mira would rise to the role now set before her. His ringed fingers tapped idly against the polished wood, his gaze steady beneath bushy brows.

Ren pulled her chair out for her, his movements fluid, practiced, as if the act had been ingrained in him since childhood. Mira hesitated for only a fraction of a second before lowering herself into the seat, her spine straight.

She folded her hands in her lap, pressing them lightly against the fabric of her dress, forcing herself to remain composed. Ren took his place on the throne. A bell chimed. A single, resounding note that echoed through the observatory, scattering silence like shattered glass.

All rose in unison. Mira followed suit, her movements controlled, careful. The weight of tradition pressed against the room as the great doors at the far end opened, their gilded frames catching the early light.

The Crowned Betrothed entered. At his side, Danlea supported him, her presence a stark contrast to the hollow shell she guided forward.

He moved slowly, his steps dragging, his expression void of recognition. His gaze drifted across the room but landed on nothing, his eyes unfocused, seeing but not seeing. Mira felt the air in the room shift.

No one spoke. No one dared to move. Queen Danlea led him to the throne beside Ren with a grace that was both deliberate and delicate, as if the very act of guiding him was something sacred. She was gentle, her hand firm but warm as she helped him settle into the seat that had once been meant for a ruler, now occupied by a man who barely seemed to exist. There was no resistance, no sign of acknowledgment from the Crowned Betrothed as he sat. Only emptiness.

Once he was placed, Queen Danlea lowered herself into the chair on the other side of Ren, her posture poised, composed. A heavy silence filled the observatory, She did not rush to speak. Instead, she took a measured breath, her silver eyes sweeping over the gathered councilors, lingering just a fraction longer on Mira.

"Last night's attack was no mere skirmish." Danlea's tone was even, but there was a steel edge beneath the words. "It was calculated. Coordinated. Our enemies struck in unison, and they did so with the knowledge of our defenses."

A murmur rippled through the room, uneasy and weighted. Lord Asric leaned forward.

"Then the question is, who was the true orchestrator?" His voice was clipped, eyes sharp as he scanned the council. "Was it Kharador? Or was it the rebels?"

The debate ignited at once.

"The resistance does not have the skill for an attack of this scale," Lord Varian interjected, his deep voice level despite the tension. "The force that breached the palace was trained, disciplined. That is not the hallmark of an unorganized rebellion."

"Then explain the uniforms" Brenna said coolly. "The insurgents bore no insignia, no unified colors. That does not scream Kharador to me."

"Perhaps because they did not need to," another countered. "Perhaps Kharador sought to disguise their involvement by scattering their men among the rebellion."

A storm of voices filled the air, each councilor offering their own interpretation, each suggestion growing more urgent, more cutting.

"Or they were separate entities," Varian argued, his voice heavy with authority. "Two blades striking at once, but not necessarily at the same target."

The voices crashed over her like waves against stone. Mira sat still, her body rigid, but inside she felt unmoored, untethered. Grief throbbed beneath her skin, sharp and raw, fraying the edges of her composure with every breath.

The sounds of the council grew louder, each voice rising to meet another, sharp with accusation, bloated with certainty.

"Torvyn Solwynd's death was the greatest loss of the night." Lord Asric, regarded her carefully, as if measuring her response before he spoke again. "His death marks the loss of not only a noble son," he continued, voice slow, deliberate, "but of a key figure in our court."

Mira's throat burned. Torvyn. Gone. Her last memory of him flashed before her. His body falling to the blood-stained marble. His hands reaching for nothing. Her stomach twisted, bile rising in her throat, but she forced it down.

Forced herself to breathe. Forced herself to keep her expression unreadable. The council watched her, waiting. Waiting to see if she would break. She wouldn't. Mira straightened, shoulders squared, her voice steady despite the weight pressing against her chest.

"What matters now," she said, "is not debating what was lost, but deciding how we move forward."

As Mira's words settled into the room, a brief hush fell. Lord Asric stood. The movement was slow, deliberate, his hands clasped behind his back as he turned toward the gathered councilors. He did not look at Mira, not at first. His gaze swept across the chamber, catching each face with quiet precision. A performance, perfectly measured.

"And yet," he said at last, "some losses are…

conveniently timed." Mira stiffened. Asric tilted his head, voice calm but laced with steel. "Lady Solwynd speaks of moving forward. Of unity. But we must ask, forward to where? And under whose direction?

"You were there, but you were not on the steps with the court. You did not fall. And you were seen after the battle, escorted by the Regent himself."

The word "Regent" landed like a blow. A few councilors shifted in their seats. Others narrowed their eyes. Mira didn't move. Asric's lips curled, almost a smile as he addressed the council.

"We have all seen the closeness between them earlier this very meeting. That is no longer speculation. It is a fact. And while I would not presume to suggest impropriety…" he trailed off, letting the implication hang in the air like a dagger balanced on its point. "It does raise questions. Of trust. Of allegiance." Mira opened her mouth, but Asric raised a hand, the picture of patience.

"Of timing," he continued smoothly. "Of who benefited from the death of Torvyn Solwynd. A man who once stood in her way. A man who knew her better than any of us. A brother." That word. It sliced through the air like a blade.

"She stood to gain," Asric said simply. "And now, she has the attention of the most powerful person in this room."

The council erupted. Some shouted objections, others spoke in hushed tones to their neighbors. The weight of suspicion rolled like thunder through the chamber. Ren stood then, sharp and sudden.

"Enough." His voice echoed through the hall like a command.

All eyes turned to him, Asric's smile only deepened. And Mira realized, with sick clarity, that this was his game.

Planting seeds of doubt, forcing them to bloom in public view. And if she wasn't careful, if Ren wasn't, those roots would twist themselves into something far worse than just doubt.

Ren's jaw was tight, his posture rigid as he faced the council, his gaze hard but composed. "Lady Solwynd suffered a loss," he said, each word deliberate, unwavering. "I comforted her. As I would any member of this court who had just lost their only living family."

He let that settle, then added, "It is not impropriety. It is duty. My duty, as Regent, is to protect this kingdom and all who serve it. Including any of you."

Asric did not flinch, but the gleam in his eyes sharpened, almost amused. The seeds had been sown. Now he would wait to see which ones would take root.

Mira rose slowly to her feet. "My brother is dead," her voice quiet but clear as a bell "And yet, instead of addressing why, you're trying to turn suspicion onto me. Instead of asking why this kingdom is tearing itself apart, primed for occupation by other kingdoms, you stand there, picking apart every word, searching for some excuse to blame me instead of facing the truth."

A hush fell over the chamber. Mira's eyes swept the room, meeting every gaze that dared to linger. She didn't beg for belief. She didn't ask. She simply stood, unflinching, the weight of her grief worn like armor.

Asric tilted his head slightly, a faint smirk curling at the edges of his mouth. "It's tragic really. That grief cannot serve as evidence."

Ren's hand clenched at his side, but he didn't move.

A voice rose. "I can provide the evidence." The words settled with unnatural weight.

Danlea stood, her silver robes brushing the stone floor,

her palms open, the light glinting off the fine rings circling her fingers. The room turned to her.

"My gift allows me to see the shape of truth within one's mind," she said calmly. "And if the council wishes it, I will see what she saw when her brother fell. When her choices were made. Not twisted. Not filtered through fear or jealousy. But as they were."

Danlea's eyes met Asric's. "And I am happy to do so with any consenting party."

She descended from her seat, bare feet silent against the marble. The sunlight in the observatory seemed to lean toward her, the shadows curling away from her touch, as if the very room recognized her presence, her gentleness.

"Mira," she said softly, her voice woven with warmth, as if calling her from somewhere far away. "Do you consent?"

Mira nodded. Danlea's movements were slow, deliberate. She stopped in the middle of the observatory, close enough that Mira could see the intricate embroidery of stars along her collar, the delicate stitching that seemed to shimmer with its own light. She beckoned Mira to her.

Mira's feet moved, the marble cool beneath her soles, the silence of the observatory pressing in like held breath. Every eye in the chamber followed her, but none of them mattered. Not Asric with his sharpened smiles. Not the council with their thrones and judgment. Only Danlea.

"You've been through so much," she murmured.

Her voice was a balm to Mira's frayed nerves, a warmth that seeped through the cracks of her composure.

"They ask so much of you." Danlea whispered.

Mira's vision blurred, and she didn't know if it was from exhaustion, grief or the sudden, aching comfort in the Queen's tone. Mira swallowed, her throat tight, something fragile lodged deep in her chest. Danlea's fingers brushed a stray lock of hair from Mira's face.

"Look at me," she asked, and Mira obeyed.

Milky white eyes met hers, and the room seemed to exhale. The light softened shadows that had seemed sharp now blurred, their edges melting into the stone.

Danlea's gaze was not merely sight, it was a soft pull, a current leading not to drowning but to something else. Mira felt herself drawn into it, the ground slipping away, her body weightless.

There was no fear. Only quiet. Only peace. Her pulse slowed, the thunder in her ears fading to a soft rhythm, like the lull of waves against the shore. Her limbs felt light, as if the burdens of truth and lies, of rebellion and loyalty, had been lifted from her shoulders.

The Queen's face remained the only anchor, her expression filled with understanding, with an unspoken promise.

Mira's knees buckled.

35

MIRA OPENED HER EYES to silence. Not the hush of a stone chamber, but real silence. Vast and alive. The ground beneath her was glass, smooth and cold, stretching into infinity. Beneath it, stars pulsed like the heartbeat of some slumbering giant, their light flickering softly, steadily, as if waiting for her to move. Above her, only blackness. Not empty. Not dead. But watching. Endless.

She stood barefoot, her breath fogging slightly in the chill that wasn't air. The quiet pressed close around her shoulders, familiar now. Too familiar. Danlea was already there. She stood some paces ahead, robed in starlight that shifted like silk in a current. Her face was calm, lined not with age but with knowledge.

When she looked at Mira, her milky eyes were clear.

"Torvyn is gone," Mira whispered, her voice barely holding. Tears streamed down her face, hot and unrelenting, as the words hung in the silence like a final breath.

Danlea didn't flinch. She only nodded once, as if acknowledging not just the death, but the wound it had left behind.

Mira took a staggering step forward. Her feet slid slightly on the glass, and her hands opened helplessly at her sides.

"They took him from me," she said, voice cracking.

Guilt churned in her chest like broken glass. She had been too late. Always too late. Her hands trembled. The glass beneath her feet seemed to pulse with her grief, each flicker of starlight echoing the tremor in her chest.

"I didn't get to choose," she said. "He didn't get to choose."

Danlea's silver gaze softened. "There were many possible choices," she murmured. A thread of sorrow wove through her voice. "But in all of them, your brother was lost at this point."

Mira clenched her fists. Her nails dug into her palms as her knees buckled.

Her voice was nothing but breath, the ghost of all the things she couldn't say. "He died alone."

Danlea stepped forward. She knelt, her starlit robe pooling across the glass, and lifted a hand, not to touch, but to gesture.

"He did not die alone." Danlea pointed to a single glowing point in the threads beneath their feet. Danlea's hand hovered above the tangled strands of gold.

The light pulsed beneath her fingers. In that glow, Mira saw him. Torvyn. A flash of him in the moment just before the end. She saw him being welcomed by celestial hands as the light faded.

"He was welcomed with open arms," Danlea whispered. "His name is written in the stars. Not as a soldier, or a traitor but as a brother. As your brother."

Her palms pressed to the stars beneath her. The guilt bled out of her. Mira wept, her shoulders trembling as her breath caught over and over in her throat. The ache in her chest was endless. A hollow cavern too vast to fill.

Danlea rose and extended a hand. "Come," she said gently. "We've lingered here long enough. Even here, I can feel Ren's concern rolling off you."

Mira hesitated, still cradling the ache that would never quite leave her. But slowly, she reached up, her fingers brushing Danlea's palm. The Queen's hand closed over hers.

Threads ignited like dawn, and the black above cracked open, just a sliver, letting something brighter pour through. And the world shifted.

Mira surfaced slowly, dragged from the depths of something vast and unknowable. Her body felt like stone, weighted and cold against the smooth marble floor of the observatory. The dim candlelight flickered at the edges of her vision, casting long, skeletal shadows that stretched across the walls like watching figures.

Voices drifted around her, muffled, distant. Echoes through water. She lay still, unable to move, her limbs numb, her thoughts sluggish. The weight of the other place pressed down on her, and yet the moment she had lived above the stars was already slipping away, retreating like the tide.

"Truly, I am sorry for the dramatics," Queen Danlea's voice wove through the murmurs, smooth as silk. "It appears Mira's mind could not withstand the intrusion. Some are simply too delicate for such direct sight."

A lie. Mira's eyelids fluttered. She had not crumbled. The Queen had not torn through her mind at all.

"She did not know of her brother's death until it occurred. She has done no wrong." Danlea declared.

A murmur rippled through the council, tension breaking like ice beneath a rising sun. Some sighed in relief. Others shifted uneasily. Ren stood tense, his hands gripping the arms of his chair, white-knuckled, barely breathing, gaze locked on Mira as if willing her to wake fully.

Danlea turned toward her, the soft sweep of her gown

whispering against the floor. Her expression remained gentle, her lips curved in a smile that might have seemed motherly.

"Mira?" Danlea whispered, her voice like a caress over the room. "Are you awake?" Mira forced her lips to part, her throat raw.

"Yes." The word was jagged, like glass against her tongue.

"There now," Danlea soothed, stepping closer. "You gave us quite a fright. I hope you do not mind my little intrusion. It was necessary, you see, to clear your name." She turned slightly, addressing the council. "And it is clear."

Silence.

"This is a farce." Asric's voice cut through the stillness like a blade.

Mira flinched, her body still weak, still aching, but her pulse spiked. Ren's head snapped toward him sharply, his dark eyes flashing with a warning.

"This is an outrage." Asric continued as he took a step forward. Toward the Queen, toward Mira.

"You expect us to believe this? That in all her time near the resistance, in the company of known conspirators, she knew nothing? That she never whispered secrets in the dark?" His teeth bared in something that was not quite a sneer, not quite a snarl.

Mira's stomach turned. He was cornering her, framing her as both too weak to be useful, but too dangerous to be free.

"She knows nothing," Danlea repeated, her voice even.

"She is a liability," Asric pressed, stepping closer. "I demand her resignation from this council."

Danlea's voice was quiet. Lethal. "Are you questioning my loyalty or my ability, Lord Asric?"

Asric stilled.

Mira glanced at Ren and saw the edges of him cracking. Saw the regret in his gaze, the apology he did not speak. His lips parted, as if to say something, as if he wanted to reach for her. But he didn't move. He couldn't.

The Queen inclined her head slightly, her voice once more filling the room. "The council extends its sincerest apologies to Mira. For both the loss of your brother and the accusations today."

Mira did not feel relief. She rose, slow, deliberate, and returned to her seat. The chair beneath her was solid, grounding, but the council chamber itself seemed distant, the voices around her blurring into something detached, something irrelevant.

Ren's voice cut through the room. "The King of Kharador has sent word this morning", each word sharp with purpose. "He is insisting on diplomatic talks in a few days time"

The effect was immediate. More than one noble stiffened in their seat. Lord Edric's mouth parted slightly before he caught himself, his frown deepening. Brenna Helmard sat back, calculating. Even Danlea's brow lifted a fraction.

Ren leaned forward, his hands braced against the polished wood. "We cannot refuse him, the guard will be split, half will remain stationed here for the peace talks, the other half deployed to reinforce the cities most vulnerable to attack. A standing force in the outer regions will not only deter Kharador, but it will remind the people that we have not abandoned them."

Edric frowned. "That will spread our forces thin."

"Less so than if we continue trying to fight a war against our own people and an invading army at the same time," Ren countered.

Danlea spoke, "My army will continue to defend

Bharalyn, doubling our forces." The murmurs quieted.

The Queen's milky eyes shone as she regarded the council. "You argue over how to end this insurgence. But what the Regent has recognized is the greater truth, it is not over.

And it will not be, until Bharalyn is united again, from its capital to its farthest villages."

Danlea's gaze swept over the council. "If you crush the resistance, another will rise. If you leave your people to suffer, they will look to Kharador for salvation."

Silence hung in the air. Ren straightened. "Then let us decide." His voice was clear, firm. "If we are to move forward, we must do so together. We vote now, on a plan that does not simply continue this war, but seeks to end it before Bharalyn collapses from within."

His gaze swept the room. "All those in favor of bolstering our defenses while also rebuilding the lands we have left to ruin, of ensuring Bharalyn is worth fighting for, raise your hand."

A beat. Then, one by one, hands lifted. First Danlea, calm and assured. Then Brenna Helmard, her sharp gaze flicking toward Ren before she raised her hand. More followed. The murmurs of uncertainty had faded, replaced by grim resolve. They cast their votes, one after another.

Mira's hand rose. She glanced at Ren across the room. His eyes met hers, steady and waiting. The knot in her chest, wound tight from grief and silence, loosened. She raised her hand higher. Clear. Unshaking. Her voice wasn't needed, her vote was enough.

All but two. Lord Asric's arms remained folded, his jaw tight with disapproval. Lord Edric hesitated but ultimately kept his hand down, glancing between Ren and the others.

Ren's eyes met Asric's. "Dissent is your right," he said evenly. "But the council has spoken."

The Queen nodded once. "Then it is decided."

✳ ✳ ✳

Council matters had dragged on until dusk, the weight of debate around supplies and allocations pressing down on Mira.

The room had thinned, nobles filing out in pairs and whispers, but Mira remained seated, spine straight despite the ache creeping into her shoulders. Her temples pulsed with the slow, steady throb of exhaustion.

Across the room, Ren stood in quiet conversation with Brenna Helmard, nodding once at something she said. But Mira saw it, the way his gaze flicked to her, just once, brief and apologetic. The unspoken words were all in that glance.

I'm sorry.

But they both knew. After Asric's accusations, after the weight of her brother's death had been turned into a political weapon, any perceived closeness between Regent and her would cost them. No words, no gesture but she knew he understood.

It's okay.

They would be careful. Distant, if they had to be. And still, even across a room, they could read each other this clearly. Mira felt a quiet, steady gratitude for that. For the kind of understanding that didn't need words.

*** *** ***

By the time Mira stepped out into the gardens, the last light of the sun clung stubbornly to the horizon, casting the sky in shades of burning amber and deepening indigo. The air was cool, crisp with the scent of damp earth and fallen leaves, thick with the quiet promise of an encroaching winter.

She walked along the winding path, her boots brushing through the golden and russet leaves that had gathered along the edges. The trees stood half-bare, their skeletal branches reaching toward the darkening sky, clutching at the remnants of a summer now lost to autumn's slow decay.

A wind stirred through her, sending leaves spiraling to the ground, their rustling the only sound beyond the distant murmurs of the palace. The palace itself still glittered behind her, its lanterns burning, reflecting off the polished marble walls and gilded spires. A monument to power, standing untouched while the world beyond its gates withered and starved. Mira turned away.

Ahead, past the final ring of the gardens, the graveyard loomed in the fading light. Her steps slowed as she approached her family's crypt. It was a simple structure, unadorned, built of smooth gray stone. No grand carvings, no towering statues, only a single crest above the arch. The sigil of House Solwynd, its once-sharp engravings now barely catching the dim candle light flickering from within. The door stood slightly ajar, the scent of melting wax drifting into the cool night air. The acolytes had left it open for her as was their customs. Open for three days for anyone wishing to pay their respects to the ascended. She stepped inside.

The chamber was quiet. The candles burned low in their sconces. Their glow cast flickering patterns along the stone walls. The walls were lined with stone recesses, each marked with a name. Her father. Her mother. And now... Torvyn.

His name was freshly carved, the stone still rough beneath her fingertips as she traced the letters. He had meant safety, guidance, home. Mira's hand trembled as it hovered there, her fingers curling slowly into a fist.

The pressure behind her eyes broke, silent tears spilling down her cheeks, sliding along her jaw. She didn't wipe them away. There was no one to see, no one left to care.

A draft slipped through the crypt, stirring the candle flames, making them tremble. A shiver ran down her spine. It was the ache of emptiness. Of being the last one standing. The last one breathing. They were all gone. She had outlived them. Mira pressed her forehead to the stone, her breath hitching. She had never felt so alone.

A movement behind her. Mira spun around, her hand hovered where the hilt of her dagger would have been.

"Torvyn deserved better than this." Brahn's voice echoed through the crypt like smoke.

Slowly, she turned. He stood in the doorway, half-draped in the flickering gold of candlelight, half-swallowed by the dark. His cloak was creased with travel, the collar still damp. But it was the sling that caught her eye. His right arm, tightly bound and cradled to his chest. He stepped forward slowly, deliberately, Brahn's expression didn't change.

"Your aim," he said, tone dry, "was better than I gave you credit for."

She snapped back at him. "You're lucky you dodged." His eyes flicked to her then.

She turned away, back to the inscription on the wall. Torvyn's name. Rough in the stone.

Brahn stepped inside, the scrape of his boot against stone

far too calm for what he was. "This is what they've done," he said quietly, "to all of us."

"No." Mira's voice cracked. "This is what you did." she whispered. The crypt went still. She turned to face him again, eyes burning. "He's dead. My brother. And I don't care how you dress it up, how righteous you make it sound, he died protecting you."

Brahn didn't move. Didn't blink. Just stood there, the flicker of candlelight throwing harsh shadows across his face.

"Did you ever try to stop him?" she spat. "Or did you just let him worship you?" Her voice cracked, breath coming hard now, uneven. Grief swelled behind her ribs, sharp and burning.

Mira hissed. "You blame the council, their golden halls, their hunger for control, but what about you? You let him believe in you. You let him think this kingdom could only be saved through blood. And when his ambition got in the way, when it stopped being about hope and became about victory, did you ever fight him? When did you protect him?"

Brahn's face remained still, unreadable, but something in his eyes faltered. Just slightly. Brahn exhaled, slow and tight. "He believed in the cause, Mira. You don't get to strip that from him."

She laughed, sharp, bitter. "I don't want to strip anything from him. I want him here. I want him breathing. I want him alive!" she yelled.

Silence fell again. The candles guttered, and the shadows lengthened. For a moment, neither of them moved. Then Brahn shifted, his voice quieter this time, almost gentle. "You forget what he is to me."

Mira flinched. The words hit harder than she expected, cutting through the haze of her fury. She had. Somewhere between the blame and the grief, she had forgotten. Not just comrades. Not just allies. Something deeper. Sacred. Bonded. Her breath caught in her throat, the fire of her anger flickering low as something heavier settled in its place.

Guilt. A slow, sinking ache in her chest.

The sling tugged slightly against his shoulder as he adjusted, wincing. "I still feel it," he said. "My bond to him didn't break, Mira. It didn't fade. It's still there."

Brahn exhaled sharply, as if he could force the feeling away. "Every breath. Every heartbeat. It's not just pain, it's a siren call. It lures me to the abyss, and there are moments that I wonder if I should stop fighting it. Because if I let go, maybe, just maybe, I'd find him again."

Mira let her tears fall, jaw trembling. Outside, the wind howled through the trees, rattling the iron gate. Brahn's voice, when it came again, was quiet. Measured.

"When the King of Kharador arrives, he will bring something that will turn the tides and ensure our victory."

"I am not one of your uprising Brahn" Mira said. Her voice was barely a whisper, but it cut cleaner than steel.

Brahn's expression stilled. His voice lost none of its certainty. Brahn sighed, "When the moment comes, you'll know your loyalty is with us, and as the sister of my bonded, there will always be a place for you... I promised him that" Mira heard Brahn step back into the cold.

For a long moment, she stared at the name carved into stone. A gust of wind surged through the crypt's entrance, the cold biting at her skin. She exhaled, slow and steady, before turning toward the door.

✳ ✳ ✳

The last traces of sunset were long gone, leaving only the pale glow of the moonlight through the clouds. The wind had picked up, making the trees scrape together with each restless gust. Mira pulled her cloak tighter around herself, her boots crunching against the path.

Tharion stood at the edge of the burial ground, waiting. He leaned against an old stone marker, arms crossed. He said nothing, simply falling into step beside her as she passed him. The palace loomed in the distance, its towers glittering, untouched by the quiet grief of the graveyard.

Finally, Mira spoke. "He hated the cold, you know." Tharion glanced at her.

"Torvyn." Mira's voice was even, but there was something heavy beneath it. "Always complained about the nights."

Tharion's expression hardened, "I remember. He used to steal extra blankets from the barracks. Claimed they were for you, but we both knew he was hoarding them."

"He always had an answer for everything," she whispered. "Especially when he was in trouble..."

Mira's expression softened, though her eyes stayed locked on the path ahead. The lanterns burned steadily along through the palace windows, their golden glow casting elongated shadows as Mira and Tharion approached the doors. As they entered, the warmth of the halls did little to chase away the cold that had settled deep in her bones.

Her gaze drifted, unconsciously. The old tapestry Torvyn used to hide behind during games of chase, the chipped vase he'd once knocked over and sworn her to secrecy about. Further down, she could see Torvyn dragging her down into the kitchens to steal sweetbread. She could almost hear his voice again. They reached her quarters. Mira pushed open the door to her room, stepping inside.

Tharion hesitated, then gestured out the hallway. "I'll be in my room. If you need anything."

She turned slightly, glancing toward it. She nodded. He lingered for a moment longer, then he gave her a short nod and turned away.

Mira closed the door. The silence pressed in even as she changed into a nightdress. She sat on the edge of the bed, staring at the wall, The cold from the graveyard still clinging to her. The shadows didn't move. The fire in the hearth had long since gone out. She didn't light another. She couldn't bring herself to fill the room with light when her chest felt so hollow.

A shift in the air. The faint creak of the window frame. She already knew exactly who it was. Ren slipped through the open window like smoke, silent and sure. His boots barely made a sound as they hit the floor. His cloak damp at the hem from mist. His brow furrowed the moment he saw her.

"You left the window unlatched," he murmured, stepping closer.

"Did I?" she asked quietly, eyes not leaving the floor. She didn't even remember unlatching the window at all.

Ren stopped a few paces from her. He crouched down, "Mira."

She blinked slowly, then met his gaze. "Brahn came to the crypt..." Ren stilled. "He tried to turn it on the council." she said, a dry huff escaping her. "And worse, he believes it."

Ren didn't speak right away. He rose slowly before sitting beside her. Just close enough that their shoulders touched. "Do you believe him?" he asked quietly.

"No," she said, then paused. "Not in the way he meant it. He thinks he's fighting to save them."

Ren leaned back on his hands, exhaling through his nose. "That's what makes him dangerous."

"I know," Her voice cracked.

Ren was silent again. Then, gently, he reached for her hand, threading his fingers through hers. His palm was warm. They sat like that for a time. Just breath and silence, the kind that didn't press but settled like a blanket.

Eventually, Ren stood and shrugged off his cloak, the damp fabric hitting the floor with a soft thud. He unlaced his shirt, his movements slow and tired. He didn't ask. Didn't need to. He lifted the covers and waited for her.

Mira slid beneath them, letting the cold be chased away by the heat of him. Ren joined her, curling around her back, one arm sliding under her waist. His other hand found hers again beneath the blankets. Slowly, Mira's eyes drifted closed.

36

DAYS PASSED IN A BLUR, each one thick with tension Mira could feel beneath her skin. Council meetings stretched for hours, exhausting, careful games of veiled words and shifting alliances. Every sentence was a blade, every agreement a trap waiting to be sprung.

She had stepped into a political minefield, and Asric was always watching. Always listening. His gaze followed her like a shadow, sharp and silent, as though waiting for her to slip. She chose her words with precision and spoke less than she wanted. The chamber held too many smiles that didn't reach the eyes, too many glances that passed between lords with histories she wasn't aware of. And in every one of them, the question lingered, who was waiting for her to fail?

Grain caravans made it to the starving towns along the western roads. Reinforcements reached outposts long forgotten by the palace. Medical tents were raised in city squares, and wounded people finally received the care they needed. The relief was far from complete, but still welcome. For the first time in months, the outlying towns had hope.

But here, in the marble halls of power, every victory tasted faintly of ash.

During the council sessions Ren led with confidence, with purpose. He carried the weight of the kingdom on his shoulders and did not falter, did not flinch under pressure. He moved through the room, a king in waiting, unshaken by opposition.

Danlea, her calm, sharp presence held the room together. Where others attempted to indulge their own interests, Danlea listened. Considered. Yet, even with them at the helm, the council was an endless battle.

Every session followed the same path. Mira sat through yet another round of nobles bickering over how much aid to divert from the palace. The same arguments circled endlessly, loud but aimless. As always, the meeting dragged until Ren finally called it to an end with small compromises. The council would disperse in familiar clusters, murmuring to one another. Already laying the groundwork for their next round of posturing and quiet scheming.

And every night, without fail, Ren came to her. Long after the palace had quieted and the halls emptied of attendants and guards, Mira would hear the soft click of her window opening. The sound of his boots on the stone, the gentle creak of the sill, had become a ritual for them both. He would slip through the darkness, silent and certain, and Mira would already be waiting, half-sitting in bed, the covers pooled around her legs and the candlelight casting shadows across the room.

He would sit beside her, sometimes taking her hand, sometimes just watching her. They spoke in whispers, voices barely audible above the soft crackle of the hearth. Words passed between them like confessions, slow and careful and wrapped in the hush of late hours.

But the space between them pulsed with unspoken grief and longing. Ren never pushed, never asked for more than she could give. He would lean in slowly, his hand brushing her jaw, his breath warm against her skin, waiting for her to meet him halfway.

When their lips met, it was never simple. Their kisses

turned desperate, urgent, as if trying to outrun everything they couldn't fix. Ren held her like she was breakable, like even in his hunger he knew where the lines were.

Mira clung to him not to invite more, but to feel safe, to feel wanted, to feel that she wasn't alone. His mouth moved against hers like he was starving, but he never let it become more than that.

He would always leave before dawn. His warmth would linger in the bed, in the imprint of his body on the bed beside her. Every morning, he left just as the sun rose.

Ren's exhale was soft, drawn from somewhere deep as Mira's fingers traced idle lines across his bare shoulder. His skin was warm against hers, their bodies tangled beneath the rumpled sheets, the early morning light seeping in through the narrow window and painting gold across the stone floor. His head tilted slightly into her touch, as if drawn to her without thought. For a while, neither of them spoke. The weight of everything, last night's council session, the looming arrival of Kharador's king, the endless demands of duty, lay between them like a third body. Mira shifted closer, the slide of her thigh against his slow and deliberate. She let her hand drift upward, threading through the dark strands of his hair.

He exhaled softly, eyes closing for a moment before he spoke. "I need to go soon. I have an early meeting with Lady Brenna to negotiate the release of more food supplies."

Mira's brow furrowed. "Why won't you announce your lineage?" she murmured, her fingers pausing at the base of his neck. "If you were the heir you wouldn't need to negotiate."

He was quiet for a moment, his hand absently curling

around her hip under the blanket, grounding himself in her presence. "Because the moment I do, the questions will never stop." His voice was rough with sleep, but steady. "Why now? Why not before? What changed?"

He turned slightly, just enough for her to see the tension behind his eyes. "And once they start asking, they'll keep digging. And the court would turn on me in a heartbeat. Anyone who is on our side will feel betrayed and we would have more enemies than friends."

She frowned. "But wouldn't it give us an opportunity to do good?"

Ren hummed quietly. The sound vibrated against her where their skin touched. "The crown won't fix this," he said, turning his face into the pillow for a moment before looking at her again. "Being king doesn't mean they'll trust me. I have to prove I'm worth following first."

Mira studied him, seeing past the casual tone, past the smirk that never quite reached his eyes. She saw the truth there, the fear, the exhaustion. The years of weight he carried in silence.

Slowly, she nodded. Ren's gaze softened. He pulled her towards him. The kiss was slow, deep, steady. A touch that said everything he couldn't. She melted into him, her hand sliding across his back, her body arching instinctively closer. The warmth between them was more than flesh, it was tethered trust.

When they broke apart, Ren rested his forehead against hers. His voice was low, reluctant. "We need to be in the observatory soon. The King of Kharador arrives tonight." Mira's eyes opened slowly. Reality crept in, cold and inevitable. She drew in a breath, steadying herself as her fingers traced the sharp line of his jaw.

"I wish you could stand with me," he murmured. She touched his face again, brushing a thumb along his cheek.

They both knew better, the implication if she did. In the stillness, in the morning hush, they stayed there just a little longer, the only place left where they were allowed to simply be.

"I'll be with Tharion though" Ren's breath hitched softly at her words, and his hand, already resting against her hip beneath the blankets, curled just a little tighter.

"I know and trust him," he said at last, voice low, threading through the hush of the morning. "I trust you."

He didn't look away. If anything, his gaze grew steadier, the storm behind his eyes quieted by something deeper. "If it has to be anyone, I'm glad it's him beside you." A pause, then something half-smile, half-sigh.

Over the course of the past few days, Mira and Tharion had found a quiet friendship. They ate meals together, sometimes laughing, sometimes just passing the time. And though the loss lingered like a shadow behind them both, there was something in Tharion that had begun to return.

A little more life in the way he carried himself. A little more light in his eyes. There was no pretense, no edges of what she had thought had once been something more. What remained between them now was something real. Grounded. Comforting. A new, fragile companionship not shaped by need or expectation.

Ren moved quietly, the soft rustle of fabric the only sound as he slipped from beneath the sheets. The early light washed over the room, pale and cool, stretching long across the floor. Mira lay still, watching him dress, memorizing the lines of his back as he fastened his belt and stepped toward the window. Then he froze, half-cloaked in shadow and early morning mist. His shirt hung open, and his hand still rested on the windowsill, body tensed for movement.

A sound split the quiet. A slow, deliberate clap. Mira sat upright in the bed, the sheets gathering at her waist, heart thudding. The sound rose again, measured and mocking.

Then a voice, smooth as oil and twice as slick.

"Well," it drawled from the garden below, "if I'd known how early you take meetings, I might've made an earlier appointment." Ren's jaw clenched.

Mira was already out of bed, yanking her robe around her shoulders as she moved to the window. Below, half-shrouded in the creeping vines and dappled morning light, was Lord Asric. He didn't smile, not really, but the glint in his eye was worse.

"I was merely out for a morning stroll," Asric continued, looking entirely too pleased with himself. "Imagine my surprise when I looked up and saw our Regent taking his leave through a chamber window."

He bowed, more performance than politeness, flashing a grin that never reached his eyes. "Still clinging to old habits, are we, heartbreaker?"

Mira's skin prickled. Her pulse thundered. Not just from fury or fear, but from the sheer brazenness of Asric.

Asric grinned, "I do believe that is Lady Solwynd's I can see. What would her bonded say, I wonder?"

Ren remained still, unmoving. Asric held up his hands in mock surrender, his smirk widening. "Do not fear, young regent. Your secret is safe with me." His voice was smooth, almost amused, but his eyes glinted with calculation. Dangerous. "Although I do have to ask a simple favor."

He stepped forward into the soft spill of dawn light, his gaze flicking between Mira and Ren before landing on the prince with feigned ease. "A rather small request, really."

Ren's jaw tightened. The air around him seemed to tighten too. Asric took another slow step as he continued casually. "I only ask that when the King of Kharador arrives, that Mira borrows something from him."

Mira's brows drew together. Asric sighed, as if explaining to a dim student. "A letter. A package. He will have both, likely tucked in the inner lining of his armor. Something meant for a different set of eyes." He smiled. "And you, my dear, have always had such quick, delicate fingers."

Ren shifted, blocking Mira from Asric's sight. His voice dropped, a blade drawn in the hush. "You want her to steal from a hostile king?"

Asric's smirk never faltered. "You think The War King of the West arrives without contingencies? He's not just here to talk. There will be something, proof of a second alliance, a threat to us. I want to see it."

Asric's gaze lingered on her, then slid to Ren. "Her work would be a gift from both of you," he said lightly. "For my continued silence."

He took his time with the next words. "You and I both know that Mira is the only one who can do this without suspicion."

"If we refuse..." Ren growled, his voice low.

Asric's smile dropped. "Secrets tend to come out when left alone too long."

The silence that followed was taut as wire. Ren's fists curled at his sides, his breath held in check by fury he didn't dare unleash.

Mira spoke first. "I'll do it," she said, her voice low and steady.

Controlled fury simmered beneath every syllable. Because what choice did she have? If she refused, Asric would not hesitate to act. He wouldn't shout her secret from the palace walls, not at first. He would whisper. Plant doubt where it hurts the most. Let it fester. Let it spread. To Danlea. To the council. To the people. She would become a liability. A traitor in the eyes of those already looking for someone to blame. And Ren, he would fall with her.

Mira's pulse throbbed beneath her skin, her body still braced, even though she stood perfectly still. This wasn't a choice. It was a trap disguised as diplomacy. She knew that. So did he. But better her hands than Ren's name.

Better to give Asric what he wanted than risk the avalanche he'd already begun to loosen.

Asric's grin widened, full of triumph. "Good."

He turned, bowed with mock grace, and began to stroll through the garden. But just before he disappeared behind the hedge, he glanced back. "Oh, and Mira?" he called softly. "Try not to get caught."

37

D ARK, SOMBER ELEGANCE filled the great hall. Long tables draped in heavy black cloth in accordance with Kharadorian traditions stretched from wall to wall. Candles flickered in their wrought-iron holders, their glow casting elongated shadows along the towering stone columns. A rich, smoky incense curled through the air , a reminder of the foreign customs now taking root beneath Bharalyn's roof.

Asric had provided a soft, pink creation that clung to Mira's frame. The fabric shimmered under the dim candlelight. Asric had dressed her as the picture of innocence, a flower in full bloom, unassuming, untouched by deceit. A perfect illusion. One that would ensure no one ever suspected what she was about to do.

The murmurs of nobles and Myrdathis soldiers filled the space, a low hum of conversation as they awaited the King's arrival. Across the hall, the dais loomed, elevated above the gathering, a stage for those who held true power in the kingdom. At the center of it sat The Crowned Betrothed, dressed in the deep, regal blue of Bharalyn's court. On either side, stood Ren and Danlea.

Danlea, poised and composed, wore a gown of shadowed emerald, a deep, near-black green trimmed with silver. A crown of delicate iron adorned her head, the filigree twisting into sharp, elegant points, an unyielding reminder of her rule. Though she exuded the quiet grace of a queen, her eyes were keen, watchful, assessing every face in the crowd, every shifting movement across the hall.

Ren was every inch a prince. Clad in deep black and gold. His high-collared cape was edged with intricate embroidery, detailing the ancient sigils of Bharalyn. His dark hair was carefully tied back at the nape, loose strands falling just enough to soften the sharp lines of his face. His shoulders were squared, his expression unreadable, but Mira knew better. She saw the tension in his stance, the controlled grip of his hands.

Next to her, Tharion stood in stark contrast, dressed in the crisp uniform of the royal guard. She hadn't seen him in a royal guard attire since they had bonded. Deep blue fabric hugged his frame, the silver fastenings gleaming under the dim lighting. A heavy belt, adorned with his rank's insignia, sat firmly at his waist, his posture rigid, prepared, as if even in this hall of decorum, he was ready for battle.

Mira's gaze flickered between them, each a piece of the grand spectacle unfolding before the court. A foreign queen, a secret prince, a lost ruler, and a warrior. And yet, beneath the polished facade, tension lay thick in the air.

The great doors slammed open with a force that sent a hush rippling through the hall. The flames of the candelabras flickered, shadows leaping against the stone walls as heavy boots echoed against the polished floor. The King of Kharador had arrived.

Violence clung to him like a second skin, exuding from every measured step. He was tall and broad, built from battles. His presence was a tangible force that sent a chill creeping down Mira's spine. A man who had earned his kingdom's obedience through blood, and steel. Through sheer, unyielding power.

The King of Kharador strode forward, his midnight-black

armor seemed to gleam like a living storm. His steps rang across the hall. Heavy with the weight of a man who had marched across battlefields and crushed empires beneath his heel. A beard framed his face, but it was not unruly, like everything else about him.

The flickering candlelight danced across his armor, catching on the jagged scars etched into the dark metal. Scars that told a history of violence, of battles neither this court nor its nobles could begin to understand. There were no embellishments of peace, no ceremonial robes. He had come dressed for war.

A hush fell over the great hall as he approached the dais, his presence swallowing the room whole. He stopped at the foot of the raised dais, his gaze sweeping over those gathered before him, assessing, measuring, as if already deciding who among them was worth his time. Then, he smiled. It was not a warm expression, nor a pleasant one. It was the slow, deliberate smile of a man who knew the fear he commanded. Who knew that no matter how finely the court dressed, how well-rehearsed their greetings, they all stood at the mercy of his whims.

"Bharalyn," he rumbled, his voice deep, with a thick Kharadorian accent carried through the hall like distant thunder. "I have been given a true Khadradorian welcome in your halls, and so I extend my thanks in return." He touched his chest in mock appreciation.

"A warrior king's appreciation." His gaze flickered toward Danlea, then to Ren, darkness glinting behind his eyes. "May we treat each other as allies, so long as we remember that alliances are built not on words, but on strength."

A ripple of uneasy murmurs skated through the gathered

nobles, though none dared voice it aloud. The king exhaled, stretching his arms slightly as if shrugging off the weight of war itself.

"It is tradition in Kharador that upon entering the court of another, one does not dance as a guest until they have first been among those they would call their equals." He let the words hang. "And so, I will know you. One by one." His sharp, assessing gaze raked over the gathered court. "Each of you will be presented." His smirk deepened. "And I will choose one among you for the pleasure of my company"

The air in the room shifted. A test. An invitation and a trap all at once. Mira swallowed, her fingers curling. The king would make his choice, a game played not with steel, but with power, with influence. And whoever he selected would hold his attention, if only for the evening. It was a game this court knew how to play. And yet, she felt the weight of it pressing against her chest. Across the hall, she caught Asric's eye. He was watching her. Not the king. Her. A slow, knowing smirk tugged at the corner of his mouth, his head tilting slightly. This is what he had intended.

The silence that followed the King of Kharador's declaration was broken by the sound of marching boots. His army was filing in. The heavy doors swung open once more, and a flood of armored figures strode inside, disciplined, unyielding, moving as one. Their presence was not that of honored guests, nor merely an escort. They were an occupation disguised as civility.

Mira stiffened. Danlea's eyes narrowed and Ren's jaw clenched. He didn't move, didn't speak, but tension rolled off him like heat. Kharadorian weapons gleamed under the dim candlelight, polished but unadorned, practical, made for battle rather than ceremony.

Each soldier was clad in dark leathers and reinforced armor, their expressions cold, their presence a stark contrast to the silks and gilded embellishments of Bharalyn's court. They lined the edges of the great hall, positioning themselves strategically, as if marking who among them could be cut down first should this negotiation turn to bloodshed.

The War King moved with slow, deliberate steps, he ascended the dais, his boots thudding against the polished wood. He approached the throne of Bharalyn, the empty throne of Queen Sarelle. He paused. Before turning to Caelric. And without hesitation, he kicked his throne. Not enough to topple. Just enough to make his message clear.

"Shall I sit here then?" He mused looking at Sarelle's throne. But it wasn't a question.

Danlea did not flinch. Not a flicker of emotion crossed her face, not a single gasp left her lips. She merely lifted her chin slightly, her milky eyes unreadable. With the same measured calm, she turned to the attendants at her side and gave a single nod.

Another throne was brought forth. It was smaller than the empty Queen's, but not by much, a twin in design, its placement beside it an unmistakable statement. A symbol of shared status. An answer to the king's challenge. But still, he said nothing. The hall held its breath as he stared at it, his expression unreadable, his hands resting at his sides, calm, still, but poised like a predator considering the moment before it struck. Then, after a long, suffocating silence, he sat in the visiting throne.

Ren stood beside Caleric. Silent, composed, but Mira saw the storm behind his stillness. His shoulders had not dropped. His fists had not loosened. He had not relaxed for even a second. Danlea remained poised. She had not spoken, had not reacted. Even with the King's blatant challenge, she had neither welcomed him nor denied him.

Instead, she let him take up space, let him position himself, but they did not acknowledge him.

The king tilted his head slightly, finally breaking the silence. "Now," he mused, his voice low, contemplative. "Begin."

The moment the King of Kharador spoke, the tension in the hall shifted, not released, but redirected. The nobles who had held their breath now whispered behind raised hands, a murmur of unease rippling through the hall.

Mira watched as the King's sharp eyes flicked toward Danlea, taking her in. A slow, knowing smirk curled at the edge of his lips. She was not bending. And he knew it.

Then, as if bored of the waiting, the King exhaled heavily, turning to Ren. "Present them."

The command rolled through the room like a slow-building storm. At once, an attendant at the far end of the hall stepped forward, a scroll tucked beneath one arm. The man's hands trembled slightly to present the scroll to the Regent.

"As is custom," Ren announced, his voice clear "each member of the court will be presented before His Majesty." He paused then, just slightly too long, his jaw tensing as his gaze flicked toward the Kharadorian king.

"In accordance with Kharadorian tradition, the King may choose whom he will honor with the first dance." His words were composed, his posture impeccably formal. Mira saw the barely concealed flicker of distaste behind his eyes.

This was not a tradition he welcomed. Not a gesture he offered willingly. But he offered it nonetheless, because the game had begun. This was not just a dance. It was a choice.

An elevation. Mira's stomach twisted. She wasn't sure if this was a symbol of favor in Kharador, or ownership.

Ren's voice rang through the hall, clear and measured. "House Veylan." A noble lord and his wife approached with careful steps, offering low bows. It was a performance. A tradition played out for generations, now sharpened under foreign eyes.

"House Ralthorne." Another family stepped forward, flanked by children taught to stand like heirs.

Ren continued, voice steady. "House Asric."

Asric rose from his seat with a lazy confidence, alone but not unadorned. A younger cousin Mira didn't recognise followed in his wake. Polished and overdressed. His bow to the dais was shallow, almost mocking. Ren didn't react. But she saw the flicker in his eyes. Felt the disdain.

Ren's voice shifted, just barely. "House Solwynd."

Mira stood. Alone. The sound of her name echoed differently than the others. Not as a legacy, not as a dynasty. As a memory. As a loss. She stepped forward, her footsteps measured, her chin lifted, though the weight in her chest made it hard to breathe. No father. No brother. No House left but herself. The hush that fell was not reverence. It was recognition of absence. Behind her, she felt the burn of stares. Pity. Expectation. She could feel Ren's eyes on her even as he remained composed. Even as he said nothing. But the energy beneath his stillness was a live wire, burning, ready to ignite.

She didn't look toward him, but she felt him like a tether, his panic a whisper against her skin.

Mira stepped into place before the War King, her shoulders squared. And she bowed, alone, unflinching. The King studied her with the kind of calculated amusement that made her skin tighten. Mira could feel the weight of his gaze, assessing, testing. A beast deciding whether the creature before it was prey or something else entirely. She did not falter. The moment stretched between them, thick with expectation.

And then he spoke, his voice slow and deep, like gravel dragged through smoke. "House Solwynd." He let the name settle on his tongue, tasting it, drawing it out as if it were something foreign to him. "You stand alone."

Mira lifted her chin, offering him a practiced, lazy smile. "That tends to happen when one's family is dead, Your Majesty."

The court shifted uneasily, an invisible ripple of discomfort sweeping through the gathered nobility. The King, however, did not react. Or rather, not in the way they expected.

A low chuckle rumbled from his chest, dark and slow, a sound that never quite reached his eyes. "And yet, here you are."

Mira tilted her head slightly, a flicker of deliberate mischief in her expression. "Here I am," she echoed, voice smooth, teasing.

A muscle twitched in Ren's jaw. The King hummed, leaning forward slightly, interest sharpening. "And does standing there frighten you?"

Mira let her lips part, then pressed them together as if in

mock consideration. Finally, she let out a soft, breathy laugh. "Should it?"

A beat of silence. His eyes narrowed. He was too experienced, too sharp to miss the details, the precision of her bow, the steadiness of her hands, the solitude of her approach. She had come alone, yes, but not unarmed. Not unknowing. And he saw it now. Whatever mask she wore, whatever part she was meant to play, he recognized the truth beneath it.

Mira knew the instant he pierced through the performance. The King's gaze darkened, not in anger, but in interest. A predator scenting something unexpected. Something that might yet bite back. The King rose. Slowly. Purposefully. The weight of his movement shifted the room. The attendants froze. The nobles sat rigid, breath caught. Even the candles seemed to still.

Ren's fear hit her like a wave. She didn't turn to him, didn't dare, but she felt it surge. No longer just concern, but panic, thick and wild and desperate. All Mira could do to keep her breath steady, her hands loose at her sides.

He descended the steps of the dais one by one, each footfall echoing through the marble chamber like the roll of distant thunder. Mira didn't move. He stopped before her, too close for comfort, close enough that she could see the fine threads of silver in his beard, the faint glint of a blade at his side. His presence was overwhelming, consuming, like smoke creeping under every door.

He looked at her, but said nothing. Mira held his gaze. The King exhaled through his nose, shaking his head slightly, as if amused, as if indulging himself.

"What is it you really want to say to me Noble Solwynd?" The smile froze on Mira's lips. Her pulse quickened, but she forced herself to hold his gaze.

If she answered wrong, it would not be Ren who suffered. It would be Bharalyn. This was a warlord in a king's armor. He was waiting. Testing her. She could feel a pulse beating like a drum in her head.

She murmured, her voice quieter now, smoother, softer. "Do you want the truth?" A sharp intake of breath, not hers. She wasn't sure if it was Ren or Tharion.

The King of Kharador studied her, his gaze sharp, unblinking. He did not seem like a man accustomed to being asked questions. Mira did not look away. Her pulse thundered beneath her skin, but she kept her stance carefully relaxed, her chin lifted, her expression curious.

The King's lips curled slightly at the edges. Not quite a smirk. Not quite a smile. "Yes." The single word was quiet, almost contemplative, yet it rolled through the hall like distant thunder. An invitation. A demand. A challenge.

Mira exhaled slowly, feigning a moment's consideration, though her mind raced. He would see through another lie. That much was clear. She chose her words carefully.

Her voice was low, smooth and quiet enough that only he could hear her. "You've made quite an entrance, Your Majesty."

His head tilted slightly, interest flickering behind his eyes. Mira let her gaze drift deliberately down, to the midnight-black armor still gleaming under the torchlight, to the soldiers lining the walls, to the way he had entered this hall as a conqueror, not a guest.

She met his gaze once more and smiled. "But I can't help but wonder… have you come as an ally or to conquer?"

The amusement in his expression did not fade. If anything, it sharpened. He had expected flattery. He had expected coyness. For a long, suffocating moment, he simply looked at her. Then, the King laughed. A deep, full sound, unexpected and unnerving as it echoed through the vast chamber. Mira did not flinch. She simply smiled wider.

"Good," the King rumbled, his voice edged with something almost approving. A shift in the room. The nobles exchanged nervous glances, uncertain whether that had been a compliment or a threat.

The King turned and returned to his throne, finally breaking his stare. "Let the presentations continue."

Just like that, the moment was over. But as Mira stepped back to her place, she felt the weight of his attention linger. And across the room, Asric's smirk had deepened.

38

THE GRAND HALL BUZZED with conversation, silverware clinking against fine porcelain, wine flowing freely into goblets of gold and crystal. But Mira hardly heard any of it. She ate in silence, her posture composed, her gaze flickering between the plates before her and the subtle movements of the court. The King of Kharador sat at the head of the hall, speaking in low tones to those bold enough to address him. His presence, even at a distance, swallowed the room whole. Mira forced herself to eat. Every bite tasted like dust.

She was aware of Tharion's stare since she had rejoined him. When the food was served, He simply picked up his utensils and began eating, jaw tight, every movement stiff and controlled. Mira chewed slowly, watching him from the corner of her eye.

Beneath that carefully constructed mask, he was barely holding himself together. She swallowed the next bite, setting down her fork before looking directly at him.

Tharion did not look at her. "What were you thinking?" His voice was quiet but sharp. "Do you know what you just did?"

Mira a took sip from her glass, unbothered. "Yes"

Tharion's grip tightened around his fork. "You provoked a warlord." Mira exhaled slowly, setting her goblet back down. "I held my own."

Tharion finally turned to face her, his eyes flashing with barely restrained emotion. "You made yourself a piece on his board, Mira. And I don't think you realize just how dangerous that is."

Mira sighed. "I do realise."

Tharion shook his head, scoffing softly. His voice dropped lower, barely more than a whisper. "Why would you bait him like that?"

Mira stared at Tharion, "Because I didn't have a choice."

Tharion stiffened. A beat of silence. She set the glass down, her fingers trailing lightly over the stem before she leaned in just enough that their conversation remained private.

"Asric knows who has been in my room." Her voice was smooth, but the weight beneath it was heavy.

Her gaze flicking toward Asric, who sat at a distance, engaged in idle conversation, or pretending to be. Mira turned back to Tharion.

He swallowed, before he forced himself to pick up his utensils again. "Why is it always you paying the price?"

Mira exhaled as she speared a piece of food onto her fork, bringing it to her lips with deliberate ease, as if they weren't discussing treachery in hushed tones over a diplomatic feast. She chewed slowly, unhurried. "I need to collect something from the King... carefully..." She set down her fork, fingers resting lightly against the polished wood of the table. "Like I collected the letter from Asric."

Tharion's fingers tightened on his knife. "Mira, "

Before Tharion could say another word, Ren's voice rang through the hall. "Honored guests, your attention, please."

The room stilled. Mira turned her head as the court's announcer stepped forward, his voice carrying over the hum of quiet conversations, cutting through the tension that had settled thick in the air.

"As is tradition in Kharador, our esteemed guest, His

Majesty, will now select a partner for the opening dance."
Ren announced.

A murmur swept through the gathered nobles,
anticipation, anxiety, calculated excitement. Mira's fingers
curled subtly against the table. Tharion's knife clinked against
his plate as he set it down a little too hard, his knuckles still
white with tension.

Across the hall, Ren stood unnervingly still, his jaw set in
rigid control. The King of Kharador leaned back in his seat,
languid, unrushed. Amused. His gaze swept across the room,
lingering on the expectant faces of the court, His eyes found
Mira. A slow, knowing look. A challenge left unspoken.
She held his gaze, refusing to shift, refusing to
acknowledge the pulse of unease curling in her stomach.
Then, just as tension gripped the room too tightly, he exhaled.

"The youngest daughter of the Vaeloria Family" he
bellowed.

The king's declaration fell into the silence like a dropped
coin. The court stilled, a flicker of surprise darting through the
gathered nobles. Mira turned her head as Nerra's breath
hitched, her bright brown eyes widening in shock. The King
had chosen her. A murmur rippled through the court, hushed
whispers traded behind raised goblets and veiled glances.

Nerra was not the daughter of a high-ranking lord. Not the
polished court beauty or the calculated political match. He
said nothing more, simply watching as Nerra stiffened, her
hands pressing against the table before she finally rose. A
quiet breath. Then, she stepped forward toward the dais.

He stood, and approached the floor. The music that
began was a deep, resonant drumbeat rippled through the hall,
steady and commanding. Strings followed, low and slow,
winding into a melody both unfamiliar and intoxicating. A

Kharadorian rhythm, slower than Bharalyn's waltzes, heavier, grounded, but no less elegant.

At the center of the hall, the King of Kharador turned to face Nerra. For a heartbeat, she hesitated. The weight of the court's attention pressed down on her, the murmurs, the silent assessments of those who had expected someone else, someone of greater standing. When he offered his hand again, she took it. A beat.

The King led with absolute control, each step measured, precise, effortlessly commanding the space around him. His midnight-black armor, though heavy, did not hinder him. On the polished stone floor, beneath flickering candlelight, he made dancing look like a battle.

Nerra followed. Though her steps were smaller, more careful, there was no trembling, no awkward faltering. She was light on her feet, her body quick to adjust, her movements unpolished yet talented. The King spun Nerra once, not with the careful gentleness of a nobleman, but with the ease of a warrior handling a blade, firm, deliberate. She let out a quiet gasp but did not stumble.

The King's lips twitched, a flicker of amusement. The court continued to watch, hushed, transfixed. The dance, at first, seemed simple. A glide, a step, a turn. But it was not the dance of Bharalyn, graceful and refined, meant for courtly flirtation. The music swelled, the tempo building as they moved across the floor, the space around them widening, clearing as if the room itself understood that this was no ordinary performance. Mira caught Asric watching too, his eyes alight with interest.

Ren had not moved. Tharion's grip on his knife had not loosened. The final notes struck, a slow, pulsing finish, the echoes of the drumbeat lingering in the vast chamber. And in one last, deliberate motion, the King of Kharador released Nerra's hand. For a moment, the world seemed to hold still. Then, the King gave her a single, approving nod. A ripple of tension broke. The court exhaled.

Without ceremony, without even a glance at the court now buzzing behind him, the War King reached out and curled an arm around Nerra's waist. It was not a gentle gesture. It was a claim. A declaration. A sharp gasp slipped from Nerra's lips as he pulled her flush against him. Firm, unyielding. Her body stiffened, startled by the suddenness, the boldness, but the King didn't stop.

He said nothing. He simply turned and began to walk. One step. Then another. His arm never leaving her. Nerra, wide-eyed and breathless, stumbled at first, caught off-guard by the possessive grip, by the weight of every eye following them. Her eyes darted around desperately. He led her forward. Up the dais. Straight toward the throne. To his lap.

Mira stood frozen. So did the court. Silence rippled outward, broken only by the rhythmic echo of the King's boots striking the marble. The moment was heavy, slow. Deliberate. Not just a dance. Not even a choice. It was a demonstration.

Danlea stepped forward from her seat, calm as always, but her expression unreadable. She did not shout. She did not panic. But there was urgency in the way her steps carried her. Ren mirrored her. Neither of them looked toward the court. They were locked on the King, on Nerra, who had not yet pulled away, who had not yet spoken.

Mira strained to hear, but whatever words passed between the rulers were lost to the crackling of the flames in the room. Danlea stepped in close. Her presence brushed the War King's shoulder, hovered near Nerra like a silent guardian. Her hand did not touch, but Mira could see it poised, watchful. Ready.

Ren said something then, low and sharp. The King did not respond at first, but Mira saw the shift in his posture. The slight turn of his head. No one else dared move. The War King gave a single nod, brief, imperious as if Danlea's presence, Ren's protest, the gaze of an entire court, were nothing but wind at his back. He sat, pulling Nerra with him.

Nerra did not move. She remained where he had placed her, perched on the edge of the throne, half on his lap, half beside him. Her posture was stiff, her hands curled into the folds of her gown, but the King's arm remained draped around her waist like a shackle.

The court rippled with the tension of it. A murmur passed through the gathered nobles, uncertain, disbelieving. Ren's expression was carved from ice and fire, his jaw locked so tightly the muscle twitched. His eyes, usually tempered even in council, burned. Mira had seen him angry in sessions before, sharp, decisive, cutting.

But this was different. This was fury. A fury barely held in check by protocol and presence. He stood still, not because he lacked the will to move, but because the room itself held its breath around him. Because he knew one wrong step now would be taken as provocation. As a challenge. And still, his hands curled at his sides, and his gaze never left the throne. Never left the War King. Never left Nerra.

The music resumed, the court scrambling to feign normalcy. Some nobles took to the floor, their movements a practiced distraction, though their gazes flickered toward the dais, toward the girl in the warlord's grasp.

Another presence loomed beside her. "A pity, isn't it?"

She didn't startle. She had expected him. Asric stood at

her side, his signature smile firmly in place, but his eyes were sharp, gleaming with a slight tinge of fear. He had seen everything, the King's choice, the way the court had shifted, the silent battle of power that had played out before them. And he was already making his next move.

"Dance with me." It was not a request.

Tharion reacted instantly. "Not happening." His voice was a low growl, his chair scraping against the floor as he turned toward Asric, shoulders tense.

Mira moved before he could finish. She placed a steadying hand on Tharion's shoulder, feeling the tight coil of tension beneath her palm. Tharion's head snapped toward her, his expression a storm of betrayal and warning.

Mira squeezed his shoulder gently, a silent reassurance. This wasn't about trust. This was about strategy. She turned to Asric. His smirk was already waiting for her, victory flickering in his gaze. He extended his hand, palm up, a courtly invitation wrapped in a demand. Mira hesitated for only a heartbeat. The moment Asric pulled her onto the floor, the dance began, a slow, deliberate waltz.

"You need to find another way." His voice was low, smooth, but the command beneath it was unmistakable.

Mira's steps faltered, just for a fraction of a second, before she forced herself back into rhythm. "Excuse me?"

Asric twirled her effortlessly, keeping them moving in time with the music. "The plan has changed."

She let out a quiet, bitter laugh. "Convenient, considering I was never given a choice in the first place."

Asric's fingers tightened around hers, not enough to hurt, but enough to warn.

"We are the same, you know," he murmured, voice smooth but laced with sharpness. "Both of us are playing this game from both sides. I'm simply trying to ensure we all survive this."

Mira held his gaze, searching for the lie in his words, for the manipulation woven between them. She let out a slow, measured breath, keeping her expression unreadable.

"And yet, somehow, I seem to be the only one at risk."

Asric's smirk didn't falter, but something in his eyes darkened. "Don't act like a martyr, Mira." He guided her into another turn, the movement precise, seamless, the illusion of an effortless courtly dance. "You chose this path the moment you chose Ren over your bonded."

Mira shot Asric a sharp glare. He met it without flinching.

"The King of Kharador is not an easy man to steal from," Asric continued, his voice lilting, casual, as if they were discussing nothing more than the wine selection at dinner. "His instincts are sharp. His trust is nonexistent. You were meant to distract him, like you did me, but now" Asric's smirk was sharp, knowing. "You're clever, Mira. You'll figure it out."

The final notes of the music faded into silence, the court offering polite applause. Mira released his hand, stepping back, her pulse steady even as her mind raced. She turned on her heel and walked back toward her seat. But even as she sat, even as she reached for her glass, her mind was already working.

She needed to get close to the King of Kharador. She needed a way in. But how did one get close to a man who trusted no one? She glanced up at the dais, watching the War King as he lounged on his throne, his presence commanding even in stillness. His hands were everywhere. Fingers skimming the curve of Nerra's waist, palm resting against her thigh, his grip firm, possessive.

Nerra was scared. It was clear in the way she held herself, in the tightness of her shoulders, the stiffness of her posture. And no one, not a single person in this damned hall was stopping it. Her heart broke for Nerra. She set down her glass with more force than necessary, pushing to her feet before she had fully decided what she was doing.

Tharion tensed beside her. "Mira, "

She ignored him. Her steps carried her forward, each one steady, deliberate, even as her pulse hammered against her ribs. Toward the dais.

Mira slowed her steps as she approached, taking in the careful game playing out before her. Danlea, ever poised, sat tall in her throne, her milky eyes fixed on the King, her voice cool and measured as she spoke.

"Kharador and Bharalyn have much to gain from true collaboration," Danlea said smoothly, her voice carrying through the hum of the hall. "It would be beneficial to both of our people if we found common ground before the battlefield." She was trying to pull him into conversation, trying to draw his attention away from the girl on his lap.

The King barely spared her a glance. "Would it?" His tone was bored, dismissive.

Danlea's fingers curled against the armrest of her throne. If she was irritated, she did not show it. "Trade routes could be expanded," she continued, unfazed. "You came here seeking negotiation, did you not?"

The King's fingers idly traced the back of Nerra's neck. "Did I?" Ren's voice cut in, "You did, Your Majesty."

Finally, the King looked at Ren. And smirked. "Ah, the bastard prince becomes Regent" His voice dripped with something close to mockery. "Do you feel threatened? That I do not offer you my full attention?"

Ren's hands curled into tight fists behind his back. "I feel nothing of the sort," he said smoothly. "Only that an ally is a valuable thing. It would be a shame to waste the opportunity before you."

The King chuckled, shaking his head. "So polite. Your step mother taught you well."

Mira's heart pounded as she stepped closer. Finally, the King's gaze flickered toward her. And held. His expression shifted, curiosity flashing in those dark, calculating eyes.

"The lonely little Solwynd." His lips curled, something dangerously close to amusement crossing his face. "Tell me, are you here to beg for your kingdom as well?"

Mira tilted her head slightly, her voice light, casual, a sharp contrast to the tension that filled the hall. "I was under the impression this was a diplomatic affair, Your Majesty." She glanced at Nerra, and back to him. "Besides, I've never begged for anything."

Danlea's gaze snapped to her. Ren's posture stiffened beside the dais, but it was more than tension, it was a sudden, visceral ripple of something Mira hadn't felt from him just before. Jealousy. It rolled off him like heat, quick and unbidden. A beat of silence.

A sharp flicker of something crossed the King's expression, a warning. Then, he laughed. A deep, rolling sound that made the room hold its breath. "You have teeth, little Solwynd," he mused. "I did wonder if I had chosen you, would you have bitten me?"

Mira tilted her head slightly, feigning consideration, before letting a slow, teasing smile curl on her lips. "Only if you had asked."

A flicker of something dangerous crossed his face, not

anger. Interest. She held the warlord's gaze, letting the challenge settle between them. Mira kept her gaze steady on the King, hiding the revulsion coiling in her stomach. The words tasted bitter on her tongue. This wasn't flirtation. It was a strategy.

Her disgust wasn't for herself, it was for Nerra, still perched like a trophy in the King's lap, her spine stiff, her silence loud. Mira's words had been a lure, bait cast into dangerous waters. Anything to pull his attention elsewhere. Anything to get him to let go. She smiled again, sharper this time. Let him look at her. Let him focus on the girl with teeth, not the one who was breaking beneath his touch.

"You would do well in my court little Solwynd, but not in my bed." Mira refused to break eye contact, refused to be the one to look away first. He knew it. And it amused him. With a slow, deliberate movement, he leaned back against his throne, exhaling as if the evening had begun to bore him.

Without ceremony, he lifted his arm from around Nerra's waist and pushed her to her feet. She blinked, startled for only a moment, before she scrambled away with careful poise. Mira's breath eased ever so slightly. The warlord-king watched Nerra go, then turned his gaze back to Mira.

"I am not a monster," he said simply, his voice devoid of its earlier mockery. "I do not make a habit of forcing women into my bed." A pause. Then, a slow smirk. "But I do enjoy watching them panic."

The King stood, his massive frame casting a shadow over the dais.

The hall fell silent. "I have no interest in your courtly games tonight," the King of Kharador announced, his tone casual, almost lazy. The words echoed in the vast hall, dismissive, unconcerned. Then, as if diplomacy were nothing more than a tedious obligation, he continued, "We will begin your diplomacy tomorrow."

He turned, stepping down from the dais, his movements calm, unhurried. A ripple of unease moved through the gathered nobles, though no one spoke. The room held its breath, waiting for the doors to close behind him. But just before he disappeared, just before he left them to stew in their own uncertainty, He glanced over his shoulder.

His eyes drifted between Ren, Danlea and Caelric. And grinned. A slow smile, one that carried no warmth, only promise.

He walked out the doors with a slam, but his army remained.

39

MIRA WAITED.

She sat through the remainder of the meal, barely tasting the food, barely hearing the murmured conversations that swirled around her. Her fork moved out of habit, not hunger. Around her, nobles whispered behind gilded goblets and diplomatic smiles. Mira's mind was already spinning. She hadn't done it. The parchment. The package. The favor Asric had demanded, it was still unfinished, untouched. The opportunity had never come. Her heart thudded, slow but deep, pulsing in her throat. She hadn't done it. And now they were vulnerable.

Asric wouldn't wait patiently. He would make them pay for not moving fast enough. Mira's palms dampened against the silk of her gown. A thousand possibilities bloomed behind her eyes, what he might reveal, what whispers he was already planting. Her breath came shallow. Too many eyes. Too many ears. And no time left.

Across the room, Ren met her gaze for a heartbeat. She looked away first.

Not now

The weight of what she hadn't done clung to her ribs like waterlogged cloth. And somewhere deep in her gut, panic began to bloom.

When the final toast was given and the nobles began to rise, she leaned toward Tharion, keeping her voice low, deliberate. "Meet me in my rooms, bring Ren"

His eyes flicked to hers, searching, already suspicious. "Mira,"

She looked at Tharion, willing him to just listen. Tharion exhaled slowly but gave a small nod. He wouldn't press, not here.

Mira slipped away. She made her way through the darkened halls, not toward their quarters, but toward where she suspected the King of Kharador would be staying.

From a shadowed alcove, she watched as the warlord stepped out, his long strides unhurried. Mira exhaled, waiting until he disappeared around the corner before moving. Then, she followed. Her steps were measured, soundless on the stone floor. She kept to the edges, letting the flickering torchlight leave her in half-shadow. Every turn he took, every pause, she mirrored at a distance.

The moment she turned a corner, only to find nothing but a wall. A dead end. Mira barely had time to react before a presence loomed behind her. She spun, but it was too late. The King of Kharador stood, waiting. His broad frame blocked the only exit, his expression unreadable. Amused, yes, but not surprised. Mira's breath hitched. He had led her here. He had known she was following him from the start.

Slowly, too calmly, he tilted his head. "Brahn said you'd be fiery."

Mira's breath hitched, just slightly, enough that she felt it, sharp and hot in her lungs. Her heart pounded, not with fear, but with fury, disgust coiling low in her stomach like something venomous. She wanted to flinch, to recoil from the weight of the War King's gaze. She didn't.

Instead, she held his gaze. She forced her pulse to slow, forced the loathing down into her bones where it couldn't be seen. She would not give him the satisfaction. Her skin crawled beneath the silk of her gown. Every instinct screamed to strike, to scream, to spit the truth of him into the air for all to hear. Mira smiled. A small, knowing smirk that curled on her lips like a blade being drawn.

She tilted her chin up. "Then Brahn knows me well."

The King of Kharador's eyes gleamed. "Does he now? He also told me you might need something from me." He raised his eyebrows. "Do you, little Solwynd?"

Her heart thudded against her ribs, the sound deafening in her ears. Not from fear, but from the sickening click of a puzzle piece sliding into place. The performance. The attention. He thought it was for the court. A show of strength.

The very thing Asric had demanded she steal from the King. The thing Brahn had said would turn the tides. They were the same. The truth slid into her mind like a blade between ribs.

That box tucked beneath the King's cloak wasn't just a precaution. It was a game. A weapon. A promise. A trap. She released her breath slowly. She couldn't afford to let the King see the crack. She couldn't afford anything but confidence.

So she smiled, slow and deliberate. "Give it to me."

The warlord only chuckled. "You'll have to be more specific, little Solwynd." His voice was deep, teasing, but beneath it, there was something else. Something testing.

Mira lifted her chin higher. "The package. Brahn told me it would ensure your victory and seal my loyalty."

A beat of silence. Slow, deliberate, He stepped forward, closing the space between them with an ease that sent a warning prickling down Mira's spine. She did not step back. She held her ground, even as he pulled back his breastplate and reached towards his chest. He pulled out a small, flat, rectangular package. Without a word, he pressed it into her hands. His fingers brushed hers, firm and deliberate. He leaned in.

His breath was warm against her ear, his voice dark with amusement. "You will make the perfect assassin."

Mira stilled. The words hung between them, coiling in the air like smoke. She said nothing. She let her fingers tighten around the package, careful, measured. Then, without breaking his gaze, she tore the paper binding it. Her breath caught.

Inside lay a dagger. A Kharadorian blade, sleek, wickedly sharp, its black steel etched with intricate engravings, sigils of war and blood. It was beautiful. Deadly. A weapon meant to be used. But it wasn't just the dagger that sent a chill down her spine.

Beneath it, nestled carefully, was a letter. Mira's throat tightened as she reached in and unfolded the parchment. A map into the Crowned Betrothed's chambers.

Royal wing passage. Second torch bracket marks the turn. Follow it to the servant stairs behind the tapestry. Guards rotate every 20 minutes. Avoid the main hall. Patrol sweeps there twice.

The letter spelled out her task with chilling efficiency. But what gutted her wasn't the instructions. It was the handwriting. Torvyn's. The War King had known exactly who she was the moment she stepped into the hall. Solwynd. A name that once meant protection, now a weapon passed from dead hands.

She forced her fingers not to tremble as she folded the parchment, closing it in her palm. She looked up at the King. His eyes bore into her, waiting. Watching. She knew what he wanted. Submission. A sign of loyalty. A sign that she understood what was being asked of her. So Mira did the only thing she could. She smiled. Slow. Measured. Deceptively soft. She bowed her head, just slightly, just enough.

The words left her lips like a vow and a curse. "Long live the Crowned Betrothed"

* * *

She ran. The corridors of the palace blurred around her, lit only by flickering sconces and the cold kiss of moonlight spilling through the windows. She hadn't dared move until she was sure the King was gone.

Her feet hit the stone in sharp, quick beats. The package with the dagger and letter remained tight in her grip, burning against her skin. The halls were still. Silent. She didn't stop. The moon broke fully above the palace, casting silver over the halls.

She just needed to get back to her quarters. There Tharion, Ren and her could make a plan. As she turned the final corner, reached for the door, and pushed inside.

Tharion and Ren stood waiting. Mira's breath caught, her body stilling as her eyes darted between them. Tharion stood near the fireplace, arms crossed, his expression carved from stone. But Ren, he was already looking at her. Not just looking, watching. His posture was too still, too controlled.

His gaze fell to the package in her grip. The air in the room tightened. Slowly she unwrapped it to reveal the blade. Ren's eyes locked on it, and Tharion's jaw tensed. His gaze flickered, not just at her, but at Ren. Something passed between them. Her mind raced. She had spent so long maneuvering through the politics of the council, navigating the shifting tides of rebellion, trying to keep her footing on a board where she was just another piece to be played.

Her fingers tightened around the dagger's hilt, the cool weight of it pressing into her palm. This wasn't about the council. This wasn't about the uprising. This was an assasination. The father of the man she loved. Ren. Her stomach lurched. Her fingers curled tighter. The man whose warmth she still carried in her skin. Whose arms she had woken up in just hours ago. The man she trusted. Who trusted her? And now she held a weapon meant for his bloodline.

She opened her mouth, but her voice caught, stumbling over the words she wasn't sure how to say. "I..."

Ren crossed the room in three swift strides, his presence sudden and unwavering. His hands came up to cradle her face, warm and grounding, thumbs brushing lightly against her cheeks. His eyes locked onto hers, sharp with alarm, worry etched deep into every line of his face.

"What do they want, Mira?" he asked, voice low but urgent.

She swallowed, throat tight. "They want me to... " She couldn't finish. The words tasted like poison. Tharion exhaled sharply, shaking his head. Ren stepped back, hands slipping from her cheek but one resting firmly on her shoulder, anchoring her.

"It's a test of loyalty," he said.

Tharion's expression didn't change, but his hand extended. "Let me see the letter"

Mira hesitated, fingers clenching around the hilt like it was the only solid thing in the room. She handed the package over. He took the dagger first, turning it over in his palm. The craftsmanship was unmistakable. Then, he unfolded the letter. His eyes flickered over the words, reading in silence. His hands folded the parchment neatly, too carefully. "Asric will want to see this."

Mira's stomach dropped. Ren didn't answer right away. His eyes met Tharion's across the space between them, No words. Ren turned back toward Mira.

His voice was quiet but resolute. "Take it to him."

Mira stiffened. The word left her lips before she could stop it. "Don't!" Mira swallowed. "I'll take it." The words came out sharp and final.

Ren studied her. Tension pulled tight across his shoulders, but instead of arguing, instead of pressing her with fear or frustration, his voice dropped, low, steady, certain.

"You owe me a favor," he said quietly. "For that first night in the observatory."

Mira blinked, confusion knitting across her brow. Her breath caught, chest tightening as a flash surfaced. Danlea, the golden threads, the vision.

He stepped closer "I'm asking you to come with me" His eyes searched hers, as if trying to weigh what she would give him, what she wouldn't. "Please..." He held out his hand to her.

The word cut through her like glass, soft, simple, but threaded with everything between them. It wasn't just a plea. It was a tether. A wave of longing crashed into her so fast it nearly knocked the breath from her. Because despite everything, despite the chaos around them, despite the weight of the dagger still clenched in her fist, despite the thousand reasons not to, she wanted to go to him.

Wanted to listen. Wanted to trust. Wanted him. Slowly, Mira turned. Her gaze met Tharion's, and in his eyes, she found no judgment, only quiet encouragement. A small nod, steady and sure, passed between them like a gift. He understood. He approved.

Carefully, she reached for Ren, giving him her hand.

40

THEY MOVED THROUGH the quiet halls, their palms a warm tether in the hush of the darkest hour of the night. No light touched the stone beneath their feet, no promise of warmth.

Only shadows stretched long and silent, curling into the corners like watchful specters.

Each step echoed off the arched ceilings, a soft rhythm, a breath between them. The garden door groaned as Ren pushed it open and the night met them. The chill wrapped around her, threading its icy fingers through the thin fabric of her pink dress. She shivered, a tremor running down her spine.

She glanced at him as they walked, the curve of his jaw, the way his hair tousled at his neck, the determined set of his shoulders. The stone path crunched softly beneath their feet, flanked by darkened hedges and trees that stood bare and skeletal, the winter stripping them down to nothing.

The full moon draped over them in silver, turning dew to diamonds, shadows to velvet. Ren's grip tightened, a grounding squeeze. He felt her faint tremor, the way her pulse fluttered beneath her skin.

They were headed towards the Tahla tree. The silver leaves shimmered, a cascade of light and shadow, the gnarled trunk twisting from the earth, bark veined with pale luminescence.

Mira stopped. Her feet refused to move, her body frozen, locked in place. Her hand slipped from his. The absence of his touch was a sudden cold. Ren turned to her. She swallowed hard, her pulse pounding against her ribs.

"I can't," she whispered, her voice unraveling. Her breath came shallow, uneven. She forced herself to speak again, her voice barely more than a breath. "I haven't been here since Tharion and I bonded."

Ren took a step closer, his voice low, steady. The words wrapped around her like a promise. "Just trust me a little further?"

She swallowed, the taste of old grief rising, thick in her throat. But she took a step forward. And then another.

The Tahla tree loomed, ancient and wise, and with every step, she felt the weight of the past pressing against her. Ren's hand found hers again, and together, they came to stand beneath the silver canopy.

"Close your eyes, Mira," he whispered, his voice curling against her ear.

Her breath hitched. She was nervous, the kind of nervous that shivered beneath her skin, that made her heart trip over itself.

Mira let her eyelids drift shut, her world shrinking to the dark behind her eyes and the warmth of his hand in hers.

She could hear the soft rustle of leaves above, the delicate crunch of frost underfoot as he shifted. Time stretched, the moment fragile, balancing on the edge of something vast.

"Ren, what are we doing here?" her voice barely more than a breath. For a moment, he didn't answer.

His fingers tightened around hers, grounding, unyielding. "I love you."

He wasn't soft. He wasn't hesitant. He was absolute. A truth spoken into the cold air, one that could never be taken back.

He didn't stop. "You have always been my heart, even when I didn't deserve you." The words cracked. "And I'm sorry, for everything that has happened. For what they did.

For what I couldn't stop."

His free hand came to cradle her face, his thumb brushing the curve of her cheek. "I can't take it back, Mira." His voice was raw, aching. "but I can try this. I can try to bring you back to me."

A rushing feeling filled her chest, like an inferno burning through her. She swayed. Ren's arms were around her, pulling her in, pressing her against the solid warmth of his body.

Her heart pounded, a wild, thunderous beat that seemed too loud, too fast. She could feel it at her wrists, her neck, a rhythm that pulsed through her entire being. It was too much. Surging, overwhelming. As if every nerve ending had been awakened at once.

She couldn't catch her breath. Her chest rose and fell too fast, the air burning in her lungs. Her hands curled into fists, fingers digging into the fabric of Ren's shirt, seeking something solid in a world that had suddenly tilted.

Her knees buckled. Ren guided them both to the ground, his movements slow and careful. The cold earth pressed against her through her dress, cooling the fire beneath her skin.

His voice whispered through the burning, low and steady, a thread to cling to. But she could barely make out his words over the rushing in her ears.

His hands cradled her face, his palms cooling against her skin. His thumbs moved in soft, grounding strokes along her cheekbones.

In the distance, the palace bells tolled. Loud. Unrelenting.

But Ren didn't move. Didn't let her go.

"Navigators please, give her back to me" he whispered.

His breath was cool against her skin, a quiet gust in the cold night. Her lashes were heavy, wet. She opened her eyes. The world came into focus, edged in silver and shadow.

As the bells continued to toll, echoing through the frozen air, the only thing she saw before her world went dark was Ren's bright green eyes.

41

Eleven years before

THE WIND RUSTLED SOFTLY through the garden leaves, warm and heavy with the scent of late-summer bloom. Ren ducked low beneath the hanging vines of the tahla tree, heart still pounding from the chase. His shoes were scuffed, his silk shirt stained with dirt, but he didn't care. Behind him, his best friend hissing in panic.

"What do we do now, idiot?" Tharion snapped. "We can't keep hiding in the same spot every time!"

"I'm thinking, okay?" Ren shot back, his voice sharp and low.

His eyes scanned the garden. Their new caretaker was relentless, faster and smarter than the last. And far more determined. She had found them twice this week already. But she hadn't found this tree. Not yet. Ren leaned against the trunk, breath shallow. The tahla tree's bark was rough beneath his fingers. He glanced toward the hedge line just as a voice rang through the air annoyed, and too close.

"Boys! I will be disappointed if you miss another appointment with your tutor!" Tharion groaned. Ren flattened himself tighter to the tree.

A whisper. "Hey. Up here."

He froze. The voice had come from above. He tilted his head, and there she was. A girl about his age, maybe younger, perched high in the branches. Auburn hair spilled over her shoulder, wild and wind-tangled, her dress torn in places from the climb.

But her face, bold and daring, held him rooted in place. There was something about the girl in the tree that made everything else fade. Her voice, her certainty, the glint in her eye. He didn't know what he was feeling exactly, only that he didn't want to look away. Only that he had to reach her.

Tharion, still clueless, whispered sharply. "Don't talk to her. She might be a tree sprite."

Ren barely heard him.

"I am not a tree spirit," she said with cutting precision. "And for all you know, I am a Navigator, and since you have insulted me, I will curse your life to sail forever through chaos."

Tharion hissed in alarm. Ren grinned. He grabbed for the first knot in the bark. "Ren, what are you doing?" Torvyn whispered in horror, but Ren ignored him.

The world narrowed to the sound of leaves, the feel of rough wood, and the girl waiting above him. She pointed, silent and sure, guiding him toward the right holds. And then, he was beside her. Breathless. Grinning.

She was even closer now. Her eyes, a sharp, startling blue, met his with sharp interest. He couldn't look away. Below, their caretaker shouted again, but Ren didn't move.

"I wouldn't mind being cursed," he said, a little breathless, "as long as it's you doing the cursing."

She stared at him for a heartbeat. Then smiled. Just a little. It hit him like lightning. Something new bloomed in his chest. He didn't know what it was. Only that he didn't want to climb back down. Not yet. Not if it meant leaving her.

✳ ✳ ✳

Ren wasn't supposed to be here. He was supposed to be anywhere else, anywhere that kept him out of sight, out of mind. But when had he ever done what was expected of him?

The championship duel was the grandest event of the season, and yet Ren hadn't come for the spectacle or the glory. He had come because he could win and feed the fires that the court already fanned. He was on the sparring sands, facing off against the one man who could potentially beat him.

Tharion, this year's Queen's Champion, was a wall of precision and strength. His blade never faltering, his footwork flawless. But Ren had been holding his own, his strikes calculated, his movements sharper than they had ever been.

Ren twisted, feinting left before striking high, forcing Tharion to step back. Ren pressed forward, catching the briefest opening. His blade flicked past Tharion's defenses, stopping just shy of his ribs. A fraction more, and it would have been a decisive blow.

Suddenly a pulse. A shift in the air, so strong it seemed to steal the breath from his lungs. It wasn't physical, wasn't something he could name, but he felt it, deep in his chest, reverberating through him like an undeniable truth.

His body hesitated. His grip faltered. And that was all Tharion needed. With a sudden twist, Tharion swept Ren's legs out from under him. The impact of his back hitting the sand sent dust rising into the air.

"Yield?" Tharion asked, extending a hand.

Ren barely heard him. His head turned instinctively, his eyes searching, pulled toward something, toward someone.

She sat in the Queen's viewing box, golden sunlight

spilling over her bare shoulders.

Her hair, twisted back, left her neck exposed. She was laughing, leaning into a conversation with the young man beside her. Some young noble boy, he remembered vaguely. But Ren didn't care about that. He only cared about her.

It had been years since he had seen her, but recognition hit him hard and fast. The tahla tree. The girl perched in the branches, grinning down at him as if she had been waiting for him to arrive. The one who had dared him to climb, who had cursed him with chaos, who had smirked as if she had already seen the rest of his life unfold before him.

* * *

Ren had never been nervous sneaking into the palace before. But tonight wasn't just sneaking out. Tonight involved more than rule-breaking, evading guards, and sneaking around undetected. Tonight was different. Tonight was for her.

He exhaled slowly, rolling his shoulders against the stone wall outside her door, arms crossed, fingers drumming against his sleeve. He was too aware of the quiet. Too aware of the way his heartbeat wasn't steady, the way his palms weren't dry, the way anticipation curled like something sharp beneath his ribs.

He planned the picnic, stolen the wine, set the blanket beneath the Tahla tree. The door cracked open. Light spilled across the stone floor, casting soft gold across bare feet, the edge of a cloak, and Mira, breathless, eyes sharp.

The fabric of her light lilac dress shimmered faintly beneath the glow, soft and weightless, like it had been spun from dusk itself. It clung delicately at the shoulders before

526

flowing in gentle folds down her frame. The color shifting with each movement, pale violet in the dim light, almost silver where the candlelight kissed it.

Ren swallowed hard. He shouldn't have noticed. Shouldn't have been so damn aware of the way the fabric brushed against her as she hesitated in the doorway, the way it swayed with her shallow breaths. But he did. And that pull, that damn pull, snapped tight inside his chest.

"How do you know where I live?" she whispered. Ren smirked, the moonlight catching in his eyes.

"Did you really think I'd let you get caught sneaking out?" His voice came out lower than he intended, but he didn't move away.

Did she really think he would wait at the tree? That he would let her slip through the halls alone. Never.

Mira exhaled sharply, glancing down the corridor before narrowing her gaze at him. "You're not supposed to be here." Her gaze locked onto his, and for a breath, one single, stupid breath, he forgot how to move.

"Come with me" He offered his hand, not grabbing, just waiting.

She stared at it too long, his heart dropped. Then, finally, she took it.

* * *

Four years before

The corridors were silent. Not just quiet, but eerily empty. Beyond the palace walls, the city prepared for the festival, candles and ribbons strung between the streets, the scent of roasted almonds and warm cider carried on the crisp winter air.

But here, deep in the heart of the palace, there was no music, no laughter, no nobles whispering behind gloved hands. Just him and Mira. And the truth waiting in oil and paint. Ren led her forward, his steps deliberate, his pulse steady, but beneath it, something simmered. A quiet anticipation.

She hadn't asked where they were going. Hadn't questioned him when he took her hand and guided her through the deserted halls, avoiding watchful eyes of the royal guards, despite the risk of being seen.

Maybe she could feel it. The tension wound tight inside him, pressing against his ribs like a cage. Maybe she already knew that this, this moment, was different.

The outer chamber of the Great Hall loomed before them, its walls lined with portraits. Massive, gilded things, immortalized in gold and history. A dynasty captured in oil and pigment.

Mira slowed beside him, her gaze flicking across the faces, the ruling bloodline, their legacies etched into eternity. The weight of it pressed against them, heavy and inescapable.

Ren exhaled slowly, stopping before the one that mattered most. The royal portrait of King Caelric and Queen Sarelle. The perfect illusion.

Caelric stood tall, regal in dark blue and gold, his presence commanding even in stillness. His expression was composed, noble and just, a king wise beyond his years.

Beside him, Sarelle, a vision in crimson silk, her delicate features shadowed with quiet strength, her brown hair woven with gold streaks. The woman the world believed to be his stepmother.

Ren stared at the painting, taking in the familiar lines of Caelric's jaw, the proud tilt of his chin. At Sarelle's unreadable gaze, the one that had never wavered, never betrayed her truth. He had looked at this painting a hundred times before. But tonight, he wanted her to really see it.

"Compare me to my father," Ren murmured.

Mira blinked, her brow furrowing slightly. She turned back to the portrait, studying Caelric's face with quiet concentration.

"You look exactly like him," she said without hesitation. Ren hummed, "And?"

Mira tilted her head, her focus sharpening. Ren felt it, the flicker of her mind piecing something together. The way her amusement faded into something more thoughtful, more searching. Her gaze flicked between the two men, the same dark hair, the same strong jawline. Then her eyes trailed lower, settling on Caelric's eyes. Deep brown.

Ren didn't move, didn't breathe. He felt her confusion spike. A pause. A hesitation. Then, she turned to him. She inhaled sharply, her brows knitting together.

"Your eyes," she murmured.

Ren said nothing. Waiting. Her breath came shallower now. Ren felt the first hints of uncertainty stir through her. She wasn't afraid. Not yet. But something inside her was beginning to shift. "You must have gotten them from your mother."

Ren nodded once, slowly. "I did."

Mira's brows drew together, her gaze snapping back to the painting. To Sarelle. To her eyes. Ren felt it before she gasped. The sharp, splintering crack of understanding breaking open inside her.

Her entire body went still. Didn't move. Shock slammed into her. Ren felt it hit him like a punch to the ribs. A sharp inhale, a staggered heartbeat. A tidal wave of realization, crashing all at once. Her hand gripped her own wrist too tightly, as if she needed something to anchor her. Something real. She turned to him, lips parting, but no words came. Ren only held her gaze. Steady. Unwavering. Silence stretched between them, thick and charged.

Ren let her sit with it. Let her feel it, all of it. Because he knew what came next. The questions. The doubt. The why. Finally, Mira exhaled shakily.

"Who else knows?" she asked, voice careful.

Ren's jaw flexed. He had never spoken this aloud. Not like this. Not to anyone outside the family.

"Aside from my parents," he said, voice even. "And Tharion?" His green eyes locked onto hers. "Nobody."

Mira stilled. A fresh wave of emotion surged through her, shock, still. Disbelief. But beneath it, something else. Something deeper. Her breath hitched.

"Why?" she whispered.

Ren's throat tightened. The truth sat heavy on his tongue. He looked back at the portrait, the careful deception painted for the court. At the woman who had risked everything to keep him safe.

"Because if the kingdoms knew who I really was, " His gaze flicked back to Mira, to the way she watched him now, eyes searching, wide.

"It would mean my life forfeited, and the kingdom's alliances would never recover." Mira's lips parted slightly. "What do you mean?"

Ren exhaled slowly, rolling his shoulders against the cold stone. "My mother was never meant to marry my father," he began.

Mira said nothing, her expression tight. Waiting. Bracing.

"She was second in line for the throne," Ren continued. "A princess meant for a political alliance. From the moment she was born, she was promised to another, a prince from another kingdom. One who would strengthen our trade, secure our borders, and ensure peace between our people."

Mira's fingers curled slightly. "But she didn't marry him."

Ren shook his head. "No. Because she loved someone else." Mira inhaled sharply.

"She was sent to his kingdom every year," Ren said. "Almost three months at a time, starting when she was fifteen. The prince was kind. Patient. He tried, Mira. He tried to make her happy."

Mira's breath hitched, just slightly. "but she fell in love with someone else..." Mira swallowed.

"Not the prince," Ren said, voice softer now. "An acolyte apprentice."

Mira stiffened. "He wasn't meant for the crown. He wasn't meant for anything more than a priest's fate. But she saw him, and he saw her. And that was it."

Ren watched as realization flickered in Mira's expression, as she began to understand. "They ran," he whispered. "For weeks. Searching for someone who would perform the bond. But no one would." Mira's fingers trembled.

"And then her brother died," Ren said. "And she had no choice but to return."

"The neighbouring kingdom had been outraged. Humiliated that their prince had been rejected for a nameless acolyte." Ren's voice darkened. "So she bargained."

Mira's posture tightened. "With her intended." Ren nodded.

"It was the only way to save the kingdom's honor. But if a new price is named and accepted..."

"The contract remains intact," Mira whispered.

Ren's jaw tightened. A long pause. Then, Mira asked, already knowing the answer. "What was the price?"

Ren hesitated only for a moment before speaking. "Their firstborn son."

✳ ✳ ✳

The great hall was bathed in opulence. Golden chandeliers hung high above the marble floors, their candlelight flickering across rich, silken banners draped along the towering columns. The scent of honeyed wine and spiced meats filled the air, mingling with the soft, breathy hum of courtly whispers.

Ren stood at the base of the throne, his hands clasped behind his back, shoulders drawn tight beneath the weight of expectation. Tonight, Ren was the subject of those whispers. The bastard prince. Unworthy. Illegitimate. Not a ruler. Hundreds of courtiers, nobles, and dignitaries filled the ballroom, their attention pinned on the dais. To him.

The lie had been whispered for years, woven carefully into the fabric of the kingdom's politics. And if the court knew the truth? Alliances would fracture. So they kept him hidden in plain sight. Raised in shadows, kept just close enough to be useful, just far enough to be ignored.

Sarelle sat upon the dais, her crown glinting under the glow of the chandeliers, her expression calm, poised, but her eyes watched everything. Beside her, King Caelric sat forward, his expression calm, composed.

Her voice rang clear. "Tonight, before the eyes of the court, we present our Prince."

Not an heir. Not the future king. Simply prince. Ren kept his face impassive. Sarelle's eyes swept the gathered nobles, commanding absolute attention. This was her declaration. Not that Ren was her son. Not that he was the future. But he was a piece on the board. And tonight, she would decide how he played.

But the moment the herald's voice rang out, the moment Ren's name was announced before the entire court, he felt the weight of it. Excited murmurs rose, whispers darting through the ranks of noble families, daughters straightening, mothers exchanging eager glances. A public display. A performance for the court.

Ren's jaw tightened. His fingers curled into fists behind his back. But before he could even swallow his irritation, he felt her. A sharp, unexpected pull beneath his ribs. It wasn't the usual tether he had, the steady ache of knowing Mira was near.

This was sharper. Hotter. Jealousy. Not his. Hers. He didn't dare turn his head to find her. Didn't have to. He could feel her watching. His pulse pounded against his throat. A small, dark thrill unfurled in his chest. Good. She was just as obsessed as he was.

He took a step forward, bowing towards Sarelle just enough to acknowledge the order. "As you command, Your Majesty."

Sarelle's smile sharpened. The music began. A noblewoman stepped forward. Lady Evelyne. Golden-haired, meticulously trained in poise and charm.

She curtsied, a perfectly measured tilt of her head. "Your Highness."

Ren offered his hand, forcing himself to keep his movements controlled, unhurried. "Lady Evelyne."

Their hands barely brushed before she set her other against his shoulder, and they began to move. She smelled of roses and something overly sweet, and her tone was carefully light.

"I heard you were raised with warriors." "You heard correctly."

"How thrilling. A prince with a sword."

Ren bit back the urge to snap back with a sarcastic comment. Instead, he spun her precisely, politely.

"Do you enjoy dancing, my lord?"

"Not particularly." Her perfectly rehearsed laugh grated on his nerves. "Then I shall consider myself honored that you suffer through it for me."

She shouldn't. Because across the room, he felt it again. A flare of heat. Mira. Her emotions lashed against his own, an unspoken protest buried beneath the fury. He risked a glance. She stood on the far side of the ballroom, dressed in soft blue, the fabric shifting like water with every movement. Her dark hair was swept back, exposing the delicate line of her throat. She was stunning. And worse, untouchable for now.

Ren's stomach twisted. Tonight, he was meant to be on display, a prize to be won. The song ended. He bowed, dismissing Evelyne with effortless ease before another woman replaced her. Another noble. Another performance.

"Prince Ren," the young woman greeted with a smile, her father lingering near the dais, watching intently.

"Lady Sienna." He held his hand, despite the wave of

jealousy. She took it. "You're much more graceful than I expected," she mused.

"Is that meant to be a compliment?" he asked.

"It is meant to be an observation." she quipped back. "Noted," he murmured.

Her fingers brushed his shoulder, her smile dipping into something bold, suggestive. The touch was light, meant to entice, to tempt. But Ren felt nothing. Mira's emotions crashing into his own through the bond, held his attention. Wild, hot and furious.

Ren barely resisted the urge to smirk, but he felt her simmering from across the ballroom. Her emotions stirred something in him, fierce and electric, as if the storm had seeded itself in his own chest. He relished it, even if she didn't know he could.

His dance partner said something else, something flirtatious, something he didn't care to hear. He didn't answer.

Ren turned to his partner with practiced ease, exhaling slowly as he forced himself to play his part. But just as the dance was ending, just as he was about to step away, Ren felt the sharp bite of her jealousy dull, replaced by something more measured, more controlled. But it wasn't gone. No, it had shifted into something far worse. Satisfaction.

His eyes searched for her as he turned, as the music swelled, as the court blurred around him until he found her. A hand extended toward her. Ren's heart stopped. Tharion knew. He knew how Ren felt about Mira, yet still offered his hand to her.

His chest went tight, burning. He trusted Tharion. He did. But something in him rebelled, twisted, roared at the sight of Mira letting herself be led onto the dance floor by someone else. The moment their hands met, she lifted her chin. Ren's steps faltered.

"Apologies," he said smoothly, releasing her hand at the final note.

Each of these women were trying to charm him. Each one failed. But their parents? Their parents were watching. Calculating. Waiting for any sign of interest. Between dances, one of them approached.

Lord Edric, father to Lady Sienna. "Your Highness," he greeted smoothly, hand outstretched. Ren took it. Firm shake. Calculated grip.

"Your daughter is a fine dancer," he said.

"She was hoping for a second." Ren offered a smile that meant nothing. "A shame, then, that the court is so full of hopeful women tonight."

Edric hesitated. A beat too long. Then, a bow, tight, forced. "Of course, Your Highness."

Ren exhaled slowly, rolling his shoulders. The next woman arrived before he had time to prepare. She was lovely enough, though her mother loomed at her side like a predator circling a meal.

Ren barely caught their names before the mother nudged her daughter forward, practically presenting her like an offering. He resisted the urge to sigh. Then, an idea struck. It was reckless. It was perfect.

Ren didn't fight the smirk that curled at the corner of his lips as he extended his hand. "Shall we?"

The young woman flushed as she placed her hand in his, her cheeks warming at his touch.

"It would be my honor, Your Highness," she said breathlessly.

He led her onto the dance floor, smoothly guiding her into position as the music swelled around them. She was eager, practically glowing with the attention.

"Your mother seems determined," Ren remarked as they stepped into the first movement of the waltz.

The young woman's eyes widened slightly before she let out a nervous laugh. "She believes we would make a good match."

Ren smiled, charming, effortless. The words meant nothing. Because even as he danced, even as he kept his movements fluid and precise, he was already positioning them carefully, subtly shifting his steps. Waiting.

His partner, oblivious to his true intention, continued, "You must be overwhelmed with all the attention tonight."

Ren's gaze flicked across the room. And then, the moment arrived. He twirled his partner away. Because when this waltz dictated they switch partners Mira spun into his arms. His fingers curled around her waist, firmer than necessary, pulling her close, closer than he had held anyone else tonight. Mira landed against his chest, breath catching, eyes widening in surprise.

Ren smirked, his grip unwavering, voice smooth as silk. "If you wanted to dance with me so badly, you could have asked."

Mira exhaled sharply, her hands instinctively pressing against his shoulders. "What are you doing?"

Ren leaned in slightly, his breath warm against her ear. "Dancing." She narrowed her eyes. "This is reckless"

"And yet, having you in my arms, is the highlight of this evening."

The music swelled around them, the ballroom blurred away as Ren moved with her, his steps slow, deliberate.

"Tell me something" he murmured, his fingers trailing along the small of her back. "Did you enjoy dancing with

Tharion?"

Mira arched a brow, amusement flickering behind her frustration. "Did you enjoy parading yourself around for every eligible noblewoman in the kingdom?"

Ren's smirk deepened. "I hardly noticed them." Mira tilted her head slightly, eyes gleaming. "You know," he mused, voice dropping lower, "I did enjoy one thing about tonight."

Mira sighed dramatically. "Let me guess. The sheer variety of available options?" Ren chuckled, spinning her effortlessly across the floor, refusing to let her go.

"Never," he said, drawing her even closer, until their bodies were flush, until he could feel the warmth of her beneath his hands. "I enjoyed those little spikes of jealousy you kept throwing my way."

Mira stiffened slightly, and Ren could feel her heartbeat hammering against his chest. "What are you talking about?" she asked, her voice careful.

She lifted her chin, forcing a look of cool indifference, but he felt the tension in her, felt the pull between them like a thread stretched taut. Mira's lips parted slightly, but her brow furrowed, a flicker of hesitation, uncertainty.

"That's not possible," she said, but the words were too soft. "We're not bonded, Ren."

Something dark and electric twisted inside him at the way she said it. Because he wanted more. Needed more. The bond between them was already woven into every part of him, pulling him toward her in ways he couldn't fight, couldn't ignore.

And yet, it wasn't enough. Because he wanted her to feel it, too. Wanted her to know, with every breath, with every heartbeat, that he was hers. Wanted her to ache for him the way he ached for her, to feel him even when he wasn't there, to wake up knowing he was part of her as much as she was part of him.

Because she already had him, fully, completely, irreversibly.

* * *

Two years before

Candlelight flickered against dark wood-paneled walls, the scent of parchment, ink, and warm embers curling through the air. The silence pressed down on Ren, heavier than any armor he had ever worn.

Near the hearth, Queen Sarelle stood poised, her golden-threaded robes pooling at her feet like liquid fire. Her expression was unreadable, but Ren knew better. She had already predicted this conversation, already weighed every possible outcome. Across from her, King Caelric lounged back in his chair, fingers steepled beneath his chin, his sharp eyes unreadable. He was calm, controlled, but Ren could sense something beneath it. Waiting.

Tharion was standing awkwardly near the door, shifting his weight like a man awaiting execution. Ren didn't need to ask why he was here. The idiot had let it slip. Ren shot him a glare, sharp, laced with silent expletives, but Tharion only grimaced, helpless.

Caelric broke the silence first. "I assume you have something important to tell us."

Ren inhaled, steadying himself. "I love her," he said simply. "And I will not be without her."

The words shattered the quiet like a hammer against

539

glass. Sarelle didn't move. Caelric exhaled slowly through his nose, unreadable. No sharp retort, no immediate anger. Just a long, unbearable silence.

Finally, Sarelle spoke, her voice soft, knowing. "And you are going to bond with her?" Ren lifted his chin. "Within the year, she has already agreed." His voice did not waver.

Sarelle inhaled sharply, but it wasn't anger that flickered across her face. It was quieter.

Knowing. A recognition that ran deeper than approval, not a blessing, but understanding.

Caelric placed his hands against the table. His voice came low, taut. "You cannot be this naïve."

Ren's jaw tightened. "I am not asking for permission."

Sarelle's eyes stayed fixed on him. "Does she know?" she asked quietly. "The truth of your lineages?"

Ren paused. "No."

Sarelle's face didn't change. But her gaze lingered on him for a beat too long. The kind of knowing only a mother possesses. She let him lie, not because he'd fooled her, but because she saw no danger in the love he had chosen to share the truth with. No threat in the girl who now held his heart. No reason to strip it bare before he was ready.

She simply inclined her head, measured and calm, an unspoken grace given without permission or need.

"At least you're smart enough to keep that to yourself," Caelric muttered.

Ren said nothing. Because if he knew the truth, if his father realized who Mira was, and that she already knew everything, this conversation would end with guards escorting her here, shackled or worse.

Caelric studied him for a long moment, sharp-eyed and unsparing, before speaking again. "Do you genuinely believe anyone will bond the two of you?"

Ren had hoped. But hope was a dangerous thing.

"Do you think you can find someone who will bind you without a blessing?" Sarelle's tone was calm, almost gentle. Beneath it was something quieter still. Sympathy.

Something that understood what it meant to want what the world would never willingly give.

"You know how difficult it is," Sarelle continued. "We, of all people, know how impossible bonding is without the Navigators' Acolyte's sanction."

Ren didn't answer. A strange weight settled over the room. Caelric let out a slow breath, his fingers tapping once against the arm of his chair.

"What your mother is saying," he said, "is that you have time, Ren." Ren's breath hitched. "And how long do you expect us to wait?"

A pause. Sarelle's lips parted, then closed. And then, finally, "Until you are both twenty-seven."

Ren blinked. "…Twenty-seven?" His pulse thundered in his throat. Caelric did not waver. "That is the law of this kingdom."

Ren laughed, but there was no humor in it. Just disbelief, bitter and raw. "The law?" He shook his head. "You tried to bend the law when it suited you. And now suddenly it's sacred? How is this any different to what you did?"

Sarelle looked at him, quiet, but there was no denial in her eyes. "You are asking us to risk everything, Ren."

Caelric's voice was still controlled, but now edged with something harder. "Your future. This kingdom. Your life. For a choice you do not have to make right now."

Ren's hands curled into fists at his sides as he exhaled sharply. "Bonding with her won't expose me."

Caelric exhaled, his tension unrelenting. "A bond will tie you together in ways you cannot imagine. And when people take notice of that, they will wonder why the bastard prince has been allowed to bond ahead of any noble-born heir." His eyes narrowed. "They will demand to know why. And if the answers do not satisfy them, they will find the truth themselves."

Ren's breath was ragged. His hands curled into fists. He forced himself to breathe, steadying his voice even as it trembled at the edges.

"We're already connected," he said quietly.

There was no triumph in the words. No challenge. Just truth, laid bare and heavy in his chest. Silence. Thick. Weighted. Sarelle's expression flickered with concern. Caelric stiffened. Barely. But Ren saw it. A fracture in his father's control.

Sarelle recovered first. "What do you mean?" Her voice was quiet now, cautious.

Ren exhaled sharply. "I feel her. Not just when she's near." He swallowed, his throat tight. "When she's anxious, I feel it. When she's happy, it's like a fire in my chest." His hands raked through his hair. "And when she's hurting..." His voice cut off. Raw.

Unraveling.

Sarelle's brows furrowed. "Ren, that's not possible." But it was. It had been happening for years.

His fists clenched. "Then explain how I can feel her."

Silence. Neither of them spoke. Ren inhaled sharply. "You bargained me away before I even drew breath. You sealed my fate before I ever had a chance to claim it. And now you tell me I have no choices left?" His voice rose, anger slipping through the cracks. Sarelle's breath caught. Cleric's expression darkened.

Ren's breath came fast, shaking. "You did this," he whispered, voice breaking. "You made a deal that will cost me my love in exchange for yours." His words cut through the silence like a blade.

And then, raw, unguarded, "If I was only ever meant to be payment, if I was only ever meant to be sacrificed for the price of your love, then why have me at all?"

The silence was suffocating. Sarelle looked at him then, and for the first time in his life, Ren saw unfathomable grief in her eyes. She turned, meeting Caelric's gaze. Something passed between them.

Sarelle exhaled sharply, her fingers trembling at her sides. "You are not a sacrifice," she whispered. "You are our son." Silence. Sarelle turned back to Ren, her voice soft, final.

"If you can find an acolyte, then you have our blessing" Ren swallowed hard. "Otherwise, you will wait until twenty-seven."

42

Mira

One Year Before

THE ALTAR CHAMBER was nearly empty. Only the distant flicker of candlelight remained, the flames swaying gently in the drafts that curled through the towering stone pillars. The scent of incense lingered, heavy with the weight of centuries of prayers whispered into the dark.

Mira stood alone before the center of the altar, her hands clasped before her, her pulse hammering against her ribs. The champagne bodice of her gown clung to her torso, its navy constellations embroidered along the boning shimmering beneath the full moon.

The fabric cinched at her waist before cascading into a waterfall of starlight, pooling around her bare feet as she moved slowly forward. Her auburn hair was unbound, wild and loose, with only a few strands woven with silver thread, catching the light like threads of spun moonlight.

Standing here, facing the towering stained-glass windows that depicted Bharas in all his celestial glory, a bead of sweat slid down the back of her neck. She had never doubted. Not when it mattered. Not even when she had stood before this very altar as a child, listening to her mother's funeral rite. But now, there was only silence.

She swallowed hard and lowered to her knees, her fingers threading together so tightly they ached. The silver glow of the stained-glass window bathed her in its fractured light, casting her shadow long against the floor. She took a steadying breath. And spoke.

"Bharas, hear me." The words echoed into the vast chamber, lost among the high ceilings and the flickering candlelight.

She exhaled slowly. She tried again. "If I have ever honored your name, then I ask you this now, not as a plea, but as a bargain." Her voice trembled. She pressed her forehead to the marble, her fingers digging into the fabric of her gown as she forced herself to be still.

"Bond us in your name, and your heart flame" The words cracked as they left her lips. "Let it be true."

She lifted her head, heart thundering, waiting, praying, for a sign. But there was nothing. No warmth curling through her veins. No whispered assurance in the back of her mind. No confirmation that the love she had chosen was a path written in the stars.

Mira's breath hitched. Her fingers clenched against the cold stone, and for the first time in her life, she felt the weight of something she had never known before. Doubt.

She squeezed her eyes shut. "I do not ask this for power," she whispered. "Not for your favor. Not for status. I only ask for him." The candles burned. The incense curled. The silence remained.

"I know nothing is given freely." The words rang out in the emptiness, firmer this time. "If there is a cost, I will bear it. Whatever the price, I will pay it."

She lifted her chin, looking up at the towering image of Bharas above her, his outstretched hands frozen in the glow of the stained glass.

"Show me what you want from me," she whispered.

Her throat tightened, her chest constricting. Slowly, she forced herself upright, blinking against the sting of unshed tears. Maybe it was foolish. Maybe Bharas did not deny her. Maybe he simply did not notice her.

The night cloaked them in moonlight, the full moon above them, casting the world in silver and shadowed quiet. There were no lanterns. No fires. Just the sky, brilliant and unflinching, and the tahla tree's ancient limbs swaying overhead. Its blossoms exhaling their perfume like a spell woven just for them.

The air was thick with something more than summer. It seemed to shimmer. The kind that held its breath for things sacred and old.

Mira stepped barefoot into the canopy, the cool grass whispering against her skin. And beneath the canopy of their tree, Ren waited. He looked like something summoned from a dream, midnight blue and golden, his tunic glinting with woven stars. A perfect echo of her.

His eyes found hers the moment she stepped into the moonlight, and her breath caught. He looked devastatingly handsome, but it wasn't his face or the cut of his jaw or the way the moonlight curved around him like it had chosen him. It was what she felt.

A wave of longing surged through her chest. Love. Fierce. Devoted. Burning. Ren. Her Ren. Her soul stretched toward him like it had been waiting lifetimes to remember the way. He extended his hand, palm open, steady and sure. No command, no urgency, only invitation. Mira took a breath as she placed her hand in his.

Their fingers laced together, and he gently guided her forward, helping her cross the circle drawn in salt and crushed tahla blossoms. The petals clung faintly to the hem of her gown, to her bare feet, like the earth itself marking the moment.

Ren's thumb brushed lightly across her knuckles as she passed the threshold, his gaze never leaving her face.

"Mira," he murmured, voice rough with awe.

He gathered her into his arms, slowly, reverently. Her heart calmed as his arms came around her, firm and warm, anchoring her to the ground and lifting her all at once. Their foreheads met, gently, deliberately and the world around them fell away. The wind held its breath. The stars shone above. Their eyes closed, pressed so close together she could feel the rise and fall of his chest match hers. Not as two people, but as one rhythm.

"Ren," she answered, just as softly, just as reverent.

She inhaled without thinking, wood smoke and something else, something distinctly Ren, and it felt like breathing for the first time.

A low chuckle sounded to her right. "I almost feel guilty interrupting." Tharion's voice held humor, but the reverence behind it rang deeper.

In his ceremonial uniform, he stood tall. He looked between them, two halves of a soul reunited, and bowed his head.

"I give each of them away willingly," he said, softer now, voice carrying not just tradition, but truth. "And I witness this bond in truth."

Above them, the wind stirred the tahla leaves. Silver petals drifted down around them, swirling. Tharion stepped back, and the circle around them seemed to glow faintly, salt and crushed tahla blossoms catching the moonlight, their scent rich and wild.

Tharion raised his hand slightly, the gesture born from friendship more than formality, and when he spoke, his voice was steady, clear. A witness, yes, but more than that.

Honored. Moved.

"You enter into this bond knowing it cannot be broken," he said. "Not by time. Not by distance. Not even in death."

The wind stirred through the clearing, rustling the leaves above them, soft as breath. A hush fell, as if the earth itself leaned closer to listen.

"You are no longer two," Tharion continued. "But one soul, shared. One path, chosen. One flame, eternal. What you build, you build together. What you carry, you do so together. Hereafter, you are not alone. Never alone."

Ren's hand tightened around her. Mira felt it, certainty, his love, his awe.

Tharion turned to them fully, eyes steady, his voice softer now, "Speak your vow, and the stars will bear witness."

Ren pulled back to face her fully, his hands still wrapped around her his thumb tracing slow circles against her back. The glow of the circle cast soft silver light across his face, catching in the tears he didn't try to hide.

For a moment, he just looked at her, like she was the first and last thing he had ever truly seen.

"I vow to be your home wherever we stand. To hold your light, and to follow you into shadows. I vow to love you in the quiet and in the storm, when you burn and when you break. To never walk ahead of you, never behind, but beside you. Always."

Mira's breath caught in her throat. Her heart thundered, but her hands were steady as she lifted them to his face, brushing her fingertips across his jaw. She saw everything in his eyes, his love, his fear, his unshakable belief in her. And when she spoke, it was not a whisper. It was a promise.

"I vow to be your shelter when the night grows cold. To guard your fire, and to meet you in every darkness unafraid. I vow to love you in stillness and in chaos, when you rise and when you fall. To never let go, whether the path is clear or wild. To walk beside you, step for step, always"

The wind picked up, spinning the petals at their feet into the air like a blessing, and the stars above seemed to pulse brighter for a breath, as if the heavens themselves had heard. Tharion bowed his head. Mira didn't wait. She leaned in, wrapped her arms around Ren's neck.

The moment her lips met his, the world fell away.

There was no palace. No queens or councils or hiding in dark corridors. There was only Ren. The shape of his mouth. The warmth of his breath. The way his arms tightened around her waist like he'd never let go again. His kiss wasn't careful. It was raw, a claiming, a surrender, a prayer answered, and a promise made.

A rush of heat flooded her chest, blooming outward, wild and uncontainable. Mira gasped against his lips, her fingers tightening in his hair as something ancient and infinite sparked to life between them.

Her pulse stuttered, then steadied, but not alone. There was his heartbeat, strong and sure, thrumming in perfect tandem with hers. She felt him. Not just the press of his hands or the taste of him, but him. His awe. His fierce, unrelenting devotion. His love, so deep it stole the air from her lungs.

Above them, the sky broke open. The first streak of silver carved across the stars, brilliant and sudden, like a divine blade slashing the dark. Then another. Then a dozen.

A celestial shower spilled across the sky in waves, silent and furious, trailing golden arcs and white-hot sparks. They fell like omens, like blessings, like the world itself was shedding its skin and becoming new. The sky pulsed with fire and wonder, and below it, they held each other, wrapped in starlight and the unbearable beauty of what they had become.

It wasn't like falling. It was like returning to something she had always known but never had the words for. Two souls folding into one. The bond burned through her like light, pure and absolute. It poured into every hollow space, every scar, every shadow she'd carried. And in that light, she felt his scars too. Echoes of pain not her own, but now shared. It didn't erase them. It didn't try to fix her. It simply met her there. Held her there. Became hers. Ren rested his forehead against hers, both of them breathless, trembling, undone.

"I felt it," she whispered, barely a sound.

His eyes searched hers, fierce and gentle all at once. "I know..."

* * *

Ren

The walk back to the palace should have been a blur. But for Ren, every step felt carved into the marrow of him.

Mira's fingers were threaded through his, warm and certain, like a vow whispered in a language older than words. The night air clung to his skin, thick with the scent of tahla blossoms in bloom. Above them, the last streaks the Navigators' blessing trailing above them.

They shouldn't have been able to bond. Not like this. No

witness. No altar. No temple rites. Yet… they had. The bond throbbed beneath his ribs like wildfire, anchoring, all-consuming. He had felt her when it snapped into place, the moment the universe tipped slightly and aligned. Something ancient and impossible had chosen them.

Ren glanced toward Mira beside him, her bare feet silent against the floors, her gown still shimmering like starlight caught in motion. Her curls were wild from the wind, loose and radiant around her shoulders. She was his. And Navigators above he had always been hers.

When they entered his chambers, their chambers, Mira let out a breath that trembled as it left her. One hand braced against the door as it clicked shut. She turned slowly, eyes wide, searching his like she was waiting for the world to catch up to what had just happened.

"I asked for the Navigator's blessing this afternoon," she said.

Her voice was steady, but the weight of her words struck Ren like a blow wrapped in wonder. For a heartbeat, all he could do was stare at her. Then he laughed. A soft, breathless sound. Not mockery. Awe.

"You clever, reckless woman." It burst out of him, half-laugh, half-prayer. He raked a hand through his hair, disbelief and joy colliding in his chest like thunder.

"You are unbelievable," he murmured, stepping toward her. "Brilliant. Perfect."

His hands found her hair, curling through it like something sacred, and he leaned in. The nearness made his heart ache. Mira let out a shaky laugh, her hands clutching his wrists, grounding both of them.

"It worked," she whispered. "Ren… it worked."

He pulled back just enough to see her face, that face he'd

never forget even if the stars burned out.

"Of course it worked," he breathed, wonder catching in his throat. "How could they say no to you?"

He cupped her cheeks, his hands trembling just slightly, the way someone trembles at the edge of a precipice, right before they fall.

"One Navigator blessed us. Without a priest. Without a ritual." His thumbs brushed along her cheekbones. Grounding. Reassuring himself she was real. "It's unheard of, Mira..." he whispered. "It's impossible..."

Here they were. The impossible made flesh. Mira's smile bloomed slow and sure, fragile at first, then bright as moonlight on open water. She pressed her hand to her chest, eyes shining. He took her other hand, guided it to his chest, let her feel the rhythm of his heart, the bond humming between them like a living thread of heat and gravity.

And then she laughed. A soft, startled sound full of disbelief and joy. Ren's breath caught, then his lips twitched, the disbelief tipping into laughter. A deep, helpless laugh that came from somewhere in his chest, sharp and bright and disbelieving. Because it was true. They had done the impossible. Together.

Mira launched forward, arms locking around his neck, laughter muffled into the curve of his shoulder. Ren caught her without thinking, arms curling around her waist, lifting her off the ground like she weighed nothing. She was solid in his arms. Real. His bonded.

"I don't care what it means," she said. "I don't care what the court says. What the laws say. The Navigators made their choice." Her fingers traced along his jaw, memorizing. Committing. Her touch was gentle, reverent. "And I would have chosen you either way."

Ren froze, the air leaving his lungs all at once. That voice, her voice, saying that. It hit him like lightning. He drew her closer, one hand cradling the nape of her neck. His thumb traced her cheek again, slow, reverent. The bond pulsed between them, strong.

He kissed her. Not desperate, but slow. Certain. Like the kiss of a man who had waited his whole life and was finally… home. Mira melted into him, her fingers knotting in his tunic like she couldn't bear to let him go.

The bond sang between them, not just emotion, not just want. But certainty. She was in his blood now. In his breath. And he would carry this moment with him for the rest of his life and beyond.

Her want. Her need. Her love. It moved through him like tidewater, slow and certain, sweeping away every thought that wasn't her. Not imagined, not hoped for. Real.

Unmistakable. She poured through the bond with a quiet, aching honesty.

And Mira felt his in return. The longing he'd buried. The devotion that had settled into his bones. The way every path he'd taken had led, inevitably, to her.

A soft sigh escaped her as he lifted her into his arms, and she pressed closer, like she needed to feel the beat of his heart to believe this was real.

Ren held her gently, carrying her across their rooms. Their home. Moonlight spilled across the bed and floor, painting the room in quiet silver. Everything felt suspended in time, wrapped in silence and stillness, like the world was waiting for them to exhale.

Ren didn't speak as he placed her on the ground. He didn't need to. His gaze found hers in the hush, and the look he gave her said everything his voice couldn't quite hold yet.

She was breathtaking in this light. Barefoot, glowing, eyes wide and steady. He let out a quiet breath, then leaned in, his lips brushing the curve of her ear.

"You're mine," he whispered. Not as a claim, but a confession. Mira's breath caught, her body giving the smallest shiver in his arms. He felt the way her heartbeat stuttered, how her hands tightened just slightly at his shoulders, the bond between them fluttering like wings caught in a breeze.

Ren smiled, soft and stunned, wonder curling around the edges of his voice. Mira tilted her chin, a spark in her eyes. He looked at her for a long moment, memorizing everything. The rise and fall of her breath. The curve of her mouth. Then he lowered his head and pressed a kiss to her throat, slow and earnest, right where her pulse beat strong beneath the skin.

"I've never wanted anything more," he murmured.

Her fingers slipped into his hair, gentle and curious, like she was trying to remember a song she hadn't heard in years. The bond pulsed between them, steady and real, an ache that was no longer painful.

She gasped softly when his tongue found her throat. His fingers traced the constellations embroidered into her dress, following the paths of stars that had led him to her again and again. Then, with one smooth motion, he pulled the ribbon loose. Letting it slide from her shoulders, pooling at her feet in a whisper of silk.

Mira. Bare before him in the soft glow of the moon. It took everything in him not to rush. Her breath hitched as his hands trailed down to her waist. As he let his fingertips memorize the shape of her, the warmth of her. He'd thought she might shy away, but no. He knew her better than that.

She smirked at him, bold and teasing, and dragged a

single finger down his chest. "You're staring."

He reached for her wrist before she could go lower, pinning it against his chest. "And you're teasing me."

Her smirk only widened. "That's a problem, why Kalren?"

The bond pulsed, the way he felt her, undid him. It wasn't just her touch, wasn't just the way she looked at him, wasn't just the way her lips parted as she whispered his name, it was her love, her hunger, her desire crashing into him through the bond, unfiltered, undeniable.

Ren exhaled sharply, forcing himself to breathe. "And if you keep looking at me like that, I'll forget how to be gentle."

A slow blink. "When did I say I wanted gentle?"

The last thread of restraint inside him broke. His hands cupped her jaw, tilting her head as he kissed her deeper, as he swallowed every gasp, every soft sound she made, every whispered plea. He let his hands roam, memorizing every curve, every soft shiver of her skin beneath his touch. She met him with equal fire, fingers working at the fastenings of his tunic, his pants, tearing them from his legs, desperate to feel him. He pressed her back into the sheets, the weight of him above her, his body caging hers.

Her lips trailed down his jaw, her breath warm against his skin, before she bit gently at his pulse point. He shuddered against her, a low growl rumbling from deep in his chest as his fingers gripped her thigh.

"I need you," she whispered, and the bond echoed it back, filling his thought with everything he wanted to do to her, with her, on her.

Ren pinned her wrists above her head, his weight pressing her into the mattress. He traced the side of her neck with his tongue, feeling the wild, erratic pulse beneath.

"I know," he murmured, lips brushing over her skin, his grip tightening just slightly. "I can feel you."

He felt her need, sharp and electric, crackling beneath her skin like a live wire. It set fire to his own, sending heat curling low, making it impossible to think of anything but her, her breathless gasps, her trembling limbs, the way she opened to him with absolute surrender. Her breath hitched. He let go of one wrist, trailing his palm down the length of her arm, down her side, gripping her thigh and pulling her flush against him.

"I will never get enough of this," Mira whispered, her voice breathless, edged with something wicked. "Feeling you through the bond is addictive"

Ren groaned, rolling his hips against hers, the friction pulling a sharp gasp from both of them. Navigators, she was right. And right now he wanted to drown in her pleasure. He wanted to take his time. To savor her. To worship her. But she had other plans.

Mira moved suddenly, a wicked glint in her eyes as she shifted, flipping them with a burst of strength that sent Ren onto his back. A breath of surprise left him, but it turned into a low, approving chuckle as she straddled him, her knees bracketing his hips, her body warm and commanding against his own.

Desire. That teasing, taunting satisfaction that she had caught him off guard. Ren felt it all, her amusement at his surprise, the satisfaction curling like smoke, the way the heat between them had turned from simmering to a sharper, more desperate fire.

It sent a shudder through him, his pulse roaring, his control slipping further from his grasp. With a slow, deliberate motion, she slid her hands down his chest, the light scrape of her nails making his muscles tensing beneath her touch. Her fingers tracing along his ribs, the scars on his back, mapping every inch of him like he was something to be studied, memorized. Possession. Affection. Awe.

Mira loved this. Loved feeling him, knowing he was hers in every way that mattered. And, Navigators, Ren could feel every moment. Her hands moved over him, soft, teasing, like she was memorizing every inch of his skin, every muscle that tensed beneath her fingertips. Her lips curved as she leaned down, pressing her mouth to his jaw, his neck, his collarbone.

She hummed against his skin, her voice a sultry whisper. "Is my bonded already falling apart?"

Ren shuddered, tilting his head back, baring his throat to her. "Mira, please." His fingers dug into her skin, his breath coming in short, uneven bursts. "I need you."

She trailed her lips lower, letting her teeth scrape lightly over his pulse, feeling the way it leaped beneath her mouth. "I know," echoing his earlier tease. "I can feel just how much."

She moved her hips, grinding on him. She shifted, slowly, deliberately, rolling her hips against him in a way that sent pleasure through his veins. Ren's breath left him in a sharp hiss, his fingers tightening where they gripped her waist. His jaw clenched, his control hanging by a thread.

"Mira." His voice was ragged, a warning, a plea, a promise all in one. Ren's grip on her thighs tightened, his fingers digging into her skin making her shiver. "Please do something about it," he growled, his voice half a plea, half a command.

Mira smirked, pressing a teasing kiss to the center of his chest. Her fingers skimming over his ribs, lower, dragging over his skin in slow, maddening strokes.

"Are you begging me, Ren?" He heard the tease, but he

felt more than that.

Through the bond, her excitement shimmered like heat. It pulsed beneath her words, bright and undeniable. She liked this, him, brought low and wanting. And Navigators help him, he liked that she liked it.

A low, desperate sound tore from his throat, his hips jerking against hers. "Yes... Navigators, yes."

Mira let her tongue flick over the hollow of his throat before whispering, "Good"

Ren stilled. A sharp inhale. His control hung by a thread, already frayed beyond reason, already unraveling at the edges. His eyes snapped back to hers, dark, demanding, burning.

"Be Patient" the words left her lips, soft, teasing, meant to provoke. She knew exactly what she was doing. Exactly how to drive him to the brink. His breath left him in a sharp exhale, his grip flexing against her.

His voice came low and ragged, "Patience is for men who don't know what they want."

Faster than she could react, he surged up, catching her mouth in a kiss that was all hunger, all fire, all the aching desperation that had been building between them.

He flipped her beneath him in one swift, fluid motion. Ren braced himself over her, caging her beneath him. A sharp intake of air that sent another pulse of heat through him. His lips hovered over hers, his own breathing ragged, uneven, his self-control slipping by the second.

He felt the sharp spike of her anticipation through the bond, felt the way her body arched instinctively toward his, felt her satisfaction curl like smoke in her chest. She wanted this. Wanted him undone. Ren growled softly, dragging his mouth over her skin, just a whisper away from touching.

"You like provoking me, don't you" he murmured, his voice rough, almost dangerous.

A slow, sinful smile curved her lips. "Always..." His control was gone. His hands slid down her thighs, gripping, pulling her leg around him. And when he slowly pushed his cock inside her, it felt like coming home.

A sharp, shattered gasp tore from her lips, her back arching, her body molding to his as if she had been made for him, as if this moment had been fated from the very beginning. The bond flared, a burst of warmth and light erupting between them, sending a deep, shuddering pulse through every fiber of their being. Her nails bit into his skin, leaving marks along his shoulders, pulling him closer, deeper, anchoring herself to him like she never intended to let go.

Ren squeezed his eyes shut, a ragged groan breaking from his chest as the intensity of it overwhelmed him. He could finish exactly like this. The way their pleasure coursed through both of them in perfect sync, like echoes of the same flame burning in two bodies.

Her name left him wrecked, raw, reverent. He pumped his hips out slowly. He felt everything. Every brush of her fingertips, every pulse of pleasure as it shot through her veins, as it shot through his.

It was a prayer, a plea, a confession whispered against her throat as he pressed open- mouthed kisses to the fluttering pulse point beneath her skin, tasting the heat of her, the salt, the sweet, breathless gasps that only he could pull from her lips.

Her muscles tensed as her emotions surged, calling to him, begging him to move faster, to give in, to let go.

"Ren..." Her breathy moan sent a shudder through him.

He could feel the way her body strained beneath him, the

way her thighs tightened around his hips, trying to pull him deeper, closer. It rushed through him like a wave, an unrelenting plea wrapped in fire and longing.

His jaw clenched, slowly shifted his hips back towards her. She arched into him, guiding him deeper, her body opening for him, welcoming him, matching him in every movement, every slow, shuddering breath, every whispered name.

"Ren... faster.." she whispered, her voice frayed at the edges, teasing and wrecked all at once. A slow exhale left him, hot against her skin.

"I know," he murmured. "if I move any faster…"

A low, ragged groan tore from his throat, the last threads of restraint holding him back, as he tilted her chin up, forcing her gaze to meet his. "Say it for me Mira" he rasped.

Her breath hitched, her fingers tangling in his hair. "I want all of you. Right now. Make me yours." The bond roared with her demand.

Ren surged, capturing her mouth, stealing the breath from her lungs as he took control. He drove into her relentlessly, each thrust sending shockwaves through them both. The sharp, dizzying rush of sensation, the overwhelming, unfiltered pleasure as she clung to him.

Their bodies and souls, their bond sealing, tightening, locking them together in ways no force, not even death, could sever.

She gasped his name, breathless, desperate, the sound so sweet, so utterly wrecked, that he nearly lost himself then and there.

Ren groaned, his hands gripping her hips, his pace faltering for half a heartbeat before he let go of the last sliver of control. Their heartbeats pounded in sync and every movement, every desperate, clinging touch. Every ragged moan and pleading sigh sent them both spiraling toward something more, something infinite.

Mira trembled beneath him, the fire building, cresting, threatening to consume them both. And when she broke, when her body tensed and shattered and fell into blissful, euphoric ruin, she dragged him with her. Ren followed her into oblivion, their bond pulsing, locking, sealing, a final, irrevocable promise etched into their very being.

As the waves of pleasure rippled through them, as their bodies melted together in the aftermath, he gathered her against his chest, pressing a slow, lazy kiss to her temple.

He could still feel her. Not just the warmth of her skin, not just the sweet, sated hum of her breathing, but her. Her love. Her contentment.

It was a truth he felt in his bones, quiet, undeniable. That she was made for him, and he for her.

43

Mira

The moments before.

BENEATH THE MIDDAY sun the altar chamber held its breath. High, arched windows spilled light in softened ribbons across the marble floor, where dust motes drifted like golden embers caught in a silent wind.

The air was thick with incense, the sharp burn of cedar and myrrh layered over the scent of wax, parchment, and stone steeped in centuries of prayer.

Mira stepped forward slowly. The altar loomed ahead, shimmering in the candlelight. Painted visages of the Navigators watched from above, their faces faded with time, yet their gaze unyielding. Unblinking.

Behind her, the great wooden doors groaned closed with a final, echoing weight. Sealed in. With him. Caelric stood at the altar. He looked unchanged, ever composed. Hands tracing lightly on sacred scripture. Every movement precise, deliberate. But there was something different today. Not sorrow. Not authority. Finality.

He had asked for her. That alone was strange enough. He never summoned her. Ren had never told him. Neither the Queen nor the Crowned Betrothed had known of their bond. She stepped forward with measured calm, spine held straight.

"You summoned me, Your Majesty," she said. Her voice was clear, cool. Caelric inclined his head, the barest acknowledgment. "I did."

Without another word, he turned from the altar and moved through a side archway. Mira hesitated only a moment, before she followed him into the adjoining study.

The shift in atmosphere was immediate. Gone was the sanctity of the altar hall. This space felt lived in. Private. Dusty shelves groaned beneath the weight of ancient tomes. A single window let in filtered light, illuminating a large mahogany desk cluttered with parchment, glass bottles of ink, and Mira stopped short.

At the center of the desk lay a book. Thick. Bound in cracked leather, its silver etchings dulled with age. The Scriptum Navigare. Her breath hitched. She had seen copies before. Tamed versions. Interpreted, softened, revised by generations of clerics and nobles.

But it looked like an original. Unaltered. Her fingers twitched with the urge to touch it. Caelric approached the desk slowly, his fingertips brushing the edge of the open page.

"I found this first edition when I was still a boy," he said, almost to himself as he opened the cover. "Apprenticing in Kharador. I thought I knew what it meant to be chosen. To be faithful."

He traced the ancient script with a kind of reverence. "I did not."

Mira swallowed, stepping closer, her gaze skimming the delicate script. The text was illuminated with gold-inked lettering, decorated with detailed illustrations of each Navigator, figures woven with celestial light and mortal flesh, their gifts etched into the pages in intricate detail.

The Gift of Myrran. To know the shape of what will come is to bear the sorrow of all that must be.

An illustration showed a veiled woman beneath a night sky, her hands outstretched toward the constellations, golden threads of fate wrapping around her wrists.

The Gift of Kharad. A voice can cut sharper than any blade. A word, once spoken, can never be undone.

Next to it, a figure stood before a kneeling army, his lips parting, his words shaping the tide of battle itself.

The Gift of Drala. Some are meant to choose not only for themselves, but for the many.

A crowned ruler stood before two diverging roads, shadowy figures waiting for judgment, hands reaching toward the unknown.

The Gift of Bharas. The Heartfire devours and all fire demands sacrifice.

An image of Bharas kneeling. His heart was depicted as a blazing flame, illuminating the night around him, burning the world.

Mira frowned. Her eyes flicked to Caelric. He nodded once, tapping the text lightly with a single finger. She read it aloud.

"It is documented that the gifts of the Navigators favor unbroken bloodlines, yet no gift is without sacrifice.

The cost must be paid before the previous bearer's final breath."

A weight settled deep in Mira's chest. She turned another page, scanning the dense script. She lifted her gaze. Sharp now. Calculating. Mira froze. These gifts weren't metaphorical. They were real. Dangerous. Ancient.

Her breath caught as her eyes met Caelric's. And in that stillness, she saw, buried beneath his composed exterior, behind the coolness of his gaze, heartfire. Banked, but burning. Controlled, but not dormant. He had hidden it. She had never noticed. No one had. Not until now.

Mira understood the danger she was in. Her blood turned cold. This wasn't some scholarly indulgence or idle remembrance of power. He had called her here. Alone. With the doors sealed behind her. And he had to know. The bond. The truth she and Ren had kept buried, he had unearthed it.

Standing here, unguarded and unarmed, Mira was suddenly very aware of just how much she didn't know about the man before her.

Her voice was barely above a whisper. "You inherited this." "Yes," he said, without flinching She hesitated, searching his face.

Her voice came softer still, but sharper, edged with the need to know. "From who?" He looked at her, quiet. Then, deliberately, "Would you like to guess?"

The blood drained from her face. "…Your father?" Caelric's laugh was low and without warmth. "No."

Mira felt the unease rise. It curled through her chest like smoke. "I took it from my bonded's father," he said softly.

"For her." She blinked. "The Queen?"

Caelric nodded once. "She was meant to inherit. But we had just suffered the lost our first child. A daughter. She wasn't strong enough."

Mira swallowed hard and looked away, "So you took it. To spare her."

He nodded. "It was not without protest. But I promised I would ensure Bharas's gift would return to their bloodline"

The weight of it all pressed down on her. Her thoughts spun, tracing backward, re- threading the tapestry. A pattern began to form.

Her voice cracked as she spoke. "Then that's why Ren felt me. Before our bond. Bharas's blood runs through him."

The words lingered between them. The way Ren had looked at her from the start. The way he reached for her, even before they knew what they were. The way he loved, not gently, not cautiously, but with the kind of fire that consumed. Ren carried that same flame. That same impossible depth. Caelric said nothing.

Mira stepped back, her pulse a thunder in her ears. "You want him to inherit Bharas' gift," she said. "But he can't. Not without..." Her voice faltered. "Not without sacrifice," she whispered.

Caelric gently closed the book. The sound was deafening.

"I had hoped," he said quietly, "to be on my deathbed." Mira's stomach turned. "I am ensuring his birthright."

"Why are you telling me this?" Caelric stepped closer. His expression was unreadable. "Because I had hoped you would understand. That you would see what must be done.

That you would accept it."

Her eyes sharpened. "I won't submit" Something flickered in his expression. Not cruelty. Not coldness. But conviction. Immovable. Mira understood. He would go through with it with or without her permission.

She stared at him, eyes burning. "Don't." "I cannot," he said before Caelric lunged.

Fire. A blinding, searing pain behind her eyes, deep in her mind. Her knees buckled as her world fractured. She felt Ren's voice. His laughter. Their whispered vows under moonlight. All of it was torn away.

The last thing she heard before the dark swallowed her whole was Caelric's voice. "Forgive me." And then, silence.

* * *

Ren

The clang of steel rang through the courtyard, sharp and rhythmic, the crisp morning air thick with the scent of sun-warmed stone and sweat. Ren barely felt the weight of his blade as he landed a strike, twisting at the last second before countering with a precise, punishing jab.

Ren scoffed, shaking the tension from his shoulders. "Still got your head full of Brahn, have you?"

Tharion grunted, stepping back just enough to bare his teeth "Careful, Ren. Too soon, even for you."

Ren's smirk faded. The space between them stilled. No more jabs, no more bravado, just a glance that held the weight of grief within Tharion but not spoken aloud. Tharion nodded once, wordless, but clear. Attack me again.

Ren lunged again. A test. A challenge. Their swords met in a flurry of movement, quick, brutal, familiar. The tempo of the fight was second nature, a comfort. A distraction.

Tharion welcomed it, sinking into the fluid exchange of blade and instinct, letting the world fade away.

Pain ripped through Ren. A jagged, brutal tear through the

bond, like being ripped open from the inside out. Ren's breath vanished. His knees buckled. His sword slipped from his grasp, the metal clattering against stone, but he didn't hear it.

A scream tore through his mind. Mira. Fear. Pain. Agony. It slammed into him, raw and unrelenting, a force so overwhelming it stole the strength from his limbs. His vision blurred, his pulse roaring, his entire body locking up beneath the weight of it. Someone called his name. Distant. Muffled. Meaningless.

Ren ran. His boots pounded against stone, his heart slamming against his ribs like it was trying to break free. The pain sharpened. Wilder. Sharper. A pull. A violent, sickening tug. Like a thread being torn from his chest.

Then, nothing. A muted, distant echo of what had once been fire. A whisper of her, so faint it barely existed. His breath tore from his throat in a ragged, panicked gasp.

His legs burned, but he didn't stop. Wouldn't stop. Stone blurred past him as he sprinted through the castle corridors, barely aware of the startled guards, the whispers, the eyes turning toward him in confusion. He couldn't feel his hands. Couldn't hear anything over the sound of his own racing pulse.

The altar doors loomed ahead. He threw them open, the wood slamming against the stone walls so hard the entire chamber seemed to shake, The world shattered.

On the dais. Under the glow of the stained-glass window. Mira lay still. Her auburn hair spilled over the cold marble, her dress fanned out around her, delicate folds of fabric like the petals of a flower wilting in winter frost.

The light from the window painted her in fractured colors, blue, gold, red, but she was pale. Too pale. The bond, the flame that had burned between them, was barely a whisper. Ren's breath left him in a ragged, gasping cry.

He stumbled down the aisle, barely catching himself as he collapsed onto the dais, his hands shaking violently as he reached for her. His fingers cupped her face, his thumb skimming over her burning cheek, his breath coming in uneven, desperate gasps.

She was breathing, barely. Her pulse weak, her body too still. She was too warm. Ren pressed his forehead against hers, his entire body shaking with the force of his desperation.

"Don't do this," he whispered against her skin, his voice breaking. "Don't leave me."

Silence. A shadow shifted in the room. Ren's head snapped up. Caelric. He stood near the stained-glass window, broad shoulders framed by the shifting colored light, his hands clasped behind his back. Watching. Waiting.

Ren's grief twisted into something violent. Something raw and ravenous. His chest heaved, his pulse thundered in his ears, his vision blurred with fury and disbelief. She was right there, but he couldn't feel her. His heart shattered.

Ren lurched forward, voice breaking open in a scream. "What have you done to her?" Caelric looked at him. Steady. Unflinching. But he said nothing. Not a word.

His arms tightened around her, like he could hold her together just by keeping her close. His fingers curled into the fabric of her dress, into her, as if anchoring himself to the only thing that mattered.

His hands trembled as he adjusted his grip, sliding one arm beneath her knees, the other around her back. He lifted her gently, carefully.

She didn't stir. Her head lolled softly against his shoulder, her breath still there, but faint. Too faint. The bond remained silent. Hollow. Ren's throat burned with everything he couldn't scream. He turned without a word, not sparing Caelric a second glance.

Ren barely felt the cold stone beneath his boots as he carried Mira through the palace corridors, his arms locked tightly around her fragile form. The halls blurred around him, but the weight in his arms was the only thing grounding him. Every step pounded against his ribs, an echo of the suffocating wrongness pressing into his chest.

Ren reached their chambers and shouldered open the door, nearly stumbling in his urgency. He crossed the threshold and lowered Mira onto their bed, his hands trembling as his fingers brushed her cheek. She was still burning up.

A strangled sound escaped his throat as he collapsed onto the edge of the mattress, his shoulders heaving with the effort to keep himself together. His hand trembled as it smoothed back Mira's hair, tucking loose strands behind her ear.

His thumb ghosted over her temple, tracing slow circles, as if that alone could tether her to him. His palm cupped her cheek, lingering there, absorbing the unnatural warmth of her skin. His vision blurred. His throat tightened. His body shook.

"You're still here," he whispered hoarsely, voice breaking on the words. "You have to be."

The bond, flickered barely, what was left of it was weak. Fragile. A thread where once there had been fire. He reached for her, desperate, willing himself to feel something, anything, but the emptiness that answered made him sick. His thumb traced the line of her jaw, the curve of her lips, the pulse at her throat. He had memorized every inch of her, yet now, she felt just out of reach.

His breath hitched. A sob broke free, raw and desperate, the weight of it crashing over him like a wave. He bent forward, pressing his forehead to hers, his fingers trembling as they smoothed over her knuckles, his grip tightening like he could anchor her here.

Sarelle stepped into the room, her golden-threaded robes whispering as she moved. The room felt too still. She lowered herself beside him, reaching out with steady hands to tilt Mira's face toward her, assessing her with the careful precision of a queen, but the quiet sorrow of a mother.

A long, tense silence. Then, finally, she spoke. "She is buried under his will."

Ren's head snapped up. His breath caught in his throat, his vision swimming with unshed tears. "What?"

Sarelle exhaled softly, her fingers running lightly over Mira's temple as if tracing something unseen beneath her skin. "The weight of him still smothers her," she murmured. "Not just the bond, Ren. It's memories of you. Your courtship. Your connection."

A beat of silence. Then, Sarelle's voice dropped lower, softer, almost apologetic. " When she wakes like this, she won't know you."

Ren's breath left him in a ragged gasp. His fingers curled into Mira's dress, gripping the fabric as if he could hold her to him through sheer force of will. He squeezed his eyes shut, trying to force back the sob clawing its way up his throat.

"She… she won't…" He shook his head violently, a broken noise tearing from his chest. "Why?"

Sarelle hesitated, searching her own bond for an answer. "He considers it a gift."

Ren's entire body snapped taut, rage curling through his veins like a slow-burning fire. His chest heaved. His breath came in sharp, ragged bursts. His grip on Mira tightened.

"I don't want his gifts." The growl rumbled low in his

throat, laced with fury, with grief.

Sarelle sighed, but there was sorrow in her eyes. "I can't undo his will." A pause. "But I may be able to guide it."

Ren's grief sharpened into suspicion. His fingers tightened around Mira's hand, his voice low and dangerous. "What do you mean?"

Sarelle met his gaze, unwavering. "If she wakes with this emptiness, there's no telling what she might do. No telling what she might believe." A pause. "Who she might trust."

Ren's thumb traced slow circles against Mira's palm, grounding himself in the last shred of her he still had.

But Sarelle wasn't finished. "I cannot lift his hold," she continued carefully. "But I could… fill the cracks."

The words slammed into him like a dagger to the chest. Ren flinched. His grip tightened around Mira's limp hand, cradling it between both of his as if sheer will could tether her to him. To fill the space he left with someone else. His jaw clenched, his head shaking violently.

"No." His voice cracked on the last word, and he hated how raw it sounded.

Sarelle's touch was light but firm as she placed a hand on his arm. "You cannot be seen with her. Not after this. He will remove her entirely if he has to."

His throat was tight. His mind roared with protest. "Then who?" The words were sharp, splintered with grief and fury. "A stranger? A noble? A priest? There is nobody we trust." The silence stretched.

"I will." Ren turned sharply at the voice. Tharion stood in the doorway. Instead, his expression was grim, resolute.

Ren blinked. Shook his head. "No."

Tharion took a step forward. "It's my fault Caelric knew

to look, Ren. Let me repay my debt"

Ren surged to his feet, grief turning to fury. "I said no, Tharion."

"She will need someone, Ren." Tharion's tone softened, but the weight of his decision lingered in his words. "Someone she trusts already. Someone she knows. Someone who can keep her safe."

Ren hated how logical it sounded. But it meant Mira would wake up believing she was bonded to Tharion. His stomach twisted violently, his grip tightening around her hand as if that alone could change what was happening. He sank back to his knees. Tharion took another step closer, his voice quiet but unwavering.

He placed a firm hand on Ren's shoulder. "It won't be real." Ren's voice was hoarse. "It will be real to her..."

A heavy silence stretched between them. Tharion swallowed hard, his voice quieter now.

"I love her like a sister Ren," he said, his throat bobbing. "and I will protect her. I give you my word."

Ren broke. His fingers tangled in Mira's hair, mapping the curve of her cheek with aching tenderness. His forehead dropped against hers, his body shaking. Tears slipped, landing against her skin. He had spent years reaching for her. Fighting for her. Now he had to let her go.

Tharion turned to Sarelle, his voice steady despite the storm lingering behind his eyes. "Do it."

Sarelle hesitated. Her gaze flickered back to Ren. Ren didn't look up. He simply pressed his lips to her forehead before finally, he nodded.

44

Ren

6 Months After

REN HAD LEARNED the contours of distance in a way he never wanted to. The aching space between them. Between what was, and what was no longer theirs. Six months of watching from afar. Mira and Tharion.

He had begged. Bargained. Raged. But no matter how many desperate prayers he whispered into the dark, nothing loosened Caelric's hold on her. Nothing severed the chains of the illusion woven into her mind. The bond remained buried beneath the weight of his father's will.

Ren became a shadow in the palace halls. A ghost in the corners of courtly gatherings. He memorized every moment he could steal, every glimpse of her. The way she tilted her head when she laughed. The curve of her fingers as she reached for a glass. The hush of her voice when she murmured something to Tharion.

He knew his friend did not touch her more than necessary. Knew Tharion played his part with careful distance. Knew he would never intentionally betray him. But it didn't matter. Because to her, it was real. And that truth destroyed Ren every single night.

* * *

The bells tolled. Deep. Sonorous. Rolling through the palace like a coming storm. Ren froze. His pulse roared in his ears. The bells did not toll for time. Not for council members, or high priests. They tolled for rulers. Only rulers.

He ran. Through the corridors, past the startled guards who did not stop him. His feet barely touched the floor. Only one hope, impossible and wild, drove him forward. He turned the final corner, heart slamming against his ribs. The doors were open.

And inside… It was not Caelric on his deathbed. Ren's breath left him in a broken exhale. His mother lay pale against the sheets, golden-threaded robes darkened with sweat, her chest rising and falling in erratic, failing gasps. Her lips tinged blue. Her body trembling. Ren staggered forward.

His gaze snapped to his father, standing at the foot of the bed, fists clenched, body rigid. Ren saw the flames. Not from torchlight. Not from the hearth. From him. Fire curled around Caelric's hands. Licked up his arms. Wreathed his shoulders like a burning crown. The heat distorted the air, making it shimmer.

Ren had seen his father wield fury. Had felt the weight of his command. But this was different. This wasn't power given. This was power unleashed. Ren stepped forward, breath ragged. "Father..."

Caelric didn't move. The flames roared brighter, licking the ceiling. Tapestries curled and blackened. The windows shuddered in their frames. Sarelle let out a soft, broken breath. Her eyes fluttered. Just barely. Her lips parted like she might speak.

Caelric inhaled sharply. His hands trembled. One final, burning kiss. The fire surged. It exploded outward in a wave of heat and light, cracking the walls, bursting the windows into glittering shards. The torches were snuffed out. Ren threw up his arm to shield himself, staggering back. The heat was unbearable. Suffocating.

Silence. The fire did not fade. It vanished. Caelric still stood. Back straight. Shoulders square. But something was wrong. His face. His eyes. Blank. Gone.

Ren swallowed hard, stepping forward. "Father?" No answer. No movement. He was breathing, but just barely. Shallow. Catatonic. Sarelle was still.

His mother was gone. A sob rose in his throat. He forced it down. Swallowed against the grief tearing through his chest. Caelric did not move. Did not blink. Did not see.

The fire had taken something of him when it vanished. Whatever had held Caelric tethered to this world had loosened, like a long, fraying leash, and now he drifted, half here, half somewhere else. Not dead. Not alive. Suspended in the space between.

Ren looked at him, his grief is a storm just beneath his skin. And still, Caelric stood. A king, unseeing. A man, undone. A part of Ren wanted to shake him. To force him to look. To feel. But another part, the part that knew loss, understood.

Part of Caelric had already followed Sarelle somewhere Ren could not reach.

✳ ✳ ✳

Through the halls. Through the whispering dark. Past the faces that turned and reached and called out. Ren ran. Until he reached the doors. Until he slammed them open, the sound echoing through the chamber like thunder.

His chest heaved. His vision blurred. He scanned the space. No sign of her. He took a step forward. She stepped out from the bathing chamber.

He gasped, a broken, reverent sound as his eyes drank her in. Damp hair curling over her shoulders. Her robe tied at the waist, skin flushed from the heat of the bathing chamber. For a moment, everything in him hoped. With Caelric lost to fire and grief, with his hold on the world loosened, maybe, just maybe, the grip he held on her had loosened too. Maybe the illusion had frayed. Maybe she had come back to him.

Ren's body moved on instinct, pulled forward by that fragile, desperate hope. His breath caught. His heart soared and ached all at once.

He took a step toward her, voice raw with everything he couldn't yet say. "Mira," She turned. "Tharion?" she called, voice light. Easy. Familiar.

Ren's breath left him like a blade through the chest. The pain tore through him. Sudden. Final. His knees hit the floor. The impact barely registered. His fists slammed against the cold stone. His body curled inward. A sound broke from his chest, raw, wounded. His shoulders shook as the grief took him.

Mira stood just feet away. He could feel her presence. Even through the bond's ragged silence. She stepped forward, hesitant. Her face was concerned, but distant. A friend's concern. Before she could speak, Tharion appeared in the doorway.

He moved fast. Shielded him. Then knelt. Between her and Ren. His hands closed around Ren's shoulders. Firm. Grounding. Ren trembled, he didn't even feel Tharion. Tharion pulled him close. Steady. Sure. Ren collapsed into him. His fists twisted in Tharion's tunic. His breath came in short, broken gasps against his friend's shoulder.

"I heard... the bells," Tharion murmured. "When she

didn't ask for you I'm sorry, Ren."

The words meant nothing. Because the truth between them was heavier. It wasn't just Sarelle he mourned. It was Mira. His Mira. Who stood just steps away, unknowing. Unseeing. Tharion's grip tightened. One hand on Ren's neck. One on his shoulder.

"Come on" he whispered. "Not like this."

Ren didn't move. Couldn't. Tharion shifted. Braced his weight. Held him together when everything inside was falling apart.

"Please, Ren." The words cut through the haze. Ren's body shook. His head bowed. His grief spilled unchecked. His mother was dead. Mira was gone.

Tharion was the only thing keeping him from drowning.

<h1 style="text-align:center">45</h1>

Mira

THE WORLD BLED BACK into existence in slow, aching fragments.

A breeze stirred the branches of the Tahla tree above her, leaves whispering against one another, their glow fractured by the moonlight spilling through the garden. The scent of damp earth and tahla filled her lungs, grounding her, tethering her to the present as the past slammed into her all at once.

Mira gasped, a sharp, broken sound, her fingers digging into the cool grass beneath her as the weight of forgotten time crashed over her like a tidal wave.

Images flickered behind her eyes, memories buried, stolen, burned away, rising now from the ashes. Ren's voice. His touch. His love. Him. The bond, once hollow and frayed, thrummed with renewed life, surging through her like a wildfire reignited. It was overwhelming. Scorching. Undeniable. Every emotion she had once lost came back tenfold. Love. Grief. Longing. Fury.

But beneath it all, one truth had never left her. Not really. Not even when Caelric had tried to erase it from her mind.

Ren. Her vision swam, but only one thing came into focus, him. Ren's face hovered just inches from hers, green eyes locked onto hers with an intensity that stole what little breath she had left.

He was shaking. His hands cradled her face, warm

against her chilled skin, thumbs brushing slowly over her cheekbones like he had done countless times before.

Through the bond, she felt everything. His raw and jagged grief. His unrelenting fear. The panic that she might vanish again if he blinked. But beneath it all, stronger than the pain, deeper than the terror, was a singular, burning thing. Love. Unyielding.

Undiminished.

Mira didn't pull away. She leaned into him, her fingers rising to press over his, grounding herself in the weight of him, in the warmth she had lost for too long.

Her voice trembled as she spoke, barely more than a whisper. "Ren…"

He drew in a sharp breath, the sound ragged in the silence. He stilled beneath her touch, afraid that if he moved, she might vanish.

His voice was fragile, reverent, laced with something between hope and dread. "Mira?"

There was a pause, just a breath, just long enough for the ache to bloom. Then softly, achingly, "My Kalren…"

She surged up and kissed him. It wasn't soft. It wasn't careful. It was everything. A collision of desperation and hunger. A kiss that held too much pain, too much time, too much longing to be anything gentle. His lips crashed against hers like a dam breaking, all restraint gone, like he needed to feel her with every part of himself just to believe she was real.

Mira clung to him, her hands fisting into his shirt, pulling him closer. She had missed this. Missed him. More than she had words for. Ren kissed her like he'd been drowning for months, like she was the first breath of air he'd been allowed to take.

His tears mixed with hers as she deepened the kiss, hands threading into his hair, anchoring herself to the only thing in the world that mattered.

The bond surged, no longer hollow. No longer broken. It roared through her. She felt Ren through it, all of him, raw, wild, and desperate. The unbearable relief. The agony of having ever lost her. The fury at the man who had stolen her. Mira pulled away suddenly, breath ragged, her fingers still tangled in the fabric of his shirt.

The bells. Loud. Droning. Unrelenting. A chill slid down her spine. If Caelric's weight was lifted from her mind. If the bond was whole again. Then that meant… Her heart lurched. She didn't explain. She couldn't. She ran.

"Mira!" Ren's voice cracked behind her, raw with confusion and fear, but she didn't stop.

His panic surged through the bond. Wild. Sharp. Desperate. It clawed at her, but she pushed forward, feet pounding against the stone path. The night air thickened around her, pressing in as she tore through the hedges, twisting through the maze.

She burst into the courtyard. The Tahla tree towered above, its silver leaves whispering. But the air was wrong. Still. Heavy. Silent. She saw him. Tharion. He stood alone, unmoving, his back turned toward them. Ren skidded to a stop at her side, chest heaving.

"Mira, what is it?" Ren's breathless voice came from behind her.

She couldn't answer. He followed her gaze and froze. Tharion hadn't moved. The space around him glowed. Her chest tightened. Her voice barely carried.

"Tharion, what have you done…"

A long pause. Then, he turned. Molten gold burned in

place of his eyes. A firestorm behind his gaze, too bright, too unnatural. As if something far greater, far older, looked out through him.

Ren staggered back a step. Flames curled in Tharion's hands, licking up his arms, twisting around his forearms like they belonged to him. The ground beneath him was scorched black, heat radiating off him in thick, suffocating waves.

His expression was empty. Blank. His body taut with something Mira had never seen before. Power like that was never given freely. Power that demanded suffering.

Sacrifice. And it had passed to the only one standing when Caelric fell.

To one who had endured an endless duty. To one who had bled, not for glory, not for legacy, but for the love of his brother. For Ren.

Through the bond, she felt Ren's horror crash into her, grief and understanding colliding in a single, unbearable wave.

Tharion had inherited Bharas' Heartfire.

ACKNOWLEDGEMENTS

Jayden, thank you for hugging me through the tears, cheering me on when I doubted every word, and believing in this story (and in me) even when I couldn't. I wouldn't have made it to the final page without you. I love you.

To my brilliant beta readers, Renee & Emma. Your feedback was thoughtful and exactly what this story needed. Thank you for cheering, questioning, and gently pointing out plotholes and spelling errors.

And to every writer who feels like they're not ready, not good enough, or not "there" yet, this quote helped me, maybe it will help you too...

> *"WRITE IT BADLY. Write it badly, write it badly, write it badly, write it badly. Stop what you're doing, open a Word document, put a pencil on some paper, just get the idea out of your head. Let it be good later. Write it down now. Otherwise it will die in there."*
>
> *- BRANDON SANDERSON*

ABOUT THE AUTHOR

Isabelle Macdowall

Isabelle MacDowall is a Melbourne-based writer who believes in the power of storytelling. With a background in education and a career spent helping people learn and grow, she now turns that same energy toward her fiction.

Her debut novel, Unravelled, is a romantic, emotionally charged fantasy about memory, sacrifice, and soul-deep connection.

When she's not writing, you'll find her drinking too much coffee or trying (and often failing) to keep her two sausage dogs from stealing her snacks.

@isy.mac.writes on Tiktok & Instagra

9 781764 105446